W9-ADF-200

CHICKAMAUGA

THE CIVIL WAR BATTLES SERIES
by James Reasoner

Manassas
Shiloh
Antietam
Chancellorsville
Vicksburg
Gettysburg

CHICKAMAUGA

James Reasoner

CUMBERLAND HOUSE
NASHVILLE, TENNESSEE

Published by
CUMBERLAND HOUSE PUBLISHING, INC.
431 Harding Industrial Drive
Nashville, Tennessee 37211
www.cumberlandhouse.com

This novel is a work of fiction. Names, characters, places, and incidents either are the
product of the author's imagination or are used fictitiously. Any resemblance to per-
sons, living or dead, events, or locales is entirely coincidental.

Cover design by Bob Bubkis, Nashville, Tennessee.

Library of Congress Cataloging-in-Publication Data

Reasoner, James.
  Chickamauga / James Reasoner.
    p. cm.
  ISBN 1-58182-253-7 (alk. paper)
    1. Chickamauga (Ga.), Battle of, 1863—Fiction. 2. Georgia—History—Civil
War, 1861–1865—Fiction. I. Title.
  PS3568.E2685 C48 2002
  813'.54—dc21   2002017515

Printed in the United States of America.

1 2 3 4 5 6 7 8 9 10—05 04 03 02

For my friend Pat Hawk

CHICKAMAUGA

Chapter One

A S A BOY GROWING up in Culpeper County, Virginia, Cory Brannon had always been fond of the color blue. After all, it was the color of the sky, and he had spent many a long hour lying on his back, a blade of grass clenched in his teeth, while staring up at the sky and dreaming of all the places he would go and all the great things he would do. There were the Blue Ridge Mountains, too, rising in the distance to the west of the Brannon farm, their forested slopes calling out to Cory to see what was on the other side of them.

No, Cory never realized that he hated that particular color until he found himself living in the conquered city of Vicksburg, Mississippi, a city now full of Yankees in their dark blue Federal uniforms. It didn't matter to Cory that the Zouaves and some of the other Union units wore more colorful outfits. When he looked at the Yankees, he saw blue, and he hated it to the very depths of his soul.

Their boots thudding against the cobblestones, a company of Union soldiers marched past in the street outside the house where Cory and his newlywed wife, Lucille, lived along with Lucille's aunt and uncle, Charles and Mildred Thompson, and their friends, Allen Carter and Carter's son, Fred. Only the day before, July 3, 1863, the commander of the Confederate forces at Vicksburg, Gen. John C. Pemberton, had ended the long, desperate siege by surrendering the city to the Federal forces under Gen. Ulysses S. Grant. And already the Yankees were parading around like they owned the place, Cory thought as he sat in a ladder-back chair on the porch and watched them go by. The taste of bitterness was strong in his mouth.

They acted like they had just waltzed in without anybody even trying to stop them, Cory thought. As if the months of

11

resistance had never happened. Battles forgotten now—Chicka-saw Bluffs, Champion's Hill, the Big Black River Bridge, the Railroad Redoubt . . . all the places where the defenders had given their blood, their very lives, to hold the invaders out of the city. Even before that, there had been the cavalry raid into Ten-nessee by Nathan Bedford Forrest that had drawn Grant away from Vicksburg and bought precious time. Cory had been there, riding alongside Forrest, wreaking havoc and making fools of the Yankees. Glorious times, ah, grand and glorious times. Less than a year in the past, and already he was forgetting the cold and the hunger, the deprivation and the danger, and recalling only the heady exhilaration of victory, forgetting even the death of his friend, Lt. Hamilton Ryder.

Because if he thought too long on it, Cory knew, he would have to admit that Ham's death had been in vain. The Yankees were here in Vicksburg now. The city that was the key to con-trolling the Mississippi River was in Union hands.

He caught his breath and started as a hand fell on his shoul-der. Turning his head, he looked up and saw Lucille standing there, a worried frown on her beautiful face.

"Cory?" she said. "You shouldn't sit out here and brood like this. It doesn't do any good."

"What will do any good now?" he asked then answered his own question. "Nothing."

He recalled a time when the sight of Lucille had been enough to make him forget everything that was wrong in the world. The first time he had ever seen her, two years earlier, he had been a starving wharf rat in New Madrid, Missouri, and she had been with her father, Ezekiel Farrell, the master of the steamboat *Missouri Zephyr*. She had been so far above him in station that only the most starry-eyed fool would ever dream that he might someday win the heart of such a lady.

Cory had been that starry-eyed fool. He had looked at Lucille's deep brown eyes and honey blonde hair and told him-self that one day she would be his. Wonder of wonders, it had come to pass, and all it had taken was bloody battles, months of separation and illness, near-starvation . . . but finally the day had come, a few weeks earlier, when a minister had pronounced them man and wife in a cave under the city while a Yankee bombardment thundered down above. Cory knew he should draw strength from the knowledge that he and Lucille were alive and together and in relatively good health. But somehow today he couldn't.

"Why don't you come inside?" she said. "Aunt Mildred has baked some biscuits."

After weeks of food being in perilously short supply in Vicksburg, a few staples such as flour and sugar and salt were becoming available again. They came from Yankee supplies that General Grant had ordered distributed. Though it pained him to do so, Cory had to give the man credit for that much: Grant had been willing to starve Vicksburg into submission, but now that the city had surrendered, he was doing what he could to alleviate the suffering. And so far there had been no reprisals against the former defenders, at least none that Cory had heard of. Instead the Confederate soldiers had been required to surrender their weapons and give their parole that they would not fight against the occupying troops. They would even be allowed to leave the city. It was a stunned peace that hung over Vicksburg now, but it was peace nonetheless.

Cory looked at the street. The Yankee soldiers who had marched by were nearly out of sight now, the shouted commands of their sergeant fading in the distance. Cory put his hands on his knees and rose to his feet, feeling a second of weakness as he did so. He had been sick for months with recurring bouts of a fever he had picked up in the swamps northeast of the city back in the winter. He was well now, but he hadn't regained all of his strength yet.

"Biscuits sound good," he said as he looked at Lucille. He summoned up a smile that he didn't feel.

"That's right. You've got to keep your strength up."

Cory nodded. He wasn't sure what Lucille meant by her comment, but he knew what was in his mind. Now that food was available, he had to eat and grow strong.

Because the day would come when he would be able to fight the Yankees again, to strike a blow for the Confederacy's freedom.

HUNDREDS OF miles to the northeast, on the road that ran west from Gettysburg, Pennsylvania, to the town of Chambersburg, a column of wagons was forming. Earlier, around midday, the clouds that had rolled in during the morning of July 4 opened up and dumped a deluge on the area. Rain fell in blinding sheets, wind howled like a lost soul, thunder crashed and rolled, and skeletal fingers of lightning clawed across the blackened sky. Hours later, the storm still raged. To the men who lay wounded and in agony in those wagons, it must have seemed as if the maelstrom would never end.

For the three days previous, a different sort of maelstrom had gripped the countryside around the crossroads town of Gettysburg. The Confederate army of Gen. Robert E. Lee, the Army of Northern Virginia, had collided with Union forces, the Army of the Potomac, under the command of Gen. George G. Meade. Some might say the resulting battle had come about by accident, and it was true that neither commander had intended to fight at this particular time and place, but it had been Lee's idea all along that by leading his men into Pennsylvania, he would draw out the Yankees. Following the Confederate victories at Fredericksburg and Chancellorsville, Lee's strategy had seemed sound. Make the Yankees fight one more time and crush them.

It had not worked out that way.

For three days, Lee and Gens. James Longstreet, A. P. Hill, and Richard Ewell had thrown their men against the Federal forces that held the long ridge south of Gettysburg. It was appropriate that a cemetery occupied that ridge, because tens of thousands of soldiers had died there, more than could ever be interred in its ground. On the final day of the battle, July 3, Lee had sent an entire division of Virginians under the command of Gen. George E. Pickett into the center of the Union line. The Yankees held, the back of the Confederate attack was broken, and now there was nothing left to do except gather the remnants of the shattered army and pull back, retreat to Virginia in hopes that there would be another day, another battle, another chance for the South to emerge victorious.

As he huddled on the seat of a wagon in the drenching rain, the young man called Roman didn't care about any of that. From his conversations with Capt. Will Brannon, he knew more about the strategy of battle and what had happened here at Gettysburg than most men would give a slave credit for understanding, but that didn't matter. All Roman wanted was for the wagons in the convoy to get moving. The sooner Cap'n Will was home, the better.

A cavalry officer in a long slicker pulled his horse to a stop next to the wagon. Water ran off the brim of his hat in a steady stream as he called to Roman, "You there! Boy! Can you handle that team?"

Roman tightened his grip on the reins attached to the team of mules in front of the wagon. "Yes suh!" he said, raising his voice to be heard over the pouring rain. "I can handle 'em just fine!"

The horse soldier raised a hand in a wave. "Carry on, then!" He rode on down the line, checking more of the wagons. It wasn't much of a line, Roman thought, more like a jumbled mass of vehicles. With luck, when they started moving they would all head in the same general direction, toward Cashtown and Chambersburg and ultimately Williamsport, where they would cross the Potomac River back into Virginia. That is, if the Yankees didn't catch them first. There had been rumors flying all day that Meade was going to attack as the Confederates began their retreat.

Roman hadn't expected to be given the job of driving one of the wagons. The Confederates were short-handed, though. As an able-bodied man, Roman had been put to work. In a way he would have preferred to be in the back of the wagon, caring for his wounded master and friend, but at the same time, he was willing to do whatever he could to help Cap'n Will. The day before, after Pickett's disastrous charge, Roman had been riding on the perimeter of the battle with Will Brannon when a stray bullet had struck the officer in the chest, knocking him off his horse. Roman had patched up the wound the best he could and had taken Cap'n Will to an aid station. The injury was a bad one, but Cap'n Will had lived for nearly a day already, and the surgeon seemed to think that was an encouraging sign. Cap'n Will's brother, Mac, had come by earlier in the day, before the rain started. A cavalryman in Gen. Fitzhugh Lee's brigade who had been involved in a different part of the battle, Mac had been looking for his brother, and Roman had called out to him when he happened to see him riding past the ambulance wagon. The reunion between the brothers had made Cap'n Will perk up, but only for a moment. Then he had lapsed back into unconsciousness.

He was still alive, though. Roman checked on him as often as he could.

This wagon, like all the others in the train, was packed with wounded men. Some moaned, some cursed, some screamed as the agony of their injuries tormented them. Roman shivered as a thin, wavery voice behind him uttered, "Oh, God, let me die!" Others lay insensible, and a few even had the spirit and courage to summon up smiles and words of encouragement for their fellows. But most cried out in one way or another, and that blended with the noises of the storm to create a melody that chilled the blood of any man who heard it for very long.

This had to be what hell sounded like, Roman thought.

The cavalryman who had stopped by the wagon a few minutes earlier—or another officer who looked the same in the bad light and pounding rain—rode toward the front of the column waving his arm and shouting, "Move out! Move out! Get these wagons rolling!"

Roman wished he had a hat to keep the rain out of his eyes. Plenty of them lay scattered about, and he knew he could have picked up one of them. But more than likely that would have meant he was wearing a dead man's hat, and he wasn't going to do that. He blinked away the water as best he could and flapped the reins as he shouted at the mules. Balky under the best of circumstances, the beasts really didn't want to move today. Roman picked up the whip that lay on the seat beside him and lashed at them. The merciless blows started the animals plodding forward. Roman tried not to think about the fact that here he was, a slave, whipping some poor creatures to make them do what he wanted them to do. He couldn't afford to feel sorry for the mules, not when Cap'n Will's life might depend on getting him back to Virginia as soon as possible.

Lurching and weaving, the mass of wagons got under way. Small groups of cavalrymen rode alongside every sixth wagon or so to protect the column from the Yankees. Other horsemen were in the rear, including the brigade in which MacBeth Brannon served. Roman had no idea how long the column was—miles, probably—but he knew the cavalry was stretched mighty thin. If the Yankees attacked in force, it was unlikely the Southern cavalry could turn them back.

So now it was a race, Roman thought, a race for the lives of the individual soldiers who lay wounded in these wagons—and for the very survival of the Army of Northern Virginia itself.

C⬥⬥

MAC BRANNON tugged his cap down as tight on his head as he could to keep the wind from plucking it off. As a captain and an aide of Brig. Gen. Fitzhugh Lee, he could have worn an officer's hat, but he had worn the old campaign cap ever since he'd joined the cavalry as a private. It was good enough then, and it was good enough for Mac now.

The huge silver gray stallion he rode plodded along in the rain, the mud from the turnpike staining its legs all the way up to its belly. Mac and the stallion had been through a lot together. The horse was so intelligent that at times Mac thought it was almost human, and its instincts were so sharp that its reactions in battle seemed supernatural. With a pride that bordered on arrogance—if such a thing could be attributed to a mere horse— the stallion was never anything less than magnificent.

Until today. Mac had never seen anything that could make the stallion's head droop until this storm had come along.

Mac's own spirits were dragging bottom, not only from the rain, though Lord knew that was bad enough to make any man depressed. Mac's thoughts went constantly to his brother Will, lying wounded in one of the wagons somewhere up ahead along the Chambersburg pike. At least Will had Roman with him to care for him and watch over him, Mac thought. Mac hadn't known Yancy Lattimer, Roman's original master, very well, but he knew that Yancy had been Will's friend and fellow officer in the Stonewall Brigade and had lost a leg in the battle along Antietam Creek, near Sharpsburg, Maryland. In time, that loss had led Yancy to take his own life, but not before he made out a will leaving ownership of his slave Roman to his friend Will Brannon. Yancy had accomplished more with that gesture than he could have dreamed. Mac was convinced that without Roman's help, Will would have died on the battlefield.

Will was far from out of the woods. He had to survive not only his wound but also the terrible, jolting, rain-soaked trip over this morass that had once been a road. And like everyone else in the miles-long column of wagons, he was in constant potential danger from the Yankees. Mac didn't like to think about what might happen if the Federals fell on the wagons now.

Fitz Lee's brigade, along with part of the brigade commanded by Gen. Wade Hampton, rode behind the column, forming a rear guard. Gen. Robert E. Lee had sent what artillery he could spare along with the wagons; those batteries, and the few thousand cavalrymen, were responsible for protecting the injured. Cavalry under Gen. John Imboden rode with the wagons themselves. Visibility in the storm was too bad to send out flankers. They would just get lost once they were out of sight of the wagons.

The pounding of hoof beats behind him made Mac raise his head and look around. For all he knew, the curtain of rain would part to reveal a brigade of Yankee cavalry about to overrun him and his companions. Instead, he recognized the mount usually ridden by his commanding officer. Fitz Lee gestured for Mac to stop and reined in beside him.

Lee leaned over in the saddle so that he was closer to Mac and shouted, "I've received reports of gunfire off to our right! Want to come with me to see about it, Mac?"

Even in this miserable weather, Lee was looking for trouble and grinning at the prospect of it. He was ever a bold cavalier, much like Gen. Jeb Stuart, his commanding officer.

Mac suggested, "Why don't you stay here, sir, and I'll scout the right flank?"

"Your discretion takes all the enjoyment out of war, Captain!" Lee said, still smiling. He waved a gauntleted hand at Mac. "Go see about it, but hurry back and let me know what's going on!"

Mac touched a finger to the brim of his cap in a semblance of a salute then turned the stallion to the right of the road and heeled it into a trot. He found himself riding up the gentle slope of one of the rolling hills that lined the Chambersburg pike. Although the stallion's hooves slipped a little on the muddy ground, the footing was better here than on the road itself, which had been chewed and cut into an incredible muddy mess by the wagon wheels and the hooves of the mule teams. At least here there was some grass to give the stallion's hooves more purchase as it trotted along.

He reached the top of the hill and paused long enough to look back. The members of the brigade were barely visible as they rode along through the rain, shapeless gray shadows in a gray world where the only color came from the lightning flashes overhead.

Mac hoped he could find his way back. He didn't want to be wandering around southern Pennsylvania, lost in enemy territory.

But orders didn't allow for worrying. Besides, he had volunteered for this job. He got the stallion moving again and rode down the hill. At the bottom, he found what was normally a little brook, no more than a few inches wide and a few inches deep. Today the rain had swelled it to a raging river. Mac pulled rein and stared at the roaring, fast-moving water. There was no way he could cross without being swept away. He wasn't going to risk his life like that, not to mention the life of the stallion.

Cracking noises came to his ears. Mac stiffened in the saddle. Those were gunshots, all right.

And they were coming from the other side of that flooded creek.

As Mac sat there, shapes came out of the rain and turned into men galloping toward him on horseback. He wasn't sure how many of them there were, three or four. But as he leaned forward in the saddle, his spine stiffening, he saw them twist around and fire handguns at something behind them. The puffs of smoke and the muzzle flashes were lost in the gloom, but Mac could hear the reports.

A moment later, as the fleeing men neared the flooded stream, their pursuers came into view. This second group was larger, at least a dozen men. They were shooting, too, a ragged scattering of gunfire that was typical of a running battle between cavalrymen. Even though visibility was too bad to make out the color of the uniforms, Mac knew the fleeing men had to be Confederate scouts who had run into a Yankee patrol. The scouts shouldn't be galloping toward the Confederate column—that would lead the Yankees right to the long line of ambulances and supply wagons—but in weather like this, the scouts probably didn't know where they were going. They were just fleeing blindly from a superior force.

With his jaw set in a taut, grim line, Mac backed the stallion into the shadows under a couple of trees. It was almost as dark as night under there, and he knew the men on the other side of the stream wouldn't be likely to see him. He patted the stallion's shoulder, settling the horse down as it stepped from side to side. The stallion was hardly ever skittish; Mac attributed the animal's restlessness to a distaste for hiding like this. The stallion wanted to be in on the action.

Across the flooded creek, two of the Confederate scouts reined in as they reached the raging waters while the third man forced his horse into the stream. The two still on the bank turned and fired their last futile shots at the onrushing enemy troopers. More shots rang out from the Yankee guns, knocking the two men from their saddles. They fell in the mud.

The man trying to ford the creek yelled and lashed at his horse with the reins as brown water swirled and raced around them. The horse struggled against the pounding of the current, its head held high, nostrils distended, eyes wide with terror. Man and horse made it halfway across the rain-swollen stream before the horse lost its footing. With a shrill whinny, the animal went over, and the rider went with it.

Mac felt sick as he watched the two of them tumble over and over in the water. The horse finally reached this side of the creek and stumbled out onto the slick, muddy bank. The scout went under, popped up, went under again, and then Mac lost sight of him. Chances were, the body would wash up somewhere downstream, snagged on a tree root.

The two scouts who had been shot off their horses hadn't moved since they fell. The Yankees rode up around them. An officer leaned down and poked them with his saber, making sure they were dead. The wind and the rain died down a little, and Mac heard the rattle of steel against brass as the officer sheathed his blade.

The stallion chose that moment to let out a displeased neigh.

Mac froze as he saw several of the Yankees turn and look across the stream in his direction. A moment later one of the men pointed toward the riderless horse that paced along the edge of the creek, unsure what to do without its master. The others must have agreed that the neigh came from that horse, because they turned and rode away from the creek, leaving the bodies of the dead scouts lying in the mud.

Mac didn't move, hardly even breathed, until the Federal troopers vanished in the storm. The Yankees didn't know they were within a quarter of a mile of the Confederate column. It had been hard for Mac to sit there and watch as three of his comrades were killed, but he knew he couldn't have saved them. All he would have accomplished by getting involved in the fight was to alert the Yankees that there were Confederates on this side of the flooded stream and maybe intrigue them enough to make them investigate. *And* get himself killed, more than likely. He had done the prudent, practical thing by hiding in the shadows under the trees.

But prudent or not, his actions—or lack of them—sickened him. War made some men do things they would never do under other circumstances. Today war had made Mac Brannon not do something that every fiber of his being had cried out for him to do.

With a sigh, he turned and rode the stallion back over the hill. He had to find Fitzhugh Lee and report what he had seen to the general. Lee would pass the word to Generals Hampton and Imboden to be on the lookout because Union cavalry patrols were in the area. They had suspected as much, and now Mac could confirm it.

Darkness began to settle over the countryside, and still the rain fell.

Chapter Two

THE WOODEN PEG THAT had replaced Allen Carter's right leg from the knee down thumped on the floor of the parlor as the man paced back and forth. Carter was somewhat stocky and of medium height, with curly brown hair liberally salted with gray. His hands were clenched together behind his back, and a scowl was etched into his broad face. He was angry, and that was evident to all who shared the room with him.

"I can't believe we just gave up like that," he said. "We should've made 'em fight house to house."

"And how would we have done that?" Charles Thompson asked from a wing chair near the fireplace that was cold now in the middle of summer. "We had little ammunition, and nearly everyone in the city is suffering from malnutrition and outright starvation." Thompson shook his head. "No, as much as I'd like to agree with you, Allen, I'm afraid that surrender was our only option. Otherwise thousands more would have died, including many more civilians."

Carter frowned, but he didn't argue. Thompson was a colonel in the Mississippi Home Guard and had been part of the inner circle that had been in charge of the defense of Vicksburg. He knew what he was talking about.

Cory sat on a divan on the other side of the room and listened to the conversation without really paying attention to it. His hands too were clenched together, and his chin rested on them as he thought.

Fred Carter sat on the other end of the divan, a happy smile on his face as he played with a piece of string, trying to lace it between his fingers. Fred was in his early twenties, a year or so older than Cory, but his mind was that of a child. As he succeeded in what he was trying to do, he laughed and thrust his hands toward Cory.

"Look, Cory! It's a cat's cradle."

"Yes, it is, Fred," Cory observed, affirming the young man. "And that's a good one."

The response was automatic. He wasn't really paying attention to Fred, either. His thoughts were on the situation in which he and Carter and the colonel found themselves. There had to be *something* they could do . . .

Lucille came into the parlor, followed by Mildred Thompson. The ladies had been washing up the dishes from the meager supper. Lucille sat down between Cory and Fred. Fred gave her a broad grin. He and she had become good friends in the months they had known each other.

Mildred took the empty wing chair beside her husband and picked up an embroidery hoop and needle and thread from the small table between the chairs. By the light of the single lamp, she resumed her stitching on the piecework that was fastened into the hoop. It was just something to keep her hands busy. After a few minutes, she broke the silence that had followed the women into the room, "What were you talking about, Charles?"

"Nothing, dear," Thompson said. "Nothing important."

From the divan, Fred said, "Pa thinks we should've fought the Yankees more."

Carter glared at his son. "Hush up, Fred."

Lucille patted Fred on the knee as he looked stricken by his father's rebuke.

Mildred asked, "Is that true, Charles?"

"The subject came up, of course," Thompson said. "Under the circumstances, what else would anyone talk about?"

"How to make the best of a bad situation, perhaps. Now that the Yankees are here, we have to learn to live with them."

"No," Cory said.

Something about his voice made everyone look toward him. Lucille touched his arm. "Cory, what are you thinking?"

Cory didn't answer. Instead, he looked over at Thompson. "Colonel, what happened to Richards and Howard?"

Thompson shifted in his chair and looked uncomfortable. "I, ah, told you, they didn't want to impose anymore, so they went to look for friends of theirs from their old units."

Richards and Howard, two wounded soldiers who had been recuperating at the Thompson home just prior to the surrender, had gone off with the colonel that afternoon to give their parole to the Yankees, as all Confederate troops were required to do. But they hadn't returned with Thompson, despite the fact that both of them were still weak from their wounds.

"I think they were going to try to get out of town before the Yankees marched them off to a prison camp," Cory said. "They couldn't stand the idea of just sitting here and doing nothing. They were going back to the fighting, weren't they, Colonel?"

"I told you what they told me," Thompson replied, his voice stiff. "I don't know anything more than that."

"I wouldn't call you a liar, sir—"

"I should hope not!" Lucille exclaimed. "After everything Uncle Charles has done for you—"

Thompson held up a hand to stop her. "No, that's all right, Lucille. Let the boy speak his mind."

Cory leaned forward, his hands clasped between his knees now. "Colonel, we all know what Howard and Richards intend to do. I'd wager that most of the fighting men in this city are thinking the same thing tonight. We have to get out of here so we can take up arms again."

"I gave my word to cease hostilities," Thompson said.

"That only applies while you're here in Vicksburg."

Thompson shook his head. "That's not what I said."

"But it's what you meant. You know it is, Colonel. Vicksburg is lost, but the war isn't. There's still plenty of fighting going on in other places."

"I don't want to hear this," Mildred said. "You've done enough, Charles. All of you have done enough."

"I'm not saying that I'm going anywhere, dear," Thompson told her.

"No, but I know you. I ought to. I've been married to you for long enough." She shot a glance at Cory. "Now that he's planted the idea in your head, there's no telling what you'll do, Charles Thompson."

Lucille leaned closer to Cory. "You have to stay here and get over that sickness, Cory—"

"I'm all right now," he said. "I haven't had a bout of fever in a long time."

"You thought you were over it before, but it always comes back."

"Not this time. I can tell."

She stared at him. "You're really thinking about doing it, aren't you? You're going to leave and go back to the fighting."

"It's not right to just give up," Cory explained, stubborn in his beliefs. "You remember what I was like when you met me, Lucille. I didn't really care about anybody but myself."

"That's not true! You risked your life to warn my father when that man roused that mob against us. They would have burned the *Zephyr* and probably killed everyone on her!"

Cory nodded. "But it was because of you I did it. And then you and the captain really taught me what it was like to care about other people. So you see, Lucille . . . ," he gave her a faint smile, "it's really your fault."

"Oh!" she exclaimed in exasperation. Turning to her aunt, she said, "Aunt Mildred, can't you talk some sense into them?"

"I'm trying," Mildred said, her expression grim. "But I'm not sure if anyone can get through to them. I'm not even sure anymore if they're men or mules."

That struck Fred as funny. He gave a loud bray. "Hee-haw!"

Everyone in the parlor laughed as the tension was broken. Carter clapped his son on the shoulder. "That's right, boy. I reckon we're makin' asses of ourselves, all right." He became more serious as he looked around at the others. "But the time may come when we can get out of here and do some good for the cause again, and if I get the chance, I intend to take it."

"Yankee patrols are watching everyone until all the paroles are processed," Thompson pointed out. "Getting out of the city wouldn't be easy right now, and even if you did, where would you go?"

"I don't know, but like Cory said, there's still fightin' goin' on elsewhere. I don't reckon it'd be much trouble findin' a battle."

"Unfortunately, you're probably right."

"Nobody's going anywhere tonight," Mildred said, "and I don't want to hear any more talk about it. My word, the Yankees have only been in town for a little over twenty-four hours!"

She didn't understand, Cory thought, and neither did Lucille.

Even an hour under the heels of the Yankees was too long.

BY NIGHTFALL, the rain was still pouring down from the sky in Pennsylvania. It had been dark all afternoon, but now the murk that hung over the Chambersburg pike was almost stygian.

Roman assumed the column would come to a halt for the night, but Imboden's cavalrymen instead told the drivers to press on. Doing his best to ignore the weariness that gripped him, Roman flapped the reins and shouted at the mules to keep them plodding along through the mud. A lantern hung inside the wagon in front of him; he could see the faint yellow glow through a gap in the canvas flaps at the back of the vehicle. He kept his eyes fixed on that feeble light, because it was the only indication that he was still going the right way. Likewise, a lantern guttered in the back of the ambulance he was driving, and the next wagon in line followed it.

Roman hoped whoever was leading the column, 'way up at the front, didn't take a wrong turn somewhere. If he did, they would all be lost.

It was quieter now in the back, although from time to time some of the wounded men still groaned. None of them were screaming and pleading for death. The Grim Reaper might have claimed some of them already, Roman thought. He wouldn't know until the next rest stop, when he would have a chance to check on them. He tried looking over his shoulder, hoping that he could tell if Cap'n Will was still breathing, but the ambulance was too crowded and badly lit for that. Will Brannon was just one more faint shape among the dozen or so wounded men crowded into the back of the wagon. Roman couldn't devote more than a glance to him, either, since it took great concentration to follow the lantern in the wagon ahead.

He wondered if he would ever be dry again.

⌒▬▬◆▬▬⌒

ALL NIGHT long, the column continued moving west through the mountainous country of southwestern Pennsylvania. The mules and horses pulling the wagons strained against their traces as they hauled the vehicles up the slopes. The trip would have been hard even without the rain and the mud. The quagmire that had been the turnpike made progress even more difficult.

Roman kept thinking that the column would have to stop to rest the animals, not to mention the men, but no halt was called. As the hours passed like an eternity, the wagons rolled on. From time to time an axle would break or a wheel would come off, and when that happened, the damaged vehicle was abandoned, and along with it, any wounded men who were unable to get out and clamber into another wagon on their own. They were left to their fate, whatever that might be. A Yankee hospital at first, more than likely, and then, if they recovered, a prison camp. No doubt most of them would have preferred death.

Dawn brought a lightening of the sky. The rain still fell, but not as hard. As blackness turned to gray, Roman could make out the shape of the wagon in front of him and then the other wagons stretching out in the long, sinuous column, the end of which was not visible. Though it was hard to tell because of the mud, the road seemed smaller than the Chambersburg pike. Roman frowned as he hoped that they hadn't taken a wrong turn during the night.

A town came into view up ahead, the roofs of several buildings and the spires of a couple of churches showing through gaps in the trees. Roman remembered skirting around Chambersburg during his long trek up here to join Cap'n Will after he found out that Massa Yancy's will had transferred his ownership to Will Brannon. The village the column was approaching wasn't big enough to be Chambersburg. It might be one of the smaller communities south of there, Roman decided, which meant that the wagon train had taken a shortcut during the night.

He hoped that was the case because it would also mean that the wagons were that much closer to Williamsport, where the column would cross the river into Virginia. Of course, there was no guarantee the Yankees wouldn't pursue them across the river. Roman didn't know what to make of it. He just wished they were all back home in Culpeper County.

The column twisted through the town. As the wagon driven by Roman reached the outskirts of it, he saw people standing in front of their houses, staring at the passing vehicles with sullen, angry expressions on their faces. These Yankees must have heard by now what had happened at Gettysburg during the past four days, and they knew these wagons rolling through their town were carrying Confederate wounded. Roman began to feel more nervous as he looked at the townspeople. Trouble was brewing here.

A man came running out of his house, brandishing an ax over his head. "Stop 'em!" he shouted. "Let's stop the filthy Rebs!"

With that, he dashed into the street and began chopping at the spokes of one of the wheels on the nearest wagon, which happened to be the one directly in front of Roman. The driver couldn't let go of the reins to try to stop him, and none of the cavalry escorts were close by.

Other townspeople took up the cry, and several more came running with axes and hatchets. The attack must have been planned or at least suggested, Roman thought, otherwise so many people wouldn't have been ready. He stiffened in fear. If the Yankee townsfolk stopped the wagon, he'd never get Cap'n Will back to Virginia.

Most of the attackers seemed to be coming from the right. Roman hauled on the reins, pulling the mules to the left. Just ahead, one of the wheels on the wagon under attack collapsed, splintering as the vehicle's weight proved too much for the spokes that hadn't been damaged. One of the rear corners dropped, and fresh screams came from inside as the wounded passengers received the roughest jolt so far.

Roman's wagon swung to the left. He didn't know if there was enough room in the street to get around the crippled wagon in front of him, but he was going to try. He snatched up the whip and started lashing at the mules. They broke into a trot. Someone inside the wagon screeched as it swayed and bumped along the edge of the road.

One of the civilians ran toward the wagon, ax in hand. Roman didn't hesitate. As soon as the man came within reach, Roman slashed the whip across his face. The man screamed and staggered back, dropping his ax.

For several hundred yards up and down the column, the Pennsylvanians attacked. A handful of wagons had been halted already, unable to move again until their damaged wheels were replaced. Once the wagons were stopped, some of the drivers were hauled down off the seats. Unarmed for the most part and outnumbered, these men stood no chance against the attackers. Axes rose and fell and rose again, now dripping with blood.

One of the townspeople lunged toward Roman from the left. Roman lifted his left leg, planted his foot in the middle of the man's chest, and shoved as hard as he could. The man flew backward and landed in the muddy ditch. Cursing, he reached under his coat and brought out a small pistol that he leveled at Roman.

A flurry of gunshots made the man glance toward the front of the column before he could fire. Roman looked in the same direction and saw several Confederate horsemen bearing down on the attackers. Pistols cracked and sabers flickered through the gloom. Most of the people fled, unwilling to continue their attack in the face of real opposition.

The man Roman had knocked down snarled his hatred and raised his pistol again, determined to get off a shot before he scrambled to his feet and ran. The blast came instead from behind Roman, making his head jerk around in surprise. From the corner of his eye, he saw the Yankee slump back in the mud, a smoking hole in the front of his coat.

"Cap'n Will!" Roman cried.

Will Brannon had roused out of his stupor and turned onto his side so that he could push up the canvas that covered the wagon bed. His pistol had been in his holster, but now it was in his hand, a tendril of smoke curling from the muzzle. He gave Roman a weary smile, then the pistol slipped from his fingers and he rolled onto his back, his eyes closing.

"Cap'n Will!" Roman exclaimed again. Without thinking, he started reining in, feeling only an urgency to get to Will Brannon's side and check his condition.

"Keep moving! Keep moving, damn it!"

The shouted order came from one of the cavalrymen who paused beside the wagon. He gestured with a drawn saber for Roman to keep the wagon rolling, the blade making a keening sound as it cut through the air. Roman looked again at Will then took up the reins and the whip.

The column couldn't be stopped in this town. If it were, the Yankee army would be on them in no time, Roman suspected. Cap'n Will had saved his life, but the captain's life still depended on speed and movement. The cavalry officer was right: The column had to keep going, no matter what.

"Get along!" Roman shouted at the mules. "Get along, you damned jugheads!"

He thought tears were rolling down his cheeks as he drove, but it was still raining, so he couldn't be sure.

GEN. FITZHUGH LEE wasn't surprised to hear Mac's report that Federal patrols were shadowing the flanks of the Confederate column. "Damn this rain," he muttered several times during the night as the brigade plodded along in the rear.

For his part, Mac didn't waste time or energy cursing the weather. He dozed in the saddle as the stallion rocked along. When he was growing up on the farm in Culpeper County, he had never given any thought to being a soldier, had never dreamed that one day he would be a cavalryman. Yet he had taken to that life with a natural ease and had no trouble sleeping in the saddle. Sometimes, in fact, it seemed to him that his true state was on horseback and that being on the ground was foreign to him.

When morning came and the rain slacked off a little, firing could be heard far in advance of the cavalry's position. Mac and Lee both heard it, and Lee said, "Sounds like General Imboden's boys have run into some trouble."

Mac expected Lee to send him galloping along the column to find out what was happening, but the general surprised him. "I'm sure he can handle it," Lee went on. "I intend to swing to the north a bit so as to screen the column more effectively from those Yankee patrols."

"What about acting as the rear guard, sir?" Mac asked.

"General Hampton and his men will continue to follow the wagon train. I believe the greater danger lies on the flanks."

Lee issued the orders, leaving a few of his men with Hampton but taking the greater part of his brigade and veering away from the road to the north. Mac wasn't sure where they were. During the trip north, he had been with General Stuart's cavalry on the great looping route that had taken them to the east of the

Union army, through Maryland and within ten miles of Washington, D.C., and into eastern Pennsylvania almost to Harrisburg. So this territory in southwestern Pennsylvania was new to him. When they stopped—if they ever stopped again—he resolved to take a good look at Fitz Lee's maps and figure out where they were.

All day, the cavalry rode through the rugged hills and valleys, looking for its counterpart in blue. After all the battles of the past weeks, all the days spent riding, all the time worrying about Will, Mac grew so weary that he didn't know if he could go on. Like all the other men, he napped when he could, catching a few winks as he swayed back and forth. He gnawed squares of hardtack and washed down the unpalatable stuff with swigs of brackish water from his canteen. And he watched Fitz Lee grow more and more frustrated and impatient.

Finally, as night fell on July 5, Lee called a halt to the foray and gathered his staff around him. "Gentlemen," he said, "perhaps it's time we returned to the column."

Several men nodded in agreement. Mac didn't say anything, but he felt relief wash through him. He hadn't wanted to leave the long line of wagons to begin with, since that meant leaving Will. But he hadn't argued with Lee's command, of course. He would follow Fitz Lee no matter what the general decided to do.

"Now," Lee continued as he held out his hand for the oilskin portfolio of maps carried by one of his aides, "does anybody know where we are?"

⊂══╪══⊃

IT WAS the village of Greencastle where the civilians had attacked the wagon train with axes and hatchets, Roman learned later that day from one of the cavalry officers. The man trotted his horse alongside the wagon for several minutes, his hat thumbed back on his head, looking more relaxed now that the rain had finally stopped and the danger from the townspeople was past.

"We rounded up a couple dozen of 'em," he told Roman. "General Imboden said to treat them as prisoners of war. I reckon if they're goin' to attack our ambulances, they can't expect any other sort of treatment."

"That's that many more mouths to feed, though, Cap'n," Roman pointed out.

The cavalryman laughed. "Yeah, that's right. Well, maybe we'll let 'em go when we get to Williamsport this afternoon."

"You think we'll get there today, suh?"

The man looked up at the sky, where the thick clouds had begun to break up in places. "Maybe, if the rain holds off."

A groan came from the back of the wagon, and a tortured voice called out. "Water . . . for God's sake, just a sip of water."

Roman looked back over his shoulder. The man pleading for water wasn't Will Brannon, but Roman's heart went out to him anyway. He wished he could stop and make all of the wounded men more comfortable.

"I can tell what you're thinkin' just by lookin' at you, boy," the horse soldier said. "Don't you stop that wagon. General Imboden has ordered that no one is to stop for any reason."

"I know that, suh," Roman said. "But it sure is hard sittin' here listenin' to those poor men."

"When we get across the Potomac, they'll be tended to then. But until we're back in Virginia . . ." The officer shrugged. "There's nothing we can do for them."

Roman nodded and kept the mules moving. After a while, the man asking for water fell silent.

True to the officer's prediction, late that afternoon the column reached the town of Williamsport, but not without more trouble along the way. Small bands of Federal cavalry attacked the column several times, dashing in at points along the line of wagons where the Confederate cavalry was not posted. On each occasion, Imboden's men came racing to the trouble, drawn by the firing of guns and the angry shouts of the Yankees, and each time they drove off the raiders. Not before damage was done, however. More wrecked wagons and dead and wounded men were left behind.

Roman recalled passing through this area on his trip north. A pontoon bridge spanned the river at Williamsport. It would probably take hours for all the wagons in the column to cross it, but once they did, they would be in Virginia again, and surely General Imboden would allow them to stop and see to the wounded. Roman didn't expect that to happen until they were on the other side of the river, though.

So he was surprised when the wagon in front of him lurched to a halt well short of the bridge. In fact, Roman's wagon was still on the northern edge of Williamsport.

"Whoa! Whoa!" he hauled back on the reins, bringing the mules to a stop. He peered ahead along the column and saw that all the wagons in front of him were stopped. Many of them had bunched up in a haphazard fashion, as if the halt had taken their drivers as much by surprise as it had Roman. Maybe there was a bottleneck of some sort at the bridge, he thought. That would slow down the column.

Whatever the cause, he was going to take advantage of this chance to check on Cap'n Will. He jumped down from the wagon seat, then had to catch hold of the front wheel to steady himself as his leg muscles, cramped from long hours of riding, refused for a moment to support him. The weakness passed, and Roman straightened, still holding on to the wagon just in case. He made his way along the side to the back then lifted himself onto the open tailgate.

"Cap'n Will?" he called softly. "Cap'n Will?"

Will Brannon was lying next to the left-hand sideboards of the wagon. Roman had to crawl on Will's legs to reach his upper body. Careful not to jar him too much, Roman leaned over and looked down into the pale, haggard face.

Cap'n Will's chest was moving, so Roman knew he was still alive. There was no sign of it in his face, however. It looked like the face of a dead man.

The man lying next to Will *was* dead, his eyes open and staring even though they would never again see anything. Roman forced himself not to look at the corpse as he picked up a canteen, poured a little water on a bit of rag, and wiped it over Will's lips. Will stirred at the touch of the moisture. Roman slipped a hand under his head and lifted it, then dribbled a few drops of water from the canteen into Will's mouth.

"Water! For the love of God, boy, give me some water!"

The hoarse cry came from the other side of the wagon, from the man who had been begging for water earlier. Roman eased Will's head down onto the folded, tattered blanket that served as a makeshift pillow, then moved across to the other man. Both of the man's legs were wrapped in bandages, and a bad smell came from them. But his arms were all right, and he snatched the canteen away from Roman and held it to his mouth, tilting it up so that water poured into his mouth and spilled down his neck and chest.

Roman grabbed the canteen away from him. "That's enough, suh," he said. "Too much'll make you sick."

"Give it back, you filthy darky!" The man flailed at Roman in an attempt to get the canteen away from him. Roman moved out of reach. "Give it back!"

Then the man saw it was hopeless and fell back on the boards of the wagon bed, covering his face with his hands and sobbing. Roman felt sorry for him, but he still stayed back.

For the next fifteen minutes, Roman did the best he could for the other men in the wagon, shifting them a little to make them more comfortable, giving them water, telling the ones who were conscious enough to understand that the Confederate column had reached Williamsport at last.

"We goin' to be back in Virginia 'fore you know it, yassuh, we sure is," he said to one of the men, slipping back into the way he talked around white people he didn't know.

The sound of hoof beats and shouted commands made him turn toward the rear of the wagon and stick his head through the gap in the canvas cover. He saw one of the cavalrymen coming along the column on horseback.

"See to your mules," the officer ordered as he spotted Roman. "We're going to be here for a while."

"How come, suh?" Roman asked.

The man looked impatient but stopped long enough to answer the question. "Because the damned Yankees got here before us. They tore up the bridge. And because of all this blasted rain, the river's come up and is too high to ford." The cavalryman shook his head in disgust. "We're stuck here until the river goes down . . . or until the Yankees come back for us."

Chapter Three

A T TWILIGHT, CAP'N WILL roused up long enough to take a little more water. He didn't speak, but he was able to press Roman's hand for a second before he slipped back into unconsciousness. Or maybe he was just asleep, Roman thought. Maybe Will was allowing slumber to begin the long process of healing his violated body. Roman hoped that was the case.

Exhaustion claimed Roman not long after nightfall. Though the ground was muddy, he stretched out underneath the wagon to give rest to his weary body. Even the stink of death and decay and the cries of pain and despair that surrounded him could not prevent him from falling asleep.

His sleep was not dreamless. He tossed and turned as images of the past few days played through his stunned brain. He saw wave after wave of soldiers clad in gray and butternut rolling toward the smoke-wreathed heights where the Yankees waited. He saw men fall, heard the roar of cannon and the whine of shells cutting through the air. He felt the earth tremble from the explosions. The entire world turned gray, the gray of powder smoke, and that gloom was shot through with streaks of fire. The only true color left was red, the red of flames belching from gun muzzles, the red of a man's blood running out onto the ground and taking his life with it.

And always, hanging over everything, the sickly sweet stench of rotting flesh.

Only now, Roman realized as he began to stir in his exhausted slumber, he smelled something else. Something out of place in this charnel house. His head was pillowed on his arms. He looked around then sniffed as he blinked open bleary eyes.

Danged if that didn't smell like stew.

Somebody kicked his foot where it stuck out from under the wagon, and a voice said, "Crawl on out o' there and get yourself somethin' to eat."

43

Roman couldn't remember when he'd had anything more than hardtack and water. The aroma of cooked food sickened him a little, mixed as it was with the stench coming from the wagons, but it was still a powerful lure.

He slid out from under the wagon and used one of the wheels to pull himself up. He saw a cavalry trooper standing beside the wagon, and there was a white lady with the soldier. She had a large china cup in her hand. The enticing smell came from the cup.

The cavalryman frowned when he saw that Roman was a slave. "You the driver of this wagon, boy?" he asked.

"Yes suh. I belong to Cap'n Will Brannon, one of the officers who's lyin' wounded inside it."

The trooper nodded, understanding now. "That's all right, then. Have some stew."

"I thank you kindly, suh," Roman said as he reached for the cup. He smiled at the woman. "And you, too, ma'am."

She flinched and then held the cup out even farther, so that Roman wouldn't have to come as close to her to take it.

"General Imboden's turned out the townspeople and made them open their homes and kitchens," the cavalryman said. "This is the first hot food our fellas have had in quite a while. The surgeons will be around in a little while, too, to have a look at the wounded."

Roman nodded, but his attention was really on the thick, savory stew in the cup. He didn't need a spoon. He brought the cup to his mouth and sucked down as much of the broth as he could. Then he used his fingers to scoop out the chunks of vegetables and meat. He tried to control himself so that he didn't wolf down the food, but it was difficult. He hadn't realized how hungry he was until he started eating.

When he finished, he ran his finger around inside the cup to get the last little bits of stew that clung to the sides. He extended the empty cup to the woman. "That was mighty good, ma'am. You don't know how much I appreciate it."

Again she shrank from him. "N-no, that's all right," she said in a choked voice. "You keep it."

Roman frowned. "But ma'am, this here is a fine cup. You best take it back."

"I told you I don't want it!" The words came out loud and harsh as the woman's control slipped away from her. She began to sob. "Can't I go home now?" she said to the trooper. "Can't you awful people leave me alone? Can't you leave us all alone?"

The cavalryman didn't say anything for a moment, just looked at her distraught face in the light of the lanterns hanging from the wagons. Then he rubbed his beard-stubbled jaw and said, not unkindly, "Funny thing, ma'am. That's just what us Confederates were sayin' to you Yanks a couple of years ago."

Still sobbing, the woman turned and ran away. The soldier looked at Roman, shrugged, and started after her, saying over his shoulder, "My orders were to see that the townsfolk stayed safe. Reckon I better make sure the lady gets home all right."

Roman was left standing there by the wagon, looking down at the cup in his hand. After a moment, he drew back his arm, as if he intended to hurl the cup away from him into the darkness. Then, slowly, he lowered his arm again. A fella who was smart didn't waste something that was useful, no matter where it came from.

As the trooper had mentioned, some surgeons were making their way along the halted column, checking on the wounded. A few minutes later, one of the doctors walked up to Roman's wagon, his shoulders slumping with weariness in the long coat he wore.

Roman was sitting on the lowered tailgate. He slid off of it onto his feet as the surgeon came up. "You've got wounded men inside?" the surgeon asked.

"Yes suh. And at least one dead one."

The physician grunted. "Burial detail will be around in a little while. In the meantime, let's see what I can do for the live ones." He started to climb into the wagon, pausing for a second and wrinkling his nose at the smell. He glanced at Roman. "You've got gangrene in here."

"Yes suh, I figured as much. But the cavalrymen all say we got to keep movin', so there wasn't nothin' I could do for the men all day."

"There's probably nothing I can do for them, either," the doctor muttered as he forced himself to step into the wagon and bend to the unpleasant task of uncovering and looking at all the injuries and wounds.

Roman watched from the back of the wagon as the man went about his work. Roman wanted to tell the man to check on Cap'n Will first, but he swallowed the impulse. The surgeon was unlikely to take his advice, and besides, Cap'n Will wouldn't have wanted anybody to play favorites. Roman knew that Will Brannon had always been a man who valued fairness, at least in the time he had been acquainted with him.

The surgeon unwrapped the bandages from the legs of the man who had been wounded in both lower limbs, and as he did so, the stink inside the wagon grew worse. "It's probably too late," the surgeon commented, as much to himself as to Roman, "but both those legs have to come off if this man is going to have a chance to survive."

The wounded man showed no reaction to that dire pronouncement, which meant he had to be unconscious. Roman thought about what had happened to Massa Yancy after he had lost only one leg. It might be kinder to just let the man in the wagon die. But the surgeon wouldn't do that, Roman knew. Even though the battles might be losing ones, this physician and all the other medical men would fight them.

"We've set up a field hospital in a tent not far from here," the surgeon said over his shoulder to Roman. "A couple of orderlies will be along in a little while. Can you tell them to take this man to the field hospital and prepare him for a double amputation?"

"Yes suh," Roman replied. "I can do that."

"Don't forget now, boy."

Roman stiffened. "No suh, I won't." He was a slave, but that didn't mean he was feeble-minded. It would be a waste of breath to point that out to the surgeon, though.

The man moved on to the other wounded in the wagon, including Will. Roman paid particular attention when he uncovered Will's wound, studied it for a moment, and then nodded in satisfaction. "Not too much putrefaction. The captain appears to be a strong, otherwise healthy young man. He might actually live through this." He looked at Roman again. "I don't suppose you know when this injury occurred."

"On the last day of the battle, suh. After Gen'ral Pickett's division charged that ridge with the Yankees on it."

"The wound could still go bad. This man needs to be in a hospital, a real hospital." A hollow laugh came from the surgeon. "Along with thousands of others." He straightened into an awkward crouch and came to the back of the wagon. He hopped down to the ground, landing with a grunt. "Don't forget what I told you to tell the orderlies."

"No suh, I won't." Now that he could see just how haggard the surgeon's face was, Roman resented the man's casual prejudice a little less.

As the doctor moved on to another wagon, Roman sat down on the tailgate again. He hadn't slept very long before the trooper and the woman with the stew came along, and he felt himself growing drowsy again. The food had given him some strength, but not enough to make up for the ordeal of the past few days. The muddy ground underneath the wagon was inviting.

But Roman knew that if he stretched out and went to sleep again, he might miss the orderlies who were working their way along the column, carrying wounded men who were deemed in need of surgery to the field hospital. Roman gave a massive yawn and shook his head, forcing himself to stay awake. Somebody would be along in a few minutes.

He sat there on the tailgate and waited for the orderlies—and the burial detail.

ROMAN GOT some more sleep before morning, but he was still yawning and knuckling gritty eyes when a renewed sense of urgency gripped the wagon train once more. Cavalrymen galloped up and down the line, and Roman wondered if somehow the pontoon bridge had been repaired and they were getting ready to cross the Potomac.

That was impossible, he told himself after he had thought about the situation for a moment. The Yankees hadn't done just minor damage to the bridge; they had almost totally destroyed it. And with the river as high and raging as it was from all the rain, no repair work could have gone on during the night. The Potomac would have to go down quite a bit before anything like that could even be attempted.

So what was going on? Roman didn't know, but he was willing to bet that it wasn't anything good.

He could have done with a nice hot breakfast, but it seemed that the citizens of Williamsport weren't being as "hospitable" this morning as they had been the night before. And General Imboden's cavalry was too busy to force them into cooking and caring for the wounded today. Roman had one small piece of hardtack left. With a sigh, he began to gnaw on it as he remembered with fondness the stew the lady had given him.

He didn't have long to enjoy the dubious pleasures of the hardtack. A few minutes later, one of the cavalry officers rode along the column, shouting, "Wagoners to me! Wagoners, form up and follow me!"

The drivers who had brought the wagons here from Gettysburg looked puzzled, but most of them followed the orders and began to form in rough ranks alongside the stalled column. Roman hesitated before following them. He looked at the wagon, knowing full well that Cap'n Will was inside and might need him, to say nothing of the other wounded men. The dead man had been taken away by the burial detail sometime in the wee hours of the morning, and the medical orderlies had come for the man who was going to have both legs amputated. But there were still more than half a dozen wounded in the wagon, and Roman didn't want to abandon them.

He didn't have any choice in the matter. The officer spotted him hesitating and rode over to him. "Damn it, didn't you hear me, boy? Form up and follow me!"

"Yes suh, I heard you," Roman said, "but my massa, he's in this wagon and he's hurt—"

"Did you drive it here?" the cavalryman interrupted.

"Yes suh."

"My orders are to gather up all the wagoners and bring them down to the river, and by God, I intend to follow orders!" The officer put his hand on the hilt of his saber. "Now get moving!"

"Yes suh," Roman muttered. Keeping his head down, he went over to join the other men in the newly formed ranks. Several of them glared at him, clearly not caring for the idea of sharing whatever they were about to do with a slave. But it hadn't been his idea, Roman told himself, so let them think whatever they wanted to think.

In a few minutes, the wagon drivers began marching toward the Potomac. The straightness of their ranks left a lot to be desired, and they were far from being in step. No one, however, seemed to care. It only mattered that they get to where they were supposed to go.

As the ragtag column advanced, more and more men joined them until Roman estimated there were upwards of five hundred in the group. He saw the guns from the few batteries General Imboden had been given being wheeled up the hills that surrounded Williamsport.

Several roads led into the town, and the wagoners were march to a position facing one of them. A small group of cavalry officers came along and divided the column into smaller groups of about a hundred men each.

If Roman didn't know better, he would have said that they were being split up into military companies so they could fight the Yankees. But fight with what? Nearly all of the wagoners were unarmed.

That problem was solved a few minutes later when men came along pulling carts loaded with muskets and ammunition pouches, along with a few handguns. They started passing out the weapons. Roman noticed dark stains on most of the ammunition pouches and realized that these guns had been scavenged from the wounded men in the wagons.

And from the dead men as well, no doubt.

The trooper issuing weapons to Roman's company stopped and grunted in surprise when he came to the young man. "Darky, huh?" he said. "You a slave?"

"Yes suh." Cap'n Will had promised to give Roman his manumission papers and make him a freedman when they got back to Virginia, but for now he was still a slave. If Will died before that could come about, he would remain a slave.

"I ain't givin' a gun to no slave," the trooper said. "You can be a courier and run messages."

Roman nodded. He didn't see any point in arguing. It wouldn't do any good. Maybe the trooper would answer one question for him, though. "Are the Yankees comin'?"

"Damn right. Word is that two whole Yankee divisions are on their way here, and maybe part of another division."

Roman's heart sank in his chest. He didn't know how many men were in General Imboden's command, but the number was considerably less than two divisions. Even with hundreds of wagon drivers recruited to help defend the column, the Confederates would still be outnumbered by what could easily be a deadly margin.

The distribution of weapons went on, and then the officers began spreading out their commands, stretching a defensive line from the river to the northeast, skirting east of Williamsport. Roman's group was not far from the river, facing level ground that looked like perfect terrain for a cavalry charge, even with the broad road that led along it. As that thought crossed his mind, he wondered where Mac Brannon and the rest of Fitzhugh Lee's brigade were. Lee was supposed to be serving as a rear guard for the column of wagons, but so far today, Roman hadn't seen hide nor hair of him or of Cap'n Mac.

Arming the wagon drivers and positioning them and the dismounted cavalrymen had taken all morning, and now the noontime sun stood directly overhead. It blared down with no mercy, baking the mud and causing steam to rise in the air. Roman sleeved sweat off his forehead. If it was this hot and miserable out here in the open where there was a little breeze, it would be even worse inside the wagons full of wounded men. Roman almost hoped that Cap'n Will was still unconscious so he wouldn't be aware of what he was being forced to endure.

Hunger gnawed at the slave's stomach, but there was no food. He didn't have a canteen, either, and by early afternoon the inside of his mouth felt like cotton. All he could do was wait, kneeling in a ditch beside the road with several other men. The lieutenant who was in command of their group paced back and forth a few yards away. Roman had told the officer that he was supposed to act as the unit's courier, but the lieutenant had waved him away. The young man was too nervous to be thinking about such things now.

Men talked in low, murmuring voices, an undercurrent of noise that Roman paid little attention to. He stiffened as he heard something else, a low, rolling rataplan that he recognized as the sound of hundreds, perhaps thousands, of approaching hoof beats.

Roman wasn't the only one to hear it. The young lieutenant called in a shrill voice, "It's the Yankees! They're coming!"

So they were. Due to the wet roads, there was no dust cloud to warn of the approach of the Union cavalry, so only a moment passed after the hoof beats became audible before the riders themselves came into sight, their horses moving at a brisk trot.

The blue uniforms were clearly visible in the sunlight, and that same sunlight struck reflections off drawn sabers.

"Steady, men, steady!" the lieutenant called. Roman had a feeling the young officer was talking as much to himself as to the wagoners who had been pressed into service as infantrymen.

From the heights that rose on the left side of the Confederate defensive line, the artillery batteries opened up. The booming of cannon and the explosion of shells served as the impetus to charge for the Yankees. They surged forward.

"Fire!" the lieutenant cried, his voice breaking a little, and along the line the other officers placed in charge of the wagoners echoed the order. A ragged volley ripped out from the men's rifles, and the fight was on.

And once more, Roman thought as he knelt in the ditch, he was right in the middle of it.

❦

FITZ LEE'S cavalry brigade had been riding all night and all morning, searching for the column it had left the day before. Mac tried to suppress the impatience and irritation he felt as he and the rest of the brigade trotted over the rolling hills and through the valleys between the mountains. They should have stayed where they were supposed to be, he thought. Yet he knew that Lee's orders from General Stuart had been rather loose and open to interpretation. The brigade was supposed to serve as the column's rear guard, but the cavalrymen had also been charged with providing a screen between the wagons and any pursuing Yankee cavalry. It was reasonable that Lee had moved his command to meet what he considered to be the greatest threat.

Still, that had meant abandoning Will and all the other wounded men, and Mac didn't have to like it.

A little after noon, Fitz Lee called a halt to give both horses and men a breather. He and Mac swung down from their saddles and stood together under the shade of some trees with a few other members of Lee's staff.

"Mac, I'm sending you to scout ahead," Lee announced. Other men had gone ahead earlier, but none of them had come back in yet. Lee continued, "That stallion of yours is the fastest horse in the brigade. We're going to continue down this road, and if you find the column, I want you to get back to us as quickly as possible and let me know its position."

"Yes sir," Mac said. "Permission to rest my horse a few minutes longer before I leave?"

"Granted. Even a mount as fine as that stallion has to catch its breath."

But not as much as the other horses in the brigade, Mac knew. The stallion's stamina was phenomenal. After five minutes and a drink from a nearby creek, the big silver gray horse was ready to go again.

Mac mounted up and lifted a gauntleted hand in a wave of farewell as he heeled his horse into a run. He thought the road he was on was the turnpike between Chambersburg and Williamsport, but he didn't know how close he was to the Potomac, or even if this was the right road. All he knew for sure was that the column had not passed along this stretch of the pike. If they had, the marks left by the wagon wheels and the hooves of the mule teams would have been visible.

Within minutes, the cavalry brigade fell out of sight behind Mac as he followed the road around several bends. The countryside was heavily wooded in places, and it occurred to Mac that he was riding alone through enemy territory. If he ran into a Union patrol riding along the road or a force of Yankee infantry lurking in the woods, he would be in a bad position. He would have to rely on the stallion's being able to outrun any pursuit.

It would be difficult, though, for even the stallion to outrun a rifle ball or an artillery shell.

Mac forced those thoughts out of his head and concentrated instead on memorizing the landmarks along his route. If he found the column, he wanted to be able to retrace his path so that he could take word of the discovery back to Fitz Lee.

The countryside seemed strangely deserted. No doubt everyone in the vicinity had heard about the great battle at Gettysburg and knew that the Confederates were likely to withdraw through this area. The civilians were lying low, staying out of the way of hostilities as best they could. Mac saw some cows and horses in the fields he passed, and the woods were full of birds and small animals, but he didn't see any people.

Several hours later, the road intersected another road, and this one was much more heavily traveled, he saw. There were no signs at the intersection, but he headed southwest along the second road anyway. A few miles farther on, he came to another crossroads, and at this one a sign told him that Williamsport was another four miles ahead in the direction he was traveling. His instincts had been right.

The column had passed through here on its way to Williamsport, he told himself. It was possible that the wagons were already across the Potomac and back home in Virginia. Mac wanted to think so. He considered turning around and racing back to Fitz Lee, but he decided to press on for a while longer until he caught up with the column. Then he could take precise information back, rather than a guess.

He had ridden only a mile farther on when he heard the sudden roar of artillery in the distance to the southwest, followed by the fainter rattle of musketry.

Mac reined in, tensing in the saddle. After hearing the soul-rattling, earthshaking bombardments at Gettysburg, he knew that this engagement was on a much smaller scale. But it was still a sizable battle, he thought, and judging from the direction of the sounds, it was taking place around Williamsport. He wondered if the Federals had caught up with the column as it was about to cross the river, or even in the act of crossing the Potomac.

There was only one way to find out.

With a shout, Mac put the stallion into a gallop.

Chapter Four

ROMAN HUGGED THE GROUND as bullets whined over his head. He was in a good position to feel the earth shake every time an artillery shell detonated. The projectiles were falling all around, both in the front of the Union advance and along the Confederate defensive line. Both sides had artillery and were more than willing to use the field pieces.

He had been wrong earlier, he told himself. He had witnessed battles before, but never until today had he truly been in the middle of one. On the third day at Gettysburg, he and Cap'n Will had watched the last great charge from a spot near the Lutheran seminary, along with an English observer named Freemantle. Will had not taken part in that fight. He had been wounded on the way back to General Ewell's headquarters, on the other side of Gettysburg. The route should have been a safe one—but on that day, nowhere in the vicinity of the town had been safe. There had been too much lead flying through the air for that. One piece of it had found Will, knocking him out of the saddle.

But even that bolt from the blue hadn't been as terrifying as this, Roman thought as another explosion assaulted his ears and shook him to his core. The attack had lasted only a few minutes so far, but already it seemed like hours to him.

"Keep firing, boys!" the lieutenant shouted. "We'll soon have them on the ru—"

A dull thud interrupted the exhortation. Roman lifted his head and saw the young officer stagger a few steps to the side. The lieutenant tried to turn. His knees folded under him, dropping him to the ground as if he were praying. Roman saw blood welling from the young man's chest where a bullet or a piece of shell had smashed into flesh. The lieutenant's mouth worked, but nothing came out except more blood. He toppled onto his side, twitched a couple of times, then lay unmoving.

Roman hunkered lower in the ditch and blinked back tears. He hadn't known the lieutenant, had never even seen the officer until today, but still he felt a wave of horror and sorrow at the man's death.

Men were dying all over the battlefield, he reminded himself. If the Yankees overran the Confederate line, he would probably be one of them. He doubted that in the heat of combat any of the Union troops would notice that he was unarmed. They might not even notice that he was a slave.

A hand gripped Roman's shoulder, hard. "Hey, there! Boy!"

Roman looked up into the bearded face of one of the wagoners. The man held a smoking rifle in his other hand.

"I heard you tell the lieutenant you was s'posed to be our runner," the man went on. "Best go find somebody in charge an' tell 'em we ain't got no officer now."

Roman hesitated. Getting up would mean exposing himself to the heavy fire going on. But he knew the wagoner was right. Word of the lieutenant's death had to be carried to the field commanders. And Cap'n Will wouldn't want him to be a coward. Roman started to clamber to his feet.

"Hold on," the wagoner said. He took a pistol from behind his belt and pressed the butt of it into Roman's hand. "I don't care what they said about not givin' a darky a gun. If you're on my side, I want you able to fight."

Roman nodded. "Yes suh." He tried not to stare in wonderment at the pistol. He had never held a handgun before. Before the war, when Massa Yancy would go hunting, Roman sometimes carried his shotgun, but those were the only times he had ever touched a firearm.

"Go on now," the wagoner told him.

Roman nodded, came all the way to his feet, and turned to run behind the line of wagoners who were peppering the advancing Yankees with rifle fire. He had gone only a few yards when another explosion roared, this one close enough to fling him forward off his feet. Badly shaken, he had to lie there on the ground for a moment before he could lift himself to his hands and knees. He looked back over his shoulder and saw that the artillery shell had landed in the ditch. The man who had given him the pistol, indeed all the men in that little group of wagoners, had been obliterated by the blast, which left a gaping, smoking crater in the ground with bodies and body parts littered around it.

Roman felt his stomach lurch and was glad now he hadn't had any breakfast except a little hardtack. He was able to force down the roiling sickness and get to his feet, where he broke into a stumbling run. Somehow when he had been knocked down he had held on to the pistol. His hand clenched on it now. He drew a meager comfort from the solidity of the walnut grips on the weapon's handle.

Roman couldn't get the sight of that crater out of his mind. If he had stayed where he was only a moment or two longer, he would have been killed when the shell landed, too. Fate had spared him for some reason.

It was so he could take care of Cap'n Will, he told himself. That was the task fate had given him. But in order to accomplish it, he had to live through today.

His stride lengthened, became surer. He was running faster now. He had a job to do.

MAC SAW the smoke from the artillery batteries rising above the trees when he was still a mile or more away from the site of the actual battle. A few minutes later he topped a rise and reined in to study the scene spread out before him. The Potomac was off to the right a mile or so, running swollen in its tree-lined banks. The town of Williamsport was nestled on the river's eastern bank. At this point, the Potomac went into a great bend that had it running almost due north and south for a stretch of several miles as it formed the boundary between Maryland and Virginia.

It was not until Mac stared at the river for a moment that he realized he was actually in Maryland now, that he had crossed the border from Pennsylvania without even being aware of it.

To Mac's left, he saw a pair of roads leading into Williamsport, one from the east, the other from the southeast. The Yankee cavalry was advancing along these roads. They had dismounted and were fighting as infantry. The Confederates had formed a stout defensive line and seemed to be holding off the Union advance. Artillery boomed from a small range of hills on the left side of the Confederate line. As Mac watched, a large number of men withdrew from the hills and shifted toward the right of the line. They were some of General Imboden's cavalry, Mac thought, and they were also fighting dismounted.

After a few moments of looking over the battlefield, he spotted the command post behind the lines. Without waiting any longer, Mac urged the stallion into a run again. He wanted to reach Imboden and urge the general to hold out. Help, in the form of Fitz Lee's cavalry brigade, was on the way.

The fire of the Federal artillery was concentrated on the front of the Confederate line, so Mac didn't have to worry about dodging shells here in the rear. And it was unlikely that any stray bullets would reach this far, since they normally didn't have that kind of carrying power. Will had been hit by a wild shot, though, Mac reminded himself. Anything was possible, especially on a battlefield.

A couple of pickets challenged him as he approached General Imboden's makeshift headquarters, which consisted of a small wagon and a tent. The guards waved Mac past when he shouted, "Message from General Fitzhugh Lee!" Imboden and several members of his staff turned around as they heard the pounding of the stallion's hooves behind them.

Mac swung out of the saddle and snapped a salute to the general. "Compliments of General Fitzhugh Lee, sir," he said.

Imboden returned the salute. "Where is the general? Not far off, I hope."

"He's a short distance behind me, sir," Mac said, hoping that Lee's brigade had indeed pushed on with all possible speed. "He should be up presently with three thousand fresh men."

Mac could see the relief that washed over the general's strained face, though Imboden tried not to be too obvious about the reaction. "We can certainly hold our own until they arrive," he said. The general turned to one of his aides. "Pass the word that reinforcements are on the way."

It didn't take long for the encouraging news to spread. Mac was still catching his breath when a cheer ran along the Confederate line. If the Yankees heard those whoops and high-pitched yells, the sounds probably struck despair in their hearts.

Mac said, "If you don't mind my asking, sir, where are the wagons?"

"Back in Williamsport," Imboden replied. "You have friends among the wounded, Captain?"

"Yes sir, and more than friends. My brother is back there, too."

"The Yankees won't take him, Captain. Not without going through all of us first, and through Fitz Lee's men, too, if they get here in time."

"They'll get here, General." Mac lifted the stallion's reins and got ready to mount. "I'll see to that."

"You propose to guide them?" Imboden asked as Mac settled himself in the saddle.

"Yes sir. As soon as possible."

"Godspeed, then." Imboden tugged the glove off his right hand and reached up to offer it to Mac. Mac returned the general's firm grip. Then he wheeled the stallion and galloped away.

Behind him, the fighting continued. Mac wished he could have seen Will, could have made sure that his brother was all right, but he knew that the best thing he could do for Will was to make sure that Lee's cavalry arrived in time to guarantee the safety of the column.

To Roman, it seemed that the shooting had been going on for days now. He knew that the great battle at Gettysburg had lasted for three days. This was nothing more than a skirmish compared to that. But he had discovered that time did strange things when a man was being shot at. Waiting for the next explosion, for the whine of the next bullet, made the seconds drag by like hours. Even the bursts of action, when he had to run from position to position along the Southerners' line, seemed to take forever.

He had stumbled onto Col. William R. Aylett, who was in charge of the wagoners on the right, next to the river. After reporting the death of the lieutenant, Roman had been ordered to take a message to Col. J. L. Black, in command on the left. Aylett had waved off Roman's feeble protest that he ought to return to his original position. There was nothing there, anyway, except a shell crater and the remains of the men who had been fighting there.

Colonel Black had had a response to the message from Colonel Aylett. He wrote it out, scrawling on a scrap of paper with a stub of pencil, and then handed the paper to Roman. "Take this back to the colonel," Black commanded, and Roman had had no choice but to comply. He had caught his breath by then, so he was able to sprint along behind the lines until he reached Aylett's position again.

That was just the beginning of the long afternoon of carrying messages. The muscles of Roman's legs began to burn with weariness, but he forced himself to ignore the pain and carry on. By late in the day, he realized that he was ignoring the bullets, too. They still whipped and whined around his head, but he no longer paid any attention to them. He was numb to the danger, numb to everything except the need to carry out his orders. In idle moments, of which there were very few, he wondered if all soldiers felt this way, so overwhelmed by the events in which they found themselves that all they could do was carry on blindly.

The sun was low in the west, and dusk wasn't far away when Lee's brigade thundered down on the scene and joined the fight.

Roman had to scurry out of the way of the shouting daredevils on horseback as they galloped past. He looked for Mac Brannon but didn't see him in the confusion. Pressed by a suddenly strengthened foe, the Union forces began to pull back. A few minutes later, the rattle of more gunfire came from the southeast. Roman had no idea what was going on over there, but it must have spooked the Yankees. They started withdrawing down the road that had brought them almost to Williamsport. It was an orderly retreat but a hurried one. Cheers of triumph went up from the Confederates, soldiers and wagoners alike, when they saw the Yankees mounting up and galloping off to the east. The artillery batteries unleashed a few last shells to speed them on their way.

Finding himself at loose ends, Roman walked toward General Imboden's command post in the center rear of the Confederate line. What he really wanted was to get back to his wagon in Williamsport and to check on Cap'n Will. He was heading in the right general direction for that.

All his life he had been given orders, he thought as he walked through the confusion of the battlefield, stepping around men who had been wounded or killed and others who were celebrating the victory. As a slave, he had hardly ever been at loose ends. There had always been somebody to tell him what to do. But then Massa Yancy had died, and Roman had trekked up to Pennsylvania to find his new master, Will Brannon. He had been nervous, traveling alone like that, and he had kept to the woods and the fields most of the time. Finding Cap'n Will had been a relief. He wouldn't have to think for himself anymore.

The thing of it was, Cap'n Will didn't boss him around like they were back on a plantation. He treated him more like one of the soldiers, giving him orders and expecting him to carry them out, but not in the same way that a slave was expected to do what he was told. Cap'n Will *trusted* him to do what was right. That was something Roman had never experienced before.

But then Cap'n Will had been wounded, and Roman had been forced to act on his own again; otherwise Will would have died. Since then he had been given orders as a driver in the column of wagons, but other than a few moments here and there, Roman hadn't really felt like a slave. He had taken part in the battle today as a soldier.

He had been scared, more scared than he had ever been in his life, but now that it was over, he felt proud that he had done his part. Pride was something else he had experienced only seldom, and it felt good.

"You there! Boy!"

Roman stopped and turned his head to see one of the officers coming toward him. The man was limping, and a bloody sling supported his left arm. "Sir?" Roman said.

The officer gestured toward Roman's waist with his uninjured arm. "What are you doin' carryin' a gun?"

Roman had forgotten all about the pistol. It was tucked in the waistband of his ragged trousers—which, come to think of it, weren't any more ragged than many of the uniforms worn by the Southern troops. Roman hadn't had any need to use the gun, but he still carried it.

He didn't let the angry glare being directed at him by the wounded officer frighten him. Instead he straightened to attention as he had seen Cap'n Will and Massa Yancy do when talking to superior officers, and he lifted his right hand in a salute. "I'm a courier for General Imboden, sir," he said.

The officer frowned in surprise. "Really? Well, then . . ." He returned the salute. "Carry on."

"Yes sir." Smartly, Roman turned on his heel and started toward General Imboden's command post once again, leaving the officer to stare after him.

He couldn't help but grin as he strode through the gathering twilight.

MAC WAS with Fitz Lee when Lee arrived at Imboden's temporary headquarters. The two cavalry commanders saluted each other and then shared a warm handclasp. "Good to see you, General Lee," Imboden said. "You and your men made a very timely arrival."

"Sorry we couldn't be here earlier," Lee replied with a smile. "But it looks as if your men did a fine job of entertaining our Northern brethren."

"We didn't let them get too bored," Imboden said.

At that moment, Mac's head jerked up in recognition of an unmistakable whining sound. The shrill sound of an incoming projectile. Nevertheless, Mac shouted a warning to the cluster of officers gathered around the generals.

There was no time for anyone to move, however. The shell slammed into the ground and burst some yards away. The force of the explosion staggered the officers and spooked the horses, but no one was knocked down. Fitz Lee had been the closest to the blast. He had been pelted by rocks and dirt but seemed unhurt. He took off his hat and slapped it up and down his uniform to get some of the dust off of him. "Good Lord!" he exclaimed. "I thought the fight was over. Where did that shell come from? Was it one of ours?"

Imboden pointed to a flash of fire as one of the Confederate cannon under the command of Maj. B. F. Eshleman discharged. "No, General, I'd say that was a parting gift from the Yankees. You can see there, Major Eshleman is returning the favor now."

Lee laughed. "That was a near thing. I'd just as soon not receive any more such gifts."

Seated nearby on the stallion, Mac breathed a sigh of relief that his commanding officer and friend was all right. Lee could laugh it off, but the blast had been much too close for Mac to feel any amusement.

He did feel a tug on the trouser leg of his uniform, however, and when he looked down on that side of the stallion, he saw a familiar face smiling up at him.

"Cap'n Mac!" Roman called out gleefully. "I was hopin' I'd run into you."

"Roman!" Mac exclaimed. He dismounted and clapped a hand on the young man's shoulder. "Are you all right? What are you doing here? Why aren't you with the wagons?" Mac knew that was a lot of questions, but Roman's presence had surprised him.

"All of us who'd been drivin' the wagons got brought up here to fight," Roman explained.

"And they did a good job of it, too," General Imboden interrupted. "This was mostly the wagoners' fight. Without them, I'm not sure we would have come through it."

The general grew more solemn as he turned back to Fitz Lee. "And I'm not sure we've won, even now. The bridge over the Potomac has been destroyed, General Lee, and the river is too high to ford."

Lee frowned, his natural ebullience diminished somewhat by the news. "My uncle was starting from Gettysburg with the infantry not long after we left. Once they get here, no Union cavalry force will be large enough to dislodge us. But until then . . ."

Imboden nodded in agreement. "Until then, we're still in danger."

Mac heard and understood that, but he knew that with darkness falling, there was little chance the Yankees would try anything else tonight. He turned to Lee. "General, would it be all right if I checked on my brother?"

Lee waved a hand toward the town. "Of course, Captain. I expect we'll be making our headquarters in Williamsport, so I'll see you there later."

Mac saluted. "Thank you, sir."

Lee returned the salute by touching a finger to the brim of his plumed hat. Mac turned to the stallion and stepped up into the saddle. He extended a hand to Roman, who eyed the stallion. "Does that horse mind carryin' double?"

"I don't think so," Mac replied. He chuckled. "I reckon the old boy could carry a lot more if he had to."

Roman clasped Mac's wrist and swung up behind him. The stallion headed toward Williamsport at an easy lope.

Roman showed Mac the way to the wagon where Will was waiting. A few men had been left behind to guard the wagons in case the people of Williamsport tried to get up to the same sort of mischief as the people of Greencastle had the day before. Roman told Mac about that misadventure.

Mac shook his head. "Bad enough we have to fight the Yankee army," he said, "without having to fight civilians, too."

When they reached Roman's wagon, he slid down from the stallion and hurried to the back of the vehicle. Mac dismounted and tied the horse's reins to one of the wheels. "Thank the Lord," Roman said as he climbed onto the tailgate. "Looks like Cap'n Will is still all right."

Mac climbed into the wagon behind Roman. A lantern was burning, its wick trimmed low so that its light was faint and wavering. But the illumination was enough to let Mac see his brother's face. Will was either sleeping or unconscious. His chest was rising and falling steadily.

The other men in the wagon were resting, too, some of them restless in their sleep but quiet. Only an occasional low moan broke the silence.

Roman knelt next to Will and whispered to Mac, "He's goin' to be all right. Cap'n Will's the strongest man I know."

"I'm sure you're right, Roman," Mac said. He rested a hand on Will's right shoulder for a moment, the touch light so as not to disturb the wounded man. Then he backed out of the wagon and dropped to the ground. Roman followed him.

"The whole time we were out there fightin', I kept thinkin' about Cap'n Will," Roman said in a quiet voice. "The doctor says he's got a good chance if he gets to a hospital 'fore too much longer. I knew that if them Yankees got him, they'd throw him in some prison camp, and he'd die, sure as shootin'."

"I think you're right," Mac said. "You helped save his life today, Roman—again."

"I figure Massa Yancy wanted me to look after him, otherwise he wouldn't have left me to Cap'n Will."

"Will told me he intends to free you as soon as he gets the chance."

Roman nodded his head. "Yes suh, I know."

Mac studied the young man's face for a moment, even though the darkness made it difficult to scrutinize his features. "But that's not the reason you keep risking your own life to help him, is it?"

Roman hesitated before answering, "Cap'n Will, he's a good man. Massa Yancy treated me just fine, 'bout as good as a master can treat a slave. But he never forgot I was a slave, and I never forgot it, either. With Cap'n Will . . . after a while, that's somethin' both of us didn't think about much."

"Brannons have never held slaves," Mac said. "Will's not used to it. He pretty much treats every man the same."

"That's true. But you and him . . ." Roman paused again, as if uncomfortable and unsure if he should go on. "You're fightin' for the right of folks like Massa Ebersole to have slaves."

Mac stiffened. "I may not agree with something," he said, "but when the law says it's legal, and the Constitution says the states have the right to decide such things . . ." His words trailed off. The words he had just spoken carried some truth to them, but they also had something of a hollow sound, even in his own ears. "Damn it," he said. "There should have been some way to solve things without them invading us. The Yankees came into our homes with rifles and cannons and sabers. *They* had no right to do *that.*"

"I reckon I agree with you there, Cap'n Mac," Roman said. "Both sides went to fightin' when they should've done more talkin'."

That summed it up about as well as anything Mac had heard. He put a hand on Roman's shoulder. "What I was getting at is that I'll see to it Will's intentions are carried out. You'll be a free man, Roman, regardless of what happens from now on."

"Ain't nothin' goin' to happen," Roman said, "except that Cap'n Will's goin' to the hospital and goin' to get well." His voice was stubborn.

Mac smiled. "That's right. And as soon as he's up to it, we'll both take him home for a visit."

"I reckon he'd like that."

So would I, Mac told himself, thinking of the Brannon farm and the other members of the family who were still there. *So would I.*

Chapter Five

H ENRY BRANNON STUDIED THE calendar that hung on the wall of the parlor in the Brannon family farmhouse in Culpeper County, Virginia. He had made the calendar himself, painstakingly laying out the grids and marking the dates on it. In the midst of war, it was easy to lose track of such things as the passage of time. Henry was determined that he would know what day it was, by God!

Not that the farm was really in the midst of the war. True, the fighting had come close to the farm on several occasions, close enough so that the rumble of artillery could be heard in the distance. On those days, Henry and his mother, Abigail, and his sister, Cordelia, had stayed close to home, sitting in the parlor and praying and talking in quiet voices. But so far combat had not touched this land that had been held by the family for decades. The Brannons had been spared that, if little else.

The invasion of Maryland and Pennsylvania by the Army of Northern Virginia had ensured that there would be no hostilities here in Culpeper County for a while. All the action had been up north. Henry, like everyone else he knew, had hoped that the daring foray would lure the Yankees into a decisive battle so that they could be crushed, once and for all.

The crushing blow had fallen instead on those Southern hopes, when word reached Virginia of the army's defeat at Gettysburg. Henry would never forget the moment when he came home from the fields to find his mother in the arms of the preacher from the Baptist church in Culpeper, the Reverend Benjamin Spanner. At one time, there had been a budding romance between those two, until Spanner's opposition to the war soured it, but there was nothing romantic about the way the preacher held Abigail Brannon that day. She had been sobbing, and he had been trying to comfort her. Spanner had brought the news of the battle at Gettysburg. Abigail had been crying because she knew her two oldest sons, Will and Mac, were there, and they might well be among the tens of thousands of Confederate casualties on the battlefield.

In the days since, Abigail had emerged from her room only seldom, and when she did, she was white-faced and puffy-eyed from the crying and praying she had been doing. Cordelia was taking things a little better, Henry thought, but she looked the same way much of the time.

For his part, Henry preferred to believe that Will and Mac were fine. He had looked up to his brothers, especially Will, for as far back as he could remember. Will had been the sheriff of Culpeper County for a while, and there wasn't a man around who was tougher or better with a gun. Will could find a way to live through any fight. And as for Mac, well, he had that big silver gray horse, and Henry knew that stallion wasn't going to let anything happen to Mac.

Still, it would be damned nice to hear something from them, Henry thought, just to be sure they were all right. He had already lost one brother, Titus, who was killed at Fredericksburg, and Cory was as good as lost, trapped like he was in Vicksburg, which was now controlled by that devil U. S. Grant.

Thinking about Titus made Henry's eyes go once more to the homemade calendar. Nearly seven months had passed since the battle of Fredericksburg.

That was long enough, Henry told himself. Six months was a proper period of time for a woman to spend mourning a lost husband. Henry had waited nearly an extra month beyond that. Now it was time.

Time for him to ask Polly Ebersole to marry him.

She wasn't his sister-in-law anymore, he reminded himself as he turned away from the calendar and stepped in front of the looking glass to adjust the string tie around his neck. He looked respectable, he decided. Not respectable enough to suit Duncan Ebersole, Polly's father, of course, but then the old Scotsman would never be satisfied that anyone was good enough to marry his daughter. Ebersole had done his level best to discourage Titus from courting Polly. Back in the days before the war, those days that now seemed a hundred years in the past, Titus had dared to dance with Polly during a ball held at Mountain Laurel, the Ebersole plantation. That audacity had gotten him a beating from some of Ebersole's overseers. But Titus had been nothing if not stubborn. He'd been bound and determined to woo Polly, and she seemed to welcome his attention. Despite everything Ebersole had done, Titus and Polly had wound up married.

For some reason that Henry had never understood, the marriage hadn't really taken. Titus had left Polly and joined the army, marching off to Fredericksburg, where he fought in his first—and last—battle. Polly had gone into mourning along with the rest of Titus's family, but lately she had shown signs of coming back to life. She had visited the Brannon farm several times and spent hours talking to Henry. In comforting each other over Titus's death, a friendship had sprung up between them with no effort at all. Then one day Polly had kissed him, and that friendship had turned into something else.

"Oh, my God," Cordelia said from behind him. "What do you think you're doing, Henry Brannon?"

Without looking around, Henry said, "You'd better not let Ma hear you using the Lord's name like that, Cordelia. She wouldn't like it."

"I don't like what I'm seeing," Cordelia said. "You're all spiffed up like you're going courting."

Henry turned away from the mirror and reached for his hat. "I thought I might take a ride over to Mountain Laurel."

"Duncan Ebersole will have you whipped—or shot."

"I don't think so," Henry said with a shake of his head. "I don't believe Ebersole is the big he-wolf he thinks he is. Polly's not going to let anything happen to me."

Cordelia stared at him. At nineteen years of age, she was two years younger than Henry, and she was the only one of the

Brannon children to inherit her father's fiery red hair. She also had something of John Brannon's Irish temper. Without warning, her left hand shot out and her fingers clamped down hard on Henry's right ear.

"Ow! Dadgum it, Cordelia, let go of me!" Henry swatted at her arm, but not hard enough to hurt her—or to make her loosen her grip.

"No! I'm not going to let you make a fool of yourself over Polly Ebersole! She'll just hurt you, Henry. Can't you see that?"

Henry twisted his head back and forth, but that just made his ear hurt worse. "You got no right to tell me what to do!"

"As long as I'm the only one left in this family who's got any sense—"

"Cordelia!" The voice came from the stairs that led to the second floor. "Let go of your brother's ear."

Cordelia released her grip and swung around to face the stairs. "Ma, you don't know what he's about to do."

Abigail Brannon came down two more steps, and as she did so, she said, "I can make a pretty good guess by looking at him. The way he's dressed up, he's going to see Polly. I think I heard her name mentioned as well . . . along with some comment about you being the only one in the family with any sense."

The fair skin of Cordelia's face turned dull red with embarrassment. "I didn't mean that like it sounded," she began.

"Yes, you did." Abigail's voice was crisp as she came the rest of the way down the stairs. "You think I'm so wrapped up in my own grief over Will and Mac and Titus that I don't see what's going on around me. That might have been true for a while, but not anymore."

Henry rubbed his ear where Cordelia had pinched it and tried to reassure his mother and sister. "Will and Mac are fine," he said. "You'll see. They'll come riding up here one of these days, big as life and twice as ugly."

"None of my children are ugly," Abigail said. "Even Titus, for all his troubles, was a sweet boy at times."

Cordelia reached out to take her mother's hand. "I'm sorry about what I said, Ma." She glanced toward Henry. "But I'm not sorry for trying to help this big lunkhead to see the light about Polly."

Again a new voice came hard on the heels of her words, this time from the porch of the farmhouse. "Oh?" it asked through the screen door. "And what light is that?"

"Polly!" Henry said, his voice rising into a yelp of surprise. He swung around toward the door and saw her standing there on the porch, her slim figure silhouetted by the afternoon sunlight behind her. As she looked into the house, she reached up and took off her hat so that her smooth blonde hair shone in the light.

"Just what is it you want Henry to understand about me, Cordelia?" Polly asked. "Do you want him to see that I'm a terrible woman who doesn't deserve his friendship?"

Cordelia raised a hand. The flush on her face was even more pronounced now. "Polly, I'm sorry . . . I didn't mean . . ."

"Of course you did." Polly's gaze moved over to Abigail. "I hope you're well, Mrs. Brannon. I'd best bid you good day and leave now." She turned and started down the porch toward the horse and buggy that had brought her here, the horse and buggy that none of the Brannons had heard approaching the house because of their argument.

"Polly!" Henry called out. He ran to the front door, slapped it open, and bounded out onto the porch. "Polly, wait!" Neither his mother nor his sister came after him or tried to stop him, and he was grateful for that.

Polly was at the buggy, reaching up to grasp the back of the seat to pull herself into the vehicle. Henry caught her arm, stopping her. She turned toward him with such a fierce look in her eyes that he let go of her and stepped back in surprise.

"I don't want your pity, Henry Brannon," she said, "and I sure as hell don't want your sister's scorn."

"Aw, you can't put any stock in what Cordelia says. She's crazy like all girls."

Despite her anger, a faint smile touched Polly's lips. "Oh?"

"I-I didn't mean that like it sounded. I just meant . . . Oh, shoot, you know what I'm trying to say . . ."

"No. I don't. Tell me what you're trying to say, Henry."

Henry reached for the reins, overwhelmed by a sudden compulsion to be anywhere else other than here. "If you're determined to go home, at least let me drive you," he said. "These days, it's not safe for a young lady to be out on the road by herself."

That was true enough; in fact, it was all too true. There were no Union troops in Culpeper County right now, but Yankees weren't the only danger in the world. There were deserters and renegades, men who had come back from the war wounded, only to find that battles had ravaged their land and destroyed their homes. Most of them were more lost than anything else, but some were pure evil.

Polly hesitated then nodded. "All right," she conceded. "You can take me home."

"Let me help you up." When he had done so, Henry went on, "I'll get my horse and tie it onto the back."

He glanced at the house as he hurried toward the barn to fetch a saddle horse. There was no sign of his mother or sister. Cordelia ought to be ashamed of herself, he thought, talking the way she had about Polly. Of course, Cordelia hadn't known that Polly was going to come up and overhear.

A few minutes later, Henry had the buggy rolling along the road toward Culpeper. Before they reached the settlement, they would come to another road that led to Mountain Laurel. It would take half an hour or so to get to the plantation. Henry intended to enjoy that time with Polly, no matter what the circumstances. But this wouldn't be a good time to ask her to marry him, he decided. He might not know much about women, but he was pretty sure she wasn't in the mood for a proposal right now.

After an awkward stretch of silence, Henry ventured, "Have you heard anything new about the war?"

Polly shook her head. She hadn't put her hat back on, and the wind of the buggy's passage blew a few strands of hair that had come loose around her face. She was so pretty she made Henry ache inside.

"All I know is that General Lee and the army are retreating from Gettysburg. My father says it was a foolish idea to go up there in the first place."

Henry felt a flash of anger. Back in the early days of the war, when the army was first recruiting, Duncan Ebersole had called himself a colonel, but he was nothing of the sort. He had never been anything but a planter. Any military experience he had was in his own head.

But he didn't have any military experience, either, Henry reminded himself. He hadn't joined up when nearly every other able-bodied man in the county had. That was a sore point with some people, including Henry himself.

Still, he wasn't going to argue with the decisions made by Robert E. Lee. General Lee had already proven himself dozens of times over in this war. He was a brilliant commander.

Henry didn't say that, didn't point out to Polly that her father was a damned idiot. He knew she didn't get along all that well with Ebersole, but she wouldn't let an outsider insult him like that.

"I just hope my brothers are all right," he said. "I tell myself they are, but sometimes I get a mite worried."

"I'm sure they're fine," Polly said. "Will and Mac have always been levelheaded, not like—"

She stopped short, catching her breath, and Henry knew what she had been about to say. Will and Mac were level-headed, not like Titus.

Not like her dead husband.

To get Polly's mind off of that subject, Henry said, "That horse of Mac's will take care of him. I never saw such a horse for being smart. He's ornery, though. We had a heck of a time catching him when he was still wild."

"I'm not sure I've heard about that," Polly said. "Why don't you tell me about it?"

Henry launched into the story of how the big silver gray stallion had haunted the Brannon farm like a ghost for months, appearing in the night then vanishing whenever anyone tried to get close to him. Mac had been the first one to see the stallion. For a while, the others had thought he was imagining things. But then Will had witnessed one of the stallion's mysterious appearances, and eventually the others in the family had seen the magnificent horse, too. Mac had begun making plans to capture the stallion, but it wasn't until Will had already joined the army and left the farm that the effort finally succeeded. Once the stallion was caught, Mac had had to tame him and get him to accept a rider. That had been easier than anyone expected. Mac and the stallion had taken to each other like long-lost relatives.

"I've always said Mac's as much critter as he is human," Henry concluded with a grin. "As far back as I can remember, he was always catching squirrels and possums and coons. He always let 'em go, though. It was like they were his friends, and he didn't want to see any harm come to them."

"Mac has a gentle soul," Polly said. "It's hard to believe he's a cavalryman fighting the Yankees."

Henry shrugged. "We all do what we have to do, even if sometimes we don't like it very much."

"Yes," Polly agreed, her voice quiet and thoughtful. "I suppose we do."

They drove on in silence for a short distance, on the road to Mountain Laurel now but still several miles from the plantation. Polly took Henry by surprise by saying, "Why don't you pull over to the side of the road? I'd like to walk a bit."

Henry didn't hesitate. "Sure," he said as he brought the team to a halt. He was willing to do anything if it meant he could spend some more time with Polly.

He hopped down from the seat and turned back to help her to the ground. When he put his hands on her waist, he felt the firm warmth of her flesh through her dress and the corset she wore underneath it. Her feet hit the ground, but he didn't take his hands away. Instead he let them linger on her for a few seconds. She looked up into his face and smiled. "We were going to take a walk," she reminded him.

"Yeah . . . yes, of course." Henry stepped back. "I'm sorry."

"No need to be sorry." She put out a hand in an obvious invitation for him to take it. "Come on."

Her hand was smooth and cool. His fingers entwined with hers. With his heart thumping in his chest, he started away from the road, walking at Polly's side.

They went up a hill that was topped by a thick stand of trees. The grass on the hillside was tall and swished around their feet. A warm breeze blew in Henry's face, carrying with it the sweet scent of honeysuckle. Or maybe that was Polly's hair he smelled, he thought. Birds flitted from branch to branch in the trees on top of the hill, bright flashes of color that drew Henry's eye. Their songs were like music on this summer day. The war and everything about it seemed far, far distant, too far away to matter.

They topped the hill, and Polly stopped in the shade of the trees. Below them was a small creek that widened out into a pond. "This is a beautiful place," she said.

"Yes, it is," Henry said. He looked over his shoulder. He couldn't see the road from here. The trees and the hilltop cut off sight of it. That meant no one down there could see them, either. He was short of breath, and he was sure the pounding of his heart was so loud that Polly could hear it. He turned toward her, only to find that she was already turning to him.

"Henry," she whispered.

He put his hand under her chin and brought his mouth down to hers. Her lips were hot and wet and sweet, and their touch sent thrills through him. He put his hands on her waist again, as he had when he was helping her down from the buggy, and after a moment he slid them around to her back so that he was embracing her. She lifted her arms around his neck. Their bodies came together.

Henry knew he was aroused. He started to pull back so that Polly wouldn't feel the evidence of his lust. She wouldn't let him get away, though. In fact, she molded her body even closer to his. A low moan came from deep inside her. Henry broke the kiss and gasped from the power of the passion she ignited in him.

"Henry, I want you," she said. "You . . . you know what I mean?"

"Yes, and I want you, too, Polly," he said, misery growing inside him. "But we can't—"

"Why not? There's a blanket down in the buggy. I'll wait here for you to get it."

Henry's eyes grew so wide with astonishment he was afraid they were going to pop out of their sockets. For a moment, he couldn't talk, couldn't even make his mouth work. Finally, he managed to say, "You . . . you really mean it?"

"Of course I do." She reached down and took hold of his left hand, moved it so that it rested on the softness of her bosom. "You're my best friend, Henry. The only true friend I have. I want to share . . . something special . . . with you."

Henry had to swallow a couple of times before he could speak again. "If . . . if you're sure."

"I'm certain."

"All right." He let go of her and stepped back. "Stay right there. I'll be right back."

Polly smiled at him. "I'm not going anywhere."

Henry turned and started walking back over the hill. By the time he reached the far side of it, he was running.

Don't think about Titus, . . . don't think about Titus . . . , he told himself as he fetched the blanket from behind the seat of the buggy. He had loved Titus as much as a brother could love another, but Titus was gone now—gone forever. Nothing Henry did now would ever hurt his brother in any way. Whatever it was that had grown between him and Polly was beautiful, marvelous.

There was nothing evil about it, nothing sinister, nothing to be ashamed of.

Don't think.

He ran back up the hill. When he reached the top and made his way through the trees, he found Polly waiting for him on the other side. She had already removed her dress and petticoats and corset and stood there in a white cotton shift that clung to the lines of her body. Her blonde hair was loose around her shoulders now. Henry stopped short at the sight of her, stunned by her beauty.

"Henry," she whispered, lifting her arms and holding them out to him.

He went to her and never looked back.

It was as if all his senses had been heightened. The dappled sunlight that shone through the trees was warmer than before, the songs of the birds were more melodic, and the scents that lingered in the air were almost impossibly fragrant. He lay on his back and looked up through the trees to the deep blue, cloud-dotted sky, and he felt contentment such as he had never known. He reached up to stroke Polly's hair as she lay snuggled against him with her head pillowed on his shoulder.

"The wedding will need to be a lot smaller this time, I think," Polly said.

Henry's eyes had almost closed as lassitude crept over him. Now they opened and he repeated, "Wedding? What wedding?"

"Our wedding, of course," Polly said. She pressed against him. "We'll be married at Mountain Laurel, but it'll be just family this time. With the war and everything, there's no need to put on airs."

Henry wanted to sit up, but he forced himself to lie still. "Polly, I . . . I haven't asked you to marry me."

She stiffened against him. "Henry . . . ?"

Now he did sit up, unable to control himself anymore. Beside him, Polly sat up as well and crossed her arms over her nudity as if she were suddenly embarrassed. He held out his hands to her and said, "Wait, don't misunderstand! I want to marry you. My God, it's all I've been thinking about for weeks now! But I wanted to do it right, to propose to you at the right time."

The worried look on her face went away and was replaced by a warm smile as she lowered her arms. "I can't think of a better time than this, can you?"

"No. No, I can't." He caught hold of her hands. "Polly, will you marry me?"

"Of course I will." She leaned against him and kissed him. "Yes, Henry, I'll marry you."

Henry put his arms around her and hugged her. His head was spinning from the suddenness of everything that had happened today. In his dreams, he might have hoped for something like this . . . but only in his wildest dreams.

Like a deep breath of freezing air on a winter day, a chill went through him as a thought occurred to him. "Your father won't like this."

"Let me handle my father. Don't worry about a thing."

"But he was so upset when you and Titus—"

A shadow passed over her eyes, and Henry cursed himself for bringing up Titus and all the memories, both good and bad, that Polly must have from her first marriage. This sure as hell wasn't the time for either of them to be thinking about Titus!

"Don't worry," Polly said again. "I promise you everything will be all right. You'll see, Henry."

He leaned closer to her and brushed her lips with his. "I'm sure it will," he said. "The way we feel about each other, how could everything not be all right?"

Even Titus, up in heaven, must be smiling down on them right now. Henry wanted very much to think that was so.

Chapter Six

ONE GOOD THING—THE *only* good thing, as far as Titus Brannon was concerned—to come out of the Yankee victory at Gettysburg was that the guards at Camp Douglas, just outside Chicago, weren't quite as vicious and brutal for a few days after the battle. They spent their time gloating over their Confederate prisoners instead of beating and tormenting them.

Titus had been in this Union prison camp since the previous winter, when he had been captured at the battle of Fredericksburg. In that time he had seen countless prisoners die from starvation, disease, and exposure to the elements. He had seen others die from beatings handed out by the guards. And still others had been shot down in cold blood for infractions of the rules, both real and imagined. It was a hell of a lot easier to die in Camp Douglas than it was to live.

But Titus had never been one to take the easy way out in anything. He had courted and married the daughter of the richest, most arrogant bastard in Culpeper County, hadn't he?

It was funny. After all this time, he was having trouble remembering what Polly looked like. He would know her if he saw her, though. That was more than she could have said about him. His dark brown beard, which he had always worn cropped close to his jaw, was now long and ragged and streaked with gray, as was his tangled, filthy hair. He had been slender before; now he was gaunt, a mere skin-and-bones shadow of the man he had been. He knew what he must look like even though he hadn't seen his image in a mirror for a long time. He knew because he could look at Nathan Hatcher and see the same changes wrought in him.

Nathan was also from Culpeper County, a former law clerk in the office of Judge Darden, the county's leading attorney. Nathan would have been a lawyer himself someday if the war hadn't come along—and if he hadn't gone north to fight on the side of the Yankees because of his opposition to the Southern cause. It was only through a series of bizarre circumstances that Nathan had wound up as a Confederate prisoner in a Northern prison camp. Now, after months of confinement in the harshest conditions imaginable, Nathan was a hardened animal concerned only with survival, just like everyone else here. The soft-handed, softhearted boy Titus's sister, Cordelia, had been smitten with was gone for good.

Titus was glad Nathan was the way he was now. Otherwise Titus wouldn't have even considered taking Nathan with him when he broke out of this hellhole.

Titus shuffled along next to Nathan, both of them taking care to avoid the deadline around their barracks. Stepping over the deadline was enough to get a prisoner shot. If the guards were in a brutal enough mood, just approaching the deadline was sufficient cause for a prisoner to get a rifle ball through the head.

More than a week had passed since the battle at Gettysburg. The prisoners had heard all about the Southern defeat from the guards. Titus was sick of the Yankee bastards laughing about it. He kept his anger and resentment under control, however. Giving in to emotions around here could get a fella dead in a hurry, too.

"Did Miss Louisa say when she'd be back?" Nathan asked, his voice low so that none of the other prisoners would hear.

"As soon as she can," Titus replied. "Later this week, maybe."

"And when she comes back . . . ?"

"She'll take us out with her," Titus said.

For a moment, Nathan didn't say anything. Then he shook his head. "Morton will never agree to that."

"Morton won't have any choice. The orders will come from Colonel Tucker. He knows that's the only way to keep the Quakers happy. He doesn't want it getting into the newspapers what it's really like here."

Capt. Floyd Morton was in charge of the guards. He was a sadistic lunatic whose religious fervor was enough to blind him to the torments handed out by the soldiers under his command. The way Morton saw it, the Lord was on the side of the Yankees, so whatever happened to the Rebels was just God's will.

Col. Joseph H. Tucker, however, was the commander of Camp Douglas, and as such he had to be more aware of the image the camp held in the mind of the public. True, most Northerners didn't gave a damn how the Confederate captives were treated, but a vocal minority did, and they were willing to stir up trouble if Tucker didn't at least make a pretense of affording the prisoners humane treatment. Chief among those troublemakers, as Tucker regarded them, was the Society of Friends, headquartered in Philadelphia. They were better known as Quakers.

It was as a representative of the Quakers that Miss Louisa Abernathy had first come to Camp Douglas.

Louisa's first visit had gotten Titus in some trouble with the guards. It had been worth it, he had reflected many times since that day. He thought about Louisa's red hair and fair skin and soft voice, and he knew the trouble had been worth it indeed.

She was his ticket out of here.

As he trudged alongside Nathan, he even smiled under his bushy beard. Women were funny creatures. He'd been an admitted no-account, a poor farm boy who drank too much whiskey, when Polly Ebersole—rich, beautiful, spoiled Polly—had decided she loved him. He had been even worse, a filthy, stinking Reb prisoner of war, when Louisa Abernathy looked at him and her heart went out to him. Titus figured it was mostly pity she felt for him. Lord knew he had looked pitiful enough. But there had been something else, a spark of interest in the eyes of the pretty, strait-laced, young woman . . . Titus was more than willing to exploit that interest for as much as it was worth. He had managed to catch a moment alone with Louisa the last time she paid one of her inspection visits to the camp, and in those few seconds he had whispered the rudiments of his plan to her. Now it was all up to her to arrange everything.

She wouldn't let him down. Titus was sure of it.

As a matter of fact, it was the very next day when Louisa returned to Camp Douglas. Titus and Nathan didn't know that until they were summoned to the administration building. Titus couldn't think of any other reason why they would be taken there. It had to be because of Louisa.

"Step lively, Rebs," Sergeant O'Neil growled from behind Titus and Nathan. O'Neil was an ugly, powerfully built Yankee who hated Titus with a special passion. From the first day Titus had entered the camp, O'Neil had done his best to make life miserable for him. Titus had had to be on his best behavior whenever O'Neil was around, because the sergeant would have seized any excuse to kill him.

"What does the colonel want with us, Sergeant?" Titus asked. Inside, he was cackling with glee because he was convinced he knew the answer to that particular question.

"How the hell should I know? Just keep moving."

Flies buzzed around Titus's head, but he didn't wave a hand to brush them away. Prisoners had been shot for making such "threatening gestures." A few of the men they passed turned their heads to watch as the little group went by, but most of the prisoners ignored them. The Confederates, clad in scraps and tatters of homespun gray or butternut uniforms, had their heads down, their eyes on the ground. They stood around dully, more like cattle or sheep than men. *Better to be dead than to live like that,* Titus thought.

If this escape attempt didn't work out, that was exactly what was going to happen.

Even inside the headquarters building, the stench from the open latrines around the prisoners' barracks lingered in the air.

But it wasn't as bad in here, and Titus was grateful for that. He and Nathan were marched down a corridor to Colonel Tucker's office, and when an aide opened the door, Titus saw Louisa sitting in front of the colonel's desk. Her back was stiff and straight as always, and she didn't turn to look at him.

That was all right. She knew he was there. And he knew she knew it.

"Here are the prisoners you asked to see, Miss Abernathy," Colonel Tucker said to her. There was a frown on his beefy face. "I still don't understand why you insisted that these men accompany you to the cemetery."

"I told you, Colonel, they were friends of the dead men. Even prisoners deserve a decent burial, and that includes mourners who aren't strangers to them."

Louisa spoke with utter conviction. That was because she meant what she was saying, Titus thought. He had figured that Louisa wouldn't be very good at lying, so when he concocted this plan, he took care to tailor it to her sensibilities. That would make the whole thing more believable.

Tucker looked at Titus and Nathan and grimaced in distaste. "At least they can dig the graves. You'll get some use out of them."

Sergeant O'Neil spoke up. "Beggin' your pardon, Colonel, but are you talkin' about sendin' these men out of the camp?"

Tucker glared at him. "That's right, Sergeant. Two of the men who died yesterday were Masons, as am I." The colonel glanced at Nathan then nodded. Titus knew that Nathan had made some sort of sign that he had learned from Judge Darden back in Culpeper. Darden was the head of the local Masonic lodge. Nathan had pointed out that Masons would often do favors for their lodge brothers, even those on the other side of a war. That had led to the escape plan they had hatched.

"They're going to be buried in the city cemetery rather than in our graveyard. This is at the direct request of Miss Abernathy and the Society of Friends."

The colonel didn't like having to explain himself. O'Neil wasn't satisfied, however, so he pressed on. "So why do these two have to go along, sir?"

"To serve as a burial detail and to mourn for their fallen comrades, as you no doubt heard Miss Abernathy and myself just discussing." Tucker spoke through clenched teeth.

O'Neil shook his head. "I don't think Cap'n Morton's goin' to like lettin' prisoners leave the camp. He won't even like the dead ones goin' out."

"The last time I checked, Sergeant, I was the commander of this camp, not Captain Morton," Tucker said. His voice was low and dangerous now.

"Yes sir," O'Neil muttered.

Titus struggled to keep a straight face and look solemn. After all, two of his closest "friends" in the camp had just died.

In truth, neither Titus nor Nathan had even known the dead men, didn't know if they were Masons or not. That was just the story Louisa had told the colonel. The frequent inspections by the Quakers and by the representatives from the War Department in Washington had put the colonel on edge and made him eager to please, in addition to his Masonic loyalties. That was what Titus had counted on.

"The prisoners will be well guarded, of course," Tucker said.

That made O'Neil perk up a little. "Request permission to head up the guard detail, sir," he said.

"I think that would be an excellent idea, Sergeant. I'll tell Captain Morton to place you in charge."

"Thank you, sir." O'Neil looked at Titus with a savage grin on his lumpy face.

Titus knew what O'Neil was thinking. Outside of the camp, it would be even easier for him to find an excuse to gun down the prisoners.

"I'll have the, ah, bodies loaded onto the wagon you brought, Miss Abernathy," Tucker went on to Louisa. "Sergeant O'Neil, escort these men outside and have Captain Morton come to my office. The captain and I will see to the details of this little expedition."

"Yes sir!" O'Neil's heavy hand fell on Titus's shoulder and propelled him toward the door. "You heard the colonel. Get movin', Reb."

Titus stumbled a little because of the shove but caught his balance and went out the door of the office. He didn't bother looking at O'Neil or letting any of his anger show.

The time was coming to settle up the score. Coming quickly, barreling down like a freight train.

THE SUN was blistering hot as Titus and Nathan stood near the camp's administration building and waited while the wagon was brought around. The heat made the smell worse. Titus did his best to ignore it. He'd had plenty of practice.

Pulled by four horses, the wagon rattled up in front of the building. A Yankee corporal was at the reins. Two long shapes lay in the uncovered back of the wagon, wrapped in moth-eaten blankets. Titus looked at the bodies and felt a touch of gratitude. Those poor dead bastards were helping him get out of here.

Louisa and the colonel emerged from the building, accompanied now by an unhappy-looking Captain Morton. At the same time, Sergeant O'Neil came around the corner at the head of a guard detail of six other troopers. Counting the corporal driving the wagon, that made eight guards who would be going to the cemetery. Not good odds. But Titus didn't care. There could have been eighty of the Yankees instead of eight, and he would still go through with his plan.

O'Neil and the other guards reached the wagon at the same time as Louisa, Tucker, and Morton. O'Neil said to Titus and Nathan, "Get in the back with those corpses."

"Sergeant, remember that this is to be a dignified occasion," Tucker said as Titus and Nathan climbed into the wagon. "Miss Abernathy will be giving an account of it to the newspapers."

"Yes sir." O'Neil's response was sullen. He didn't give a hang for the press, Titus knew. All O'Neil cared about was torturing Reb prisoners. But he couldn't keep on doing that unless he stayed on Tucker's good side, so he would try to follow orders. Titus was counting on that.

Morton said, "I still believe this to be a mistake, sir. Our own burial facilities are quite satisfactory."

Camp Douglas's burial facilities, which Morton referred to, consisted of a series of long ditches in the rear of the camp. The bodies of dead prisoners were thrown into one of the open ditches and left to rot. When a ditch was full, it was covered up and a new ditch was dug. Titus knew a great deal about that part of the camp. He had helped to dig more than one of these ditches during his months in captivity.

"There will be no more discussion of this issue, Captain," Tucker snapped. "The decision has been made."

Titus and Nathan had settled down cross-legged on the floor of the wagon bed, next to the blanket-wrapped bodies and a pair of shovels. The smell of death already came from those shapes in their crude shrouds.

Louisa stepped up to the wagon. Tucker took her arm to help her onto the seat. Then he moved back and motioned for the driver to get the horses moving. The wagon lurched into motion. The corporal swung the team toward the gate. The wagon went out, moving at a slow pace so that O'Neil and the other guards could keep up with it on foot.

Oak Wood Cemetery wasn't far from the camp, but the trek there seemed endless to Titus. When they had been gone from the camp for several minutes, Louisa turned around on the seat and took a small pouch out of her handbag. She started to hand it to Titus when O'Neil called out, "Hold it, ma'am! What've you got there?"

"A Bible, Sergeant," she replied in a scornful voice. "Something quite necessary for a burial ceremony."

"Yes, ma'am," O'Neil said in a grudging voice.

Titus opened the drawstring pouch Louisa handed to him and took out the black book. He had been raised a Baptist back in Culpeper County, but he wasn't sure he even believed in God anymore. If there was a higher power, He was bound to be a Yank. Otherwise He wouldn't allow such places as Camp Douglas to exist.

Titus placed the pouch on the floor of the wagon beside him. He was careful about that, because he didn't want the two pistols still in the pouch to bang together and make a racket. O'Neil probably wouldn't be able to hear such sounds over the rattle and creak of the wagon wheels, but there was no point in taking chances now, not when they were so close to freedom.

Titus started mumbling and paging through the Bible. He kept his head down as if he were praying, but his eyes cut from side to side, taking in the details of their surroundings. The camp was on the outskirts of Chicago, and so was the cemetery. But there were quite a few buildings and pedestrians around. That might make getting away a little harder when the time came. There was nothing that could be done about it.

Even riding next to a couple of corpses, the air smelled better once they were out of the camp. Titus took a deep breath and felt it invigorate him. He kept pretending to pray. It was good to be out of that place. Even if he died today, it wouldn't be in that den of pestilence.

And he would take that bastard O'Neil to hell with him if it was the last thing he ever did.

The wagon reached the cemetery entrance at last and passed through the open gates between two large stone pillars. The guard detail tramped through the gates behind the wagon. The cemetery itself was quite large, Titus saw. Rolling green hills were dotted with tombstones and monuments. There were quite a few trees as well, casting their shade over the ground.

The corporal sent the wagon along a dirt track that twisted and turned between the burial plots. It was almost pleasant here among the trees and flowers and grass, Titus thought. Compared to the prison camp, even a graveyard seemed like paradise.

The corporal brought the horses to a stop next to a pair of burial plots that were marked off with ropes strung between short stakes pounded into the ground. "Here we are, ma'am," he announced to Louisa.

"Thank you, Corporal." She turned to look at Nathan and Titus. "You can proceed now, gentlemen."

"She means get out of the wagon and get to diggin'," O'Neil snapped. "Hop to it, Rebs."

Titus's eyes flashed around. The other guards looked hot and tired and bored. They weren't paying much attention to what was going on. O'Neil was the only one really watching.

"Sure, Sarge," Titus said. He picked up the pouch to drop the Bible back inside. As he did so, his fingers closed over the butt of one of the hidden pistols. He pulled it out, and with a smooth continuation of the same movement, he tossed the pouch to Nathan.

Titus lifted the pistol in his hand, earing back the hammer as he did so, and lined the barrel on the bridge of O'Neil's nose. For a split second, the Irishman failed to comprehend what was happening. When that moment passed, his eyes widened with both surprise and anger.

"Drop that rifle, you bastard," Titus said, "or I'll blow your brains out."

Beside him, Nathan jerked the other pistol from the pouch. His movements were more awkward than Titus's, but with the element of surprise on his side, he was able to get the gun out and reach up to grab the collar of the corporal's uniform before the man knew what was going on. Nathan hauled him over backward. The corporal sprawled on top of the blanket-wrapped corpses. Nathan dug the barrel of the pistol into his throat. "Don't move," Nathan warned him.

O'Neil quivered from the power of the rage gripping him. "You bastard," he grated at Titus. "You filthy Reb bastard. You can't get away with this."

"I reckon we can," Titus said. "I told you to drop that rifle."

O'Neil hesitated. The other guards knew what was going on by now, but they looked to O'Neil to see what to do about it.

"There's eight of us," O'Neil said. "You can't get all of us."

"Nope, we can't," Titus agreed. "But unless you order the others to go along, you'll die, O'Neil. All I have to do is let this hammer down, and there'll be a bullet in your brain. The corporal will be dead, too. And if your boys don't kill us with their first shots, we're liable to get two or three more of them before we go down. You'll die first, O'Neil." Titus grinned. "Who wants to be second?"

He knew the answer to that—none of them did. Just as he had thought all along, the Yankees were cowards. Gutless sons of bitches who wouldn't take a chance on dying even though the odds were heavily in their favor. None of them wanted to risk it.

"Titus," Louisa said from behind him, her voice low and urgent. "Titus, there can be no killing. Please."

He bit back an angry reply. What the hell had she thought was going to happen when she agreed to get them out of the camp and smuggle guns to them? Did she really believe the guards would allow him and Nathan to just walk away?

"What's it goin' to be, O'Neil?" he demanded.

The sergeant drew in a deep breath. For a second Titus thought he was going to put his rifle on the ground. Then O'Neil said, "If it was anybody but you, Brannon. Anybody but you . . ."

He jerked the rifle up and fired.

He was already dead when the blast sounded. Titus was the best shot in Culpeper County with a rifle, and he was almost as good with a handgun. Only his brother Will was better. Even with an unfamiliar weapon, Titus couldn't miss at this range.

The pistol cracked as soon as O'Neil started to move, and the bullet struck him between the eyes and bored on into his brain, throwing him backward so that the shot he fired went high in the air.

It was a quick death, too quick and easy for that son of a bitch, Titus thought.

Then he was too busy for thinking. He went over the side of the wagon in a headlong dive.

Louisa screamed. Titus hoped she would get down and stay down while the bullets were flying. He struck the ground hard. Rolling over onto his hands and knees, he threw another shot at the guards, who were still slow to react. One of them staggered as Titus's bullet hit him somewhere in the body. Titus flung himself under the wagon, triggering twice more as he did so.

He heard the sounds of a struggle above him. Nathan was fighting with the corporal. Damn that boy! He should have pulled the trigger and blown the Yankee's throat out as soon as the shooting started. One less enemy to deal with that way. Instead, Nathan had hesitated as his old doubts about killing had surfaced at just the wrong moment. Even without seeing what had happened, Titus was sure of it.

He wound up on his belly under the wagon. From here he could see the legs of the remaining guards. He sent a bullet into a blue-clad kneecap, blasting it into bloody white splinters of bone. The soldier screeched in agony and fell, dropping his rifle. Another one out of the fight. He might just come through this alive, Titus realized.

Louisa yelled, "Hyaaahhh!" and the wagon jolted forward. *What the hell is she doing!* Titus thought. She was taking his cover away from him.

He twisted around on the ground and dropped the gun as he reached up to grab one of the iron cross-braces underneath the wagon. The vehicle left the path and started across the cemetery. The horses were running wild now. Louisa must not have been able to control them, Titus realized. He hung on as tightly as he could. Every few feet his body bounced and then slammed back into the ground. At this rate, he couldn't hold on for very long.

There was another brace at the back of the wagon. If he could catch hold of it, he might be able to pull himself up and climb over the tailgate. In desperation, Titus let go of his hold and reached for the rear brace as it passed over him.

He shouted in pain as the jolt seemed to pull his arms right out of their sockets. He managed to hold on, though, and after a moment the burning agony in his shoulders lessened a little. From here he could see the surviving guards. The wagon was at least a hundred yards away from them now. They were firing after the wagon, but Titus figured the shots were going wild. He didn't hear any of them strike the vehicle.

He released his right hand grip and twisted his arm to grasp the brace from the top. Then he let go with the left and turned over. His right hand almost slipped off before he got the left hand on the brace again. Breathless, he hung there facedown for a second as the racing wagon dragged him along behind it.

Summoning all the strength in his gaunt body, he made an upward lunge with his right hand and grabbed the top of the tailgate. If the latch had come open at that moment, dropping the gate, he would have been jarred loose. But the latch held, and he was able to pull himself up so that he could catch hold with his left hand, too. His toes cut furrows in the ground as he was pulled along.

He was almost done in. Months of bad food and horrible conditions had left him weakened. But the will to live burned inside him, and so did his desire to be free of the Yankees. The corded muscles in his arms and shoulders bunched as he levered himself higher. He hooked a toe on the tiny lip at the bottom of the tailgate. With a groan of effort, he hauled himself up and over. He landed in a sprawl next to the bodies of the dead men.

He saw Nathan on the seat, trying to grab the dangling reins and bring the runaway team under control. Louisa was slumped beside him, fainted maybe. The Yankee corporal was still in the back of the wagon, unconscious. Blood seeped from a gash on his head where Nathan must have clouted him with something, probably the pistol.

Titus lay there for a long moment catching his breath. Then he got onto his knees, picked up the nearest shovel, and brought it down hard so that the side of the blade slammed into the corporal's head at the same spot Nathan had hit him. He felt the satisfying crunch of the Yankee's skull shattering. The corporal twitched once and didn't move again. That was one more dead Yankee, Titus thought.

Nathan finally had hold of the reins. He started hauling back on them and shouting at the horses to stop. Titus dropped the shovel and grabbed Nathan's shoulder. Nathan jerked around, unaware until then that Titus was in the back of the wagon.

"Keep goin'!" Titus shouted over the pounding of the hoof beats. "Head for the back of the cemetery!"

Nathan looked around, confused, and then nodded as he understood what Titus wanted. Someone must have heard all the shooting. Soldiers would come to investigate. By that time, Titus and Nathan—and Louisa—needed to be long gone.

Titus turned back to the dead corporal and thought about stripping the uniform off him. A Yankee uniform might come in handy. Titus's nose wrinkled. The corporal had voided his bowels when he died, and it had soaked through the long underwear to the trousers. The jacket was covered with blood from the head wound. Titus decided a dirty, bloody Yankee uniform would probably just get him into more trouble.

Louisa moaned. Titus looked around and saw her trying to sit up. He put a hand on Louisa's shoulder. "It's all right," he told her. "We got away from them."

They were coming to the rear of the cemetery. A high stone wall marked the boundary. Nathan brought the team to a stop next to the wall and stood up on the wagon seat. "There are fields on the other side. No buildings that I can see."

"Let's go. Climb over that wall and drop on the other side." Titus tugged at Louisa's arm. "Come on. You can make it."

She looked stunned. "I . . . I can't. I'll stay here."

"The hell you will. The Yankees will know you got those guns to us and helped us escape. You'll go to prison yourself."

"No . . . no."

"Some of those guards were killed. They'll blame you for that, Louisa. You've got to go with us."

"Hey!" Nathan exclaimed from the top of the wall, where he had paused to look down into the wagon. "That man is dead!" He was looking at the corporal.

Titus grinned up at him for a second. "Reckon you must've hit him a little too hard, Nathan."

"I didn't!" Nathan protested. "He was still alive. I . . . I just knocked him out."

"Like you said, he's dead now. Get movin'!"

Nathan swallowed and then turned to lower himself to the ground on the far side of the wall. He hung from his hands and dropped the last couple of feet.

Louisa was still being stubborn. "I didn't want anyone to die," she said.

"It couldn't be helped," Titus snapped. His only regret was that he hadn't been able to gutshoot O'Neil so that the bastard would have taken hours to die. He tugged at Louisa's arm again. "Come on, or so help me I'll leave you here."

She looked up at him, her gaze showing an unusual defiance. "Perhaps you should," she said. "I deserve to go to prison. That's the least of my worries. I've damned myself by helping you."

"You know what they say." Titus grinned at her. "In for a penny, in for a pound."

For a second he thought she was going to slap him. Then she sighed. "You're right."

A shot blasted in the distance, and a bullet whined past them to smack into the wall.

"The rest of those guards will catch up in a minute," Titus said. He held out a hand. "Are you comin'?"

"I'm coming." Louisa took hold of his hand. "God help me, I'm coming with you."

A minute later, they were both over the wall and running through the field behind the cemetery. Nathan was a good distance ahead of them, but they were catching up. The sun was bright and hot on Titus's face. He heard shouting behind them as the Yankees reached the wall. The Yankees wouldn't give up. They would come after the escaped prisoners. Pretty soon they would probably have bloodhounds on the scent. Titus didn't care. He knew all the tricks of throwing off pursuit. If he and his companions could reach the woods, the Yankees would never catch them.

Louisa stumbled and cried out. Titus reached over and took her hand, steadying her and pulling her along. He heard the faint crack of a rifle, and a bullet whispered through the tall grass off to his right. He smiled, unafraid.

For the first time in months he felt good, damned good.

Chapter Seven

T HE SHOOTING ROMAN HAD heard in the distance to the southeast during the final stages of the battle near Williamsport had heralded the arrival of Gen. Jeb Stuart and more Confederate cavalry. Having been reinforced by Generals Stuart and Fitzhugh Lee, and the Union cavalry having fled, the Confederate column was safe enough for the time being, even though the Potomac River was still too high to cross.

General Imboden was not content to rest on his laurels and wait for the rest of the Army of Northern Virginia to arrive. He found two flatboats moored along the river in Williamsport. Each of the vessels was large enough to carry about thirty men. Ferrying the wounded soldiers across the river in such small numbers would be a long, difficult task, but at least it was making a start. Imboden ordered his subordinates to put the flatboats to use and get as many of the wounded men on the other side of the river as soon as possible.

Roman felt a nagging impatience as he waited for it to be Will's turn to be ferried across on one of the flatboats. Getting Will across the Potomac might not get him to a hospital any faster, but remaining here in Williamsport meant that they were still in danger from a Federal attack. If the entire Army of the Potomac showed up, as it was rumored was going to happen any day, the Confederates would be very vulnerable. It didn't seem that the river was going to recede anytime soon, either, because heavy rain fell nearly every day and every drop swelled the already swollen stream that much more.

On July 7, the Confederate infantry arrived, led by Gen. James Longstreet's corps. A. P. Hill and Richard Ewell weren't far behind, though Ewell's troops had been harassed almost every step of the way by Federal cavalry and had suffered considerable losses the night before during a battle in the hills at

Monterey Pass. Gen. Robert E. Lee set up his headquarters in a house on the road between Williamsport and Hagerstown and began trying to remedy the ills that had plagued this retreat. Confederate scouts reported that General Meade and the rest of the Union army weren't moving yet, for some unaccountable reason, but they couldn't count on that bit of good luck holding. Lee ordered a defensive line established east of Williamsport. The line stretched from Conococheague Creek north of the town to Falling Waters, some six miles south and west of Williamsport. Engineers erected earthworks, and the infantry-men dug in behind them. The artillery batteries were placed along this earthen parapet, and what had been in the minds of the men a desperate situation changed into a position of strength. The disastrous battle of a few days earlier was not for-gotten; it could never be forgotten. But now an air of eagerness and anticipation hung over the Confederate line. Let the Yan-kees come, the men seemed to be saying. This time, they were ready, and the results might be completely different.

Roman wasn't anxious for a battle. A couple of days dragged past while he waited for Cap'n Will's turn on one of the flat-boats. Mac Brannon, who spent his days scouting with Fitz Lee's cavalry, came by in the evenings and talked with Roman, telling him what was going on with the army and the defensive line that had been established. It was some comfort to know that the Yankees wouldn't be able to overrun them without one hell of a fight. Still, Roman was going to feel a lot better when they had a river between them and the Union army.

The rain continued. Maj. John A. Harmon, quartermaster of the Army of Northern Virginia, was placed in charge of tearing down any buildings in Williamsport and floating the salvaged timbers downstream to Falling Waters for the construction of a pontoon bridge at that point in the river. While that work was under way, the flatboats continued to make the crossings at Williamsport, carrying the wounded men to Virginia soil. Finally, after several more days, Will Brannon's turn came.

Will was still unconscious most of the time, but when he was awake, he seemed to Roman to be more lucid, more alert. His color was a little better, too. He was still very weak, still very much in danger from the chest wound, but according to the surgeon who checked on him, every day he lived was a sign that he was going to recover. Roman held on to that hope as he maneuvered the wagon through the narrow streets of the town to the river landing where the flatboats were waiting.

Two more of the wounded men who had been in the wagon during the nightmarish journey from Gettysburg had died while waiting to be ferried across the river. There were only half a dozen men in the back of the wagon now. Some of them still moaned in pain, night and day. The sound of misery had been so constant that Roman had gotten used to it and sometimes didn't even hear it anymore. When he became aware of what was going on, he felt a surge of guilt that he could be so callous. But there was nothing he could do about it, he told himself as he kept the wagon rolling. Every jolt, every rough place in the street, brought more cries of pain from the injured men.

The rolling pound of hoof beats coming up behind him made Roman lean over on the seat and look back. He saw Mac riding the big stallion along the street after him. He raised a hand in greeting as he drew alongside.

"Surprised to see you here, Cap'n Mac," Roman greeted him. "I thought you and the rest of the cavalry was keepin' an eye out for the Yankees."

Mac grinned as he held the stallion to an easy walk. "I convinced General Lee that he could do without me for one day. When I saw that your wagon wasn't where it was the last time I visited, I figured you might be on your way to the river."

"Yes suh. Got the word this mornin' that it was Cap'n Will's turn, along with those other fellas back there. You hear anything about the Yankees?"

"Meade's moved his army down to Frederick, but he's not in any hurry to come this way. I suspect President Lincoln and

General Halleck are foaming at the mouth with impatience back in Washington, but Meade can't be rushed."

"I reckon that's good."

Mac looked to the east, as if he could see over the miles all the way to the Union army's position. "Some of our officers want Meade to attack," he said. "They think that this time, since we'd be the ones holding the defensive line, that we'd win. But I don't know. We lost so many men up there at Gettysburg . . . so many men . . ." Mac gave a little shake of his head to break out of the memories before they got a good grip on him. "The important thing is that Meade's delay has given us a chance to get our wounded across the river. And I'm told the bridge down at Falling Waters is coming along. If we can have just a few more days, we'll get all the army back on Virginia soil."

"Hope so." Roman craned his neck to look ahead a couple of blocks. "There's the river landin'."

"I'll ride on up there and make sure they're ready for you," Mac said. With the barest touch of his heels, the stallion surged ahead in a trot.

Roman kept his team moving forward as Mac rode on to the landing. When Roman got there, he saw that one of the flatboats was pulled up to the rough dock while the other one was being poled across the Potomac. A small group of medical orderlies waited on shore to transfer the wounded men from the wagons to the flatboat.

Roman had to wait again behind a couple of other ambulances, but finally his turn arrived. He pulled the wagon up next to the dock, set the brake, and jumped down from the seat. He hurried around to the back to watch as the orderlies began unloading the patients. The wounded men were placed on stretchers as they were lifted out of the vehicle. Roman noticed that the canvas from which the stretchers were made was heavily stained. Those litters had soaked up a lot of Confederate blood.

When it came time for Will to be loaded, Roman couldn't restrain himself. He said, "You be mighty careful with Cap'n Will."

The pair of orderlies who were placing Will on one of the stretchers looked at Roman in surprise. "You talkin' to us, boy?" one of them asked.

Roman didn't back down. "That there is Cap'n Will Brannon," he said. "You handle him gentlelike, you hear?"

"Who the hell are you to be givin' us orders, darky?"

"I'm Cap'n Will's civilian aide, wrote down on the company roster all proper."

The two men laughed as they lifted the stretcher. "You're an uppity slave, that's what you are," the second one said. "But we'll be careful with the cap'n anyway."

Roman watched anxiously as they carried Will onto the dock then across a gangplank to the flatboat. Will was unconscious, his head swaying a little from the motion of the stretcher. The orderlies set the stretcher down and moved Will from it to the deck of the flatboat.

Roman looked from the boat out across the surface of the Potomac. The river was muddy and still flowing fast. The flatboats couldn't go straight across but were always carried by the current a half-mile or so downriver during the crossing. Roman didn't like the looks of the swollen stream. If that boat were to capsize, all the wounded men on it would drown. He started to step onto the gangplank. He was going to stay at Will's side, just to make sure nothing happened to the cap'n.

"Hold it!" The voice that spoke was sharp with command. Roman stopped and looked over his shoulder to see one of the Confederate officers coming toward him. "Where do you think you're goin'?" the man asked.

Roman gestured toward the flatboat. "With my cap'n, suh. I got to look after him."

"Didn't you drive up in that wagon?"

"Yes suh, but—"

"Get back on it and get it out of here," the officer snapped. "Take it back where you've been parked until the orders come to move out."

Roman frowned, feeling fear growing inside him. "Move out, suh? I don't understand."

"You don't have to. Just do as you're told."

Roman looked around as panic crowded into his brain at the idea of being separated from Will. He was about to argue with the officer when Mac stepped up beside him and asked, "Is there a problem here, Lieutenant?"

The young officer saluted. "No sir, no problem, I was just explainin' to this boy that he's got to take his wagon back where he came from. The column will be headin' down to Fallin' Waters tomorrow to cross the river on the bridge there."

Mac nodded. "I see. What about the wounded men he's been caring for ever since the wagons left Gettysburg?"

"There are surgeons and orderlies on the other side of the river to take care of them, sir," the lieutenant explained.

Not liking the way this conversation was going, Roman said, "Cap'n Mac, I really think I ought to stay with Cap'n Will."

Mac turned to him. "I wish you could, Roman, but the lieutenant's right. We have to get all the wagons downstream so that they can cross. Once that's been done, I'm sure everyone will link up again."

"But Cap'n Mac, I been watchin' over Cap'n Will and takin' care of him—"

Mac gripped Roman's arm. "And you don't know how much I appreciate that. Will couldn't have a better friend than you, Roman. We can't do anything about these orders, though."

Roman looked at the boat, at Will's pale face and the gaunt shape of his body under the blanket in which he was wrapped as he lay on the deck. "You sure . . . you sure he'll be all right all by himself, Cap'n Mac?"

"Like the lieutenant said, there are surgeons and orderlies waiting on the other side. I'm sure they'll take good care of him."

From what Roman had seen of the army's surgeons, some of them were little better than butchers. But many of them seemed to be skilled medical men, and they did their best for their patients. With his spirits sinking, Roman realized that Mac was right. They were going to have to let Will go and hope for the best.

"Yes suh," he said. "I'll get this wagon back where it's supposed to be."

"Thanks, Roman. I'll be down at Falling Waters, too. I'm sure I'll see you there, and if we can, we'll look for Will together once everyone is across the river."

"Yes suh. That'll be fine."

Roman climbed onto the seat of the now-empty wagon and swung it away from the landing. A few minutes later more rain began to fall. He paused for a moment and turned his head to look out onto the river. He saw the flatboat carrying Will bobbing on the current as the men poling it struggled to keep it moving toward the opposite shore. Then the rain started to fall even harder, and it was as if someone had drawn a gray curtain over the river. Roman could no longer see the boat.

And inside him, gnawing on his vitals like a rat, was the fear that he would never see Will Brannon again.

⊙══╪══⊙

RAIN LASHED at Roman's face as he used the whip to lash at the backs of his team. The tired mules strained against their harness and the wagon lurched forward. The mud of the road made a sucking sound as it reluctantly released its tenacious grip on the wheels. That release was only momentary. The wagon rolled only a few feet before bogging down again in the quagmire that had been the road between Williamsport and Falling Waters.

The movement of the army was under way despite the downpour and the utter blackness that ruled the night. Roman steered more by sound than sight, listening over the racket of the rain for the shouts of the driver in front of him. He shouted at his own team, not so much to urge them on as to provide a beacon for the wagon following him.

The troops of the Army of Northern Virginia moved along the road, too, trudging through mud that was ankle-deep and sometimes calf-deep. Roman caught glimpses of the soldiers in the erratic flashes of lightning. Ragged, gaunt-faced, walking with a hand on the shoulder of the man in front of them so they wouldn't get lost, they might have been a column of ghosts, doomed spirits marching to hell instead of Virginia.

At least they didn't have to worry about the Yankees, Roman told himself. Yankees had more sense than to be out on a night like this. It was scant comfort, and he knew he was just trying to reassure himself, but tonight he was going to take whatever comfort and reassurance he could get.

Nothing was going to ease his mind of worry about Will Brannon, though.

Long, miserable hours passed. The six-mile trip between Williamsport and Falling Waters took all night and part of the morning. When Roman finally came within sight of the pontoon bridge that had been constructed over the past few days, he felt even more unease. The bridge was bobbing and swaying in the river current. Cobbled together out of beams and lumber and barrels, it had a sort of crazy quilt look to it. But men and horses and wagons were moving over it, Roman saw as he drew closer. Maybe it was strong enough to hold up until all the army had crossed over.

A lot of the troops were already on the other side of the river. The rain had stopped, and Roman could see the soldiers moving around over there. He wondered where Cap'n Will was and how difficult it would be to find him. Maybe the wounded men had been brought down here and were being kept someplace nearby until the wagons arrived, so that they could be put back on the same vehicles that had carried them this far.

Ever so slowly, the column drew nearer the bridge. At last, Roman drove out onto the rickety thing. The mules shied at the moving surface under their feet, but Roman shouted at them and flapped the reins until they plodded forward. The bridge tilted to the right. Roman's heart was in his throat as he kept the team moving. The bridge swayed and then tilted back to the left. It was fairly wide, but there were no rails along the sides to stop anything from sliding off if it came too near the edge. Roman tried to keep the team and the wagon pointed right down the center of the span.

It took him less than five minutes to cross the stream, but the time seemed much longer than that. He was limp with relief when the wagon finally rolled onto the muddy ground on the far side of the river. He was back in Virginia at last, but that wasn't what mattered to him at this moment. Right now all he was feeling was gratitude that he hadn't gone into the river and drowned.

A trail ran up the bluff that led down to the Potomac. A Confederate sergeant bellowed at Roman, "Get that wagon up the hill! Get movin', boy!"

"Yes suh!" Roman called back. He had to use the whip again to get the tired mules to move. Almost staggering with weariness, the animals strained and hauled the wagon up the slope.

Roman had just reached the top when he heard shooting across the river. He brought the wagon to a halt and turned to look back the direction he'd come. Only one infantry division remained on the Maryland side of the river, and Roman saw that the group of wagons in which he was traveling was the last one. All the other wagons had crossed already.

Blue-clad riders swooped down toward the lone division still on the wrong side of the Potomac. The Confederates fired back at the Yankee cavalry, providing a rear-guard action to protect the wagons and men still on the bridge. Soldiers began running, dashing along the very edge of the span. They would rather risk falling off the bridge than let themselves be captured by the Yankees. Most of them made it, Roman noted. The few who tumbled into the Potomac started swimming desperately toward Virginia soil.

Clouds of smoke rose from the guns of those engaged in the battle, though the smoke was hard to see against the gray overcast of the sky. No one came along and ordered Roman to move, so he stayed where he was, watching the fight. The Confederates, wet, exhausted, and miserable, low on ammunition and weak from short rations, put up a determined fight, turning back charge after charge by the Union cavalry. More of the troops pulled back across the bridge, and the ones who stayed behind fought that much harder to give their fellows a chance to escape. As more Federal cavalry arrived and threw themselves into the battle, the outcome became a foregone conclusion. Sure enough, the Confederate positions soon were overrun.

That left the Yankees with a clear path to the river. All they had to do was ride down the bluff on the Maryland shore and cross the pontoon bridge after their quarry.

Movement nearby caught Roman's eye and made him turn to look. He saw an elderly Confederate officer ride up on a fine-looking white horse, accompanied by several other officers. The old man wore a long gray coat and had a short white beard. His face was lined and weathered, but his eyes were alert. He looked down at the river and the bridge for a moment, then lifted his eyes to the far shore where the victorious Yankee cavalrymen were rounding up prisoners.

"Have the bridge cut loose," the old man said in a strong, clear voice that belied his age. Some of the officers with him raced down the hill on horseback to see that the order was carried out. While they were doing that, the old man turned and rode away, followed by the rest of his entourage.

Roman realized that he had just seen Robert E. Lee.

Moments later, the sound of axes chopping at the cables that held the bridge in place floated up the hill. Roman saw the Yankees rushing down the slope on their side, but they were too late. The bridge tore loose, and the Potomac broke it into pieces and carried them downstream. The Yankees reined in. Even from this distance, Roman could see their frustration. One of them, an officer with long yellow hair, tore off his hat and flung it on the ground in disgust.

Roman turned back to his team and took up the reins. He had places to go and things to do.

And the most important was to find Cap'n Will.

THE FIRST thing Roman did was to look for Mac. The captain had said that he would be down here and that he would help him find Cap'n Will. But no one Roman asked could tell him where to find Fitzhugh Lee's cavalry, and he saw no sign of Mac himself among the cavalrymen moving around the hastily established camp a mile or so from the river.

Roman had parked his wagon with the others. He thought about returning to it, but he was afraid that if he did, some officer would come along with orders for the wagons to be moved elsewhere, and then Roman would have to leave without finding Cap'n Will. The wagon was empty, and all of Roman's belongings were in the small pack he wore slung over his shoulder. He had no reason to go back to the vehicle. As a slave, he could move around the camp without anyone's paying much attention to him. He decided he had had enough of driving an ambulance wagon. He avoided that part of the camp and began looking for the wounded instead.

"Excuse me, suh," he said to an officer a few minutes later. "Can you tell me where I'll find the wounded men who were brought over at Williamsport?"

The officer gave him a harried glance. "What? Are you talkin' to me?"

"Yes suh. I'm lookin' for the wounded men. My massa, Cap'n Will Brannon, is one of 'em."

"Well, they're not here," the officer snapped. "You said it yourself—they came across the river at Williamsport. Lord knows where they were taken from there."

"You ain't goin' back up there to get 'em?"

"I'm not privy to the plans of General Lee. Now get the hell away from me."

"Yes suh. I'm sorry, suh."

Roman hurried away, hoping he could find a more sympathetic officer to approach next time. Before that could happen, however, someone rode up behind him and called, "Roman? Is that you?"

With a sigh of relief, Roman recognized Mac's voice. He turned and saw the cavalry captain reining in. "Cap'n Mac, have you seen Cap'n Will?" he asked, his anxiousness prompting him not to give Mac a polite greeting.

Mac didn't seem to care. He shared Roman's worry. He shook his head. "I'm told all the wounded were gotten across the river safely, but they weren't brought down here to rejoin the rest of the army."

"Yes suh, I found out the same thing."

"We'll ride back upriver. I don't know what else to do." Mac extended a hand. "Come on."

Roman didn't hesitate. He grasped Mac's hand and swung up behind him on the stallion.

By midafternoon they were approaching a spot on the Potomac opposite the town of Williamsport. Smoke from quite a few campfires caught their eye and made Mac turn the stallion away from the river. Several minutes later they rode up to a sprawling collection of tents. "This must be a temporary hospital they set up to care for the wounded until they could be moved out," Mac commented.

Roman felt a tingle of hope and excitement. "Then Cap'n Will must be here," he said.

"We'll find out soon enough." Mac headed for a tent where a Confederate flag was flying. "That must be the headquarters."

They dismounted in front of the tent, which was guarded by several haggard, tired-looking soldiers. In a quiet voice that the guards couldn't overhear, Mac said to Roman, "Hang on to the stallion's reins. If anyone asks, you're my servant."

"Yes suh," Roman agreed, knowing that things would go more smoothly if he appeared to be an officer's slave—which, of course, he was, just not Mac Brannon's.

Mac returned the salutes of the guards. "Is the camp commander inside?"

"Yes sir," one of them replied. "That'll be Colonel Rose."

"Is he a doctor?"

"Yes sir, Cap'n. Assistant chief surgeon to Dr. Guild."

"Is he in surgery now?"

"Naw, they don't do any doctorin' in this tent. Just paperwork, mostly."

Mac nodded. "Much obliged, private." He stepped to the entrance flap of the tent. None of the guards made a move to stop him. Roman edged closer in hopes of being able to hear what was said inside.

Mac pulled back the canvas. "Colonel Rose?"

A man sat at a folding table inside the tent. Short and stocky, he was hatless and had wispy blond hair. A notebook was open on the table in front of him, and he had been making notations in it with a pen. He set the pen aside, capped the inkwell, and returned Mac's salute. "Yes, Captain, what can I do for you?"

"I'm looking for my brother, sir," Mac explained. "He was wounded at Gettysburg."

"Along with thousands of others," Colonel Rose said, his tone sharp and angry. Then he sighed and shook his head. "My apologies, Captain. Dealing with all these injuries has been quite a trying task. What unit was your brother in?"

"The Thirty-third Virginia, sir. His name is Will Brannon."

"Stonewall Brigade, eh? What little is left of it, at any rate." Rose turned several pages in his notebook and scanned the columns of cramped writing. "Ah, here he is. Brannon, Captain William S. Is that him?"

"Yes sir."

Shakespeare. That was what the initial in Cap'n Will's name stood for, Roman recalled. William Shakespeare was some sort of Englishman who wrote plays that Cap'n Will's pa, old Mr. John Brannon, had been mighty fond of. Roman had never read any of them, but he hoped to, one of these days.

"Gone," Colonel Rose said.

Roman's breath caught in his throat, and he saw Mac flinch at the single short word from the colonel. "Gone?" Mac repeated, his voice hollow. "You mean . . . he died?"

"Oh, no." Rose shook his head. "My apologies again, Captain. I didn't mean to make it sound like that. What I meant is that your brother is gone from here. Late yesterday afternoon we sent a group of the most seriously wounded men on to Richmond, using wagons we were able to commandeer in the area. They had waited long enough; we didn't want to delay their arrival at the hospital there any longer."

"Richmond, you say? Will's been sent to Richmond?"

"That's right. That's what I just said." Rose was beginning to look and sound a bit impatient now. "Is there anything else I can do for you, Captain?"

"No sir. I reckon not."

The colonel reached for his pen. "I'm sure your brother will be fine. He'll have the best possible care in Richmond."

"Yes sir, I'm certain he will. Thank you."

"Good day, Captain."

"Good day, sir." Mac saluted and backed out of the tent. He came over to Roman and took the stallion's reins.

"Cap'n Mac . . ."

"You heard?"

Roman nodded. "They sent him to Richmond."

"He'll be better off there in the hospital. It's what he's needed all along." Mac hesitated then sighed. "But I sure wish I'd gotten to see him before he left."

"I ought to be with him, lookin' after him."

"I know you feel that way, but that's not possible now. And I can't leave the brigade long enough to go chasing after that wagon train. But you might be able to catch up on foot, although that would be pretty hard to do. And there's also the risk that you might get picked up as a runaway."

Roman touched the front of his shirt. Tucked away underneath the garment and wrapped in oilcloth to protect them against the nearly constant rains were the documents Judge Darden had drawn up, stating that Roman was the legal property of Capt. Will Brannon. "If I was to get picked up, they'd send me to Cap'n Will," he said. "And that's where I want to go."

Mac frowned as he thought it over. "You may be right. I can't stop you from doing what you want to do, Roman. At least, I *won't* stop you."

"I thank you for that, Cap'n Mac. I got to go after him."

Mac smiled and nodded. "Yes, I suppose you do." He held out his hand. "This is good-bye, then. And good luck."

Roman drew in a breath. "You'd shake hands . . . with a slave, Cap'n Mac?"

"I'd shake hands with one of my brother's best friends."

"Thank you, suh." Roman clasped Mac's hand, swallowing hard and thinking that despite the things that Mac was fighting for, he was a good man, one of the best men Roman had ever met.

Neither of them paid any attention to the stares they received from the soldiers around them, stares directed at the uncommon sight of a Confederate cavalry officer shaking hands with a slave. At that moment, neither of them cared what anyone else thought. They had formed a bond of friendship based on their affection for Will Brannon.

"I'll find him," Roman said. "I'll see that he gets home when he's well enough."

"See that he gets home . . . either way."

"Y-yes, suh."

But Roman wasn't going to let himself think about that, wasn't even going to consider the possibility that Cap'n Will might not be all right. Cap'n Will was going to be fine. He was going to be just fine.

Chapter Eight

G EN. JOHN C. PEMBERTON'S forces at Vicksburg numbered more than thirty-one thousand men. It took several days after the surrender before the Yankees were able to obtain the paroles of all of them. Each Confederate soldier was required to sign, or make his mark on, two copies of the parole form. One copy stayed with the clerks in the Union army; the other was supposed to be carried at all times by the paroled soldier. Being caught without the parole form would lead to punishment, it was warned.

By July 8, the Federal occupation of Vicksburg was in full force. The Stars and Stripes flew from the dome of the court-house that loomed high on the bluff overlooking the river. Down below, along the riverfront, numerous Yankee gunboats and supply boats were tied up at the wharves and levees. Blue-clad soldiers prowled the streets, behaving more like sightseers than conquerors as they inspected the artillery-battered buildings of the city and explored the caves in which the citizens had sought shelter from the months-long bombardment. The whole process was remarkably peaceful, perhaps because General Grant had issued orders to his troops that there were to be no celebrations. The people of Vicksburg were fellow countrymen now, not van-quished foes. Looting was forbidden as well, though some minor instances of it did occur.

With the surrender of the Confederate army finally com-pleted, the former defenders marched out of the city under a light guard, heading east toward Jackson, Mississippi. Some of Grant's forces had already started in the same direction, intend-ing to drive the Confederate troops under the command of Gen. Joseph E. Johnston out of Jackson. What the fate of the parolees would be, no one left behind in Vicksburg could say. Nor did it matter much to the citizens of that devastated city. After the past six or seven months, what most of them wanted more than anything else was a return to some semblance of normalcy.

As members of the Mississippi Home Guard, rather than the regular army, Colonel Thompson and Allen Carter were not required to depart with the parolees. They stayed behind in the house with Cory and Lucille, Mildred Thompson, and Fred Carter. Cory was still restless. He spent his days pacing in the parlor or sitting on the front porch, staring at the courthouse in the distance and the flag that now flew above it.

Cory was on the porch when Colonel Thompson came along the street, his steps slow and weary. Thompson had been down-town, summoned to Federal headquarters. As one of the few remaining Confederate military officials in the city, the Yankees intended to utilize him as a liaison between the occupying army and the townspeople.

"More bad news today," Thompson announced as he came up onto the porch. "The garrison at Port Hudson surrendered the day before yesterday."

Cory looked up at the colonel. He wasn't really surprised. Port Hudson, a hundred miles or so downriver from Vicksburg, had been the final Confederate bastion on the Mississippi. It had been under siege by the Yankees for over a month. The defenders there had held out as stubbornly and gallantly as those in Vicksburg, but in Port Hudson, too, the end result had been inevitable.

Now the Yankees really did rule the river.

Thompson sat down in one of the chairs next to Cory and rubbed his eyes, as if in weariness. Cory thought he detected a glint of tears. The colonel knew as well or better than any of them what the developments of the past week and a half meant.

"I'm afraid it's just a matter of time now," Thompson said.

Just a matter of time . . . before the entire Confederacy was forced to surrender. Though the words were unsaid, both Cory and Thompson knew the truth. With the Confederacy split in two, with no possibility of bringing in supplies or reinforcements from the western states, with the Yankees pressing them from two sides now, defeat was inevitable. Unless there was some sort of miracle . . .

But even without a miracle, they couldn't just give up, Cory told himself. They had to keep fighting.

After a few moments of silence, Thompson added, "The Yankees are going to appoint a board of civilian commissioners from among the townspeople to make sure the occupation is peaceful. They'll address any grievances that the people might have with the Federal troops."

"That sounds like a good idea," Cory commented, surprised.

"Perhaps it is," Thompson noted. "But one of the commissioners is a man named Jason Gill."

Cory bolted upright, jerking up in the chair as if lightning had struck him. For a moment he was too startled to even talk. When he was able to make his tongue work again, he asked, "Gill? The same Jason Gill?"

"I suppose it's possible there could be more than one, but somehow I doubt it under these circumstances."

"Did you see him?"

Thompson shook his head. "No. But I'm convinced he's the same man you told me about."

"He's not a citizen of Vicksburg! He's a damned agitator, an agent for the Yankees!"

Gill had been a thorn in Cory's side, and vice versa, ever since Cory had first seen the man on the docks at New Madrid, Missouri. It had been Gill who had organized and led the mob that intended to burn the *Missouri Zephyr.* Cory had warned Captain Farrell of the plot, and the riverboat captain had turned the mob away with the aid of a small deck cannon. That had been the beginning of Cory's friendship with Farrell, which in turn had led to his meeting Lucille and falling in love with her and marrying her. Since then, Cory and Gill had crossed paths indirectly on several occasions, though Cory hadn't ruined any more of Gill's plans, as far as he knew.

Still, Gill harbored a burning hatred for him. Cory had seen that in the man's eyes the first time they met, and he could tell that Gill was not the sort to ever forgive a grudge. He would nurse the hate and resentment he felt for years if necessary, allowing it to grow stronger and stronger, until he finally got the chance to take his revenge.

"Yankee or not, he's one of the people overseeing things in Vicksburg now," Thompson said.

"Does he know who you are, that you're connected to me?"

"I have no idea. I'll be attending a meeting of the board of commissioners tomorrow, though. I'm sure we'll meet then."

"Be careful, Colonel," Cory warned. "Treat Gill the same way you would a cottonmouth, and you can't go far wrong."

"I'll bear that in mind," Thompson said. "However, I usually chop the heads off of snakes."

Cory nodded. "In Gill's case, that'd be a good idea. Before it's all over, we may be wishing that's exactly what we did."

❦

THE ROOM was tiny and squalid, sparsely furnished and tucked under the eaves of a boarding house on the south side of Chicago. Titus didn't like the looks of the old woman who ran the place. She reminded him of a spider—a tiny, wrinkled spider. But Louisa swore she was trustworthy.

Nathan paced back and forth as much as he could in the cramped quarters. "This is almost like being back in the camp," he said.

Titus grunted. "Not hardly." He took a deep breath, smelling the odors of rancid food and unwashed flesh and urine that had seeped into the room over the years. "It ain't what I'd call fragrant, but the stink ain't near as bad here as it was in the camp."

"Well, no," Nathan admitted.

"And there ain't no guards to throw us up on the Mule or beat us or shoot us."

"You're right," Nathan said. "I just wish Miss Abernathy would get back. I'm nervous."

"Never would have known if you hadn't told me," Titus drawled with a grin. He grew more serious as he went on, "Louisa wouldn't sell us out, if that's what you're worried about. Not after everything she did to get us out of there."

"Oh, no, I trust Miss Abernathy. I'm still not sure why she would risk so much to help us, but I know she won't betray us. She might be followed, though. She might lead the authorities back here without even being aware of it."

Titus shook his head. "You heard what she said when she brought us here. She used to help runaway slaves come through here on their way to Canada. She knows how to duck the law."

Louisa had referred to this hidden room as a stop on the Underground Railroad. Titus had never heard the term before, hadn't known that such a thing even existed. It struck him as funny, though, that a system put into place to assist runaway slaves was now going to help a couple of escaped Confederate prisoners get back to the South. If a railroad ran one direction, it could also run the other way, he supposed.

Louisa had brought them here after they had given their pursuers the slip near the cemetery. The fugitives had stolen a couple of coats off a clothesline behind a house and covered up enough of their tattered Confederate uniforms so they didn't stand out too much. To continue passing as Yankees, though, they had to have better clothes and their beards and hair needed to be trimmed as well. Louisa had gone to get some clothes. When she returned, she would tend to the haircutting.

Despite what he had said to Nathan, Titus was nervous, too. Being hundreds of miles behind enemy lines like this, there was no truly safe place. No matter where they went or what they did, they risked discovery and recapture.

Discovery, anyway, Titus thought. Nobody was going to recapture him. He would make sure of that. He would die fighting before he'd go back to that hellhole of a prison camp.

A soft footstep outside the door made him tense and come to his feet. He had been sitting cross-legged on the floor, but now he stood there, ready for trouble but stooped a little because the ceiling was so low. A key rattled in the lock, and the door swung open to reveal Louisa with a carpetbag in her hand. She stepped into the room and handed the bag to Nathan.

"Here," she said coldly. "You can change clothes now. When you're done I'll come back and cut your hair and beard."

She started to leave the room, but Titus stopped her by saying, "Hold on. Did anybody see you?"

She looked at him and snapped, "Of course people saw me. I had to go out in public to buy those clothes."

What was she so touchy about? he wondered. "I meant, did you run into any problems with any soldiers?"

Louisa shook her head. "No. But I heard people talking about the escape. Both the authorities and the soldiers are furious about what happened."

Titus was tired of her attitude. He said, "Seems like your nose is a mite out of joint, too."

"And why shouldn't it be?" she shot back at him, taking him by surprise with the vehemence of her reaction. "There wasn't supposed to be any killing! You murdered several men!"

Nathan set the carpetbag on the floor and made shushing motions with his hands. "Please, Miss Abernathy—"

"What did you expect?" Titus cut in. "You didn't think those Yankee bastards would let us just walk away, did you?"

"I thought . . . I thought the threat of the guns would be enough . . ." Louisa lifted her hands to her face as her voice trailed away. Her anger was fading, replaced now by grief and guilt. "Lord, forgive me," she said, the words muffled by her hands. "I never meant for anyone to die! I just wanted to help."

Titus moved closer to her. He and Nathan couldn't afford for her to act like this. If she kept wallowing in her guilt and torturing herself over what had happened, she would do something to give them away and put the Yankees on their trail. She might not mean to, but it could happen anyway. He grabbed her arms and dug his fingers into her flesh.

"Listen to me," he said over her surprised gasp. "I didn't murder anybody. O'Neil was never going to let me go. He hated me too much for that. It was him or me, Louisa. Him or me. I didn't have a choice."

"What about . . . what about the other men?"

"They were shooting at us, too. It was war, that was what it was. And killing a man in war isn't murder."

"I'm not so sure about that," she murmured. "Violence is always wrong." She looked at Nathan. "And there was that poor man who was driving the wagon."

Titus suppressed the grin that tried to tug at his mouth. "Well, that was just bad luck. The fella shouldn't have been fightin' with Nathan. He wouldn't have gotten hit so hard it busted his skull."

Nathan looked pale and sick. "I still don't see how I hit him that hard."

"Dead's dead," Titus said then turned his attention back to Louisa. "And it's over and done with now. If you help us, nobody else will get hurt. All we want is to get home safely."

So that he could get back in the war and kill more Yankees, he added silently to himself. He was sure Nathan didn't feel that way, but the desire to see more of those Northern bastards fall under his gun was the only thing that had kept Titus going all those months in the camp.

"All right," Louisa said. She still sounded miserable, but her voice was a little stronger now. "I don't understand . . . I'll never understand violence and war . . . but there's nothing that can be done about it now." She gestured toward the carpetbag. "Change clothes. I'll wait outside."

When she had pulled the door closed behind her, Titus and Nathan stripped off the foul-smelling rags they wore and dressed in the new clothes. The shirts and trousers weren't actually new; in fact, they were worn and patched. But they felt wonderful to Titus. So did the socks and boots he pulled onto his feet. When he was dressed, he gathered the remnants of their Confederate uniforms into a bundle. "That old lady better burn these," he commented.

Nathan opened the door. "We're ready."

Louisa came in and took a small pair of scissors out of her bag. The little room had one ladder-back chair in it. Nathan sat in it first after Titus motioned that he would wait. Louisa began cutting his hair.

A quarter of an hour later, she had trimmed his hair and beard, and in the clean clothes, he looked almost respectable. Titus grinned. "You could pass for a damned Yankee, all right."

"Please don't curse," Louisa said without looking at him. To Nathan, she said, "All right, I'm finished with you."

He stood up and brushed the hair off his shoulders. "Wish I had a looking glass," he said.

"Don't worry, you're a handsome son of a . . . gun," Titus told him. Louisa gave him a frown, and he shrugged his shoulders. Then he sat down in the chair and waited for her to get to work on him.

As she stepped closer, he could smell her. Mostly she smelled of strong lye soap, with just a hint of sweat underneath it, but there was something else, too, something uniquely and indefinably female. He hadn't been this close to a woman for a long time. A damned long time. And her nearness was starting to have an effect on him.

He swallowed and tried not to think about her soft, milky white skin and red hair. Despite his resolve, his arousal grew. When Louisa finished cutting his hair and came around in front to trim his beard, her breasts were only inches from his face. He closed his eyes so he wouldn't have to look at them.

That didn't work, either. He couldn't stand the temptation. He opened his eyes and saw her breasts and thought about how they would look naked and what it would feel like to bury his face between those creamy mounds of female flesh—

"Oh, my," Louisa said. "My goodness."

"What is it?" Nathan asked from across the room. "Something wrong?"

Slowly, Titus lifted his head so that he could look up at Louisa. She was peering down at him, at the evidence of his excitement. A wave of redness crept up her neck and into her face. She looked horrified and fascinated at the same time.

"Nothin's wrong," Titus said. "I reckon Miss Abernathy was afraid she'd nicked me with the scissors, but she didn't."

"Oh." Nathan didn't sound too interested. He was running his hand over his close-cropped beard. After months without shaving, the beard must have felt pretty strange to him.

Titus thought he saw relief and maybe even a little gratitude in Louisa's eyes, along with a modicum of shame. As low an opinion of him as she seemed to have, she might have been afraid that he would blurt out what she was looking at. She took a deep breath—which didn't really help matters because it made her bosom even more prominent—and went back to trimming Titus's beard.

She really would be upset if she had known that he was a married man. He didn't feel married. He had left Polly at Mountain Laurel and gone back to the Brannon farm before joining the army. The marriage was over as far as he was concerned, even if it still existed in the eyes of God and the law. And if he'd had trouble before with remembering what Polly looked like, now it was even worse. Louisa had driven Polly right out of his head.

He was mighty anxious to get back to Virginia, but not yet, he decided. Not just yet. And wouldn't that high-and-mighty Polly be shocked if he showed up with Miss Louisa Abernathy on his arm?

He was getting ahead of himself. He still had a lot of miles to go before he was back safely in the Confederacy. But the scene that had just played out in his head was something to think about, all right. Yes sir, it sure was.

HENRY WAS in one of the cornfields, hoeing up weeds between the rows, when he heard the drumming of hoof beats. Somebody was in a hurry. It was unusual for anyone around here to be riding that fast on a hot summer day like this.

Giving in to his curiosity, he carried the hoe to the end of the row and looked toward the lane that led to the Brannon farm. The first thing he saw was the dust being kicked up into the air by the hooves of the horse. Then he looked at the horse itself and the rider on its back. The man was hatless and coatless, and his long, reddish-gray hair streamed out behind his head as he galloped along the lane, slashing at his mount with the long quirt in his hand. He rode like a man possessed—or a demon himself.

"Henry!"

That was Cordelia's voice. Henry jerked his head around and saw his sister standing about halfway between the edge of the field and the farmhouse. She had a bucket in her hand, with the handle of a dipper sticking out the top. Henry knew she had been bringing him some water when the approaching rider caught her attention, too.

Trouble was on the way, bad trouble. That was Duncan Ebersole on the horse, and he wasn't coming to pay a social call on the Brannons.

"Get back to the house, Cordelia!" Henry waved her away. "Go on. Hurry!"

"Henry?" she said again, her tone doubtful and a little frightened now.

Henry was scared, too. But he tightened his grip on the hoe. "Go to the house, Cordelia. Now!"

Ebersole veered the horse off the road and headed for the cornfield and Henry. Cordelia let out a sharp cry and turned to run toward the house. She dropped the bucket. The water splashed out, unnoticed.

Henry had every intention of standing his ground. He was not going to let Ebersole frighten him. He wasn't going to show that fear, anyway.

But the horse was galloping straight at him, and Ebersole's face was like that of a madman, twisted and ugly with rage. Despite Henry's courageous intentions, his nerve broke and he turned and plunged into the corn, running for his life.

Ebersole came after him. Henry heard the horse's hooves pounding on the ground, heard the rustling and crashing of the cornstalks as they were beaten down by the animal's weight. He heard something else, too, something even more frightening. After a few seconds, he recognized it as a human voice. In high, shrill tones, Ebersole was cursing him.

Henry didn't have to think about why Duncan Ebersole was after him. It had been several days since he and Polly had made love on that hillside and decided to get married. Polly had promised him that she would tell her father about their plans. Henry had wanted to do that himself; after all, it was only proper that he ask Ebersole for his daughter's hand in marriage. But Polly had insisted on handling it herself, in her own time.

Obviously, the time had come. And just as obviously, Ebersole hadn't taken the news well.

Henry realized he couldn't outrun the horse. He stopped short and threw himself to the side, thrashing through several rows of corn. Ebersole had been close behind him and wasn't able to bring the horse to a halt right away. When he succeeded in doing so, he wheeled the animal around and sent it crashing through the rows after Henry.

By that time, however, Henry had doubled back and was heading for the edge of the field. If he could reach the house and get his hands on a gun, he might be able to make Ebersole listen to reason. Otherwise, Ebersole might kill him. The Scotsman was threatening to do that and worse.

Henry burst out of the field, but as he did so, he tripped and went sprawling and rolling on the ground. The hoe slipped out of his fingers and flew off to the side. He couldn't even use it as a weapon now. Before he could get to his hands and knees, let alone his feet, Ebersole was there, looming over him on the horse, which looked gigantic from this angle. With a hoarse cry, Henry threw himself to the side and rolled away from the pounding hooves of the horse.

Ebersole jerked back on the reins, hauling the horse to a stop again. He leaned over in the saddle and used the quirt to lash at Henry.

"I'll flay th' bloody hide off ye, ye bastard!" he shouted. "Teach ye t' come sniffin' 'round yer betters! Ye bloody little—"

Henry flung up his hands to protect his face from the whip. He felt it cut across his palms and cried out in pain. He rolled again and wound up lying almost on top of the hoe. Snatching it up, he swung the tool blindly in Ebersole's direction.

He felt the hoe handle hit something but didn't know where the blow had landed. Ebersole let out a groan and fell off his mount, landing with a thud not far from Henry. With a spryness that belied his age, he scrambled to his feet and kicked the hoe out of Henry's hands before Henry could strike again. Then he stood over Henry, blood dripping from the cut on his forehead where the hoe handle had hit him, and began whipping the young man with the quirt.

"I'll lash ye wi'in an inch o' yer worthless life!" Ebersole declared.

The blast of a shotgun made him freeze with the quirt poised above his head, ready to fall again.

"If you touch my son again with that whip, I'll use the next barrel on you, Mr. Ebersole. As God is my witness, I will."

Henry's breath burned in his throat as he turned his head and saw his mother standing there, the old shotgun that had belonged to John Brannon in her hands. The twin barrels were unwavering as she pointed them at Ebersole. Behind Abigail, Cordelia was hurrying up, along with the burly, white-haired preacher from Culpeper, Benjamin Spanner.

"Abby, don't do it!" Spanner called. "You're not a murderer!"

"Defending one of my family from a mad dog is not murder," Abigail said, her voice cool and determined. Henry had never before seen this side of her, but he was mighty glad she had picked today for it to surface. He had glimpsed the insanity on Ebersole's face. The plantation owner wouldn't have beaten him within an inch of his life, as he had threatened. Ebersole would not have stopped until Henry was dead, and Henry knew it.

"Mad dog, am I?" Ebersole demanded, his voice shaking with indignation. "Then what d'ye call this pup o' yers—" He pointed the quirt at Henry, who was climbing shakily to his feet while he had the chance. Ebersole finished by thundering, "Who raped my daughter!"

Henry's eyes widened in shock. Cordelia gasped. Reverend Spanner muttered, "Good Lord!"

"That's a lie!" Henry shouted. "I never . . . I never did anything of the sort! I'd never hurt Polly!"

"She's wi' child! D'ye deny that?"

Henry could only blink in silence, stunned by what Ebersole said. Polly . . . pregnant? This was the first he had heard of it. He felt sick, not only from the physical shock of being attacked by Ebersole, but from the sudden doubts that assailed him as well. He thought he knew Polly. He believed he could trust her. Yet, what if she had had second thoughts about what had happened between them? What if she had decided that she regretted it, and fearing that she might be pregnant, had told her father that Henry had attacked her? A wave of dizziness hit him. He almost stumbled and fell. What if . . . what if . . .

"Henry," Abigail said, "you had best explain yourself." She lowered the gun but continued to point it at Ebersole.

Henry swallowed hard. "I . . . I don't know what to say, Ma."

"The truth is always a good idea, son," Reverend Spanner put in. He must have been visiting the Brannon farm for some reason, though he wasn't really welcome there anymore. While working in the field, Henry hadn't heard the preacher come up.

"Tell us how ye defiled my daughter," Ebersole said. "Beg fer forgiveness, not that ye're goin' t' get it."

Henry's face and hands and arms stung. He knew he was bleeding from the scourging Ebersole had given him. Maybe it was what he deserved, he told himself. Polly had gone along with what they had done, had seemed just as eager and willing as he was, maybe even more so. But she was a woman. It had been up to him to put a stop to things before they went too far, and he hadn't done that. Hell, he had hurried them along, he thought. He deserved whatever happened to him.

But Polly didn't. She didn't deserve the shame. It would be bad enough for her if others thought that he had raped her. But it would be much worse for her if the truth came out.

Henry took a deep breath, ready to lie, ready to confess that he had attacked her and was to blame for the whole thing—

"Look!" Cordelia called out. "That's Polly's buggy, isn't it?"

Everyone swung around toward the road. Henry recognized the buggy. It was the one Polly used, all right, and it was coming toward the farm in a hurry. The Brannons were having more visitors today than they'd had in a month of Sundays.

No one else said anything until Polly had brought the vehicle to a stop in the yard between the house and the barns and leaped down from it to run toward the cornfield. Then Ebersole took a step in her direction and shouted, "Go back, Polly! Dinna come out here!"

She ignored him. She was hatless like her father, and her hair had come loose to fall around her face. Even hot and upset, she looked as beautiful as ever, Henry thought.

"Henry!" she called. "Henry, are you all right?"

He took a step toward her, and Ebersole moved to get in his way, the quirt rising again in Ebersole's hand. But the shotgun in Abigail's hands came up, too, and she said, "I'm warning you, Mr. Ebersole . . ."

"Oh, my God!" Polly said as she came up to Henry. "You're hurt!" She reached up as if to touch the bloody welts on his face, then drew back in horror as she turned to look at her father. "*You* did this!"

"Wha' did ye expect me t' do, after ye told me tha' this lout attacked ye?"

"I never said that!" Polly turned back to Henry. "I swear, Henry, I never told him that you attacked me."

He smiled and touched her cheek with the back of his hand, since his palm was bloody. "I know," he said. "You don't have to tell me that." He would never mention the momentary doubts that had plagued him about her. As far as he was concerned, such thoughts had never entered his head.

"Someone had better explain to me what's going on here," Abigail said.

"I can do that, Mrs. Brannon." Polly stood next to Henry as she spoke. "Henry and I are in love. We're going to be married."

"Never!" Ebersole shouted. "I'll not allow it!"

Polly's chin came up in defiance as she turned her head to look at her father. "Then the child I'm carrying will be born out of wedlock. Do you really want your first grandchild to be a bastard, Father?"

For a second longer, Ebersole met her gaze with a stubborn glare. But then the fight seemed to go out of him. His shoulders sagged. A gray look of despair replaced the flush of anger on his face. "Th' boy did no' attack ye?" he asked in a half-whisper.

"No. I tried to tell you that, but you were so crazy you wouldn't listen. You just rushed off like a madman. I knew you had to be coming here."

Ebersole stared down at the ground and didn't say anything.

After a moment, Abigail spoke up. "Mr. Ebersole, it appears that we both have good reason to be disappointed in our children. However, what's done is done. I'm not prepared to forgive you for coming onto my land and attacking one of my children—even an apparently wayward child such as Henry—but I'm willing to put that aside for the good of both of our families." She paused then added, "It appears that a connection between the Brannons and the Ebersoles still exists. Will you come to the house and sit down so that we can discuss the matter? There are . . . arrangements . . . to be made."

Ebersole lifted a trembling hand and wiped the back of it across his mouth. "Aye," he said. "Aye, missus."

"Good," Abigail said. "Cordelia, see to your brother. He's hurt."

"I can help," Polly said.

Abigail looked at her, and Henry saw that his mother's eyes were as cold and hard as stone again. "I believe you've done enough already," she said.

Chapter Nine

L UCILLE KNEW THAT SOMETHING was wrong. Cory could feel her watching him, but when he looked at her, she glanced away, as if to hide the speculative expression on her face. She couldn't hide her worry from him, though. By now, he knew her too well for that.

He didn't want to tell her that once again Jason Gill might pose a threat to them. The strain of the past few months had been bad enough for her. She had had to take care of him when he was sick. Her wedding day, a day that should be special for any woman, had been spent in the cave underneath the house while Yankee artillery shells fell above. And she was just as devoted to the cause of the Confederacy as he was, Cory knew. The loss of Vicksburg had to hurt.

So he put on a brave face about the matter, but it did no good. Lucille still knew something was wrong. For now, though, she didn't demand to know what it was.

When Colonel Thompson returned from the meeting of the civilian commissioners, Cory was anxious to ask him about Gill, but he had to wait until he could catch a moment alone with the colonel. Finally he was able to do so in the parlor that evening while Lucille and Mildred were preparing supper and Allen and Fred Carter were out back, bringing in more wood for the stove.

"What happened at the meeting, Colonel?" Cory asked in a quiet voice as they stood in front of the fireplace. "Did you see Jason Gill?"

Thompson nodded. "I was even introduced to him. He looked quite unhealthy, as if he were suffering from some injury or illness."

"You didn't feel sorry for him, did you?"

With a thin smile, Thompson shook his head. "Not at all. Evil fairly radiates from the man like heat from a stove."

141

"Maybe he really is sick. Maybe he'll die." There was a wistful note in Cory's voice.

"Perhaps. But I wouldn't count on that. Whatever his condition, he struck me as having the strength of a fanatic."

Cory nodded. "He's always been that way, ever since I've known him."

"At any rate, he's only one man, and the other commissioners seemed reasonable enough. The Federal officers are putting some rather stringent rules into effect, though. Movement in and out of the city will be quite restricted."

"I was afraid of that," Cory said. "If we decide to leave, we'll have to avoid the Yankee patrols."

"Exactly. They allowed the paroled soldiers to leave, but they don't want a mass exodus from the city. They need the rest of us." Thompson chuckled, but there was no humor in the sound. "Without its citizens, Vicksburg cannot function. And the Yankees need the city. They plan to bring a great deal of men and supplies through here and make it their headquarters for operations in the western states and territories."

"If they think I'm going to stay here and help them—" Cory began. He stopped when he heard footsteps in the hall. A moment later, Lucille and Mildred came into the parlor.

"Come on to supper, you two," Mildred said. "You can solve the problems of the world later."

Cory and Thompson exchanged a glance. It was not the problems of the world they sought to solve, Cory thought. Just the problems of Vicksburg—and Jason Gill.

⊙━━◆━━⊙

DURING THE long siege, Vicksburg had been cut off completely from the outside world. Little news had come in about how the war was going elsewhere. Back in the winter of '62–'63, before the siege began, the townspeople had heard of Fredericksburg, the battle in which Gen. Ambrose E. Burnside's attempt to cross the Rappahannock River had been turned back. Not every clash had been a Confederate triumph, however. Gen. Braxton Bragg's army had been defeated at the battle of Stones River, and Bragg had been pushed back to Tullahoma by Gen. William Rosecrans. Cory was familiar with Bragg. During the same time that Bragg had clashed with Rosecrans in Middle Tennessee, Cory had been with Nathan Bedford Forrest on a raid into western Tennessee. That had come about after Cory had traveled from Vicksburg to Tullahoma with a message for Bragg from General Pemberton, beseeching Bragg to come to Vicksburg's aid. Bragg had refused, and eventually U. S. Grant had been able to lay siege to the city and capture it. Because of that, Cory had little respect for Bragg, either as a general or as a man.

Now, with information filtering into the city again, Cory learned from Colonel Thompson that over the past weeks Bragg's forces had withdrawn all the way to Chattanooga, forced to do so by a series of flanking maneuvers carried out by Rosecrans. The Army of Tennessee was in Chattanooga now, waiting to see what Rosecrans would do next.

"What about Bedford Forrest?" Cory asked the colonel on the porch the day after the commissioners meeting. "Where is he? What's he been doing while Bragg was retreating?"

"Making life as miserable as possible for General Rosecrans, I'm told." Thompson smiled as he packed tobacco into the bowl of his pipe. "I know General Forrest is a friend of yours, Cory, but to the Yankees he's the very devil himself. I'm told his cavalry destroyed nearly every railroad bridge along General Rosecrans's supply line. He made it quite difficult for the Federals to advance." The colonel shook his head. "Unfortunately, there's only so much that one man, or the forces under one man, can do. Forrest was unable to prevent Rosecrans from forcing General Bragg to retreat to Chattanooga."

Cory clasped his hands between his knees and peered off into the distance, not really seeing the buildings of Vicksburg. "So our army's in Chattanooga now," he said.

"Indeed." Thompson's voice sharpened. "And if you're thinking of joining them, I'm not sure it's a good idea."

"Is Forrest there?"

"I'm told that he is."

"I wouldn't mind seeing the general again."

"And how do you intend to do that? If you meant to leave Vicksburg, the time to do it was during the first few days after the surrender, when there was still some confusion. Now the Union patrols are in place."

Cory knew the colonel was right. There had been a time for decisive action, but he had missed it. He had thought too much, brooded too much, instead of taking action.

But he was still practically a newlywed. How could he have gone off and left Lucille like that?

The same way you went off and left her every other time some adventure beckoned.

The bitterly cynical words sounded in his brain. He couldn't deny the truth of them, either. When he had been separated from Lucille against his will, he had sworn that if he ever found her, he would never leave her side again. Yet he had done exactly that more than once, leaving her to go gallivanting off with Forrest's cavalry then traipsing up into the swamps northeast of Vicksburg to help fight a delaying action against the Yankees. It was during that expedition he had contracted the fever that had almost killed him. If he had died, Lucille really would have been left in a bad situation. How could he even think of abandoning her yet again?

But when he thought about those days he had spent riding with Forrest, the siren call was undeniable. He had always had a restless nature; that was what had led him to come west from Virginia in the first place. And he was a patriot as well, wanting to do whatever he could to help the Southern cause. This time, though, it would be sheer foolishness to run off to war. No one man could make a difference, he told himself. Win or lose, the Confederacy could carry on without him just the same. His place was here, he told himself as he sat there and looked down at the boards of the porch. Here—with Lucille.

"I know what you're thinking, lad," Thompson said in warning tones.

Cory shook his head. "No sir. This time, I don't think you do." He looked over at the colonel. "This time, I'm staying put."

From the doorway, where he hadn't heard her come up, Lucille announced her presence. "Thank God."

Cory came to his feet in surprise and turned toward the door. Lucille stepped onto the porch and embraced him. She put her arms around his waist and rested her head against his chest.

"I've been so worried you were going to leave again," she confessed. "I could tell it was bothering you to stay here, out of the fight."

What had been bothering him more than anything else, however, was the vague threat in the sudden appearance of Jason Gill, Cory thought, but he still didn't want to tell her about that. Instead he stroked her hair and said, "I'm not going to leave you. I'm going to stay right here, Lucille."

He hoped, for both their sakes, that he was telling the truth this time.

CORY HEFTED the wicker basket. It wasn't very heavy, containing as it did only a small bag of flour, an even smaller bag of sugar, and a slab of bacon. The provisions had come off of one of the Yankee supply boats from the fleet of Adm. David G. Farragut. Cory didn't like the idea of accepting supplies from the Yankees, but given the situation there was little choice other than starvation. Almost every bit of food in Vicksburg had been eaten during the siege. Since that long, bitter standoff had ended, the only way for the townspeople to live was to accept the charity of their conquerors.

Cory started up the path that led from the riverfront to the top of the bluff. He joined a long line of civilians who had been down to the Mississippi this morning to draw supplies. Even more people were still waiting below at the boats for their turn.

Halfway up the bluff, Cory paused for a moment to look along the river. The Confederate batteries were still in place, but Yankees manned them now. Once those guns had ruled the river for the Confederacy. Lucille had brought homemade pastries down here in a wicker basket much like the one Cory carried now. The treats had been for the gun crews. That was where Cory had found her when he arrived in Vicksburg the first time. That seemed like such a long time in the past now. It was hard to believe less than a year had passed since that day. So much had changed . . .

With a sigh, Cory started walking up the path again. Longing for the past wasn't going to bring it back. Besides, in actuality those days hadn't been all that good. Even then, there had been the threat of the Yankees looming over the town. Everyone knew that sooner or later they would try to capture Vicksburg. And now, they had.

"Brannon? Cory Brannon?"

Cory froze on the path. The voice had come from above him. Slowly, he lifted his head and found himself looking into the deep-set, burning eyes of Jason Gill.

How did Gill know his name? That question, irrelevant though it was at this moment, went through Cory's mind. And then, a second later, the answer came to him. Gill knew his name because he hated him enough to have found it out.

Gill hadn't changed much in the past couple of years. He was still tall and slender, with dark hair that fell nearly to his shoulders and a lantern jaw. The colonel had been right about him looking ill, though. Gill was thinner than ever. His face was pale and drawn. He stood stiffly on the path, as if moving too much or too quickly would cause him pain. But he managed to smile as he looked down at Cory.

"We've never been properly introduced, I don't believe," Gill went on. "I feel like we're old friends, though. After all, we go all the way back to a cold night in New Madrid, don't we?"

Maybe he could bluff his way through this, Cory thought. "I don't know what you're talking about, mister," he said. "I never saw you before."

Gill lifted a finger and wiggled it back and forth. "Don't lie like that. You interfered with my plans then, and you've kept it up ever since."

Cory shook his head and started up the path again, intending to brush past Gill. "Sorry, I don't know—"

Gill's hand shot out and closed over Cory's arm, stopping him. "*I* know," he hissed, leaning in closer. "I know all about you, Brannon. I've made it a habit to be well acquainted with my enemies. I know how you and Colonel Thompson set up that supply line through Louisiana using the railroad and wagon trains. I lost some valuable men because of you."

So Gill had been behind the raids on those supply wagons! Cory had suspected as much at the time, and now his guess had been confirmed. That didn't make him feel any better, though.

Gill's voice was a menacing purr as he continued, "Yes, Palmer Kincaid told me all about you."

That took Cory by surprise. He couldn't keep it from showing on his face, either. Gill chuckled.

"You weren't aware that I knew Kincaid, were you? I told you, Brannon, I like to be well informed."

Cory's heart pounded in his chest. Palmer Kincaid had owned a saloon in Cairo, Illinois, when Zeke Farrell had been making the Mississippi run in the *Missouri Zephyr.* When the Yankees had closed the river at Cairo, trapping the steamboat there, Kincaid had helped in the daring escape carried out by Farrell. Despite that, Cory had never trusted the man even though Lucille regarded him as an uncle. Later, Kincaid had shown up in Vicksburg, probably having fled Cairo one step ahead of trouble. After several months, he had disappeared.

Cory had no idea what had happened to him, but he had assumed that Kincaid had either gotten in trouble again or found that he could make more money somewhere else. Either way, it was good riddance as far as Cory was concerned. He never had liked the way Kincaid looked at Lucille.

"Kincaid was a treacherous bastard, but at least he had good information," Gill went on.

"He was working with you?" Cory couldn't stop the words from coming out of his mouth.

"For someone who manages to get in the middle of things as often as you do, Brannon, you're remarkably ignorant." Gill waved a hand. "We won't go into my dealings with Palmer Kincaid. Suffice to say that he's out of the picture now. You won't ever have to worry about him again." Gill's smile widened. "You will, however, have to worry about me. I'm one of the newly appointed commissioners for public safety, you know."

Gill made it sound like Kincaid was dead. Cory couldn't bring himself to feel sorry about that. What he felt was anger that a Northern agitator such as Jason Gill could wield power in a Southern city.

"I know what you are," Cory said, his voice trembling a little. "You're a damned Yankee agitator. I don't know how you managed to pass yourself off as a citizen of Vicksburg, but it doesn't matter."

"You're right about that. The Federal officers know that I'm not a resident of this fair city. They appointed me to the commission anyway."

"To cause trouble, more than likely! Isn't it enough that you've captured Vicksburg? Isn't it enough—"

Again Gill's clawlike hand closed on Cory's arm, tight enough this time to make him gasp in pain. With his lips drawing back from his teeth in a grimace of hatred, he said, "No, it's not enough! No matter what we do, it'll never be enough to punish you Rebels for what you've done. You all deserve to burn in hell, every man, woman, and child of you!"

Gill's voice rose and grew shriller as he spoke. Quite a few people on the path heard what he was saying and stopped to stare at him. He seemed unaware of them. All his attention was focused on Cory.

There were soldiers close by, but Cory didn't care. He put his free hand on Gill's chest and shoved him away, at the same time yanking his other arm loose from the Northerner's grasp. Gill staggered, and his mouth opened in a soundless gasp. Cory had hurt him, just with that simple push. There really was something wrong with Gill, he thought.

"You'll . . . pay for that," Gill said. "You and that . . . pretty little wife of yours."

Cory shook inside from the power of the anger he felt. A red haze threatened to creep in from the edges of his vision. He wasn't afraid of Gill, but when the man started threatening Lucille—

Forcing himself to calm down and look around, Cory saw that not only were some of the townspeople on the path watching, but so were several Union troops. In fact, a couple of the soldiers started walking toward him and Gill, obviously intending to forestall any trouble.

"Listen, Gill," Cory said, his voice quiet but intense. "Whatever happened between us, it's in the past. I'm not looking for trouble now. But if you do anything to hurt Lucille . . ." His voice dropped even more. "I'll kill you. I swear it."

Gill straightened, holding himself in the same stiff manner that he had before. He laughed. "You're in no position to threaten anyone. You're just one more poor, defeated Reb. You'd better get that through your head, Brannon. Otherwise you won't live to see the end of this war."

"If you're waiting for me to apologize—"

Gill shook his head. "Go on about your business. But I'll be seeing you again. Count on that."

He turned and ascended the path, his stiffness making his gait awkward. When he encountered the two soldiers, he stopped and talked to them for a moment, shaking his head and turning and smiling. Cory stayed where he was and watched the conversation. The two soldiers turned and went on up the bluff with the provocateur.

So it was over. For now. But Gill wasn't given to making empty threats. His words might have sounded like the blustering of a villain in a penny dreadful, but Cory knew he meant them. As long as he stayed in Vicksburg, he was in danger.

And more important, so was Lucille.

"LEAVE TOWN? Cory, I don't understand."

"Wait until everyone's here," Cory said. "Then I'll explain."

Lucille frowned in confusion as she looked at him. After a moment, she sighed and shook her head. "All right. But I swear, you look like you've seen a ghost."

Cory would have liked it a lot better if Jason Gill *had* been a ghost. That would mean that the man was dead and could no longer harm any of them.

He paced back and forth in the parlor while Lucille sat on the divan with her hands folded in her lap. Cory had sent Fred Carter upstairs to fetch his father and Colonel and Mrs. Thompson. Now, with a clatter of footsteps, Fred came back down the staircase and hurried into the room, grinning.

"They're coming, Cory," he said. "Why do you want to talk to everybody?" Eagerness came into his voice as he went on, "Is it a surprise?"

"Maybe a little one," Cory said, returning the young man's smile. He and Fred were about the same age, he thought, but he felt much, much older. And it wasn't just the fact that Fred was simple-minded. It was the war that had aged Cory.

The other members of the household came into the parlor a few minutes later. "Well, here we are, lad," Thompson said. "What's this about?"

"Jason Gill," Cory said, his voice flat and hard.

"Gill?" Lucille repeated. "My God, Cory. He's not . . . here in Vicksburg, is he?"

Cory nodded. "I'm afraid so. In fact, he's one of the commissioners that the Yankees have appointed to run the city."

Lucille's hand went to her mouth. "You knew about this?"

Cory took a deep breath. "I did, and so did the colonel. We didn't want to tell the rest of you unless we had to. We didn't want to—"

"Let me finish that for you," Lucille said as she came to her feet. "You didn't want to worry us. My God, Cory! Haven't you learned anything?"

He stared at her, flabbergasted by her reaction. When he could make his mouth work, he said, "Lucille, I . . . I didn't mean . . ."

"The boy's trying to say that he didn't mean any harm," Thompson put in. "Neither did I. You see, it was possible that Gill wouldn't cause any trouble for us." He looked at Cory. "I take it that has changed?"

"I encountered him today on my way back from the riverfront with the supplies." Cory glanced at Lucille, saw the anger on her face, and felt miserable. "He recognized me. I couldn't get past him. He forced a confrontation, told me that he knows all about me." Again Cory looked at Lucille. "He knows about you, too, Lucille."

Fear crept into her eyes, replacing some of the indignation. "He must remember me from the riverboat."

"More than that. He knows we're married." Cory didn't mention that Gill claimed to have some connection with Palmer Kincaid. Lucille might still have some fondness for absent Kincaid. He didn't want to destroy any more of her illusions than he had to.

Lucille folded her arms across her chest and regarded him calmly. "So this is why you think we have to leave town?"

"Leave town?" Mildred repeated in surprise.

"We're goin' on a trip?" Fred asked. His father shushed him. Carter was looking at Cory with an intent expression on his face.

Cory took a deep breath. "I think, under the circumstances, it might be a good idea to get out of Vicksburg."

"And go where?" Lucille asked. "To Chattanooga, so you can join General Bragg's army like you've been wanting to for days now?"

"No," Cory said. "I think we should go to Texas."

That made all five of them stare at him in surprise. Then Fred let out a whoop. "Texas! I like Texas!"

When the supply line had been set up between Vicksburg and Marshall, Texas, Fred had driven one of the wagons, as had his father and Cory and Colonel Thompson. They had made the trip across Louisiana several times. Lucille had even come along. Cory's friend Pie Jones had been a member of the group that had set up the supply line, but when he had fallen in love with a young woman who had turned out to be a runaway slave, Pie had fled with her even deeper into Texas, much of which was still untamed frontier. It was remembering Pie and Rachel that had given Cory the idea of heading for Texas now.

Thompson was shaking his head. "I don't . . . I'm not sure . . . Texas?"

"If we can get across the river to Louisiana, we can follow the railroad to Monroe, and we know the road from there. We wouldn't have any trouble getting to Marshall."

"Getting there in what?" Carter asked. "We'd need a wagon and some horses."

"We could get some in Louisiana," Cory said. He knew he was glossing over some of the problems . . . well, nearly all the problems, to be honest . . . but he was convinced they could do it. They could get to Texas. And he *knew* it was important that they get out of Vicksburg, no matter what obstacles they might encounter on their way elsewhere.

Carter rubbed his jaw. "I'm with the colonel," he said. "I ain't sure about this."

Mildred nodded in agreement. "The idea of traipsing all the way over to Texas because of some Yankee . . . well, it just seems like too much."

"Jason Gill's not just some Yankee," Cory argued. "You don't know how dangerous he is. None of you do except Lucille. She saw the way he nearly got a mob to destroy her father's boat."

"Gill tried to get them to burn the *Zephyr*," Lucille said. "He would have succeeded if not for Cory."

"And now he's vowed revenge on us," Cory said. "On all of us." Actually, Gill had threatened only him and Lucille, but he didn't think the man would stop there. Given the chance, Gill would vent his hatred on the others, too.

Fred tugged on his father's sleeve. "Pa, I want to go to Texas. Can we? Can we go? That's where Mr. Pie and Miss Rachel went, ain't it? Maybe we could find them and live wherever they settled down."

"Yeah, maybe." Carter frowned in thought. "But from what I've heard, Texas is a mighty big place. We just saw a little of it. We might not ever find Pie and that gal."

"I doubt if Gill's reach extends that far," Thompson said. "The whole idea certainly presents some problems, but . . ."

They were wavering, Cory sensed. "But we can do it," he said. "If we can get out of town, we can find somebody with a boat downriver to take us across. You know we can do it, Colonel. You know it."

"I suppose it's worth a try."

Carter gave an abrupt nod. "I'm for it," he said.

"Aunt Mildred, what should we do?" Lucille asked the older woman.

Mildred looked around the room at the men and then sighed. "What women have always done, I suppose," she said. "Follow their menfolks. They're determined to go."

Lucille looked at Cory. "Yes, I can see that." She took his hand. "You're sure about this, aren't you? You know how dangerous this is going to be?"

"I'm sure," he told her. "And it can't be any more dangerous than staying here in Vicksburg with Gill."

"All right, then." Lucille summoned up a smile. "I suppose we're going to Texas."

Fred let out another shout of excitement as Cory drew Lucille into his arms and hugged her, holding her tightly to him.

Chapter Ten

SOMEONE WAS CRYING, A low, wretched whimpering that went on and on. That sound was the first thing Will Brannon became fully aware of. It came from somewhere nearby. Curious about the crying, he opened his eyes and turned his head to look.

The whole world began to spin crazily around him, as if it had been knocked out of its orbit to go careening through the universe. Will gasped and closed his eyes again. Closed them tight this time.

Something cool touched his forehead. "It's all right, Captain," a voice said. "Just lie there and rest."

The voice seemed to come from far, far away. Will couldn't tell anything about it. Young, old, male, female—he didn't know. The words were disembodied, just like the sobbing that still went on somewhere close by.

He took a deep breath and felt something pull in his chest, a twinge of pain that reminded him of when he was a boy and had run so hard that he got a stitch in his side. This wasn't a stitch, though. It was higher up and more in the front. And when the sharp pain faded away, it left behind a dull ache, sort of like a bad tooth.

Where was he? What was wrong with him?

He lay as still as he could, taking only shallow breaths. He was aware that he was lying in a bed, on a mattress that was thin and hard but still luxurious to him. Moving his hand a little, he felt clean sheets underneath him.

Little by little, the memories came back to him. The clearest ones were those of standing near the seminary with Roman and that Englishman and watching the massive Confederate bombardment of a long ridge in the distance, followed by wave after wave of Southern troops marching toward the distant ridge. Will recalled a small clump of trees . . . a low, crumbling rock wall . . . an officer's hat on an upraised saber, rallying the troops forward . . . clouds of smoke that rolled over the battle-field, and men who came stumbling back out of that smoke covered in blood . . .

After that, nothing except a jumbled nightmare of jolting pain and the screams of the damned. And a gun . . . a pistol. He'd held it in his hand and fired it. Will remembered that. The way a pistol bucked against his palm when it went off was something very familiar to Will Brannon.

Was he remembering that time in Michael Davis's store when Joe Fogarty had drawn on him? Will didn't think so, but he couldn't be sure. He'd had to kill Joe that day, he recalled. No great loss, because Joe was a Fogarty and a more no-account bunch of thieves and murderers had never plagued Culpeper County. As sheriff, it was Will's job to deal with renegades like the Fogartys.

But he wasn't the sheriff anymore, he reminded himself, and all three of the Fogarty brothers were dead now. Ranse and George had died at Manassas. First Manassas, Will thought. There had been a second battle there, along the creek called Bull Run. He had fought in it, too. He had fought in a lot of battles . . .

Like the one at Gettysburg.

Will groaned. Gettysburg. Culp's Hill. The place where his friend and sergeant, Darcy Bennett, had died. Where the guns on top of the hill had rained down death on countless men under Will's command, until nearly all of his company was wiped out. Gettysburg.

"Roman?" Will said without opening his eyes.

Again the cool touch on his forehead. "There are no Romans here," the voice said. "Only Confederates." A pause then the voice, soft now, added, "But no more noble gladiators ever trod the sands of the Coliseum."

Will couldn't make any sense of that. He pried his eyes open and said again, "Roman?" Where was he? Roman should have been close by. Will tried to lift himself in the bed.

The pain in his chest knocked him back like the blow of a fist. This time the world didn't start spinning, but he still couldn't move. The pain had him paralyzed. All he could do was look up at the whitewashed plaster ceiling above the bed where he lay.

Something moved between him and the ceiling. For several seconds his vision was so blurred that he couldn't make it out. The voice spoke again, and Will realized it was coming from the person who was leaning over him.

"Please, Captain, you mustn't excite yourself. If you open that wound, you'll be in serious trouble."

"Wh-where . . . ?"

"Where are you? I can answer that question, at least. Nearly everyone asks it when they wake up the first time. You're in a hospital. In Richmond."

Will's vision finally steadied and focused enough so that he could make out the face of the person talking to him. It took him by surprise.

He was looking up at a woman. And not just any woman, but one of the most beautiful women he had ever seen.

TITUS HANDLED the buggy horse's reins with ease. He had driven plenty of buggies in his life, including the one that Polly favored whenever she wanted to travel off of her father's plantation. He frowned. He didn't want to think about Polly or her father. That part of his life was over.

What was important now was staying out of the hands of the Yankees and getting home. Not home to Polly, but to the rest of his family. To his ma and Cordelia and Henry, maybe even Will and Mac if they ever got to visit. Titus wasn't sure where the

Confederate army was these days, but if they were anywhere in northern Virginia, Culpeper County wasn't too far away.

He and Nathan were a lot farther away from home than most, he thought. They were somewhere in Indiana; Titus didn't know where, exactly. With Louisa sitting on the seat beside him, he drove the buggy down a country lane between seemingly endless fields. Nathan rode behind on a chestnut mare that had seen better days. The saddle was old and in bad shape, like the mare. So were the buggy and the horse that was pulling it. But they had done the best they could, Titus told himself. The money Louisa had brought with her had bought them transportation and supplies, and Louisa's knowledge of the so-called Underground Railroad had enabled them to avoid the authorities during the week since they had left Chicago.

Titus and Nathan didn't talk much, leaving that to Louisa. And when they did have to speak, they pretended to be Quakers. "Say 'thee' and 'thou' a lot," Louisa had told them. "And pretend to pray as much as you can."

"I won't be pretending," Nathan had responded with a smile, but Titus asked, "Why do we have to talk that Scripture talk? You're a Quaker, and you don't."

"I do when I'm around other Friends," Louisa had explained. "Sometimes it makes other people uncomfortable, though, so I don't always speak in the proper manner." She had blushed again, as she did quite often. "I fear that I have never been as pious and God-fearing as I should be."

That just meant that sometimes she gave in to the human side of her nature, Titus thought. He was glad of that. If she hadn't, she wouldn't have felt enough pity for him and Nathan to help them escape. Nor would she stay with them and help them get back to Virginia. She was coming along on this journey for reasons that had nothing to do with religion and everything with what she felt for him as a man. She was in love with him, or at least consumed by curiosity and a desire for him. That didn't bother him a bit. He was going to take things slow and easy.

Like a deer in the forest, Louisa would be easy to spook, and if she ran away, she might not stop—but sooner or later she was going to have to act on what she was feeling.

And when she did, Titus was going to enjoy every minute of it . . . as long as it didn't interfere with getting back to the business of killing Yankees.

They were coming to a crossroads. Titus's eyes narrowed as he spotted a cloud of dust coming from the road that intersected the one they were on. That much dust had to be kicked up by a good-sized bunch of riders. It looked to him like those riders would reach the crossroads about the same time as the buggy.

Nathan put the mare into a trot and drew alongside the buggy. "There are riders on that other road, Titus," he said over the pounding of the hooves and the rattling of the wheels.

"I see them," Titus replied. They had only one pistol; he carried it now. But one gun wouldn't do much good against a party of armed men, especially soldiers.

Louisa's fingers dug into Titus's arm as she clutched it. "What are we going to do?"

"Nothing we can do except go on," Titus said. "If we've seen them, you can bet they've seen us. It'd look too suspicious if we was to turn tail and run."

He wished he had his pipe, or even a cheroot. During the first few weeks of his captivity, he had missed tobacco something fierce, but the craving had gone away after so long a time. It returned at moments such as this one, however, when all his nerves were drawn tight and all his senses seemed magnified. He clenched his jaw and drove on, trying to look as if he didn't have a care in the world.

As the buggy drew closer to the junction of the two roads, Titus saw blue uniforms in the sunlight. Yankee cavalrymen. He pulled back on the reins, slowing the horse a little but not so much that the soldiers would notice it—he hoped. Maybe they would just ride on past and not pay any attention to the buggy and the lone horseman who accompanied it.

No such luck, Titus saw with a grimace. The cavalrymen reined in and stopped at the crossroads. They were just letting their horses rest, he told himself. Any minute now, they would ride on.

That didn't happen. Several of the riders moved their mounts to the side of the road, but that was as far as they went. They were making room for the buggy to pass, Titus realized. "Smile and nod to them," he said from the corner of his mouth to Louisa. Maybe Nathan would have sense enough to follow their lead.

But as the buggy reached the crossroads, one of the Yankees moved his horse forward, partially blocking their path. The man held up his gauntleted hand in a gesture that plainly meant for them to stop. He wore the insignia of a major on his broad-brimmed black hat.

There were more than a dozen Yankees in the party. Titus knew that he and Louisa and Nathan couldn't outrun them, nor would it do any good to fight. He did the only thing he could. He hauled back on the reins and brought the buggy to a halt.

The major edged his horse closer to the buggy, touched his fingers to the brim of his hat, and said in a pleasant voice, "Good day to you, ma'am. And you, too, sir."

"Hello, Colonel," Louisa said with a smile. "How are you?"

"Why, I'm fine, thank you, but I'm not a colonel, just a major." The man seemed pleased by the "mistake" Louisa had made. "Do you mind if I ask where you folks are going today?"

"We're on our way to my sister's in Peru."

Titus had never heard of a town in Indiana called Peru. He hoped Louisa knew what she was doing. So far she had, but one mistake could easily be their last.

"You don't have much farther to go, then, only about eight miles or so."

"Yes, I know."

The major glanced at Titus, who had said nothing so far. "I assume this is your husband?"

Louisa linked her arm with Titus's and moved a little closer to him on the seat of the buggy. Even at this tense moment, he was aware of the soft warmth of her breast as it pressed against his arm.

"Yes, of course." Louisa nodded toward Nathan, who was sitting on the mare, trying—and failing—not to look nervous. "And this is his brother."

Titus wasn't sure if he and Nathan could pass for brothers. Titus himself didn't look that much like either Cory or Mac, so he supposed it was possible. Especially considering that the major didn't seem to be too interested in anything except flirting with Louisa.

That hope exploded a second later when the major asked, "How come you boys aren't in the army?"

Titus knew he couldn't let Louisa continue to answer all the major's questions. He had to take a chance with his drawl, which he hoped had grown less noticeable during the months of confinement in the prison camp. Keeping his response deliberately curt, he said, "Well, I was." He slapped his left thigh. "Got a bum leg at Fredericksburg."

That was the only battle in which he had participated, the only one he might be able to talk about without sounding like a fool—or a liar.

"Sorry to hear that," the major said. "I've heard it was mighty bad there at Marye's Heights."

That was where Titus had been, all right, holding off the Yankees' attempt to take the long ridge just west of the Rappahannock. He gave the officer a grim smile. "Bad enough."

"What about your brother?"

"Nathan?" Titus lifted his hand and tapped a finger against his temple. "Not quite right in the head. He couldn't go off to fight those damned Rebels."

"That's a shame." The major moved his horse back. "Well, don't let me keep you folks. Have a pleasant day, and enjoy your visit with your sister, ma'am."

"I'm sure I will, Major," Louisa said sweetly. "Good-bye."

Titus flapped the reins and got the horse moving again. Nathan rode along beside the buggy, a vacant expression on his face until they were out of earshot of the cavalrymen. Then he said, "Not quite right in the head?"

Titus laughed. "It did the job, didn't it? Not even a Yankee'd be suspicious of an idiot boy."

"Do you really think he believed us?" Louisa asked.

"Are they coming after us?"

She turned to look behind them. "No, they're riding on to the south."

"Then they believed us," Titus said. "We made it through all right—this time."

The next time might be a different story. And it would remain that way, the threat of capture hanging over their heads until they reached Virginia and the Confederate lines.

"Huh," Nathan said. "Idiot boy."

Mac Brannon and Fitzhugh Lee reined in their horses and looked out across the multitude of tents that covered the open fields near Culpeper. Lee crossed his hands on his saddle in front of him and leaned on them. "Beauty's decided to call it Camp von Borcke," he said.

Mac wasn't surprised. Heros von Borcke, the giant Prussian aristocrat who had traveled across an ocean to fight for the Confederate cause, had been a member of Stuart's staff and one of the general's closest friends. Von Borcke was one of the few officers who could match Stuart's flamboyance and zest for life.

But during an engagement near Upperville, Virginia, while Stuart's cavalry was screening the Confederate infantry during their movement north toward the Potomac, von Borcke had been seriously wounded by a rifle ball that had torn through his neck. Mac had helped save von Borcke's life and had gotten him away before the Yankees could capture him, but the surgeons and everyone else thought that the Prussian was going to die.

Von Borcke had fooled all of them by surviving, and the last Mac had heard, the burly German was still alive, though probably he would never recuperate enough so that he could take the field of battle again. Naming the Confederate cavalry camp after his wounded friend was a typical gesture for Stuart, who was very much a sentimentalist.

The important thing to Mac was that the camp was near Culpeper, which meant the Brannon farm was only a few miles away. He was anxious to pay his family a visit. He hadn't seen them or been in touch with them since the battle at Gettysburg; the cavalry had been moving around too much and too quickly for that. Fitz Lee's forces had helped screen the Confederate retreat, and once the army had gone into bivouac, there were scouting missions to carry out to make sure the Yankees hadn't followed them.

Now, though, even the cavalry was going to get a chance to rest for a bit after the brutal first half of the summer of 1863. Perhaps Mac would be allowed to visit his family and let them know that he was all right.

And tell them about Will.

Mac could only hope that Will was all right. There had been no way of checking with the hospitals in Richmond to find him or ascertain his condition. Mac couldn't even be sure that Will had made it to Richmond. If there was time, he intended to ride there and see. The rest of the family might want to go, too. Before the war, the Brannons had gone to Richmond to attend fairs and horse races. Those pleasant days were long gone and might never come again. Mac regretted their loss, but right now he would settle for knowing that Will was all right.

"I know what you're thinking," Fitz Lee said. "You want to go home."

"Yes sir," Mac admitted. "For a few hours, anyway."

"You're one of the best aides on my staff," Lee said. "You know how much I depend on you, Mac."

Mac felt his heart sinking. Lee wasn't going to give him leave to visit the Brannon farm.

Then a broad grin spread across the general's face. "Go on," he said with a friendly wave of his hand. "Go see about your family. I'll let the adjutant know where you've gone and that you have my permission."

Mac returned Lee's grin and snapped a crisp salute. "Thank you, sir."

Lee sketched a casual salute in response. "One more thing . . . take your time, Captain. I don't want to see you back here for a couple of days."

Mac's grin got wider. "Yes sir!" He wheeled the stallion and urged it into a ground-eating trot that carried them away from Camp von Borcke.

He went around the town of Culpeper itself; there was nothing there now to attract his interest. Michael Davis, a long-time friend of the Brannon family, had closed his store and left town. Judge Darden was still there, but even though the elderly, florid-faced attorney had once been a good friend and drinking companion of John Brannon, the rest of the family had never been that close to him. Cordelia had been fond of Nathan Hatcher, Darden's clerk, but Nathan was long gone. He had left Culpeper to fight for the Union, of all things. No, there was no reason to pause in town, Mac told himself, not when his family was waiting on the farm.

A half-hour later he turned from the road into the lane that led to the house. The place looked good, he thought as he slowed the stallion to a walk and studied his surroundings. Some of the fields were still being worked, no doubt by Henry and Cordelia. That cultivation put the Brannon farm ahead of many others these days. Most of the fields in the South were lying fallow, the men who had tilled them in the past having gone off to war. Some of those men had come back crippled and unable to work; others had fallen in battle or died of sickness and would never return. Those who were still healthy were still fighting. The job of caring for the farms had fallen to the women and children, and in many cases they simply weren't up to the task. The plantation owners, with their slaves still around to do the work, had fared somewhat better. Mac was sure that Duncan Ebersole, for example, had found a way to maintain an iron grip on his slaves. Mountain Laurel was probably doing just fine.

Mac didn't see anyone in the fields or around the house or the barn as he approached. It was late in the afternoon, though, so that wasn't too unusual. Maybe all the day's chores were already done. But even as that thought crossed his mind, a shiver of fear went through him. A lot of farms in the South had been abandoned since the beginning of the war. Could that have happened here? Would the rest of the family just up and leave without letting him know?

But how could they have let him know? he asked himself. He hadn't been able to get word to them. How could he expect them to have been in touch with him?

Anyway, the farm hadn't been abandoned. The fences were in good repair, and the corn was high. Somebody had been tending to things around here. Confident that he would get an answer, Mac rode up in front of the house and called out a hello.

Silence was the only response.

Mac frowned. He had seen plenty of deserted farms since joining the cavalry, and he knew that hadn't happened here. But where was everybody? He swung down from the saddle and stepped onto the porch. A practiced flick of his wrist looped the stallion's reins around the railing. The front door was closed. Mac opened it then called out again. "Ma? Henry? Cordelia? Anybody home?"

His voice echoed in the house. He felt his nerves drawing taut. Something was wrong.

They've just gone somewhere for a little while, he thought. *They'll be back.*

He took a quick look around inside. Nothing was out of place. All the furniture was there; nothing looked disturbed. That convinced him even more that his family's absence was only temporary. He supposed he should have gone through Culpeper; he might well have found them there.

One thing that was a little unusual caught his eye. The big family Bible was lying open on a lace-covered table in the parlor. Mac stepped closer to it, and as he looked down at the thick, leather-bound volume, he saw that it was open to the pages between the Old and New Testaments where births, deaths, and marriages were recorded.

The light in the room was growing a little dim, but there was enough for him to be able to make out the words written there in his mother's firm and unmistakable hand. Mac's eyes widened as he saw today's date and the names of his brother Henry—and Polly Ebersole.

Mac put a hand on the table as he leaned closer to study the family Bible. With the index finger of his other hand, he touched the names. The ink wasn't completely dry. The date had convinced him, but this was even more proof.

Henry was getting married to Polly Ebersole—Polly Ebersole *Brannon*, the widow of their brother Titus—and the wedding was taking place today. Might have already taken place, Mac corrected himself.

But where? At one of the churches in Culpeper? Mac recalled that when Titus and Polly had gotten married, the ceremony had been held at Mountain Laurel. In all likelihood, that was where Henry and Polly would tie the knot, too.

Mac gave a little shake of his head. What was he doing wondering about where the wedding was occurring when he should have been asking himself how in blazes it had come to pass that Henry and Polly were getting married in the first place? He hadn't been aware that there was any sort of romance between those two. And it had only been a little over seven months since Titus's death at Fredericksburg. That was hardly enough time for a proper mourning period. Polly should have waited at least a year before entertaining suitors.

And why the hell would Henry be courting Polly? As far as Mac knew, Henry had never been interested in her in the past.

But maybe that was because Titus had always been crazy in love with Polly. Henry looked up to Titus, the same as he looked up to all his older brothers. Even if he'd been attracted to Polly, he would have kept it to himself rather than do anything to hurt Titus.

Now, though, Titus was beyond being hurt. Still, for Henry to woo his former sister-in-law, and only months after Titus's death . . . Mac's jaw tightened. He wished he had been here to have a long talk with Henry. He would have set the boy straight. Now it was too late.

There was only one reason Mac could think of for Henry and Polly to rush into marriage: Polly was in a family way.

"Damn it, Henry," Mac muttered. He needed a good old-fashioned thrashing, and Mac was just the one to give it to him. Leaving the Bible open on the table behind him, Mac strode out of the house. He jerked the stallion's reins loose and mounted up, then headed down the lane and turned the horse toward the Ebersole plantation.

As he rode across Culpeper County in the fading light of day, he thought about what sort of reaction his mother must have had to the news that Henry and Polly were getting married. Forgiveness of any sort of sin came hard to Abigail Brannon. She had forced Will out of the family for a while because of the trouble he'd had with the Fogarty bunch. And that had come about because Will had been doing his duty as sheriff! True, Abigail had welcomed Will home when he and Mac returned for a visit following the battle of Sharpsburg, but it hadn't been easy for her. Mac couldn't imagine her being as quick to forgive Henry for getting Polly with child.

Dusk was settling down over the landscape as he approached Mountain Laurel. He could see lights burning in the windows of the plantation house as he rode up the lane lined with the trees that gave the place its name. When he came closer, he spotted several buggies and wagons parked in front of the house, including the wagon from the Brannon farm. He had come to the right place. He was sure of that now.

A young boy came running out to meet him. As he swung down from the stallion and handed the reins to the slave, Mac inquired, "Is there a wedding going on inside?"

"Yes suh," the boy replied. "But I reckon it's 'bout over by now."

"Loosen the cinch and give him a little water, but no grain."

"Yes suh. I knows how to take care of a horse."

Mac gave the boy a distracted smile and then headed for the front door of the house. He took off his kepi and knocked on the door with the lion's-head knocker. The door was opened a moment later by an elderly slave in butler's livery.

"Why, Mr. MacBeth Brannon!" the man exclaimed. "Is that really you, suh?"

At first Mac didn't answer the question. Instead, stepping inside and forcing the butler to move back, he asked, "Is my family here?"

"They sho' is, the ones that's left 'round these parts. Your mama, your sister Miss Cordelia, and Mister Henry—" The butler stopped short as he mentioned Henry's name. After a moment he resumed, "Yes suh, they's all here. Right down yonder in the ballroom."

He swept a hand down a broad hallway toward a pair of double doors. Mac remembered them from the party he and his family had attended here during the early days of the war, when it had seemed as if the whole thing were little more than a lark, a glorious adventure that would end in a matter of weeks when the Yankees ran back home with their tails between their legs.

It hadn't worked out that way, of course, and at that party, Titus had wound up being beaten by some of Duncan Ebersole's overseers. Life had a habit of turning on people like that,

Mac thought as he handed his cap to the butler then walked toward the doors of the ballroom.

On that other night, musicians had been playing so that the partygoers could swirl around the floor in gay waltzes. Tonight, there was no music, only the murmur of conversation and some muted laughter. And all of that came to a stop as Mac opened the door and stepped into the room.

He saw a small group of people at the other end of the room, near the French windows that led out into the garden. He saw his mother, attractive in a dark brown dress, and Cordelia stood near her in a green gown that went well with her red hair. Not far from them, Duncan Ebersole had been talking to Judge Darden. Both men wore sober black suits. Standing together in front of the windows were Henry and Polly. Henry looked handsome but rather uncomfortable in a suit with a stiff collar, while Polly was downright beautiful and radiant—there was no other word for it—in a yellow gown. Her thick blonde hair was piled on top of her head in an elaborate arrangement and held in place with dark blue ribbons. She had a bouquet of flowers in her left hand, and her right arm was linked with Henry's left. A few other people were scattered around the room, men and women whom Mac recognized only vaguely. They were friends of Ebersole's, he supposed. He didn't pay much attention to them. As he walked across the ballroom, he summoned up a smile for his family, and for the woman who was now his sister-in-law—again.

"Mac?" Cordelia said, breaking into the surprised silence. "Is . . . is it really you?"

"It's me," he said.

"Oh!" She rushed forward and came into his arms. "It's so good to see you!"

He hugged her and patted her on the back. "It's good to be home," he said as he looked over her shoulder at Henry and Polly. "Looks like I got here too late for the wedding. But like they say . . . better late than never."

Chapter Eleven

THEY CROWDED AROUND MAC. His mother hugged him and started to cry. Henry slipped his arm out of Polly's and came over to him to pound him on the back. Mac hugged Abigail and thought about how much things had changed. When he'd been a boy, she had always been rigid in her control of herself. He couldn't remember her crying on more than a handful of occasions. Now she was sniffling and had to slip a handkerchief out of the sleeve of her dress to wipe her eyes as she took a step back to look at him.

"Are you all right?" she asked.

"I'm fine," he told her with a reassuring smile. "Not a scratch."

"What about your brother? What about Will?"

Mac had thought a great deal about what he would tell them concerning Will. There was no way they could understand what it had been like at Gettysburg. They hadn't been there, nor had they been through any of the other battles in which Will and Mac had fought. But they loved Will, and they deserved as much of the truth as Mac could give to anyone who hadn't been through combat.

"He was wounded at Gettysburg, on the third day of the battle. His company had been through a lot of fighting, bad fighting. Darcy Bennett was killed. Will was taking a message to General Ewell when a bullet hit him in the chest and knocked him off his horse."

Abigail and Cordelia each lifted a hand and pressed it to their mouths as Mac spoke, mother and daughter mirroring their concern with their gestures. Now Abigail whispered, "Dear Lord. Was . . . was he . . ."

"He was hurt bad but not killed," Mac said. "Roman was with him—"

175

"Roman?" Cordelia said.

"That boy of Yancy Lattimer's," Mac explained. "Yancy left him to Will."

Judge Darden had come close enough to hear Mac's statement. He rumbled, "That's right. I drew up the papers."

Mac looked at him and nodded. "Yes, Judge. There'll be more papers for you to draw up. Manumission papers. Will wants Roman to have his freedom."

Darden frowned in disapproval at the idea of freeing a slave, but he nodded, more concerned with his potential client's wishes than with politics or morality. "Whatever Will wants. He's still alive, then?"

Mac nodded again. "Yes, he's alive. After the army withdrew back across the Potomac, he was one of the lucky ones sent to Richmond to recover."

"Richmond!" Abigail said. "Why didn't they just bring him here? Bring my boy home?"

"I don't know, Ma," Mac said with a shake of his head. "The surgeons must have thought he'd be better off in a hospital in Richmond."

"Better off in some hospital in Richmond than at home with his family?" Abigail's tone made it clear what she thought of that idea. "I never heard of such a thing!"

Henry clutched Mac's arm. "But he's going to be all right? Really?"

"As far as I know."

That was the truth, Mac thought, but only part of the truth. He had no idea how Will's recovery was going or even if his older brother was still alive. But he had to hope for the best, and he wanted the rest of his family to do that, too.

"Looks like I owe you some congratulations," Mac went on as he smiled at Henry and extended a hand.

"Thanks," Henry said with a sheepish smile as he shook hands with Mac.

"And to the bride," Mac said as he turned toward Polly.

She came forward. "It's good to see you, Mac." She held out her hand.

Mac took it, but he put his other arm around her and used it to draw her into a hug. "I can't say I'm not surprised," he told her, "but I hope everything turns out for the best."

"I . . . I'm sure it will."

She was pale, he thought, and obviously she had been under quite a strain lately. When he glanced over at her father and saw the dark glower on Duncan Ebersole's face, Mac could guess why. Ebersole had been bitterly opposed to Polly marrying Titus; he must have been livid when he found out that she was going to wed yet another of the Brannon boys.

But of course Ebersole had a right to be upset, Mac thought. Any father would be if he found out that his unmarried daughter was going to have a baby. Though nothing had been said here in the ballroom about Polly's being pregnant, Mac was still convinced that was the case. Nothing else could have brought on a second marriage less than eight months after Polly had been widowed.

With Polly's hand still clasped in his, Mac asked, "The wedding *is* over, isn't it?"

Henry grinned. "The wedding is, but not the party." He held out his hand. "If you'll give me back my wife, I'd like to dance with her."

"But Henry, there's no music," Polly said.

"Don't need any. All I need is you."

She went up to him, and as they embraced, they began to sway as if both of them heard the beautiful strains of a waltz.

Duncan Ebersole looked like he had just bitten into a green persimmon.

Mac had to suppress a chuckle as he saw Ebersole's sour expression. He still wasn't happy with Henry and intended to have a serious talk with his little brother as soon as he had the chance, but anything that bothered Duncan Ebersole that much couldn't be all bad, Mac thought.

Cordelia slipped her arm through his. "I wouldn't mind dancing, either," she said. "It's been a long time."

"Even if it's with your brother?"

"There's a war on," she said, trying to make her tone light. "We all have to make sacrifices."

Mac felt a surge of anger, but he stopped himself from responding with harsh words to Cordelia's comment. She didn't mean anything by it, he told himself. She was just like the rest of them, trying to get through a bad situation the best she could.

Judge Darden waddled over to Abigail, but she held up a hand to stop him before he could say anything. "I don't hold with dancing, so don't even ask," she said.

"Oh, yes, I'd forgotten that you're a Baptist, ma'am. No offense meant."

But Abigail looked offended, Mac thought as he took Cordelia in his arms and began to dance with her to the same imaginary music that Henry and Polly seemed to hear. Dancing was a terrible sin in Abigail's eyes. With her glaring at them from one direction and Ebersole staring daggers from the other, the atmosphere in the room was becoming rather icy.

Mac didn't care. He was just glad to be home.

⌒═══╫═══⌒

"TELL ME the truth," he said later, when he was sitting on the front porch of the Brannon farmhouse with his pipe and a warm breeze blowing through the night. "What happened between Henry and Polly?"

From where she sat on the steps with her knees drawn up and her arms clasped around them, Cordelia laughed. "I'm your little sister, Mac. I don't think it's proper for me to go into detail about such things."

For a second, Mac was irritated, then he chuckled. "You're old enough. You'd be married by now if there were still any suitable young men in the county, and you were raised on a farm. Polly *is* in a family way, isn't she?"

"She is," Cordelia agreed.

"I'll bet Ma wasn't happy when she found out."

"No, she wasn't happy at all. Neither was Mr. Ebersole. He tried to kill Henry, but Ma stopped him."

"What?"

Cordelia explained about the confrontation in the cornfield when Ebersole had whipped Henry with the quirt.

"I wish I'd been here," Mac said when she was finished. "I might not have fired that old shotgun into the air."

"Yes, you would have," Cordelia said. "You're not a killer."

Mac didn't say anything in response to that. He *was* a killer, dozens of times over. But those deaths had come in battle, and he knew that wasn't what Cordelia was talking about.

There hadn't been much of a celebration after the wedding. The other guests had left, and so had Ebersole. He'd had one of the slaves saddle his horse and then he had ridden off into the night without telling anyone where he was going. Once the Brannons were gone, that had left Henry and Polly alone at Mountain Laurel except for the servants. After a few hugs, Mac and Abigail and Cordelia had left, too, coming back here to the farm. Abigail was still upset and had gone straight inside, leaving Mac and Cordelia to sit on the porch for a while as they had done so often in the past.

Only it hadn't been just the two of them then, Mac told himself as he puffed on his pipe. There had been a time when all six of them would sit out here on warm summer evenings, talking quietly and listening to the sounds of the night and smelling the sweet fragrance of honeysuckle and magnolia.

Of course, it probably hadn't been as idyllic as he was remembering it now, he mused. Cory would have been talking about how much he hated being tied down here, how he was going to travel all over the world and see all sorts of exciting things. And Titus likely would have been sulled up, angry over something or other, because he usually was. That boy had taken offense over the least little thing, Mac recalled. As the oldest one, Will would have been solemn, and Mac knew that he himself had often been distracted, too, by thoughts of woods to explore and animals to see. He had always been happier by himself in the forest than with people, even his own family.

But the two youngsters, Henry and Cordelia, would have been laughing and carrying on, and as those merry sounds went out into the night, the older children would smile and forget about their own worries for a while, and they would all wrap themselves in the warmth of family. As Mac thought about those times now, he missed them so much that their loss was like a knife inside him, tearing at his vitals.

Titus was dead, and Cory was gone. Will was off in Richmond, lying in a hospital while he fought to recover from the wound that threatened his life. And Henry was a married man now, with a wife to worry about and care for and a child on the way. Mac knew that even in times of peace, things had to change. That was the nature of life. War just made it worse, ensuring that nothing could stay the same, tearing asunder the very fabric of a man's . . . a family's life.

"Henry will be all right, Mac," Cordelia said into the brooding silence. "He's not a little boy anymore."

"Don't reckon there are very many little boys anywhere south of the Mason-Dixon Line these days," Mac said. "They've all had to grow up in a hurry, no matter how old they really are."

⊖═══◆═══⊖

Virginia. CORY sighed as he thought about his home. Would he ever see the Old Dominion—and his family—again?

Lucille was his family now, he told himself as he tried to push those homesick thoughts out of his head. Lucille and her Aunt Mildred and the colonel. Even Allen Carter and Fred felt like family to Cory now. And after all, a few years earlier he couldn't wait to leave home. He had been so restless he wouldn't have cared if he never went back to Virginia.

A man got to feeling a little different, though, when he realized there were people he loved that he might never see again. And Texas was a long way from Virginia.

"One good thing about the war," Lucille said from the other side of their bedroom. "It hasn't left us a lot in the way of possessions. Packing for the trip should be easy."

Her voice shook a little. Cory went to her and took her in his arms. She turned to him and rested her head against his chest. He stroked her hair.

"I know it's asking a lot of you to uproot yourself again like this," he said.

Lucille shook her head. "No, it's all right, Cory. It really is. It's not like Vicksburg is really my home. The only home I ever really knew was the *Zephyr,* and she's gone."

That was true enough. The riverboat had been blown to kindling by Union gunboats during the last-ditch defense of Fort Henry, over on the Tennessee River. That explosion had killed the *Zephyr*'s pilot, Ike Judson, and the rest of its crew except for Cory and Lucille's father. By that time, Lucille had gone overland with some of the fort's troops to Fort Donelson, on the Cumberland River. After the fall of Fort Henry, Cory and Captain Farrell had walked to Fort Donelson, but Lucille was gone by the time they got there. Farrell had died during the ensuing battle, but before his death, Cory had promised him that he would find Lucille and look after her. Months of searching had led Cory to Nashville, where Lucille had gone to stay with her aunt and uncle, Charles and Mildred Thompson. But once again he was too late, and Lucille was already gone. She and the Thompsons had gotten out of town just before a Yankee army under the command of Gen. Don Carlos Buell occupied it. Cory's search had gone on, interrupted by a little fracas with the Yankees near a place called Pittsburg Landing, in the woods around a tiny church known as Shiloh . . .

Now, as he held Lucille in the little upstairs room in the house in Vicksburg, Cory reflected that she was right. Nashville had never been her home, and neither had Vicksburg. They were just places she had found herself, buffeted on the currents of war. He cupped her chin and lifted her head so that he could look into her brown eyes. "It's a home you really want, isn't it?" he whispered.

She nodded. Tears glistened in her eyes. "Yes . . . but I'm afraid we'll never have one of our own as long as we're running from the Yankees."

He couldn't bring himself to tell her that they might not have to worry about that much longer. With Federal forces now completely in control of the Mississippi River and Robert E. Lee's invasion of the North turned back at Gettysburg, the war might not go on much longer. Cory was sure the Confederacy would hang on as long as it could—from generals such as Lee down to the lowliest privates, the Southern army was made up of fighting men who never liked to admit defeat—but barring a miracle, the cause was lost. The best the Confederacy would hope for was a negotiated peace that would allow it to retain at least a degree of self-control. In his darkest moment, Cory didn't think even that would ever come about. What was it they called Grant? *Unconditional Surrender.* That was what the Yankees would hold out for.

"Once we get there, our home will be in Texas," he said. "I met a soldier from there while I was at Fort Donelson. He told me about a river called the Brazos and said some of the best farming and ranching land in the world is there. I told Pie all about it, and I think that was where he and Rachel were headed. When we get there, we'll find them and start up a place of our own, a place where we can raise a family."

Lucille smiled, but her cheeks were still wet with tears. "It's a nice dream, Cory, but I'm not Fred. I know it won't be easy. It won't be just an adventure. There'll be so much hardship and danger . . ."

"But it'll be worth it in the end," he told her. "You'll see." He drew her tightly against him again.

He was standing there holding her like that when someone began to pound on the front door downstairs.

Lucille lifted her head. "What in the world?"

Whatever it was, it couldn't be good, Cory thought. "I'd better go see," he said. "Why don't you stay here and go on packing?"

Lucille stepped back and caught hold of his hand. "No, I'm going with you. I'm scared, Cory."

"Don't be," he told her as he squeezed her hand. He even managed to smile.

But inside, panic lurked at the back of his mind. Something about the hard, brutal sound of the knocking told him that whatever this was, it was going to be bad.

He wanted Lucille to stay in the bedroom but knew that arguing with her would be a waste of time. He hurried out into the upstairs hall and headed for the staircase. When he reached the top of it, the pounding on the door down below stopped, and he heard voices.

Colonel Thompson's was first. "What is it? What do you men want?"

"We're lookin' for Cory Brannon," a harsh voice replied. "We got orders to take him into custody."

Cory froze at the top of the stairs. From where he stood, he could see the lower half of Thompson's body as the colonel stood in the foyer by the open front door. Several men crowded in around him; all of them were clad in the blue trousers of Union army uniforms.

The Yankees had come for him! Even as that chilling thought went through his head, Cory knew who was to blame for this.

Jason Gill.

Gill had vowed to get revenge, and this sudden intrusion demonstrated that he would not hesitate to use his powerful new position to get it. Rage and fear mingled together and rose in Cory's throat, tasting as bitter as wormwood.

"What the devil are you talking about?" the colonel demanded. "Mr. Brannon is a civilian. You have no right—"

"Vicksburg's under martial law, and we got our orders. Now get out of the way, old man."

Lucille's fingers dug into Cory's arm. He turned to look at her as desperation grew inside him. He couldn't fight a whole Yankee patrol.

"Go!" Lucille hissed at him. "Get out of here, Cory!"

"I can't just leave you here—"

"Please!" Lucille came up on her toes and pressed her mouth to his. "I love you, Cory. Now go!"

He knew she was right. He gripped her shoulders. "Go on with the plan. Get to Texas. I'll find you, I swear it."

She kissed him again and held him for a second in an embrace so tight it took his breath away. Then she stepped aside, and he ran back down the hall toward their bedroom.

Cory heard shouting below as Colonel Thompson continued to argue with the Yankees and get in their way. He ran into the bedroom and went straight to the window. Several of the panes had shattered from the concussion of nearby explosions during the siege of the city, and they had been covered over with oil-cloth. He slid the window up, tearing the cloth away when it snagged on the upper panes. Outside the window was a bois d'arc tree with several of the branches within reach. Cory threw a leg over the sill, sat down, and slid his other leg over. He balanced there for a second then threw himself forward, reaching out for the nearest branch. His palms slapped against it, slid for a heart-stopping second, and then his fingers closed around the bark. He hung there for a moment, his feet dangling, before he was able to stand up on a lower branch. With his heart pounding like mad in his chest, he started working his way toward the trunk. He was glad he had learned how to climb trees as a kid back home on the farm. That skill was going to come in handy now.

When he was close enough to the ground, he hung full length and dropped. He landed lightly, bending his knees on impact so that he wound up in a crouch. He could still hear shouting coming from the front of the house. He also heard women's voices and knew that Lucille and Mildred were getting in on the argument.

The Yankee soldiers wouldn't hurt women, Cory thought. He was fairly sure of that. But if the colonel or Allen Carter tried to stop them, they might wind up being arrested, too. Cory prayed it wouldn't come to that.

He broke into a run up the alley behind the houses. He was fleeing with nothing more than the clothes on his back. This wasn't the first time he had done that, though.

He had gone only ten yards when someone yelled behind him, "Lieutenant! There he goes!"

Cory darted a glance over his shoulder and saw Yankees hurrying around the rear corner of the house. He stumbled, almost falling, then caught his balance and raced on, his eyes in front of him again. The alley, like almost everywhere else in Vicksburg, was pocked with shell craters. He weaved between them, expecting at any second to hear the crackling of rifle fire behind him. The Yankees weren't shooting, though. He wondered if Gill had given orders that he was to be taken alive. He wouldn't be at all surprised.

Gill had vowed to take out his vengeance on Lucille, too. Colonel Thompson knew that. The colonel was a smart man. He would act quickly to get his wife and niece out of town and on their way to Texas. He had Allen and Fred Carter to help him. They would make it, Cory told himself.

But inside, he was filled with bleak despair. Gill might act quickly, too. If he had sent troops to arrest Cory today, then his moves against the rest of the family might come tomorrow, or even sooner.

He wished that he had killed Gill when he had the chance. When he met the Northerner there on the bluff, he should have wrapped his fingers around the man's scrawny neck and held on until he was dead. He would have been arrested for murder, but at least Lucille and the others would be all right.

Cory darted around a house and into another alley. All the houses along here were abandoned because they had been damaged in the shelling. Nearly all the roofs were gone, and some of the walls had collapsed, too. Maybe he could hide somewhere in the ruins . . .

He whipped around a corner, vaulted over a pile of rubble into one of the abandoned houses, and fell to his knees. He caught himself on his hands and felt pain shoot through one of them as he ripped his palm open on a piece of jagged wood. To his left was the house's fireplace. Cory glanced up through the gaping hole where the house's second floor and roof had been and saw that the chimney had the top blown off of it. Some of the bricks must have fallen down inside the fireplace, but if there was still room for him to crawl into it, the Yankees might not find him there. The patrol might not be willing to take the time to conduct a house-to-house search. It would all depend on how important Jason Gill had made it sound that he be captured.

Cory scrambled into the fireplace, ignoring the pain in his gashed hand. He had to duck low and push some tumbled bricks aside, but he made it. Soot and ashes billowed up around his feet, and the smell was so bad he wanted to sneeze. He suppressed the impulse, not knowing how close the searchers were. If they overheard him now, he was lost.

He tilted his head back to look up the chimney. Sunlight slanted down through the ruined top. The chimney was clear, Cory saw, realizing that he could climb it. He reached up as high as he could, searching for finger holds between the bricks.

Grunting with the effort, he pulled himself up. He was able to reach more handholds and after a moment got a foot braced against the side of the chimney. He climbed higher until he was above the level of the fireplace opening. Now anyone looking into the ruined house wouldn't be able to see him.

The strain of hanging there sent waves of pain through his hands and arms and shoulders. He was able to take some of his weight on his toes, but not much. He knew he couldn't stay there for very long.

"Look over there!"

The voice was muffled by the stones of the chimney around him, but Cory heard it clearly enough to recognize the Northern accent. The soldiers were right outside this house. The officer in charge shouted more commands, spreading his patrol through the neighborhood. Cory forced himself to breathe shallowly and quietly as he heard footsteps very near his hiding place.

A second voice announced, "He ain't in here, Lieutenant. How long we gonna look for him?"

"Until we find him," the officer replied.

Cory's spirits sank. Gill must have made it sound important indeed that he be taken into custody. But there was still a chance he could get away, if only the Yankees would move on and give him the opportunity to double back. He might even be able to get back to Lucille and the others.

No, he thought, that was the last thing he needed to do. The Yankees, for all their faults, weren't fools. They would have left someone to watch the colonel's house, just in case Cory came back. He had to stay as far away from there as he could. Sooner or later, the guards would leave, and Lucille and the others could slip away.

Cory's right hand started to cramp. He grimaced in pain and hung on tighter with his left. The spasm in his right passed after a few seconds. He heard footsteps again, fainter now.

"Check the houses in the next block," the Yankee lieutenant called. He was farther away than he'd been. He was leaving, Cory thought, closing his eyes in relief. All he had to do was hide for a little while longer, then he could risk sneaking out.

The seconds seemed endless as they stretched into minutes. Cory wasn't sure how much time had passed. After he didn't hear anything to indicate that the Yankees were still in the area, he waited a little longer before trying to climb down out of the chimney. When he did move, he found that he couldn't hold on. His fingers slipped, and he fell into the fireplace.

Fiery knives jabbed into his ankle as he crumpled into a heap amidst the ashes. He knew he had turned his ankle, but it wouldn't stop him from getting around. Nothing was going to stop him. Again soot billowed up and clogged his nose and mouth. This time he couldn't keep himself from sneezing. He was still doing it as he pulled himself out of the fireplace.

"I'd say God bless you, Reb, but I don't really care whether He does or not."

Cory's head jerked up at the sound of the voice, and he found himself staring in horror at the Yankee lieutenant, who stood on the other side of the ruined room with a cocked pistol in his hand. He saw several other members of the patrol standing on the outside of the collapsed wall, rifles held at the ready.

"No point in trying to run again," the lieutenant went on. "You ain't goin' anywhere. You're our prisoner now."

"H-how . . ." The soot was still choking Cory, and the single word was all he could get out.

"How'd we know you were in here?" The lieutenant pointed to the floor. "I spotted that fresh blood. Drops of it led right to the fireplace. I sent most of the boys away and had the rest keep mighty quiet. Figured you'd crawl out of your hidey-hole in a little while."

Sickness filled Cory. All his life he'd had a habit of acting rashly, of overlooking things that he should have seen. He had thought that he'd gotten better about that over the past couple of years, but now, with his freedom and perhaps his very life on the line, he had made another mistake.

The worst of it was, Lucille and her aunt and uncle and their friends might wind up paying for that mistake, too.

If the soldiers had wanted to shoot him, they'd had their chances before now. Gill wanted him alive. Cory was sure of it. So maybe he could take one more slim chance . . .

He started to climb to his feet, the very picture of weary dejection, but as he did so, his hand closed over a chunk of brick that had been blown off the chimney. Straightening suddenly, he flung it as hard as he could at the lieutenant's head.

The Yankee officer let out a yell and jerked aside. The gun in his hand went off, blasting a shot into the floor. Cory followed the brick, jumping the lieutenant. The soldiers outside couldn't fire for fear of hitting their commander, even if they hadn't been ordered to take the prisoner alive. Cory crashed into the lieutenant and knocked him to the floor. The fingers of his uninjured hand closed around the cylinder of the revolver as he tried to wrest it from the lieutenant's grip.

He heard the other soldiers yelling surprised curses. Heavy footsteps sounded close by Cory's head, and the next second something smashed into the back of his skull. A rifle butt, he realized as he went limp and consciousness started to slip away from him. He had known he couldn't outfight the whole bunch of them. But he hadn't been able to surrender, either. Maybe in the back of his mind he had been hoping he could force them to kill him, because then Gill might leave Lucille and the others alone.

But that hope had been a futile one. All hopes were futile, Cory thought as he tried to fight off the darkness. All of a man's dreams died when he did, and life came to nothing.

Nothingness was what claimed him then, a darkness that carried him far, far away.

Chapter Twelve

THE WOMAN'S NAME WAS Dorothy Chamberlain. Dorothy Willingham Chamberlain. Or Mrs. Horace Chamberlain, of the Norfolk Willinghams who had married one of the Richmond Chamberlains. She explained all that to Will, but he didn't pay much attention to what she was saying. Part of the time he spent wondering if the bullet wound in his chest was going to kill him, and the rest of the time he thought about how incredibly lovely she was.

This was one hell of a time and place to be thinking about whether or not a woman was pretty, he told himself.

He had lost track of the days he had been here in the hospital in Richmond. Most of the time, he slept. When he was awake, he listened to the moans of the wounded men in the beds around him in the hospital ward. There was nothing else to do. That was why he looked forward so much to Dorothy Chamberlain's visits. It didn't have anything to do with the way she looked. When she came to see him, it was a break in the monotony; that was all.

If he told himself that often enough, Will thought, he might even come to believe it.

It wasn't as if there had never been any women in his life before. He'd had a few lady friends in Culpeper, and there were places where a fella could discreetly relieve the urges of his flesh, even if he was the sheriff of the county. But he had never met a woman quite as beautiful or as nice as Dorothy Chamberlain. It was a damned shame she was married.

He'd noticed the wedding ring on her hand that first day when she used a damp cloth to wipe the sweat from his forehead. She came to the hospital to do what she could to help, she explained. There were never enough medical orderlies to take care of all the patients' needs. Being a married woman, she was

193

able to wash the men and empty chamber pots and things like that without too much embarrassment. Her main job, though, was just visiting with the men and keeping their spirits up. She was good at that.

One of the doctors came by every day to check on Will. The surgeon would remove the bandages around Will's chest and check the red, puckered hole where the bullet had gone in. "You're healing nicely, Captain," was always the verdict.

At least he was healing on the outside, Will thought. Inside might be another matter. The doctors couldn't peer into his body and see how much damage the Yankee bullet had done, nor could they be sure that the injury was getting better. All Will knew was that after weeks in the hospital, he was still weak as a kitten and felt a sharp pain inside whenever he took too deep a breath. Maybe the bullet had broken a rib and the jagged end was poking him. Maybe the muscles were torn and had not knitted up the way they should. He didn't know and neither did the surgeons. But they weren't going to let him out of here until his strength returned. At this rate, the war might be over by the time he got out of the hospital.

Dorothy brought news of the war, though sometimes she was reluctant to deliver it if it was bad for the Confederacy. Will knew that the Union forces had prevailed at Gettysburg. After the failure of that glorious but doomed charge, General Lee would have had no choice but to withdraw from the field of battle. Dorothy knew some of the details of the army's retreat to Williamsport and the crossing of the Potomac at Falling Waters. She sat beside the bed and told Will all about it.

Roman must have looked after him, Will knew. He had vague memories of the young man's face and suspected that Roman had done whatever was necessary to get him to safety. But then they had gotten separated somehow. Will wondered where Roman was now and hoped that he was all right.

Until Dorothy told him about it, he had no idea that Vicksburg had fallen to the Yankees. He hadn't even known about the siege. A few days after Vicksburg's fall, according to Dorothy, Port Hudson, farther south on the Mississippi, had surrendered to the Yankees, too. Now they controlled the entire length of the great river.

In Tennessee, Federal forces under General Rosecrans had occupied Tullahoma, the former headquarters of the Army of Tennessee under Gen. Braxton Bragg. Bragg had fallen back to Chattanooga and was still there. Everyone expected Rosecrans to follow him there and try to drive out the Confederates, but so far that hadn't happened. Rosecrans was sitting in Tullahoma, taking his time before his next move, whatever it was to be.

"What about the cavalry?" Will asked Dorothy as she sat beside his cot on a stool. "Where's Jeb Stuart these days?"

"I'm told the cavalry has gone into bivouac. Isn't that what it's called when they camp for a long period of time?"

"That's right. Do you know where?"

"Near Culpeper, I believe. Isn't that where you're from, Captain?"

Will nodded and closed his eyes in relief. Mac would get a break from combat as long as Stuart's cavalry was camped. Not only that, but he was close to home and would probably be able to get back to the farm sooner or later for a visit, if he hadn't already. He wondered if Mac knew he was in Richmond. If Mac knew, he would tell the family. At least they would know he was still alive.

Just in case Mac couldn't get away, though, Will decided he ought to get in touch himself. "If I write a letter," he said to Dorothy, "can you see that it gets mailed?"

"Yes, of course. But the post isn't too dependable these days. Sometimes letters don't reach their destinations."

Of course they don't, Will thought. War played hell with everything, right down to the mundane details of life like sending a letter. But he would try anyway. "If you could find me some paper and a pen . . ."

"I'll look for some right now."

Dorothy came back a short time later with a piece of paper, a pen, and an inkwell. With a smile, she explained that she had pilfered them from the office of one of the surgeons. "Actually, he was quite nice about it and volunteered the use of his pen and ink."

Will wasn't surprised. Most men would have trouble saying no to a woman like Dorothy Chamberlain.

She helped him sit up. Her hands were warm and strong, and despite his condition, Will found himself enjoying her touch. But when he tried to sit on the cot and take the paper and pen from her, his head began spinning and he felt almost too weak to draw another breath. She must have realized he was about to pass out, because she quickly put an arm around his shoulders to support him. With great care, she lowered him until he was stretched out full-length on the cot again.

"Well, that didn't work very well," Will said in disgust at his weakness.

"Don't worry about it," Dorothy told him. "I'll be glad to write the letter for you. Just tell me what you want to say."

That seemed to be the only solution. Will nodded. "All right. Address it to my mother: Mrs. Abigail Brannon, Culpeper County."

Dorothy settled back on the stool with a board across her lap to serve as a desk. As Will dictated the letter, telling his mother and the rest of the family that he was all right and would be home as soon as he could, he looked at Dorothy. She was in her late twenties, with ash blonde hair that was pulled back and tied behind her head with a ribbon. She wore a dress made of gaily colored plaid fabric, so that she stood out in the drab surroundings of the ward. There was nothing gaudy about her, though. She was every inch a lady.

Will had nearly finished dictating the letter when he noticed that she was crying.

A single teardrop had trickled down each cheek, and her hand shook a little as she moved the pen over the paper. Will stopped talking, and after a second she looked up to see why. She started to blush as she found him staring at her.

"Please, go ahead, Captain," she said. "I'm quite all right, I assure you."

"Not hardly," Will said. "What's wrong, Mrs. Chamberlain?"

She shook her head. "Nothing. It's just so kind of you to let your family know that you're all right. You must care for them very much."

"Sure. They're my family." Will paused. "But that's not why you're crying."

More tears welled from her eyes. Though it was an obvious struggle, she maintained her composure as she said, "Your letter reminded me of the ones I received from my husband, that's all."

"He doesn't write to you anymore?"

"He was killed at Chancellorsville."

Will swallowed the angry curse that tried to come up his throat. He was furious at himself for being such a double-damned idiot. He should have figured it out for himself. Dorothy had mentioned being married, but in all the time she had been coming to visit Will here in the hospital, she had never said anything about getting a letter from Horace Chamberlain or about his coming home for a visit. Will had just assumed that Chamberlain was still alive, but looking back on it now, he realized that Dorothy had never said that he was.

"I'm sorry," he said, knowing how inadequate that sounded. "I should have known better, ma'am. I never meant to cause you any discomfort."

She slipped a lacy handkerchief out of a pocket in her dress and wiped her eyes. "That's all right, Captain," she said. "You had no way of knowing. I tend not to say anything about Horace's death unless someone asks. I'm not looking for sympathy."

Will could see that was true. He would be willing to bet that most of the men Dorothy visited here in the hospital didn't know the truth about her husband. She was only interested in helping them, not in burdening anyone else with her grief.

Dorothy tucked the handkerchief away and summoned up a smile. "It's not as bad as it was during the first month or so. One never fully adjusts to such a loss, but with time, the hurt grows less . . ."

"Yes, ma'am," Will said. Though losing a brother was not the same as losing a spouse, he knew from the way he had felt after Titus's death that Dorothy was right. The pain had subsided somewhat, had become a dull ache of loss rather than the sharp, wrenching, knife-edge grief he had felt when he heard that his brother had been killed by the Yankees. "If there's anything I can do for you . . ." It was a ridiculous offer to make, what with his being stuck flat on his back on this damned cot, but he said it anyway.

Dorothy smiled again. "Thank you, Captain, but I'm fine." She picked up the pen and dipped it in the inkwell. "Now, we'll just get back to this letter to your family. I'm sure they'll be very glad to hear from you."

Will figured they would be, too. He just wished that he had better news for them.

Although the fact that he was still alive, when they might have been afraid that he was dead, was pretty good news by itself, he thought.

TITUS FIGURED they were somewhere in Ohio now. Louisa seemed to know where they were going and how to get there, so that was good enough for him. He had never been one to think too highly of a woman's ability to find her way around, but considering the way he and Nathan had put their lives in Louisa's hands, he supposed he ought to give her the benefit of the doubt.

The buggy was parked inside some farmer's barn. Louisa had talked to the man, who was old and had a long white beard. Titus wasn't sure what she had told the farmer and didn't care. The story, whatever it was, had gotten them a place to sleep tonight where they would be out of the weather. And since the sky had grown overcast during the late afternoon and now thunder was rumbling in the distance, Titus was glad for the roof over their heads, even if they did have to share the barn with some cows and mules.

He sprawled on his back on a pile of fresh hay, his hands clasped behind his neck. A lantern with its flame turned low hung from a nail beside the big double doors, and it cast enough light for Titus to see the center aisle of the barn from where he lay in one of the rear stalls. The corners of the cavernous structure were in shadow, as was the loft overhead.

A feeling of contentment stole over Titus. Lying here in the barn like this made him think of being back home. He had spent hours in the barn there, taking life easy and dreaming of the day when he would be rich and powerful and married to Polly Ebersole. The last part of that dream had come true, but not the rest of it. The marriage hadn't worked out, either, and that had taught Titus not to put too much stock in dreams. The ones that came true never made a man happy, and no dream had ever kept a man from dying when his time was up. Better to live in the here and now, Titus had learned, and to hell with the future.

Of course, he hadn't felt like that while he was stuck in the Yankee prison camp. Then his dreams of escaping had been the only things he could cling to, the only things that had kept him alive.

He wished he had a jug of Israel Quinn's corn liquor right now. Those squeezin's went down mighty fine and really lit up a man's insides with their warmth.

He was alone in the barn. Nathan was outside somewhere, standing guard with the pistol. Titus figured it was unlikely any Yankee patrols would come nosing around a farm deep in their own territory, but it didn't hurt to keep an eye out. Besides, as long as Nathan was occupied with standing guard, he wasn't in here prattling to Titus about this, that, and the other. As he felt himself growing sleepy, Titus wondered where Louisa was.

Tending to personal business, more than likely. Titus had spotted a privy behind the farmhouse.

His eyelids had just about drooped closed when he heard one of the double doors open. He sat up, his gaze going to a pitchfork that hung on a couple of pegs nearby. If it came down to trouble, a pitchfork made a wicked weapon with its row of razor-sharp tines. Titus relaxed, however, as he saw the slender figure slipping into the barn. Louisa closed the door behind her.

She came toward him, and as she drew nearer he saw droplets of moisture sparkling in her hair. "Is it raining?" he asked.

"It started to sprinkle a few minutes ago." There was another roll of distant thunder as Louisa spoke. "I think there'll be a storm in a little while."

"You're probably right. I'm glad we're inside. Some of them summer thunderstorms can get pretty bad."

She looked back toward the door. "I should go find Nathan . . ."

"He'll come in if it starts rainin' too hard. Even Nathan's got sense enough to come in out of the rain."

"I don't know why you talk about Nathan like that," Louisa said with a frown. "He's very nice, and he seems very intelligent to me."

"A fella can be smart without havin' a lick of sense, and as for bein' nice, Nathan's too nice for his own good most of the time." Titus shrugged. "But I reckon he's all right. He ain't been a burden so far."

"I should say not." Louisa came closer and shook her head, getting some of the water out of her hair. Titus felt his chest get tight as he watched those thick red curls jump and swirl around her head. Earlier she had taken off her hat and gloves and left them in the buggy. Now that she wasn't dressed up, she looked more vulnerable somehow, and prettier than ever.

Titus got to his feet. "You sure you can trust that old man?"

"Mr. Egilholtzer? Of course. We have mutual friends."

"From the Underground Railroad."

She looked at him with an intent expression. "Does it bother you that we're making use of the route used to bring runaway slaves to freedom?"

"Hell, no. I think it's funny."

"I don't think there's anything humorous about slavery." Her voice was cold now.

This conversation wasn't going the way he wanted it to. "I don't much care one way or the other about slavery," Titus said. "My family has never held any slaves, but we're strong for the Confederacy and states' rights. Besides, it was the South that was invaded."

Damn it! Why was he standing there arguing politics when all he really wanted to do was look at Louisa and appreciate how pretty she was? She was the one who'd brought it up, but he hadn't had to take the bait.

"I'll never understand that attitude," she said. "How can you support the South without supporting slavery?"

Titus shrugged. "A man's home is his home. If you can't understand that, I can't explain it any better."

After a moment, Louisa sighed. "I suppose we'll have to agree to disagree on this matter."

"Sounds good to me." Titus couldn't resist a parting shot. "I ain't sure why you decided to help a couple of raggedy-ass Rebels like Nathan and me escape in the first place."

"Because cruelty is cruelty, no matter who is carrying it out or what the reason," she replied without hesitation. "I don't believe the ends justify the means. There is no excuse for the brutal, inhumane treatment you and the others received at Camp Douglas." Her voice rose with passion. "I would have gotten all of you out of there if I could. All I could manage was you and Nathan, so I had to do what I could."

"Well, we're much obliged," Titus said in a dry tone. He moved closer to her and put a hand on her arm, feeling the warmth of her flesh through the sleeve of her dress. "If there's ever anything I can do to pay you back . . ."

He halfway expected her to pull away, to jerk her arm out of his loose grip. But she didn't. Instead, she tipped her head back to look up into his lean face. He knew he wasn't as gaunt as he'd been when they left Chicago. Their meals had been sort of haphazard while they were on the road, but he was still eating better than he had all those months in the camp. He'd put on a little weight, and he felt much stronger.

"Titus, you . . . you have the wrong idea," Louisa said. "Thou . . . thou are not a Friend . . ."

His fingers tightened on her arm. "Don't start that Quaker talk," he said, his voice rough with the feelings that were rising inside him. He had been holding them in for weeks, and he was getting damned tired of it. He was convinced that Louisa felt the same things he did. She was just better at not expressing them, that's all. Well, he told himself, the time had come for both of them to let go for a while.

"Please, Titus," she said, her voice almost a whimper. "I need—"

"I know what you need," he said.

He pulled her against him and brought his mouth down on hers.

He wouldn't have been surprised if she had fought him. He wasn't sure what he would do if she tried to get free. He might let her go . . . or he might kiss her until she had to admit that she wanted him as much as he wanted her.

She didn't fight, though. She stood there inside the circle of his arms, her body stiff and unresponsive at first, just like her lips. But then her lips softened and so did the rest of her, sagging against him almost like she couldn't stand up by herself anymore. Her body molded against his. He turned a little, taking her with him. One little push and she would be on her back in the hay, ready to have her dress hiked up and her legs spread . . .

One of the barn doors flew open behind them, and Nathan ran into the barn, hissing, "Titus! . . . Titus! . . . There's Yankees out there!"

Titus let go of Louisa and spun toward the front of the barn. "Shut the door!" he said, pointing at the door Nathan had left open behind him.

Nathan stopped short, looked surprised, and whirled back to close the door and drop the bar that fastened it. Titus ran over to him. Louisa was forgotten now. All Titus was concerned about was this new threat to their lives—and their freedom.

"How many? Where are they?"

Nathan's eyes were wide with fear, and the rain had plastered his hair to his head. "I saw them come up to the house. I don't know how many . . . ten or twelve, I think . . ."

Louisa moved up beside Titus. "They can't be looking for us. No one knows we're here."

"Unless that old man sent for them!"

"No," Louisa said with a disbelieving shake of her head. "Mr. Egilholtzer wouldn't do that."

Titus felt a surge of disgust. Anybody was capable of anything if they thought they had the right reasons for it. The fact that Louisa didn't seem to know that just showed how naive she really was.

He turned toward the lantern, intending to blow out the flame so the light wouldn't draw attention to the barn. Before he could do so, a shout came from outside.

"You Rebels in there! Come out with your hands up!"

"Son of a bitch!" Titus said. That pretty well answered the question of whether or not the old farmer had betrayed them.

"Titus, what are we going to do?" Nathan asked. His voice was frantic with fear.

"Give me the pistol," Titus snapped. When Nathan fumbled the pistol out from behind his belt, Titus snatched it from his fingers. "Grab that pitchfork, and if you have to—use it!"

Louisa clutched at his arm. "No!" she pleaded. "There can't be any more killing!"

Titus shook off her hand. "I won't go back to that camp or any other prison. Not ever."

Again one of the soldiers outside called to them. "Hear me, Rebs! You ain't got a chance! Give up now!"

There was a small rear door in the barn. Titus turned toward it, saying to his companions, "Come on!" but before he could reach it, the door was kicked open from outside. Lightning flashed, revealing the Union trooper standing there with a rifle held across his chest.

"They're in here, Cap'n!" the Yankee shouted, and then he tried to bring his rifle to bear on Titus and Nathan.

Titus shot him in the head.

Had there been more time, Titus might have appreciated the shot more. The light was bad and his heart was pounding, but his aim with the pistol had been true. The Yankee flipped backward, arms and legs flailing, the rifle flying out of his hands.

Titus twisted and fired again, this time at the lantern. It exploded, sending flames and coal oil spraying over the dried wood of the barn's front wall. The planks blazed up, and so did the straw scattered on the floor.

Something slammed against the double doors. The Yankees were trying to break in. They could probably see the fire through the cracks between the boards and knew that the front part of the barn would be an inferno in a matter of minutes. Someone yelled, "Get around back!"

There was no time to hitch up the buggy. "Grab the horses!" Titus called to Nathan and Louisa. He snatched up a halter and slapped it on the buggy horse, cursing as the animal tried to shy away from him. Both horses were spooked by the shots and the smell of smoke from the growing blaze.

Titus yanked the horse toward the rear door. It would be a close fit, but he thought he could get the horse through there. He didn't look over his shoulder to see if Nathan and Louisa were following him.

A figure loomed up just as Titus reached the doorway. Knowing that anyone moving in the night was an enemy, Titus fired. He saw the figure double over as the bullet drove into its midsection. Another rifle clattered on the hard-packed ground just inside the door. Titus kicked the wounded Yankee out of the way, jammed the pistol behind his belt, and picked up the fallen rifle. He burst out of the barn, dragging the frightened horse behind him. The rain, falling hard now, lashed at him.

Louisa was right behind him, he saw as he turned back toward the burning building. Titus vaulted onto the horse and settled himself on its back. He had grown up riding without a saddle, so the lack of one didn't bother him now. He held a hand down to Louisa. "Come on!"

She hesitated then clasped his wrist. He pulled her up behind him.

"Hang on!" he said as he kneed the horse around. Nathan hadn't come out of the barn yet, but that was Nathan's problem. Titus kicked the horse into a run.

More than likely, the Yankee patrol was infantry, not cavalry. Titus wanted to believe that, anyway. If they were cavalry, he was doomed. If they were foot soldiers, though, even the buggy horse could outrun them.

Rifles cracked from the corner of the barn. Titus guided the horse with his knees and pulled the pistol again. He threw two shots toward the Yankees who were coming around the barn and had the satisfaction of seeing one of the men spin off his feet. There was still no sign of Nathan. That was too damned bad. Titus wasn't going to wait for him.

"Hyyaaahhh!" Titus sent the horse galloping toward the woods that bordered the old man's fields. A red glow from the blazing barn rose into the rain-shrouded sky behind him and Louisa. With all the old wood and straw for fuel, the fire was burning too fiercely for the rain to put it out.

Louisa had her arms wrapped around Titus's waist and was hanging on for dear life. More rifles went off behind them. One of the bullets came close enough for Titus to hear it sing past his ear, but the rest of the shots were wild. The darkness of the woods loomed ahead, a welcoming haven.

"Nathan's not with us!" Louisa shouted into Titus's ear. "We have to go back!"

Titus ignored her. He didn't pause until they reached the edge of the woods. Then he stuck the pistol behind his belt and grabbed the halter. Hauling back on it, he brought the animal to a stop.

He turned the horse so that he could look back at the farm. The barn was fully ablaze by now, flames shooting high in the sky from its burning roof. Even from several hundred yards away, the fire cast enough light for Titus to be able to see the Yankees milling around near the barn. He also saw the old farmer, his long white beard bobbing up and down as he capered around and waved his arms and yelled at the Yankee captain who had led the patrol. Titus figured the farmer was complaining because the soldiers had let the escaped Rebels burn down his barn.

In one smooth motion, Titus lifted the rifle he had picked up, settled the butt against his shoulder, laid the sights on the old man, and fired. Louisa let out a startled cry. Titus had no way of knowing how accurate the rifle was, but he did the best he could.

It was good enough. The old man jumped then crumpled into a motionless heap.

"Old bastard won't sell out anybody else," Titus muttered.

Louisa sobbed, "How . . . how could you?"

"He had it comin'," Titus said. With that, he wheeled the horse again and sent it deeper into the woods. He thought Louisa might slip off and go back, but she didn't. She hung on to him, and after a while she stopped sniffling.

Titus was sorry they'd had to leave the buggy behind. He supposed he was sorry about Nathan, too. When they reached the top of a long ridge a mile from the farm, he paused and looked back. The rain had stopped. The barn's roof and walls had collapsed by now, but the fire was still burning fiercely.

So long, Nathan, Titus thought. *Better a funeral pyre than goin' back to that camp.*

Titus turned the horse and rode down the far side of the ridge. Louisa was close behind him, her body warm against his.

TASTING DIRT in his mouth from where he had been flung face-down on the ground, Nathan heard one of the soldiers say, "We'll get the other two, Cap'n. Soon's we get word to the nearest cavalry barracks, they'll be rounded up." The toe of a boot slammed into Nathan's side and made him curl into a ball of pain. "At least we got this one."

The captain knelt in front of Nathan, grabbed his hair, and jerked his head up. Nathan gasped in pain.

"You're going back to prison, Reb, but it won't be like before. Your friend shot down a civilian. Since you escaped with him, you're just as guilty as he is." The Yankee officer laughed. "This time, I expect you'll hang."

Chapter Thirteen

CORY WASN'T SURE HOW long he had been locked up in the old jail in the basement of the Warren County courthouse. At least a week. But it was difficult to keep up with the days when his jailers fed him only occasionally and he never saw anyone else. There was a tiny barred window in the stonewalled cell, set just below street level, but it was too high above him to see out of it. He could tell whether it was day or night by how much light came through the window, but he slept so much that he was never sure if it was the same day as the last time he'd been awake or the next one.

He was a little surprised that Jason Gill hadn't shown up to gloat over him. He supposed that Gill was letting him stew in his own juices for a while. It would be just like the bastard to stay away and let Cory hope that somehow he would get out of this, before showing up to torment him again.

The worst torture of all was worrying about Lucille and the others. He had asked his jailers about them at first, figuring that he was wasting his time but unable to stop himself. The soldiers and the civilians working for them had ignored all his questions, so after a while Cory had stopped asking them. But the worry still haunted him, and the fear for his loved ones gnawed at his vitals.

The cell was six feet wide and eight feet long, built completely of stone except for the heavy wooden door, which also had a small barred window in it. The windows allowed a little circulation, but not enough to keep the heat from building up during the day until it was so stifling Cory could hardly breathe. Only after hours of darkness at night did the air cool off a little.

Cory awoke from a drowse covered in sweat. Only a faint gray light came through the window. He could tell from the heat that it was dusk, not dawn. He yawned as he pushed himself to a sitting position on the iron-framed bunk that hung from chains attached to the wall. His stomach rumbled. Had they given him any breakfast that morning? He couldn't remember. He hadn't had anything to eat at midday; he was certain of that. Surely it wouldn't be too much longer before the Yankees brought him something to eat.

A few minutes later, footsteps sounded in the corridor. A key rattled in the big, heavy lock on the door. Cory swung his feet to the floor. "Damned well about time," he said as the door scraped open.

"Cory," Col. Charles Thompson answered. "Come along, lad. Quickly."

For a second, Cory's brain refused to accept what he had just heard. He was sure he was imagining things. But then as his eyes grew wide with surprise, he saw the tall, erect figure of the colonel standing there in the dim corridor, and he shot to his feet. It took a second for him to comprehend that Thompson was dressed in the uniform of a Union officer.

"Colonel! What—"

"Quiet," Thompson said, his voice little more than a whisper. "We don't want any of the other prisoners to know what's going on. They might raise a ruckus and alert the rest of the guards."

Cory's heart was pounding as he stepped through the open door into the corridor. Thompson pressed a small pistol into his hand. "Put this behind your belt and drape your shirt over it so it can't be seen," the colonel said. "Don't use it unless you absolutely have to, though."

Cory nodded his understanding. He tucked the gun away. "Am I getting out of here, Colonel?"

"God willing, we both will." Thompson gripped Cory's arm. "Come on. This way."

Cory didn't hesitate. All he had were his clothes; he wasn't leaving anything behind him in the cell except hours of nightmares and anxiety. He and Thompson walked at a brisk pace along the corridor that ran the length of the cellblock here in Vicksburg's county jail, which had been taken over by the Yankee troops. They didn't encounter anyone, and in a matter of minutes they had reached the stairs at the end of the corridor that led up to an alley behind the jail.

Cory had no idea how Thompson had managed to get in here, let alone get his hands on a Yankee uniform and a set of keys. All that mattered was that a minute later, Thompson had unlocked the door at the top of the stairs and they were outside in the alley. The air smelled like rotting garbage, but since it was the first free breath Cory had drawn in days, it smelled sweet to him.

A wagon was waiting in the alley. The back of it was covered with canvas. There was some sort of cargo underneath the canvas. At the front of the wagon, two mules stood in harness with the stolid patience of their breed. Thompson climbed onto the seat and motioned for Cory to join him. "You'll need to drive," he said. "A Yankee major wouldn't be handling the reins himself."

Cory understood. After releasing the brake lever and picking up the reins, he slapped at the rumps of the mules with the trailing ends of the leathers until the animals began to move. The wagon started down the alley with a rattle of wheels.

Cory found himself having trouble breathing as he sat there beside the colonel. His throat seemed to be blocked by his heart. He swallowed hard and tried to force himself to calm down. The wagon was approaching the end of the alley. They would be out on the street in a moment, and he had to look normal, not like a prisoner who had just escaped from jail.

"Colonel, how in the world did you manage—"

Thompson interrupted him again. "Later. I'll explain everything later."

That was good enough for Cory, as long as he wasn't in jail anymore. Maybe the colonel would take him to Lucille, wherever she was. He couldn't wait to see her.

Not many people were out and about now that it was growing dark. Cory saw only a handful of civilians and not many more Union soldiers. None of the Yankees seemed to be paying any attention to the wagon and the two men on it. They probably didn't dream that anyone could escape from the jail right under their noses.

Cory followed the colonel's low-voiced directions. Gradually, he became aware that they were heading east, away from the river. "Where are we going, sir?" he asked.

"You'll see."

Cory frowned. It wasn't like Thompson to be coy about anything. The colonel was one of the most forthright men he had ever met. But he knew it wouldn't do any good to press the issue. Thompson could also be quite stubborn when he wanted to be.

They were on the edge of town, rolling along the road that led to Jackson, before anyone stopped them. A sentry post was set up there, and a Yankee lieutenant in a campaign cap with crossed sabers on it stepped into the road and held up his hand. Cory was tense, but Thompson seemed relaxed and unworried as he returned the salute the lieutenant gave him.

"Begging the major's pardon, but could you tell us where you're bound tonight, sir?" the lieutenant asked. Several Union troopers stood by, holding rifles.

Thompson jerked a thumb at the cargo in the wagon bed behind him. "Got a load of grain for the artillery horses," he said. "You're welcome to take a look, Lieutenant."

"I'll have to, sir. Orders." The young officer turned to the men with him. "Get that cover off of there and take a look."

A couple of the soldiers handed their rifles to their companions and moved forward to untie the cords that held down the canvas cover. When they stripped it back, nothing was revealed except several dozen bags of grain. The lieutenant ordered them to unload the bags.

"There's no need for that," Thompson protested.

"Sorry, sir," the lieutenant said. "We've heard that some of the Rebs are trying to sneak out of town to get back into the fighting, even though they surrendered. You might be carrying some of the bastards under those bags without even knowing it."

The colonel nodded. "Go right ahead, then."

The soldiers removed the bags from the wagon and stacked them in the road until it was obvious no one was hiding in the wagon. "That's all there is, Lieutenant," one of the men said. "Just grain." He tossed the bag he was holding back into the wagon.

"Very well. You can proceed, sir. Sorry for any inconvenience."

"Not at all. You were just doing your duty, Lieutenant."

The sentries put the unloaded grain into the wagon and pulled the canvas back into place but didn't tie it down. Thompson and the lieutenant exchanged salutes again, and then Cory flapped the reins and got the mules moving once more. The wagon rolled on down the Jackson road, leaving Vicksburg behind.

Cory closed his eyes, wiped a hand over his sweating face, and shuddered a little. "I thought they'd arrest me for sure," he said as he opened his eyes.

"No reason for them to do that," the colonel said. "Quite a few of the civilians hereabouts have been pressed into service. The Yankees think that just because the siege forced General Pemberton to surrender, we're all beaten." His voice strengthened as he went on, "They'll find out how wrong they are about that."

Cory looked back over his shoulder. They were well out of earshot of the Federal checkpoint. "Where's Lucille, Colonel? Is she all right?"

"She's fine, I imagine."

"You imagine?" Cory repeated. "Colonel, tell me where my wife is!"

"On her way to Texas with Mildred, of course, just as we planned. Allen and young Fred are with them, too, looking out for them."

Cory heaved a sigh of relief, glad that Lucille had gotten out of Vicksburg before Jason Gill could get his hands on her. "I reckon we're going to circle around and go after them?"

"Well . . . not exactly."

Cory stiffened on the seat and looked over at Thompson. "What do you mean by 'not exactly,' Colonel?"

"It's rather a complex situation—"

Cory gripped Thompson's arm. "Colonel, where are you and I going?"

Without answering, Thompson took the reins from Cory and swung the wagon off the road and brought the team of mules to a halt in the thick shadows at the edge of a stand of trees. He turned to Cory. "I was able to arrange passage across the river for Mildred and Lucille and the Carters, but no sooner were they in Louisiana than the Federal forces clamped down on the city. The river is being heavily patrolled from Memphis to New Orleans. They don't want anyone fleeing to the west."

"There's got to be a way across!" Cory protested.

"Perhaps, but it would be very dangerous."

"To hell with that! Lucille's over there."

Thompson nodded. "I know. And I'd remind you that my wife is on her way to Texas, as well. But there's more, Cory. A couple of days ago I received a message that was smuggled into the city."

"A message from who?"

"Bedford Forrest."

Cory's eyebrows rose. "General Forrest sent you a letter?"

"The message was not addressed to me specifically, no. It was to be brought to the highest-ranking Confederate military officer still in the city. Until tonight, that was me. Our men who gave their paroles and were allowed to march out of the city are still being held at Raymond. General Bragg is now ensconced at Chattanooga and needs men, and it is General Forrest's hope that some fighters may be recruited from the civilians left behind in Vicksburg."

Despite his worry over Lucille, Cory's spirits rose. If he and Thompson could get to Chattanooga, he could ride again with Forrest—

He yanked those wildly galloping thoughts to a sudden stop. Once again adventure had called out to him, and without thinking, he had started to answer. Having narrowly escaped Vicksburg, he had to do the sensible thing for once in his life and make his way to Texas so that he could rejoin his wife.

"I'm sorry, Colonel, but I've had enough war. I hate to let General Forrest down, but I'm going west instead of east."

"You'll wind up a prisoner again, I tell you," Thompson insisted. "Now that they have split the Confederacy in two, the Yankees are determined to keep the sections apart. We'll do the cause more good by assisting Forrest and Bragg than we will rotting in some Federal prison camp."

With weariness and indecision threatening to overwhelm him, Cory rubbed his forehead and tried to think. It was possible the colonel was right: Texas might be beyond their reach right now. To clear up some of his confusion, and to postpone the decision a little longer, he asked, "How did you manage to get me out of that jail tonight?"

"Bribed one of the Southern jailers who's been forced to work for the Union army and the commissioners. It took all the cash I had left . . . but under the circumstances, money means very little to me now."

"The commissioners . . . What about Gill? I don't understand why he had me arrested and then just left me there in jail."

"Jason Gill has other things on his mind right now. Or perhaps I should say, he has nothing on his mind. In my role as liaison to the commissioners, I learned that he collapsed on the day he had the orders issued for your arrest. He was badly wounded somehow, several months ago, and has never fully recovered."

"He looked sick when I saw him," Cory said, remembering their sudden encounter on the bluff and how pale and weak Gill had been.

"He's quite ill," Thompson reported. "He lost consciousness, and the last I heard, he never regained it. For all I know, he's passed on by now."

"If there's any justice in the world . . . ," Cory started to say then stopped. He knew from bitter experience that all too often there wasn't any justice.

"At any rate, with Gill in the hospital or dead, you might have languished there in that cell for months before anyone even tried to figure out what to do with you. I decided I had to act quickly, while we still had a chance of getting out of the city and joining General Bragg's army."

"Are we the only ones answering General Forrest's call?"

Thompson shook his head. "No, I spread the word among some trusted men, the remnants of the Home Guard and others. There are quite a few of us who plan to slip out and make our way by ones and twos to Chattanooga."

"That's a long way," Cory said, doubt in his voice. "And we'd have to dodge the Yankees all the way."

"Yes, but I know the country through which we will be traveling, and the Union forces don't. I can get us there," the colonel said, confident.

Cory turned on the wagon seat and looked back at Vicksburg. He knew that he was also looking westward, also looking toward Texas.

Toward Lucille.

But she and Mildred, along with Carter and Fred, were out of Yankee hands now. They might encounter dangers on their way across Louisiana, but Allen Carter, despite his missing leg, was one of the toughest men Cory knew. Carter was a battle-hardened veteran, and he also had a native cunning. And Fred . . . well, Fred might not have the mind of a man, Cory thought, but he had the heart and soul and courage of one, and he was devoted to Lucille. Anyone who tried to hurt her would have his hands full with Fred Carter.

"All right," Cory said. "We'll go to Chattanooga."

But he knew that his mind was already in Texas, somewhere along the river called Brazos, on the land that someday he and Lucille would call home.

IT WAS four hundred miles from Vicksburg to Chattanooga, northwest across Mississippi and Alabama and a corner of Georgia. Cory had covered part of the ground before during his trek from Nashville to Vicksburg when he was searching for Lucille. That journey had taken him months on foot. With the wagon and the mules, he and Thompson expected to make better time. Even though the mules were unimpressive in appearance, they were strong and hardy and could pull the wagon all day.

At night they camped well off the road. There were plenty of woods to conceal them from curious eyes. By the light of a small campfire, the colonel studied a map he had brought with him from Vicksburg, planning their route for the next day. They had to swing far to the north to avoid Grant's army, which was moving toward Jackson with the obvious intention of pushing the Confederate army under Gen. Joseph E. Johnston out of Mississippi's capital. Once the Yankees were behind them, Cory and Thompson were able to turn more to the east. They followed the back roads, the small, sparsely traveled roads, and did their best to avoid people. When they forded the Tombigbee River, Thompson announced, "It won't be long now until we're in Alabama."

Cory wished they were crossing into Texas instead, but that would have to wait. Every night he dreamed of Lucille. While he was asleep, he couldn't keep her image and the memories of what it was like to be with her from haunting him, but during the day he tried to concentrate on the matter at hand—getting to Chattanooga and joining Nathan Bedford Forrest in helping to protect that city from the Yankees.

The weather was miserable, with rain falling most days and making the roads muddy. But the bad weather kept most people inside unless they had a good reason for going out, so that made it easier for Cory and Thompson to avoid being seen. Some days they encountered absolutely no one along the roads.

It was difficult to keep track of the date, but Cory judged it was early September when the road they were following skirted the southern end of a long ridge and led onto a bridge across a shallow, fast-moving stream. Thompson reined the mules to a halt on the bank and looked at the river. "I expect that's the Tennessee," he said.

"It's smaller here than it is downriver at Fort Henry," Cory said.

"Well, yes, that's to be expected." Thompson looked over at Cory. "You were at Fort Henry when it fell, weren't you? I remember Lucille's speaking of it."

Cory nodded. "That's where we lost the *Zephyr*."

"And knowing Zeke, I'm sure he was never the same afterward." Thompson sighed. "This war has taken a lot from everyone. I hope the Yankees are satisfied with themselves."

With that bitter comment, he got the mules moving again and sent the wagon rattling onto the bridge and over the Tennessee River.

After the flatlands of Mississippi and northern Alabama, the terrain became much more rugged as they approached the Georgia border. High, rocky, heavily wooded ridges with narrow valleys between them ran from southwest to northeast, with few crossable gaps. The road went to the south of the ridges, taking Cory and the colonel away from Chattanooga rather than toward the city that was their destination. Yet that would be the quickest way to get there, Thompson indicated. Traversing the ridges in the wagon would be difficult if not impossible.

"According to the map, we'll intersect another road that will take us north into Chattanooga," Thompson explained. "Besides, following this route will make it much less likely we'll run into any Union forces that might be attempting to flank General Bragg on his left."

Cory recalled his earlier meeting of Gen. Braxton Bragg and his own role in a cavalry raid into western Tennessee. All of the attached memories were not particularly thrilling in Cory's mind. He didn't look forward to seeing Bragg again. Cory was no military man, but even he could find fault with the way Bragg had conducted his campaigns so far. The joke making the rounds in the Confederate army was that General Bragg would never enter the kingdom of heaven, for if ever Saint Peter should throw open the pearly gates for him, Bragg would retreat.

But Bragg wasn't the only general in Chattanooga. Forrest was there, too, and Cory was eager to see him again. The cavalryman was known to the Yankees as a devil for his quick, daring strikes and unequalled success as a commander of cavalry. Forrest had also been a good friend to Cory, putting him onto Lucille's trail after the fighting at Shiloh. Forrest's men would ride to hell and back for him, and Cory had to admit that probably he would follow right along with them.

The next day, they struck the road that ran north toward Chattanooga and turned to follow it. With the rugged heights of a long ridge running for miles and miles on their left, they cut through the northwestern corner of Georgia. This was the first time Cory had been in Georgia, and that fact prompted him to count up in his head the number of different states he had visited. He figured it at eleven—Virginia, Kentucky, Illinois, Missouri, Arkansas, Tennessee, Georgia, Alabama, Mississippi, Louisiana, and Texas. Back in the days when he had wanted so much to leave home and see something else of the world besides Culpeper County, the thought of visiting eleven different states would have been quite exciting to him. He hadn't realized then that a man's troubles usually follow him, no matter where he goes or how far he travels from his home.

During the afternoon of the next day, they began to hear a rumbling in the distance that sounded almost like thunder. Almost, but not quite. Cory and the colonel both recognized the sound of artillery.

"The Federals must be moving on Chattanooga," Thompson said, his forehead creasing in a worried frown.

"We knew we were heading into trouble," Cory pointed out.

"Yes, but I was hoping General Rosecrans would act with his usual deliberation so that we would have time to reach the city before he attacked."

"What do you know about Rosecrans, Colonel?"

"A good commander, but slow—very slow—to move. That's a trait he shares with most Yankee generals, save Grant and Sherman. That's why Lee, and Jackson before his untimely death, have been so successful against them. Quickness can win some battles that should go the other way, based on sheer numbers."

Cory laughed. "General Forrest says the side that gets where it's going 'fustest with the mostest' usually wins."

"I don't know how much formal education your General Forrest has, but he sounds like a very astute man."

"When it comes to war, he's probably the smartest man I've ever met," Cory said.

The sound of the shelling grew louder as they pressed on. After following the narrow valley for more than fifty miles, the road began to climb, angling to the left toward a gap in the ridges. Before they could reach that gap, Cory and Thompson saw wagons moving through it and heading for them.

Weeks earlier, as soon as they had cleared the ring of Federal troops outside Vicksburg, Colonel Thompson had taken off the Yankee uniform and put on civilian clothing. Now, with some sort of military column heading for them, Cory wondered if the colonel ought to dress as a Yankee again. If those wagons and the soldiers with them belonged to the Union . . .

That was impossible, he told himself. Chattanooga hadn't fallen. If it had, those cannons wouldn't still be firing. He was just letting his imagination, and his fears, run away with him.

The movement up ahead had to mean something, though. As the colonel brought the wagon to a halt, Cory asked, "Do you reckon we ought to push on?"

Thompson frowned in thought for a moment. "I didn't come this far only to turn back. Those must be our boys up there. We ought to at least find out from them what's going on."

Cory hoped Thompson was right.

The colonel got the wagon moving again. A few minutes later, a group of horsemen rode into sight. As the riders came closer, Thompson pulled the wagon to the side of the road, and he and Cory waited tensely.

The riders were Confederate cavalrymen. Their commander halted his troops. Cory didn't recognize the officer from his previous time with Forrest's cavalry. This patrol must belong to a different brigade.

"This isn't a good time for civilians to be abroad, mister," the officer said to Thompson. "I'd turn around and head the other way, if I was you."

"Perhaps I would, if I were a civilian. I'm Colonel Charles Thompson of the Mississippi Home Guard, late of Vicksburg, Mississippi, at your service, sir."

The officer stiffened in his saddle and saluted. "I'm pleased to make your acquaintance, Colonel."

"What's going on up there, Major?" Thompson asked.

"The Yankees are doing their damnedest to encircle Chattanooga and trap us there. We're falling back."

"General Bragg is retreating again, eh?"

For a second, the major looked as if he didn't know whether to be offended or amused. Then he chuckled. "It might've been better this time if the general had been quicker to retreat. That Yankee bastard Rosecrans feinted right then swung left." He waved a hand toward the ridges to the west. "According to our scouts, he's over there now with most of his army, trying to come in behind us."

Thompson nodded. "I appreciate the information, Major. I take it you and your men are the advance guard for General Bragg's supply train?"

"That's right, sir."

"Good luck to you, sir. Can you tell me if General Bragg himself is still in Chattanooga?"

"As far as I know."

Thompson lifted the reins. "We'll push on, then, and report to him when we get there."

The major looked worried. "Colonel, I swear, you might not want to go on to Chattanooga. If you do, you might not get out."

Cory spoke up for the first time. "Is General Forrest there?"

"I'm not sure. I expect so, though. Who might you be?"

"Aide and scout for General Forrest," Cory replied. That had been his position in the past, even though he had never actually joined the Confederate army. If this major wanted to assume he was a soldier, that was his mistake.

Understanding dawned in the major's eyes. At least, he thought that he understood the situation. "You know what'll happen if the Yankees catch you out of uniform," he said, his face and voice grim.

"I suppose we'll be shot as spies," Thompson said. "But we'll have to take that chance. Thank you, Major."

"It's your own funeral, Colonel. The boys and me got to be moving on." After an exchange of salutes, the cavalry patrol galloped on down the road.

"Maybe we ought to take his advice and turn around," Cory said when the wagon was rolling toward Chattanooga again.

"It would be the prudent thing to do," the colonel agreed. "We could report to General Bragg wherever he establishes his new headquarters." Thompson paused. "I do hate to flee in the face of the enemy until it's absolutely necessary, though."

Cory grinned. He supposed the colonel was right. He was anxious to see General Forrest again, too. "Well, then, let's keep going," he said.

Their pace slowed, because often they had to pull to the side of the road to let supply wagons and groups of riders move past them. Some of the Southern soldiers called out to them to turn around and go back, but Cory and Thompson just waved at them and smiled. *They must think we're crazy as loons,* Cory thought. *They're probably right, too.*

When they reached the point where the road passed through the gap in the ridge, they could look down and see the winding course of the Tennessee River, which made a great horseshoe bend right in front of them. The small town of Chattanooga, visible through the trees as the roofs of houses and the steeples of several churches, was nestled on the eastern bank of the river. The place didn't look like much, Cory thought, and in truth the town would not have been of much strategic importance if not for the fact that several railroads intersected either in Chattanooga or nearby. He had learned that much from the map Thompson had brought with them from Vicksburg.

Before hostilities had broken out between North and South, Cory would have said that the outcome of battles—and wars—depended entirely on the soldiers who fought them. Armies clashed, and whichever side killed more of the enemy emerged victorious. It all seemed so simple.

In the past two years, though, he had learned just how important supply lines were to the armies, and therefore to the wars. Without supplies, an army couldn't fight. The Confederacy had already lost the great lifeline of the Mississippi River. If the Yankees took Chattanooga as well and shut off rail traffic to the south and east, the Confederate army would be that much closer to defeat.

As they paused in the gap, Thompson observed, "It's a rugged land hereabouts, but quite beautiful."

Cory nodded. "It won't be easy fighting here, with all these woods and ridges and ravines."

"No, but the terrain should give us something of an advantage, if it comes to that. The Yankees will have to come to us."

He sent the mules down the slope on the northwestern side of the gap. At the foot of the hill, another road merged with it and led on into Chattanooga. The closer they came to town, the more heavily traveled the road was, with companies of infantry now moving out. As the men marched past the wagons, Cory was struck by how weary they looked, how gaunt and tired, both physically and spiritually. Their uniforms were ragged, many had no shoes or boots, and their packs were light because they had few supplies to carry with them. "They've given everything, but it hasn't been enough," he said, as much to himself as to the colonel.

"Not everything," Thompson said, and Cory knew what he meant. These Southern soldiers still had one more thing to give in defense of their homeland.

Their lives.

The road became the main street of the town, and as the colonel drove along it, Cory looked up and down both sides of the street. Most of the buildings appeared to be deserted. Some had boarded-up doors and windows. The townspeople had gotten out while they could, before the city became even more of a battleground. Cory saw homes and businesses with gaping holes in their roofs and walls where Yankee artillery shells had landed. The street was pocked with craters.

While they were looking for General Bragg's headquarters, a group of riders came around a corner into the street in front of them. The man who rode in the forefront was lean, almost gaunt, with deep-set, burning eyes, and a jutting beard. He reined in, stared at Cory and the colonel as Thompson brought the wagon to a stop. He drawled, "Welcome back to the war, Mr. Brannon."

They had found Nathan Bedford Forrest.

Chapter Fourteen

FORREST SPURRED HIS HORSE forward, removed the gauntlet on his right hand, and leaned over in the saddle to extend his hand. Cory took it.

"It's good to see you again, General. I wish it was under better circumstances, that's all."

Forrest grinned and nodded. "Damned right. I'd rather be going out to meet Rosecrans, rather than running away from him. We have our orders, though." He turned to Thompson. "I don't believe I've had the honor, sir."

"Colonel Charles Thompson, late of the Mississippi Home Guard. I was the last recipient of your missive requesting that the men of Vicksburg make their way here." The colonel shook hands with Forrest. "I've heard a great deal about you from our young friend."

"The young are inclined to lie," Forrest said with a grin. "I've heard about you, too, Colonel, and a great deal about that niece of yours with whom young Brannon is so smitten."

Cory blushed. "Lucille and I are married now, sir."

"Really? I'm pleased to hear it. Where is she? Back in Vicksburg? What are you doin' here?"

Cory took a deep breath. "She's on her way to Texas with the colonel's wife and some friends. The colonel and I have come to join the fight with you and General Bragg."

Forrest threw back his head and laughed. Possessed of a grim, savage demeanor in battle, in more relaxed times he had a dry wit and an appreciation for irony. "You're one of the least enthusiastic soldiers I've ever seen, Mr. Brannon, and yet you continually find yourself in the middle of history. How is that?"

Cory could only shake his head. "I wish I knew, General. I sure wish I knew."

Thompson then inquired, "Can you direct us to General Bragg's headquarters, . . ."

"No need for that. Bragg's either left town or will be leaving shortly. He plans to set up a defensive line southeast of here around La Fayette. We'll meet up with him there. For now, come along with me. My men are helping to screen the retreat."

Cory looked over at Thompson. "Do you think that would be all right, Colonel?"

"I don't see why not." He turned to Forrest. "This wagon may slow you down, though, General."

Forrest gave a casual wave of his hand. "If it does, we'll leave you behind for the Yankees."

Cory doubted that. Some of Forrest's men had been captured in the past, but Cory couldn't remember a time when the general had deliberately abandoned anyone in his command.

Thompson turned the vehicle, swinging it wide around a shell crater in the street, then headed it on a different road southeast out of Chattanooga, following Forrest and the general's staff. More troops and wagons were leaving the city in this direction. Once Chattanooga was evacuated, if the Confederate forces that had pulled out were able to link up in the hills, they could form a formidable defensive line.

While they were moving into the rugged country outside Chattanooga, Forrest dropped back to ride alongside the wagon. "Tell me about Vicksburg," he said to Cory. "We've had reports that it was very bad there during the siege."

"It was plenty bad, sir," Cory said. "The shelling went on night and day for more than a month, and most of the time there was nothing for anyone to eat." He went on to describe in detail the hazardous, harrowing existence of Vicksburg's townspeople during the weeks of the siege and how they had been forced to burrow into the ground in hopes of escaping the Federal barrage. "The bluff along the river is honeycombed with caves now," Cory said. "It's so hollow I'm surprised the whole place doesn't fall in."

Forrest snorted in contempt. "If it does, I hope some of the blasted Yankees are caught in it. What a terrible way to treat a beautiful city. Does the courthouse still stand?"

"It does," Cory said. "In fact, it suffered only minor damage during the bombardment. Some providence protected it."

"Would that the same providence had protected the entire city," Thompson said. Forrest grunted in agreement.

The road they were following, along with a large portion of Bragg's army, curved more southerly once it left Chattanooga. It led through a gap in one of the many ridges and across a heavily wooded valley through which a creek meandered. The army, in its orderly retreat, passed a two-story, whitewashed building on the east bank of the creek. Written on the front of the building was the legend LEE & GORDON'S MILLS.

The creek twisted and turned but was almost always within sight to the right of the column as it moved south. Forrest pointed to the stream, which was easy to see through the trees because of the way the sunlight sparkled on the water. "That's Chickamauga Creek," he said. "The name comes from a Cherokee word that means *river of blood*." Forrest grinned.

Cory looked at the creek and thought the name wasn't very appropriate. The stream winding through the valley made for a peaceful, pretty scene.

And the word *Shiloh*, he recalled, meant "place of peace."

Late in the afternoon, having covered some twenty miles, they came to the Georgia village of La Fayette. The column halted there. Forrest bid farewell to Cory and Colonel Thompson here.

"Now that we're here, I'd better see to organizing a little scouting," the general explained. "We don't want the Yankees to catch us nappin'." He lifted a gauntleted hand in farewell. "Come see me. I could use you, Cory."

When Forrest had galloped off with his aides, Thompson commented, "Meeting the general in Chattanooga was a stroke of good fortune. I know you want to ride with him again."

"If I can get my hands on a horse," Cory said. "But what about you, Colonel?"

Thompson laughed. "I'm afraid I'm too old and stiff to serve as a cavalryman."

"When we went to Louisiana the first time, you outrode me and Pie both."

"That was only because you lads were inexperienced on horseback." The colonel shook his head. "No, I'd only be a hindrance when it comes to dashing about the countryside and bedeviling the Yankees. But don't let that stop you, Cory."

Cory frowned. "I sort of figured we'd stick together . . ."

"I intend to seek a position on the staff of General Bragg. From the sound of things, the general could use some good advice, eh?"

Cory wasn't sure Bragg would listen to military advice from the Lord God Almighty, but it was worth a try, he supposed. "If that's what you want, Colonel, that's fine with me. Let's go find the general's headquarters, if he's got 'em set up yet."

By inquiring of the officers they met, they were able to locate Bragg. Dusk was settling over La Fayette as Cory and Colonel Thompson entered the hotel that the general had commandeered to house himself and his staff. A sentry stopped them and asked their business.

"We've come to offer our services to General Bragg," Thompson said. "I'm Colonel Charles Thompson of the Mississippi Home Guard."

The sentry thumbed back the ragged, shapeless hat he wore and grinned. "If that's s'posed to mean anything to me, you're out o' luck, pap. The Miss'sippi Home Guard don't carry no weight 'round here."

Thompson stiffened, and his face darkened with anger. "How dare you speak that way to me!" he said.

"I fit the Yankees in the gaps all the way down here from Stones River, that's how come I dare. Ain't no civilians goin' to waltz in an' demand to see the gen'ral on my watch."

"We came here from Vicksburg," Cory said, his voice cold and hard. "And before that I rode with General Forrest into western Tennessee last winter, *after* meeting with General Bragg." The sentry started to say something, but Cory went on, overriding him, "Before *that*, the colonel and I established a supply line between Vicksburg and Texas, and I have fought at Forts Henry and Donelson, Shiloh, and Big Black River. Now do you want to let us in to see the general?"

The soldier's expression was sullen, but he nodded his head. "I reckon it'd be all right." He stepped aside and motioned for Cory and Thompson to go into what had been the hotel's dining room until tonight.

Now it was home to a council of war. Several tables had been pushed together, and maps were spread out on them. Cory spotted Gen. Braxton Bragg leaning over one of the maps, surrounded by several of his aides. The general had changed very little in the months since Cory had last seen him. The lines on his face were perhaps a bit deeper, but the bushy eyebrows and the gray-shot beard were the same. Bragg looked up as Cory and Thompson approached. He stared at Cory and frowned. "Have we met before, sir?" he said without preamble.

"Last November, sir," Cory said. He hesitated. The letter he had carried from General Pemberton to Bragg had been unofficial, not a part of the military record. Pemberton had appealed for help, and the man's pride had not allowed him to do so openly. Cory wasn't sure how much to say, so he summarized, "I brought you a message from a comrade in arms."

For a moment, Bragg's frown deepened as he struggled to remember. His expression cleared as the memory came back to him. "I recall that. Your name is Baxter, Bannister, something like that."

"Brannon, sir. Cory Brannon. And this is Colonel Charles Thompson. We've come from Vicksburg to offer our services."

Bragg's eyebrows, which looked like a thick, hairy worm on his forehead, drew together even more than usual. "The men who surrendered at Vicksburg were paroled and are still under Federal guard at Raymond, the last I heard."

"That may well be, General," Thompson said. "But Mr. Brannon is a civilian, and I was a member of the Mississippi Home Guard. Mr. Brannon gave no parole, and mine prohibits me only from taking up arms against the enemy. I can assist in other ways."

Bragg grunted and glared at Cory. "You're a spy, sir," he said bluntly.

Cory shook his head. "With all due respect, sir, I was carried on the books of General Forrest's brigade as a civilian scout. I intend to perform that duty again, if the general will have me."

"You'll have to join the army," Bragg announced.

Now it was Cory's turn to frown. He had no problem with swearing allegiance to the Confederacy, but something inside him made him hesitate. His natural rebelliousness, he supposed. It had been quite a vexation to his mother when he was young. He had his father's stubbornness and dislike for authority.

Yet there was nothing else that could be done. He intended to fight the Yankees, no matter what. "I'll recite the oath and mark my name down in the regimental records, General, especially if you'll give me a horse and a gun."

Bragg glared at him for a moment. "You'll have to take that up with General Forrest. For now, both of you can consider yourselves members of the Army of Tennessee. Can you read a map, Colonel Thompson?"

"Of course, sir. Quite well, in fact."

Bragg pointed to one of the other tables. "Then look at that one and tell me what General Rosecrans is planning to do next. He thinks he's got us on the run, but he's mistaken."

From what Cory had seen today, he wasn't sure but what Rosecrans was right. Bragg's army had left Chattanooga in a hurry, abandoning the city to the Yankees. Unless Bragg intended to turn and fight, what he had just said was nothing but bravado.

Unless he intended to turn and fight, Cory thought again, and suddenly he knew that was exactly what Bragg was going to do.

THE COLONEL was in his element again, studying and discussing strategy with Bragg's staff. After a while Cory left the hotel and went to look for Forrest.

The cavalry was encamped on the outskirts of the village. As soon as Cory halted the wagon, he heard Forrest's drawl from near one of the campfires. "That's a mighty fine chariot you've got there, Mr. Brannon, and an impressive pair of steeds."

Cory brought the mules to a halt and dropped from the wagon seat to the ground. "I'll need a horse, no question about that, General," he said. "And a rifle, too, if you've got a spare."

Forrest motioned for him to join the circle of men sitting around the fire. "I seem to recall givin' you a pistol at one time," he said. "What happened to it?"

Cory shook his head. "I'm afraid I lost it, General. I hope some Yankee didn't pick it up, but I reckon there's a good chance that's what happened."

Forrest sighed. "If I give you a horse and a gun now, I trust you'll be more careful with them"

"I'll do my best, sir."

"Did General Bragg swear you in?"

"Not really, but he told the colonel and me to consider ourselves members of his army."

"Good enough for me," Forrest said. "Welcome to army life, Lieutenant Brannon."

Cory raised his eyebrows. "I'm an officer?"

"Don't let it go to your head," Forrest told him. "That just means the Yankees'll be tryin' that much harder to kill you. Don't it, boys?"

The other horse soldiers gathered around the fire laughed. Several of them leaned over to congratulate Cory and slap him on the back. The heat from the flames wasn't the only warmth he felt, Cory discovered.

The camaraderie of these men and their easy acceptance of him made him feel as if he belonged here. He recognized many of the troopers from his time with Forrest the previous winter, and they remembered him. They recalled how he and Ham Ryder had gone into Yankee-occupied Memphis and brought back the precious percussion caps without which their rifles would have been useless. They respected him for that. Him, shiftless Cory Brannon who was never going to amount to much of anything, at least to hear his mother and the preacher back home tell it.

Maybe this business of being in the army wasn't going to be so bad after all.

"Have you had anything to eat?" Forrest asked.

Cory thought back. "Not today, sir."

"We don't have much to offer except coffee and hardtack and beans."

Beans? Cory couldn't remember the last time he'd had beans. "That would be just fine, sir," he said, trying not to sound too eager.

The coffee was the usual roasted and boiled grain, and the hardtack lived up to its name, but the beans tasted wonderful. He ate his fill, which didn't take as much food as it had before his stomach had shrunk during his long illness and the siege of Vicksburg. When he was finished he took the pipe that Forrest offered him. He had never been much of a smoker, but tonight, like the beans, the tobacco tasted mighty good.

Giving in to his curiosity, Cory asked Forrest, "What happened, sir, after I left you at the river crossing last January?"

"We guarded the infantry for a few weeks while they were in bivouac and then rode over to Fort Donelson to disrupt traffic on the Cumberland River. Wound up in a little skirmish with the Yankees."

One of the other officers laughed. "It was more than a little skirmish, General. If I recall, you had two horses shot out from under you that day and were slightly wounded yourself."

"Yes, and we lost many good men," Forrest said, his expression so bleak now that Cory wished he hadn't asked the question. "Frank McNairy among them."

Cory remembered Colonel McNairy from Forrest's staff and was sorry to hear that he was dead.

"I advised against that attack," Forrest went on, "but General Wheeler was insistent . . . as, of course, was his right, since he commands the entire cavalry. I told him that night, though, that I would never fight under him again."

A strained silence hung in the air around the campfire. After a moment, Forrest shook off the bitter memories and continued. "We camped at Columbia for a time and then as spring approached moved north toward Nashville. The Yankees chose to send out a reconnaissance in force, and we wanted to put a stop to that. We fought them at Thompson's Station, Brentwood, and Franklin, and carried the day in each case, though not without great loss. Captain Freeman was killed at Franklin."

Cory remembered the artilleryman and knew that he had been one of Forrest's favorite officers. Clearly, the past months had been a difficult time for the general.

"Then we chased down and caught a bunch of Yankee cavalry that had come down here to try to burn our trestles and tear up our railroads," Forrest went on. "The same sort of thing that we did to the Yankees last winter, only these boys didn't get away with it like we did."

Cory had a feeling that wasn't the simple story Forrest made it sound like, but he didn't press the general. Later, he could get the details from some of Forrest's staff.

"Following that, a great deal of picket and scout duty for General Bragg as he withdrew first to Tullahoma and then to Chattanooga," Forrest said, his tone dry, his dislike for retreat evident. His natural military skills told him there were times when it was necessary to run, but he didn't have to like that necessity. "Now you know the entire story, Lieutenant Brannon. Do you still wish to join our band?"

"More than ever, sir," Cory replied without hesitation.

"I think I'll put you with the scouts," Forrest mused. "You seem to have a talent for finding the enemy, and you served me well in that capacity before."

Cory nodded. "Yes sir. I'll do my best."

Forrest put his hands on his knees and pushed himself to his feet. "I'll say goodnight, then, boys. Get a good night's sleep, Cory. You'll be goin' to work tomorrow."

"Yes sir," Cory said again. With the other officers, he came to his feet and saluted. Forrest returned the salute and then turned to walk stiffly toward his tent.

Cory frowned as he watched the general go. There was something odd about the way Forrest carried himself. He turned to one of the other officers. "Is General Forrest all right?"

"He didn't tell you about what happened after we pursued and captured Colonel Streight and his 'Mule Brigade.'"

"That was the Yankee cavalry that tried to raid down here?"

The officer nodded. "That's right. One of the places we fought them was called Sand Mountain. The general was unhappy with the way one of the artillery batteries performed that day, so after it was all over he had the officer in charge of the battery transferred to another command. The fellow was a hot-head, a young lieutenant named Gould. He pressed the general for an explanation of the transfer, but the general refused to even discuss it with him. Gould was so upset he came to the quartermaster's office in Columbia where the general and some of the rest of us were discussing some matters of supply. General Forrest stepped out into the hall to speak with Gould privately, probably hoping to spare him some embarrassment. Gould drew a gun and shot him."

Cory's eyes widened in astonishment. "What?" he exclaimed.

The officer nodded, his face solemn in the firelight as he continued the story. "The general had a clasp knife in his right hand. He'd been toying with it while we talked to the quartermaster. Just something to keep his hands busy, you know.

Gould got off the one shot, but before he could fire again, the general grabbed his wrist and turned the gun aside. He used his teeth to open the blade on the knife he had in his other hand, and he plunged it into Gould's belly." The officer shook his head. "Those of us still in the quartermaster's office ran out into the hall at the sound of the shot, of course. I saw the wound the general inflicted on Gould. He ripped his belly wide open. Gould was able to pull free and run off, though. The general walked down the street to the doctor's office and asked if he was mortally wounded. The doctor made a cursory examination and said that he feared the wound was fatal."

"But General Forrest is still alive!" Cory said.

"So he is," the officer said. "But he thought he was going to die. So he took my pistol and set off after Gould. He was determined that the lieutenant was going to die, too. Gould was down the street. He had run into a tailor shop and collapsed on the counter. The general found him there and would have shot him, but he saw there was no need. Gould couldn't possibly recover from his wound. The general ordered that Gould be taken to the doctor and cared for, then he turned and walked away. He was so pale and weak from loss of blood that we all thought he would collapse, too, but he didn't. He didn't die, either. But Gould did, a couple of days later. Not until he had asked the general for forgiveness, though. A forgiveness that General Forrest granted without hesitation or reserve."

Cory took a deep breath and shook his head. "So the general has recovered from that gunshot?"

"For the most part. I think it still troubles him at times. He won't allow it to hold him back, though."

"No," Cory said. "He wouldn't."

"And he never speaks of the incident, either. Once the rage he felt at being attacked had passed, he was quite sorrowful at the loss of Lieutenant Gould."

"I won't bring it up," Cory said.

"You'd be wise not to."

Cory talked for a while longer with the other officers and then asked where he could sleep. "You can share my tent," one of them offered. He extended his hand. "I'm John Cullum from the Great Smokies, also one of the general's scouts."

Cory shook Cullum's hand and accepted the offer of the shared tent. "I expect we'll be kept busy," he observed.

"I reckon so," Cullum agreed. "We'll have to be on the lookout for ol' Rosy. He'll be comin' after us."

"You think so?"

Cullum nodded, as did several of the men gathered around the fire. "If there's one thing you can count on, that's it," Cullum said. "Rosy is mighty slow to move, but now that he thinks he's got us on the run, he ain't goin' to stop in Chattanooga."

"We don't want him to stop, do we?"

A grin spread across Cullum's lean face. "Say, old son, if you've got that much figured out, you might just make a soldier after all."

THE PILE of grain sacks in the rear of the wagon had diminished during the journey from Vicksburg, because it was used to feed the mules. Some nights they had slept on those bags, and other nights they had rolled up in their blankets on the ground underneath the wagon. It had rained a great deal, so during the trip Cory spent many a wet, uncomfortable night. This wasn't the first time he'd had to suffer through the elements, but his familiarity with such things hadn't made them any less miserable.

Having spent weeks like that on the road, the chance to sleep on a cot inside a tent seemed like a real luxury to him. It felt as if he had just dozed off when a hand on his shoulder shook him awake.

"Let's go, Brannon," Cullum said. "General Forrest says that if the enemy won't advance on us, we've got to move on him, so we're goin' lookin' for him today."

Cory sat up, yawned, and rubbed his eyes. Those words sounded like Forrest's, all right. He was seldom content to sit and wait to see what was going to happen. General Forrest preferred to be making things happen himself.

As Cory stood up, Cullum said, "I found this for you," and handed him a lieutenant's jacket. "That's all the uniform you're goin' to get, I'm afraid."

Cory looked at the jacket and saw several dark stains as well as a small, ragged hole in the front. "Do I want to ask what happened to the man who used to own this?"

"I reckon not," Cullum replied with a grin.

Cory shrugged into the jacket, hoping that he wouldn't add any more bloodstains to it.

Cullum led the way to where the other scouts were assembling. In the gray dawn light, Cory saw that General Forrest himself was there along with a good-sized group of cavalrymen, some of whom were already mounted, some still milling around on foot. Cullum pointed to the riders. "Looks like we're goin' on what they call a 'reconnaissance in force.'"

Forrest overheard the comment. "That's right, Lieutenant. You never know when you might need some force."

Cullum grinned at him. "I reckon that's the truth, General."

"Sleep well, Lieutenant Brannon?" Forrest asked.

"Yes sir, just not long enough," Cory answered.

"Well, you can't lay a-bed while there are Yankees about." Forrest waved toward a good-looking chestnut horse with a white blaze on its nose and four white stockings. "Think this animal will do you for a mount, Lieutenant?"

Cory moved closer to the horse, studying it with something close to awe. "Yes sir," he said. "He's a fine one, sir, just fine."

"His name is Dash. If you're goin' to be a cavalryman, you need a mount. I see you've got part of a uniform already."

"Yes sir. Lieutenant Cullum advised me that I might not want to ask what happened to the previous owner, though. I suspect the same holds true for Dash here."

"Actually, he was one of the mounts used by my brother William. He was wounded in the leg at Sand Mountain while we were chasing that fool Streight. William is back home recuperating. He won't be needing Dash for a while, so I want to entrust his horse to someone who'll take good care of him."

"I'll do my best, General," Cory said. "You've got my word on that."

"That's good enough for me. Mount up, Lieutenant."

Dash was already saddled. Cory swung up onto the horse's back. It felt good. He wasn't as skilled a horseman as his brother Mac, but he thought he was a pretty good rider. He would need to be, to keep up with Forrest.

Cullum took a pair of rifles from a stack and handed one of them up to Cory, along with an ammunition pouch. "I don't reckon the percussion caps in there are some of the ones you brought back from Memphis last winter. We probably shot all them up already."

"You know about that?" Cory asked, surprised.

"Sure. You're next thing to famous in this here cavalry, Mr. Brannon. You best live up to your reputation."

Cory's hands tightened on the rifle. He didn't want to be famous. He just wanted to do his job and fight.

"Mount up!" Forrest called to the men who weren't already on horseback. "We've got us some Yankees to find—and if we're lucky, to fight!"

Chapter Fifteen

T HE GROUP OF THREE hundred men rode west, toward the high, wooded ridges. Out in front of the others, Cory and John Cullum rode side by side. Cullum pointed to the nearest height. "That's Pigeon Mountain. It shoots off from Lookout Mountain. That's the longer ridge yonder. It runs 'way off down into Alabama. We got word that some bluebellies are movin' across Lookout through the gaps. If we can get 'em separated and get some of 'em bottled up, we can bust 'em to pieces."

"Won't they suspect they're walking into a trap?" Cory asked.

Cullum chuckled and shook his head. "Not if they've paid any attention to the deserters who've been comin' into their camps and the country folk they've passed along the way. Everybody's tellin' the Yankees the same story—that we're runnin' away like rabbits and probably won't stop until we get to Atlanta."

Cory thought about that and a slow grin spread across his face. "And that's exactly what we want them to think, isn't it?" he said.

"Yep. And after a while, those so-called deserters will slip away and come right back here to fight with us again."

It was a good plan, Cory thought. Make Rosecrans and his commanders overconfident and then use that against them.

"We got to be ready to move fast, though, once we've got 'em where we want 'em," Cullum went on. "That's what we're doin' today, seein' if the Yanks have taken the bait."

Cullum led the way toward Pigeon Mountain, gradually veering so their route led to the south of the ridge. Another scouting force would head north of Pigeon, he explained. He and Cory skirted around the little village of Alpine and found themselves on a narrow road that wound through an area of thick woods. The woods were cut through in places with deep, steep-sided ravines, as if the earth itself had been slashed here by giant claws. Those ravines were choked with brush that would make it almost impossible to get across. Any army moving through here would have to travel by way of the narrow, twisting roads.

When Cory looked back over his shoulder, he saw that General Forrest and the rest of the troops were out of sight. He and Cullum were alone, far out in front of the rest of the party. That made him a little nervous, but not too much, he decided. He could tell that his horse had plenty of speed. If they ran into trouble, he was confident they could outrun it.

He hoped he wasn't getting as overconfident as the Yankees.

The two men paused from time to time to listen. During the morning, they heard nothing except birds singing in the trees and small animals rustling around in the woods. Not long after noon, though, different sounds came to their ears and made both men stiffen in their saddles.

For men who had been around war, the tramp of thousands of marching feet, the jingle of harness chains, the creaking of wagon wheels, all of these and a myriad other sounds were unmistakable. And they could mean only one thing: Up ahead, a large column was on the move.

Cory looked over at Cullum. "You know where all of our people are," he said. "Any chance that could be some of them we're hearing?"

"I reckon not. We'd best be sure, though. Come on, let's get off the road."

The trees and underbrush were so thick that the two scouts had to dismount and lead their horses into the woods. The heavy growth made for slow going.

Cory and Cullum penetrated fifty yards into the woods then turned to start making their way forward again, toward the sounds they had heard a few minutes earlier. They were careful in their movements, with every sense alert. It made sense that the Federals would have scouts out, too, even if they believed that all the Confederates had fled the area.

Cullum motioned for Cory to stop. They stood motionless except for the rise and fall of their chests as they breathed. Cory had his hand over the nose of his horse to prevent the animal from neighing if it caught the scent of another horse. Cullum did likewise.

After a moment, Cory heard the same thing that had made the lean mountaineer halt. Someone else was in these woods, moving toward them. Cory figured it had to be Yankee scouts. Nobody else would have any reason to be out here.

Cullum pointed to Cory, then to the left, then made walking motions with his fingers. Cory understood. They were splitting up. That way, if anything happened to one of them, the other would still have a chance to get back to Forrest.

Cory continued to keep one hand on the chestnut's nose and used his other to lead the animal through the vegetation. He knew that it was impossible for the horse to move through the underbrush without making some noise, but Cory could still hear the rustling and cracking of branches coming from the direction of the Yankee column. He hoped the Union scouts were overlooking whatever sounds he and Cullum and their animals were making.

Instinct told him when to halt. He did so, freezing in position again. He heard the thud of hoof beats nearby, coming from his right. Crouching behind a bush, he watched as a horse came into view, making its way between the trees.

It took Cory a second to realize that the horse's saddle was empty, and then another instant passed before he knew what that meant. A tiny noise sounded behind him, like the scuff of shoe leather on dirt. He started to turn, but before he could get all the way around, something slammed into his side and knocked him away from his horse. He went sprawling on the ground with a heavy weight on top of him, crushing him and forcing the air out of his lungs.

Gasping for breath, Cory stared up into the face of a man and at the blue uniform of a Union soldier. The man had a knife in his hand. He swung it up, poised to bring the blade sweeping down into Cory's body.

Cory convulsed, twisting and writhing so that his back was off the ground. At the same time, he drove a fist at the face of the man sitting on him. The Yankee managed to block the punch, but he couldn't retain his balance. He toppled off to the side, taking the knife with him.

Cory's heart pounded wildly, the same as it did every time he found himself locked in hand-to-hand combat with an enemy. His brain was still working, though. He wasn't fighting completely on instinct. He lunged after the Yankee, reaching for the wrist of the hand that held the knife.

The Yankee scout had a pistol in a holster on his hip, but the holster's flap was fastened down. He didn't try to pull the weapon. Not knowing how close the rest of the Rebels were, or how many of them were in these woods, he wanted silence as much as Cory did. This would be a fight to the death, but a fight with no words, only grunts of effort as the two men strained against each other. Cory locked his fingers around the man's wrist, pinning the knife hand to the ground, but the Yankee's other fist sledged into Cory's belly, knocking even more of the wind out of him. He felt sick. Tears blurred his vision. With a desperate effort, he pulled himself back from the edge of passing out.

He was damned if he was going to die here so far from home, so far from everyone he cared about.

He brought his leg up and smashed his knee into the Yankee's groin. The man wheezed in pain. Cory kept his left hand on the man's right wrist but shifted his right hand to the Yankee's neck. The Yankee tried to fend him off, but Cory's fingers locked around his throat.

The smell of rich earth was in Cory's nostrils. The sunlight that filtered down through the trees was tinted green by the thick growth so that everything looked a little like it was underwater. The toes of Cory's boots scrabbled around in the dirt as he pushed himself farther on top of the Yankee scout, using his weight to hold the man down. The man made small whining noises. That was all he could manage with Cory's fingers clamped hard on his windpipe. He used his free hand to strike at Cory's head. Cory hunched his right shoulder and took most of the blows on it. He concentrated on two things: keeping his left elbow straight, so that the Yankee couldn't use the knife against him, and keeping up the pressure on the man's throat. Everything else was unimportant. One of the punches landed and made Cory's head ring and his vision spin, but none of that mattered. Keep the knife away, and keep the Yankee from breathing. If he did those two things, Cory knew, he would live. If he didn't, he would die.

The Yankee stopped trying to raise the knife. His fingers relaxed, and the blade slipped out of his hand. His body bucked a couple of times and then went still. Cory realized that he had closed his eyes without being aware of it. He opened them now and saw the way the Yankee's eyes bulged in their sockets, the way his tongue protruded from his mouth, stiff between bluish-tinged lips. The sharp stink of voided bowels and bladder filled the air. The Yankee scout was dead.

He let go of the man and rolled off him. Lying on his side, Cory retched, unable to control the reaction. He had killed men before, sometimes close enough to them so that he could see the life go out of their eyes as they died. But it never got any easier. Nor did dealing with the knowledge that if the fight had gone just a little differently, it could well be him lying there dead on the floor of the forest, never to see his home or his loved ones again.

After a few minutes, Cory was able to push himself to his hands and knees and then onto his feet. He looked around. Nothing was moving in the woods around him. He didn't see his horse or the Yankee's horse—the horse that had nearly gotten Cory killed. The Yankee must have sensed that someone was lurking in the trees and had sent the horse walking ahead of him to draw out whoever it was. The trick had almost worked.

"Brannon!"

Cory tensed. That was Cullum's voice, of course, he told himself. His fellow scout was the only one out here who could know his name. Cullum sounded all right, not like he was wounded. Of course, the Yankees could have taken him prisoner and forced him to lead them to Cory. Cory didn't think that was very likely, though. Cullum didn't strike him as the sort to surrender without one hell of a fight.

"Over here!" Cory hissed. He wished he had his rifle, but it was slung on his saddle, wherever his horse was.

As it turned out, Cullum had the horse, and three more besides, including his own. The animals made a considerable racket as Cullum led them through the woods. When Cory saw the horses, he knew that Cullum must have encountered a Yankee scout, too. That was where the fourth horse had come from. Which meant the Yankee wouldn't be needing his mount anymore . . .

Cullum had a long scratch on his cheek, but he was grinning as he approached. "I took a look around, but I don't think there are any more of 'em out here. Just these two Yankees, and we already took care of them. Yours is dead, ain't he?"

Cory nodded. "Just outside the pearly gates as we speak. Thanks for rounding up the horses."

"They came to me. Wasn't no roundin' up to it. These two Yankee horses look like good mounts. The cavalry can always use more animals."

Cory listened for a moment. "I can still hear that column moving."

"So can I. Come on. I think there's a little rise up ahead. Maybe we can get a look at 'em."

They moved forward, Cory taking the reins of his chestnut and one of the other horses to lead them. The sounds of marching men grew louder. The two Confederate scouts made their way up a wooded slope, and when they came to the top of it, Cory stopped and took a sharp breath.

He and Cullum were looking across one of the numerous ravines in this area. On the other side of it, no more than a hundred yards away, scores of Union infantry troops marched along a trail that led down from one of the gaps in Lookout Mountain.

Cory and Cullum stood motionless, the horses behind them. The screen of brush was so thick no one could see them from the far side of the ravine unless it was by sheer accident. But accidents could happen, Cory knew, so he remained as still as possible. Beside him, Cullum spoke in a whisper, even though it would be impossible for the Yankees to hear him at this distance.

"See that flag yonder? It belongs to the Eighty-first Indiana. Those boys are from McCook's corps."

"How do you know that?" Cory asked.

"I've studied up on 'em." Cullum grinned. "Got to know your enemy. Come on." He drifted backward, away from the edge of the ravine.

When the trees had closed in so that the two were well out of sight of the Federal forces, the experienced scout mounted up and motioned for Cory to do likewise. "We'd best hightail it back to General Forrest. He'll want to know what we've found up here. Probably want to take a gander at it for himself, if I know the general."

Cory agreed with that sentiment. Forrest wouldn't come this close to the Yankees without taking a look, at the very least. As he swung up into the saddle, he said, "You don't think General Forrest will want to attack that column, do you?"

"You've ridden with him before. What do you think?"

"He'll want to attack," Cory said without hesitation, "but he brought only three hundred men with him. It would be crazy to attack an entire corps with that many men."

"Yep. So we'd best hope for most ever'body's sake that the general ain't in a crazy mood."

Cory grunted in agreement as he set out through the woods with Cullum, following the other scout and leading one of the spare horses. Now that they had found the enemy, they didn't have to be quite as cautious in their movements and so were able to proceed at a faster pace. In less than an hour, they came around a bend in the trail they were following and found themselves riding toward the group of cavalry being led by Forrest.

The general held up a hand to halt his men and waited for Cory and Cullum to come to him. As the two scouts rode up, Forrest called, "What luck, boys?"

With a jerk of his head back in the direction they had come from, Cullum reported, "They're up there, all right, General. McCook's corps, from the look of it. They're crossin' through Winston's Gap and swingin' round in this direction."

Forrest looked at Cory. "Do you agree with that, Lieutenant Brannon?"

"I don't know the names of all these places, General," Cory said, "but Lieutenant Cullum's right about there being a whole column of Yankees moving toward us."

"Just what we expected," Forrest said with a nod. "Let's go take a look."

Cullum glanced over at Cory and grinned. Both of them had been right about the general's reaction to the news of the Federal movement.

Following Forrest's orders, the cavalry strung out even more. The general rode at the head of the group, accompanied by Cory and Cullum. They showed him the paths to take. Soon the sounds of the Yankee column were audible again. McCook was moving quickly to the east.

Cullum reined in and pointed. "There's a good view from that little ridge, General," he suggested. "From there you can see the road the Yankees are usin', but they won't be able to see us."

Forrest nodded in agreement. "Let's go," he said, impatience in his voice. He could hear the enemy; now he wanted to see them for himself.

Cory, Cullum, Forrest, and a few members of the general's staff rode to the crest of the ridge. They stopped their horses under the line of trees that ran along the ridge. In the distance below, perhaps three hundred yards away, the Yankee column moved along the road that ran from Winston's Gap to Alpine. Probably the village was their destination, Cory thought. The Yankees had time to reach Alpine before night fell, and then they could camp there. Given General Rosecrans's tendency to move his troops for a while and then settle down to wait, the Union army might even go into bivouac until they found out for sure what Bragg was doing.

Forrest leaned forward in his saddle as he watched the Yankees. His expression was intent, his normally piercing eyes even more so now that the enemy was in sight. Cory could tell by looking at him that the general wanted to attack. Even with a small force such as Forrest had at hand today, a swift strike into the column's flank could do some damage. And since the Yankees wouldn't be expecting it, chances were the Confederate cavalrymen could wreak their havoc and get away unscathed.

After a moment, Forrest took a deep breath. "My orders today were to scout out the position of the enemy in this area, and that's what we've done, boys. Time to get back and report." Cory could tell that the decision not to attack had cost the general quite a bit of effort.

Forrest wheeled his horse and led the way back down the ridge, away from the Yankees. His jaw was clenched, and his beard jutted out in defiance. What Forrest was defying were his own natural inclinations, Cory thought. He could understand. Reluctant soldier that he was, even he had found himself wondering just how much damage they could do to the Federal column if they had swooped down on it.

That question would have to remain unanswered. As Forrest had said, today the cavalry had already done its job.

But there would be other days, Cory knew, and other jobs. Bloody jobs, more than likely.

THAT NIGHT, the Confederate camps around La Fayette were buzzing with speculation. The Yankees under Gen. Alexander McCook had moved through Winston's Gap, as reported by Forrest and his scouts, while Gen. George H. Thomas's corps had come through Stevens' Gap and into McLemore's Cove, the little valley between Lookout Mountain and Pigeon Mountain. The only way out of the cove was a bottleneck to the northeast, so Thomas's corps would be sitting ducks if the Confederates could close up that bolthole. Farther to the north, the Union corps under the command of Gen. Thomas L. Crittenden had moved out of Chattanooga and through McFarland's Gap to march down the valley of Chickamauga Creek to the vicinity of Lee and Gordon's Mills. When Cory heard about that, he remembered passing through there and thinking what a peaceful-looking place it was. That wouldn't be the case now, with thousands of Yankee soldiers tramping over the ground.

For some reason General Rosecrans had divided his army, always a risky move. The three Federal corps were isolated from each other. Now was the time to strike. Even Cory could see that, and he said as much that evening to Cullum as they shared coffee and hardtack by the campfire in front of their tent.

"Yep," Cullum said, nodding in agreement. "But just because it's the thing to do don't mean that Bragg'll do it."

"No one likes him much, do they?"

Cullum shook his head. "Hell, not even his own staff cares overmuch for the old boy. I don't reckon he's a coward—never heard anybody say that about him—but he ain't much of a commander, neither. Was it up to me, I'd put Forrest in charge, or Joe Wheeler, or even Joe Johnston. Johnston was here carryin' out an inspection for Jeff Davis not long ago, and we all figured he'd replace Bragg when it was over. Davis likes Bragg, though. I heard tell that when they were both fightin' in the Mexican

War, Bragg saved Davis's bacon one day when the Mexes were about to overrun his command. Could be Davis won't ever replace Bragg."

"Maybe the general will surprise all of us," Cory said. Remembering Bragg's reaction to Pemberton's plea for help for Vicksburg, he went on, "I wouldn't count on it, though."

The night passed without the army moving. Murmurs of speculation became mutters of discontent. The Yankees were ripe for plucking, especially in McLemore's Cove. Why weren't they attacking, the Confederate soldiers asked themselves.

More rumors flew the next morning. Reinforcements were on the way. Two divisions led by Gen. James Longstreet, who had fought at Gettysburg back in July, were supposed to have boarded trains in Virginia so that they could hurry west and come to the aid of the Army of Tennessee. These troops would be in addition to some eight thousand men who had been brought from Knoxville by Gen. Simon Bolivar Buckner and an even larger force under Gens. John C. Breckinridge and William H. T. Walker that had moved in from the west. Not only that, but Bragg's ranks were swelled a little more each day by men like Cory and Colonel Thompson, who answered the call from all over Alabama, Mississippi, Georgia, and Tennessee, showing up one or two or a dozen at a time, all of them coming to fight the Northern invaders. Bragg's army had been badly outnumbered when it pulled out of Chattanooga; at the rate reinforcements were pouring in, the odds would soon be much closer to even, though it was likely the Federal forces would remain larger.

No matter. A fighting spirit gripped the camps around La Fayette. These men were ready for combat.

And still they sat and waited.

Before midnight the night before, Forrest's cavalry had mounted up and pulled out of the camp. Cory could tell they were heading northeast, and as he saw the way Forrest dispersed the various brigades under his command so as to form a long line of cavalry along a northeast-southwest axis, he could tell that the general was setting up a screen for the right flank and rear of Bragg's army in case Crittenden's corps tried to swing around them. Rosecrans wouldn't have split up his own forces the way he had if he hadn't been thinking of trying to encircle the Southerners.

At dawn, while the infantry back at La Fayette was still wondering what was going to happen and gossiping about reinforcements, Forrest and his escort, including Cory and John Cullum, rode into the little railroad town of Dalton, Georgia, some twenty miles from La Fayette. The Western and Atlanta Railroad, one of the handful of rail lines that converged near Chattanooga, ran through here, though no trains were moving on the tracks this morning.

Making the railroad station his headquarters, Forrest waited there for word from Bragg that an attack had been launched against Thomas's corps in McLemore's Cove. In addition, he received dispatches from his brigade commanders, who were reconnoitering along the ridges, keeping an eye out for any Yankees trying to move east.

Cory and Cullum sat on the station platform, their legs dangling over the edge, and watched Forrest pace back and forth, his impatience and eagerness to fight evident in every stride. He wore a long white linen coat, and each time he turned, the movement was so abrupt that the tails of the coat swirled around him. In a quiet voice, Cullum said, "The old boy can't hardly stand it, he wants to hit the Yankees so bad."

"Someone needs to," Cory said. "They took the bait. They did just what we wanted them to do. Why doesn't Bragg attack?"

Cullum shrugged, "You're askin' the wrong man, Brannon. I just ride around and figure out where the Yankees are. It's up to the officers to decide what to do about 'em."

Cory knew the other scout was right, but still he grew impatient, almost as much so as Forrest. The news came almost as a relief when a rider galloped in bringing word that Gen. John Pegram's brigade had encountered some of Crittenden's force moving south along the railroad in the vicinity of Ringgold, not far from the Tennessee border. The fighting had been scattered but fierce.

"I knew Crittenden would try to slip around us," Forrest said with satisfaction when he heard of the engagement. "Pegram will turn 'em back."

The general sounded confident, but Cory wasn't surprised a couple of hours later when Forrest decided to take a look for himself and lend a hand if Pegram needed it. He'd had all he could stand. "Mount up!" he called, and his subordinates passed along the order. "We're ridin' to Ringgold!"

It was a beautiful late afternoon, but as the cavalry rode north, Cory began to hear the distant popping of rifle fire. When they came closer to Ringgold, the air took on a hazy look, which Cory knew came from all the powder smoke generated by a battle. Even at a distance, he could smell the distinctive tang in the air of burned powder.

Forrest called a halt when they were close enough for him to scan the fighting through his field glasses. Instead of being out front today, Cory and Cullum rode with the rest of Forrest's escort. Cory couldn't see much from where he was, but he could hear the ebb and flow of the firing.

Pegram was using his men as dismounted infantry. There would be no dashing, breakneck cavalry charges in this rugged terrain. The cavalry's only advantage was that they could move from place to place faster than foot soldiers. And even that was not always true in this land of ridges and ravines.

Forrest lowered his glasses. "Definitely Crittenden's men," he muttered, as much to himself as to his aides. "An attack by the infantry now would smash them. I have to get word to General Polk."

A message had arrived earlier in the afternoon from La Fayette, notifying Forrest that Bragg's army had finally begun to move. A force under Gen. Leonidas Polk had marched north to the area of Lee and Gordon's Mill in preparation for striking at

Thomas's corps in McLemore's Cove. Gen. D. H. Hill was also in the vicinity with a sizable number of Confederate troops. Forrest expected that Polk and Hill would both be engaged with the enemy by morning, if they weren't already, but surely Polk could spare some men to crush Crittenden's advance up north.

Forrest said as much as he dictated a dispatch in rapid-fire fashion that a galloper would carry to Polk. Once the messenger had ridden off, Forrest and the men with him settled down to watch Pegram's continued skirmishing with the Yankees. Cory sat in his saddle and wiped the back of one hand across his mouth while with the other he clutched the rifle he carried. Part of him wanted to get down there and pitch in, but another part was glad that he was up here on a ridge, safe for the moment. He knew those feelings didn't make him a coward. When he had been called on in the past to fight, he had always answered without hesitation. He didn't doubt his courage.

But he was a married man now. He had to think about Lucille. And thinking of her only made him miss her that much more, as well as worrying about her safety. It was a long trip to Texas from Vicksburg. Deserters and renegades roamed the roads in Louisiana, and there could be danger as well from Union patrols as the Yankees secured their grip on the state. Cory wanted to believe that even Yankees wouldn't bother a couple of women, a cripple, and a boy who was weak in the head, but he had learned that nothing was certain in war. There was no way to be sure how someone would behave. All he could do was hope for the best.

The afternoon faded into dusk, then night settled down over the countryside. "Hell's fire!" Forrest exploded after a couple of hours of darkness. "Where's that infantry from Polk?"

Cory didn't know the answer to that question. None of them did. He was sitting under a tree and gnawing on a piece of hardtack he had taken from his pack. He put it away hastily as Forrest stalked by and snapped, "I'm goin' back to Dalton to see if they've had word from Polk there."

Cory knew that he and Cullum and the rest of the general's escort were expected to come along. They mounted up in a hurry and put their horses into a ground-eating trot as they followed along behind Forrest. Despite the darkness, Forrest set a fast pace. The men who trailed him could only hope that he knew where he was going.

The news that awaited them at Dalton wasn't good. Polk and Hill had been slow to move and even slower to attack. In fact, they had not attacked the Yankees in McLemore's Cove at all during the day. Bragg was said to be furious, but that fury came too late. The advance units of Thomas's corps must have realized the danger in which they had placed themselves by entering the cul-de-sac, because they had pulled back through the gap to the other side of Lookout Mountain.

The Yankees had waltzed into the trap—and waltzed right back out again when the jaws didn't clamp shut.

Forrest was incensed when he heard about this from the men he had left at the station in Dalton. "Where's Polk now?" he demanded.

The subordinate to whom he addressed the question could only shake his head. "I don't know, sir."

Forrest clenched a fist. "That was all we had to do," he said. "If we had just closed our fist on them . . ." He gave a little shake of his head. "I had planned to circle around the Yankees and hit 'em in the rear while the infantry struck them in front. That way we could have taken Red House Bridge and cut 'em off from Chattanooga for good. They would have been ours, no doubt about it." Again he shook his head, even more disgusted this time. "Crittenden's boys won't stay where they are. They'll come on down the railroad line. Pegram can't hold them by himself. I'll have to reinforce him with at least a brigade. But by God, the Yankees won't come through here without getting past me, and I don't intend to let that happen!"

Forrest swung into the saddle again and dashed out of Dalton, headed north to where the guns had fallen silent with the coming of night. General Pegram had stymied the Yankee advance all day, but he couldn't be expected to hold them back forever, not without help. As Cory galloped along through the night after Forrest, he knew that barring unforeseen circumstances, the wait was over.

Tomorrow, Forrest would get the fight he had been wanting all along—and so would the men with him.

Chapter Sixteen

FORREST SPREAD HIS MEN in a long line that stretched west from the tracks of the Western and Atlanta Railroad just north of Ringgold. The border with Tennessee was only a few miles away.

The general paused in positioning his men to look at Cory and Cullum. "You two stay close. I may need you to carry messages for me."

Cullum drawled, "I'm a scout, General, not a messenger."

Cory tensed. That was the sort of insubordinate remark that was liable to make Forrest explode with anger. His short temper was legendary. Instead, unpredictable as always, the general gave a short, barking laugh. "I'm aware of that, Lieutenant Cullum," he said. "But just what is the purpose of a scout?"

The question seemed to take Cullum by surprise. "Why, to find out where the enemy is, I reckon."

Forrest leveled an arm and pointed off into the darkness to the north. "He's right over yonder." The general paused and then went on as if the conversation had never taken place. "Where's Colonel Scott? I need his brigade in the center of the line . . ."

Preparations continued as dawn approached. Colonel Scott moved his brigade to the front and center of the defensive line, as Forrest had ordered, and as shafts of daylight began to spread through the eastern sky, the crackle of rifle fire from the area where Scott's men were deployed told everyone within hearing that the battle was under way.

The firing quickly became furious. Cory stood with General Forrest and watched as blue-clad figures poured out of the woods and tried to move south along the railroad right-of-way. Confederate soldiers blocked their path. This was no long-distance fight;

almost as soon as it began, the troops from each side were in each other's faces, shooting, thrusting with bayonets, swinging empty rifles as clubs, grappling hand to hand. Thick clouds of smoke rolled back and forth, obscuring the scene for seconds at a time then clearing to show how things had changed. Cory had been in the middle of such hellish melees before, most notably at the Hornet's Nest during the battle of Shiloh, so he knew what they were like: loud, confusing, terrifying. Most of the orders shouted by the officers went unheard. At this point, the battle was in the hands of the poor devils fighting it, the soldiers choking and coughing from the stench of burned powder, gagging on the coppery smell of fresh-spilled blood, too scared to do anything except keep fighting until bullets ripped through them or bayonets disemboweled them or bursting artillery shells blew them apart.

Forrest turned to Cullum. "Tell Captain Arnold to move up behind Scott."

"Yes sir," Cullum replied as he turned to his horse and rode off at a gallop.

Cory remained beside Forrest, close enough to hear the general mutter, "We can't hold 'em here . . . May have to pull back to Ringgold."

A frown of surprise creased Cory's forehead. He had never heard Forrest talk about retreat before. When under attack, the general's first impulse had always been to charge the enemy, and that tactic had proven successful more often than not, even against overwhelming odds such as they appeared to be facing now. Maybe Forrest had come up against odds that were too much even for him. If General Polk had sent a couple of brigades of infantry, as Forrest had requested . . . if they hadn't been forced to try to hold back the Union advance with only unmounted cavalry . . .

Cory forced those thoughts out of his head. Battles had to be fought with things the way they were, not the way one might wish them to be.

The Federal fire became heavier. Cory looked around and saw more men heading toward the front. That would be Captain Arnold's regiment moving into position to support Colonel Scott. Sure enough, Cory spotted Cullum galloping back toward him and Forrest, the message having been delivered.

Cory cried out in shock as Cullum and his horse disappeared in a huge explosion from a bursting artillery shell. Forrest swung around and demanded, "What is it?"

Cory pointed. The smoke and dust began to clear, revealing a shell crater and a couple of heaps of bloody flesh that seconds earlier had been Cullum and his mount. "Lieutenant Cullum, sir," Cory choked out. "He was hit."

Forrest looked where Cory was pointing, but his expression didn't change other than a slight narrowing of his eyes. "Damned shame. He was a good man." Forrest turned his gaze back toward the battlefield. Without looking at Cory, he ordered, "Start the rear guard toward Ringgold. We'll delay the Yankees here as long as we can, but we'll make our real stand farther down the line."

"Yes sir," Cory managed to say. He had known Cullum only a few days, but the man's death had hit him hard. It was best not to make friends, Cory thought, because war could snatch them away in an instant. But it was hard to go against his instincts and his natural friendliness. He swung up into the saddle and put Dash into a gallop that carried him toward the rear of the Confederate force to deliver Forrest's orders.

As the morning passed, Forrest's men fought a delaying action as they gradually retreated to Ringgold. The general began to concentrate his forces around the village, pulling in the stretched-out line. The Yankees were coming straight down the tracks and seemed to be intent on following the railroad. It was easier to move along the cleared right-of-way than it would have been to go through the thick woods on either side.

Forrest set up his headquarters at the tiny station. He drew his pistol and held it in one hand while he clutched his saber in the other. He used the blade to point out where he wanted his people positioned and slapped the saber against the barrel of a light artillery piece when its crew didn't swing the cannon around fast enough to suit him. "The Yankees ain't goin' to wait for you to get situated," he said.

The last companies from Colonel Scott's brigade straggled in, most of them bloody and limping. As the men moved past him, Forrest turned toward the north and muttered, "Good work, boys. You've done a fine job. The Yankees just think they know what fightin' is. Now we'll really give 'em hell!"

Cory made sure Dash was safe with the other horses and then moved up alongside Forrest. He couldn't quite shake the image of Cullum's being trapped in that explosion, but he tried to force it to the back of his mind. He held his carbine ready for use and followed Forrest's example, looking northward along the railroad tracks that seemed to converge into a single line in the distance.

Mere minutes later, Yankee cavalry came roaring along that line toward them.

The Confederates scattered around the depot and in the edge of the woods began firing. As bullets whined around them, the Yankees reined in their horses and dropped out of their saddles. They went to one knee and returned the fire. A volley ripped out from their rifles, and then, amazingly, another round of shots followed almost immediately.

Cory crouched next to Forrest. "They didn't have time to reload!" he cried out.

"Those must be some of Wilder's men," Forrest said, his voice calm despite the storm of lead that clawed through the air around him. "I've heard that they've got those new seven-shot Spencer repeaters. What I'd give for a thousand of those!"

Cory hadn't heard anything about repeating rifles, but it was obvious that was what the Yankees were using as they came down the railroad tracks toward Ringgold. Cory lifted his single-shot carbine and fired toward the mass of blue-uniformed figures. He dropped to a knee behind a rain barrel that sat next to the wall of the station building and reached for his ammunition pouch to reload. A few feet away, Forrest paced restlessly, heedless of the danger. His long white coat would make him an easy target for Yankee sharpshooters, and Cory gave some thought to grabbing the general and pulling him to safety. No doubt Forrest would take offense at that, however, and he might even attack Cory if his temper blazed up. Some men just didn't know what it was like to be afraid, and Nathan Bedford Forrest was one of them.

With his carbine reloaded, Cory stood up and drew another bead on the Yankees. He fired, the butt of the weapon's stock kicking hard against his shoulder. At this range, he couldn't tell if his shot hit anything or not. He dropped down to reload again.

For the next two hours, Cory followed that pattern over and over as the Confederates made a gallant stand and stopped the Union advance down the railroad. The Yankees had repeating rifles, but the Southern defenders had better cover here at Ringgold to offset any advantage the Spencers might give the enemy. The Rebels were packed into all the houses and businesses in the little hamlet, and they rained gunfire on the Yankees from every window and doorway. Forrest had his batteries of light artillery set up as well, so that the wicked little cannons added their weight to the fight. The Yankees charged several times but were thrown back again and again.

At first, Cory had been able to smell the raw pine lumber out of which the depot was constructed, but as the battle wore on, his nose became clogged with smoke and dust so that he couldn't really smell anything. Heat rose from the barrel and breech of his carbine and made sweat trickle down his face. Bullets thudded almost constantly into the building, the impacts like a drumbeat that counterpointed the hammering of his heart.

Forrest never sought shelter. He mounted his horse so that he could gallop around the battlefield. He directed the artillery fire and moved his men himself, rather than trusting the orders to subordinates. His saber slashed through the air to point out what he wanted, and his pistol jumped in his hand as he joined the battle. Every time the Yankees tried to thrust out a salient or make a charge, they found Forrest waiting for them, yelling and prodding his troops into position to turn back the attempted advance. Cory had never seen anything like it, even during the desperate raid into West Tennessee. Forrest was a whirlwind, moving from place to place so fast it must have seemed to the Yankees like there was more than one of him, like he was a veritable host of devils.

The knowledge that death was sizzling through the air around him kept Cory from getting bored, but at the same time, the fighting had an air of sameness to it that deadened the mind. He lost track of how long the battle had been going on. He wasn't really aware that he had been fighting for nearly two hours until he realized that he was running low on ammunition. He would have to slow down and pace himself, or he would run out of powder and shot and percussion caps.

Before that could become a problem, Forrest turned and strode toward the depot, his coat flapping around his legs. He waved the saber in the air and bellowed, "Fall back! Fall back!"

Men heard the order and scrambled for their horses. Cory waited until the general came up to him. "Are we retreating, sir?" he asked.

Forrest wore a savage grin on his face. He was untouched despite all the bullets that had flown through the air around him. "I've just received word that a Yankee division is movin' up on our left. We can't let them flank us. We'll fall back to a better defensive position."

Again, Forrest was going against his usual mode of operation by going on the defensive. Cory couldn't argue with the decision, though, not if an entire division was moving into position to strike their flank. He had been so busy shooting at the Yankees he hadn't even noticed Forrest talking to the courier who had brought the news of the Federal maneuver.

Cory ran toward the horses, grabbed Dash's reins, and vaulted into the saddle. Forrest raced up alongside him, also mounted now. The general had holstered his pistol, but he was still waving his saber in the air. With the rest of his staff trailing him, Forrest rode south along the tracks, taking to the roadbed itself wherever the rail line crossed a ravine or gully. The horses had to slow down then and pick their way across the trestles. Behind Forrest at Ringgold, the firing began to dwindle as one by one the units of Confederate cavalry joined the retreat.

Within three or four miles, Forrest and his escort came within sight of a wooded hill that seemed to be squatting right on the railroad tracks. Cory remembered passing that height several times during the past couple of days. It was called Tunnel Hill because a tunnel had been cut into it to allow the railroad tracks to pass through it, rather than having to go around.

Forrest reined and turned in his saddle. "Bring up the artillery! I want the batteries set up on that hill! Quick, boys, quick!"

The general moved off to the side of the right-of-way to supervise the redeployment of his men. "Dig in up there!" he ordered his brigade commanders as they rode past with their men. "The Yankees won't be able to push us off that hill!"

Cory hoped the general was right. In combat, the advantage usually lay with those who held the high ground. From what he had heard of the great battle at Gettysburg, the Yankees had established defensive positions atop a long ridge and several hills, and they had been able to withstand everything that Lee's army could throw at them. Maybe, on a much smaller scale and with the sides reversed, the same would be true today at Tunnel Hill.

Despite the hard fighting in which they had been engaged since dawn that morning, the horse soldiers' pace was brisk and their movements crisp. With Forrest galloping around the hill and up and down its slopes, shouting orders, the men took their places, hunkered down, and prepared to fight once again. It was a good thing they were still able to move quickly, Cory realized, because minutes after the last of Forrest's soldiers reached the hill, the blue-clad foe came boiling along the railroad tracks, firing scattered shots.

On horseback at the base of the hill, Forrest shouted for the batteries to fire at will. The order was relayed up the slope, and seconds later, the light guns began to boom.

Grinning with satisfaction, the general wheeled his horse to ride up the hill. He would command the action from the top of the height. Before he moved in that direction, however, he grunted and sagged in the saddle.

Cory witnessed what happened and exclaimed, "General! Are you hit?"

The answer was evident. Blood streaked the side of the linen coat. Forrest tightened his knees on the horse and straightened from his slumped position. He shook his head. "I'm all right. Get up that hill, Lieutenant Brannon."

"Sir, I can help you—"

"I said get up the hill!" Forrest roared.

For a second, Cory believed the general might swing at him with the saber. He kneed Dash forward, ascending the slope as Forrest had commanded. A moment later, the general passed him, riding as stiff and erect in the saddle as if Yankee lead had never touched him.

For hours, Forrest had exposed himself to enemy fire at Ringgold and never been hit. Now, as the battle at Tunnel Hill was just getting under way, the general had been struck. Cory had no idea how bad the injury was, but at least Forrest was able to stay in the saddle.

With their horses straining under them, the general and his aides approached the top of the hill. As he reached the crest of the slope and reined in, Forrest swayed a little. Cory leaped off his horse and hurried to help the general to the ground. The staff surgeon came up on the other side of him.

"General," the physician said, "you had better turn over command and let me have a look at that wound."

Forrest's head jerked around. "Relinquish command! No need for that. I'm fine." He shook off Cory's hand and turned so that he could see the action below. Cory noticed how pale he was, and the general's lean face was more haggard than ever. Obviously, he had lost a lot of blood and was weaker for it.

Looking and sounding somewhat tentative, because he didn't want to risk an explosion of Forrest's temper, the surgeon whispered, "If you won't come back beneath the trees and lie down, General, perhaps you'll take a small bracer . . ." He held out a silver flask.

"You know I never touch liquor," Forrest said.

"With all due respect, sir, in this case I think it might be a good idea. You might consider it a medical order."

Forrest glared at the doctor, but the surgeon stiffened his back and gave the general a level stare in return. After a moment, Forrest muttered under his breath and reached for the flask. He swallowed a healthy slug of the whiskey and then handed the flask back to the surgeon. The liquor brought some color back into his face, and it seemed to Cory that he stood a bit straighter and seemed a little stronger.

"Don't expect me to make a habit of that," Forrest commented.

"No sir, of course not." After looking at the flask for a second, as if tempted to take a drink himself, the surgeon tucked the small flask under his coat.

Cory could have used a shot of whiskey, but he knew it wouldn't be a good idea. He hadn't eaten anything all day, and the liquor wouldn't have a good effect on an empty stomach. During the months he had worked on the docks at New Madrid, he had drunk too much, stumbling into the squalid tavern called Red Mike's anytime he had an extra coin in his pocket. He recalled that because he had been drinking one night, he had almost failed to warn Captain Farrell in time of the danger that threatened the *Missouri Zephyr.* How different his life would have been if things had worked out that way. He would probably be dead by now, he thought, starved to death or frozen from sleeping outside on the docks during the winter. Farrell had saved his life by taking him under his wing.

Cory gave a little shake of his head and put the past out of his thoughts. The present was enough for anyone. More than enough, because the Federals were assailing the base of the hill.

Forrest had positioned his men so that the enemy could be driven back, concentrating his forces where he thought the Yankees would launch their heaviest attack. As Cory watched the battle unfold, he saw that the general hadn't neglected the flanks, either. Every time some of the Union troops tried to circle around the height, Confederate artillery drove them back with a barrage of canister, grape, and shell. In the middle, the dismounted Yankee cavalrymen charged ahead, elbow to elbow like true infantrymen. Waves of fire from the defenders on the hill scythed them down.

Cory had seen worse carnage. Relative to some other battles in which he had participated, the forces engaged here at Tunnel Hill were small. But blood was blood and death was death, and Cory never failed to be both horrified and awed by what he saw as the fighting spread out before him. Yankee bullets whipped through the cedars on the top of the hill, clipping off branches, but Forrest stayed where he was, guiding the battle, and Cory and the rest of the general's aides stayed with him. That one swallow of whiskey must have had quite an effect on Forrest, because he never faltered again during the long afternoon.

The Confederate defenders had the advantage of high ground, but the Federals had those repeating rifles—and superior numbers. Cory tried to estimate the size of the Union force but was unable to do so. All he knew for sure was that it was larger than Forrest's. The Confederates would hold out for as long as they could, but sooner or later, if the Yankees didn't care how many men got killed, they might overrun the hill.

Late in the afternoon, a rider galloped in from the south. Cory saw the man coming, using his hat to slap the rump of his horse and drive it faster up the slope. "General," Cory announced, "rider coming."

Forrest swung around as the courier galloped up and brought his mount to a sliding stop. "Colonel Dibrell's compliments, sir," the man gasped out. "He said to tell you that his brigade is on the way and will be here momentarily to join you."

One of Forrest's hands clenched into a fist, but that was the only reaction he showed to the news other than a curt nod. "Much obliged, son," he drawled. "Get off that horse and catch your breath."

Forrest turned to look down the slope again. "Wilder has scouts, too," he mused. "If he doesn't know already that Dibrell's on the way, he will soon."

"You think he'll pull back, sir?" Cory asked.

"If he doesn't, he'll lose every man he's got, because as soon as Colonel Dibrell gets here, we're comin' down off this hill."

Cory knew what the general meant. Forrest had fought enough delaying actions, had established enough defensive lines for one day. He was ready to attack again.

He didn't get the chance. Within minutes of learning that Dibrell's brigade was approaching, the Confederates on Tunnel Hill saw the Yankees begin to pull back. The firing from the Union side dwindled. Clouds of dust rose as cavalrymen mounted their horses and rode northward. Cory suspected they would withdraw as far as Ringgold and camp there to lick their wounds. One thing was certain: The Yankees weren't going to get past Tunnel Hill. Not today, anyway.

When the Federals had withdrawn and the shooting had stopped, Forrest looked around and announced, "I reckon we'll camp right here." No one questioned his decision, but he explained it anyway, standing there with drying blood on his coat and his saber still in his hand. "I like the view."

THE NEWS that filtered into Forrest's camp was uniformly bad. For some reason, Polk had grown indecisive and had failed to attack the Yankees in McLemore's Cove. Furthermore, a force under the command of Gen. Thomas Hindman, which was supposed to come to Polk's aid, did not move as scheduled; did not, in fact, move at all. And when Confederate scouts slipped into McLemore's Cove to check on the Union positions, they found the Yankees gone.

Forrest raged when he heard this, blaming the debacle on Bragg. Cory had little sympathy for Bragg, having found the man sour and resentful of just about everything and everyone around him, but in this case it sounded as if there were plenty of blame to go around. Bragg could only order his field commanders, such as Polk and Hindman, to move. He couldn't get out there and prod the troops into motion himself.

The next day, Pegram's cavalry brigade was once again scouting the valley of Chickamauga Creek and along La Fayette Road. At Leet's Tan Yard, they ran into a Federal column heading west, toward Lee and Gordon's Mills, on the banks of the Chickamauga. These were the same Yankees who had fallen back to Ringgold the day before after failing to advance past Tunnel Hill. Part of Crittenden's corps, they were moving west to re-form with the rest of the corps.

It appeared that Rosecrans had gotten the message: His troops were too spread out, and if he didn't pull them together, he ran the risk of their being destroyed separately.

Pegram's cavalry put up a brisk fight, as was reported later to Forrest, but in the end they were unable to keep the Yankees from pushing on to where they wanted to go.

Rumors still abounded that Gen. James Longstreet, affectionately known as "Old Pete" to his fellow officers and foot soldiers alike, was on his way with reinforcements, but so far there was no sign of him.

Four days dragged by: September 14 to 17. Little happened during that time except a few skirmishes between scouts and pickets of both sides. The Yankees were on the move, pulling closer and closer together on the west banks of the creek.

Cory knew that from personal observation, because he carried out several scouting missions for Forrest during this time. In this wooded, hilly terrain, much of which was so thickly forested with trees and bushes and creepers that it was like a jungle, keeping up with the enemy's movements was difficult. There were times when Cory could hear the enemy but not see them.

The scouts brought back vague information to the generals, who strategized over maps that often possessed a dubious accuracy. Even knowing that, Cory shared Forrest's growing frustration with the lack of action. The army was ready and waiting, eager to join battle with the foe. Surely it would be better to do *something*, rather than just sit and wait.

As far as Cory was concerned, the only good thing about the delay was that it gave him an opportunity to seek out Charles Thompson and visit with the colonel.

With permission from Forrest, Cory rode to Bragg's headquarters, which was now at Rock Spring, on Pea Vine Creek about midway between Ringgold and Lee and Gordon's Mills. It was the evening of the seventeenth, and as Cory rode along through the warm, dusky air, he looked to the west and could sense the Yankees over there. They seemed not more than a stone's throw away, and in some places along the line, that might be literally true. He had heard stories about how the pickets had called to each other across the scant yards that separated them, carrying on conversations that could only be described as friendly.

Tomorrow those soldiers in blue and gray might be doing their best to kill each other, but on this warm evening, no one wanted to think of that. It was easy to forget, if only for a moment, that the men on the other side were the hated enemy. Some of them might be neighbors, even kin. Cory recalled learning from one of Cordelia's letters that Nathan Hatcher had gone off to join the Yankee army. He remembered Nathan quite well, though they had never been friends. Nathan might be on the other side of the line this evening, wearing Union blue. Anyway, it would be good to talk to somebody, anybody from back home, Cory thought.

Bragg's headquarters were in a log farmhouse. Cory found Colonel Thompson outside the crude building and sitting on a three-legged stool, a map spread out on his bony knees. Thompson looked up as Cory approached, and even in the fading light, he could see a smile spread across the colonel's face.

"Cory!" Thompson exclaimed as he came to his feet. "By God, it's good to see you, lad! I heard about that scrap General Forrest got into up at Tunnel Hill. I take it you were with him for that?"

"Yes sir," Cory said as he dismounted. "From beginning to end."

Thompson extended his hand, and when Cory took it, the colonel pulled him into a bear hug. When Thompson let go of him and stepped back, he said, "You look well. You weren't wounded in the hostilities?"

Cory shook his head. "No sir. Not even a scratch."

"I heard that General Forrest was injured, though."

"A bullet dug a pretty good furrow across his side. It wasn't bad enough to knock him out of the saddle, though, and he never left the field."

"That doesn't surprise me." Thompson looked around. "I'm afraid I don't have much in the way of amenities to offer you but that stump over there" He pulled his stool closer, and the two men settled on their rough seats.

"Tell me what you've been doing, Colonel."

"A bit of this and a bit of that. Working with supplies for the most part and helping out a little with planning." Thompson shot a glance toward the cabin, and Cory inferred that General Bragg was probably inside. The colonel lowered his voice.

"The general is not one to seek a great deal of advice from subordinates. He knows what he wants to do."

"Just not how to do it, eh?"

Thompson frowned. "Talk like that from a lieutenant borders on insubordination . . . but considering what everyone else is saying, I suppose there's no point in worrying about such things." He sighed. "That man is the most . . . unpleasant . . . officer I've ever served with. He hasn't a good word for anyone or anything and seems to think that the entire world is against him. However, if everything happens tomorrow the way it's supposed to, we'll win a smashing victory."

"Tomorrow?" Cory's pulse leaped. "We attack tomorrow?"

Thompson looked around again. "I wouldn't discuss this with any other junior officer, you understand. But you and I have been through so much together, Cory . . . and there's Lucille to consider. You're her husband. You're family now."

Cory leaned forward, the war forgotten for the moment. "Have you heard anything from—"

"Nothing," Thompson said. "Of course, I didn't expect to. Still, a message telling us that they were safe would do a great deal to ease the mind."

That was the truth, Cory thought. During these past few days, there had been periods of inactivity between the scouting missions, and all it took was a spare moment for him to start thinking about Lucille. He missed Mrs. Thompson and Allen and Fred Carter, too, of course, but his longing for Lucille was an ache inside him. He wanted to be with her, but even more he wanted to know that she was all right, that wherever she was, she was safe.

"I'm sure they're all fine," Cory said, but even he could hear the hollowness in his voice.

"Certainly. No doubt about it." Thompson sounded as unconvinced as Cory did.

After a few moments of awkward silence, Cory said, "You were talking about tomorrow . . ."

The colonel nodded. "The general has ordered a swinging-gate maneuver. The right end of our line will attack across the creek at dawn tomorrow, and then the rest of our troops will follow along, one brigade after another, all the way to the left end of the line, where the attack will be anchored. As our forces swing around, they'll drive the Yankees to the south, into McLemore's Cove. They'll be trapped there so that we can destroy them."

Cory thought about it for a moment then commented, "It sounds like it could work."

"I'm told General Forrest and his men will be posted near the right end of the line," Thompson said. "That means you'll be part of the action early on, lad."

"The sooner the better. You know me, Colonel." Cory flashed a grin. "I hate waiting."

"Yes, the impatience of youth. Often that can be a good thing on the battlefield."

Cory didn't make any reply, but he heard what the colonel left unsaid. If Cory was among the men who launched the attack across Chickamauga Creek, it meant he would get one of the first chances to strike at the enemy.

And one of the first chances to be killed.

He would also be in the fighting longer that way, and in combat, each minute meant that the odds of survival went down.

Still and all, Cory found himself almost looking forward to it. "Maybe by this time tomorrow, we'll have won," he said.

"Yes," Thompson agreed. "By this time tomorrow."

Chapter Seventeen

CORY DIDN'T SLEEP WELL that night after returning to Forrest's camp, which had been moved from Tunnel Hill to a point northeast of Rock Spring. Part of him wished that Colonel Thompson hadn't told him of the coming attack, yet he knew that for more than a week now, nearly everyone in the Army of Tennessee had gone to sleep thinking that the next day might bring battle. There was a certain amount of relief in knowing that one way or another, the waiting would be over soon.

Thompson had sworn him to silence regarding Bragg's plan. Since Cullum's death, Cory had been sharing a tent with a young Tennessee lieutenant named Gardenhire. The man seemed to sleep soundly that night, but Cory tossed and turned, thinking not only of the attack but also of Lucille.

He managed to doze for an hour or two then got up before dawn. Rubbing eyes that felt so gritty he wondered if their sockets were lined with sand, Cory stumbled out of the tent. From beside the small campfire, Gardenhire offered him a cup of coffee. Cory sat on a log and took the tin cup. Curls of steam rose from it.

"General Forrest rode by a few minutes ago," Gardenhire said. "The cavalry is being split up today."

Cory frowned. That wasn't the news he was expecting to hear. "What do you mean?" he asked.

"General Bragg wants us to cover all the divisions up and down the creek," Gardenhire explained. "I reckon it means we're getting ready to move."

It meant that Bragg was making another mistake, Cory thought. The cavalry was the eyes and ears of the army. If Bragg would leave Forrest alone to operate independently, Forrest would soon know where almost every Yankee was on the other side of the creek. Not only that, but Forrest would also hit the

Federal force and disrupt them, keep them from mounting an effective defense when the infantry started their advance across the Chickamauga. Forrest would need all his men at his command to do that, though.

That wasn't the way things were meant to be. Cory knew that Forrest had little if any respect for Bragg, but Forrest was not one to disobey orders. At least, not without some kind of provocation. If Bragg wanted the cavalry spread out, Forrest would do so.

"The general said to tell you that you're riding with him today," Gardenhire went on. "I'm hoping I will be, too."

"The general will be where most of the action is," Cory agreed. "He seems to attract it."

He finished his coffee but declined the hardtack Gardenhire offered him. He wasn't hungry this morning. Before the day was over, he might regret the decision to pass up breakfast. If he was still alive, that is.

The sky lightened with the approach of dawn. Forrest's camp was busy as the general separated his brigades and sent them to new positions up and down the line. Everyone knew by now that there would be an attack this morning; once that word started going around the camp, it moved with remarkable speed. Men saw to their horses and weapons and talked together in low, excited voices. Quite a few prayed. Nearly every soldier in the Confederate army considered himself a religious man, and most of them were convinced that the Almighty was on their side.

Cory, unable to shake the cynicism that had always been a part of his makeup, assumed that most of the Yankees likely felt the same way on this morning and were also equally fervent in their belief.

While Cory was saddling Dash, Gardenhire came up to him. "I have a favor to ask of you, Brannon."

"What's that?" Cory asked, thinking that in all likelihood he already knew the answer.

"I don't know if we'll fight together today or not, but if I fall, and if you hear of it, will you write to my family and tell them . . . tell them . . ."

"That you died fighting valiantly for the cause?"

Gardenhire nodded. "Exactly."

"You're assuming that I'll make it through the battle."

"Of course you will," Gardenhire said. "You always ride with General Forrest. Some of his luck is bound to have rubbed off on you by now."

Cory laughed. "I hope you're right about that, but not about your own fate." He put out a hand. "I'll see you after the battle, Mr. Gardenhire."

"Thanks, Brannon." The two men shook hands.

A short time later, Forrest rode by with his staff and escort. Cory was already mounted and joined the group of riders. It was still dark under the trees, but a glow filtering down through the branches told Cory that morning had broken. The air was silent, though, except for the songs of the birds.

Where was the attack? Gen. Bushrod Johnson was supposed to be at the far right of the Confederate line, the farthest right of all except Forrest. Cory wondered why Johnson wasn't in position and moving.

Forrest looked impatient, and Cory figured that if he just kept quiet, he would have the answers to his questions sooner or later. The general wasn't the sort to keep his complaints to himself. That was one of the few qualities he shared with General Bragg. Unlike Bragg, however, if something was bothering Forrest, he usually did something about it instead of dithering and blaming.

"I'm told that General Johnson received conflictin' orders this morning," Forrest announced. "He got sent in the wrong direction, but he's on his way back now. Same thing happened with some of the other divisions." Under his breath, but loud enough so that Cory could hear him, he added, "Bragg should've got everybody in place yesterday or the day before."

Cory knew that was true. Anytime an army had to move, it encountered unexpected delays. He had learned that much, even in his limited military experience. If something could go wrong, it would. That was why a plan had to allow for such things.

The sun rose higher in the sky, and still Forrest and the men with him sat and waited. Silence hung over the valley of the Chickamauga, broken only by an occasional burst of hammering from the other side of the creek. The Yankees had been sawing down trees and building something over there for several days now. Cory could guess what it was. He was sure the Union troops had thrown up breastworks to provide even more cover for them and make any Confederate advance that much harder.

Around eleven o'clock, with a great tramping of feet, Johnson's division came marching from the east. Forrest rode to meet the general, an old friend and comrade in arms who had fought at Fort Donelson with him the year before. The two generals shook hands, then Forrest glanced over his shoulder to Cory. He ordered, "Lieutenant Brannon, go take a look at the Yankee lines and see if they've moved."

Cory acknowledged, turned, and started his horse along a narrow trail that led west. He knew that behind him, General Johnson would be getting his troops into position to begin the advance. Once that was under way, it was inevitable that the battle would soon be joined.

Several times during the past few days, Cory had been over the path he followed now. It led through the woods, across Pea Vine Creek at a shallow ford, and out of the trees into a narrow strip of cleared land just east of Chickamauga Creek. Then he would come to Reed's Bridge, which crossed the creek just above a spot where it made a short bend to the west. If all went as planned, that bridge would soon accommodate General Johnson's men so they could begin the attack and start the gate swinging shut on the Federal forces.

Cory's every sense was alert not only for any signs of the enemy but also for everything else around him. He drank in his surroundings, keenly aware that this might be his last day on earth. The previous night, when he had tried so futilely to sleep, had been chilly, but the sun had warmed the air considerably and burned off the mist as it rose this morning. The air was still and heavy in the woods. There might be a breeze along the creek, where the landscape was more open. It was Friday, Cory told himself as his mount splashed across the ford at Pea Vine Creek. Friday, September 18, 1863.

And there were Yankees on this side of Chickamauga Creek.

Cory reined Dash to an abrupt halt then sat stiffly in the saddle as he stared through a narrow gap in the trees up ahead, where the trail took another turn. He caught a glimpse of movement up there. He had a pair of field glasses in a pouch strapped to his saddle. Forrest himself had given him the glasses a couple of days earlier. Cory peered through them, already knowing somehow what he was going to see.

Blue-clad troops were nearly at the bend up ahead. Cory saw the uniforms plainly. The blue stood out much more than the brown trousers and butternut jacket that he wore. He started backing Dash away as he lowered the glasses and put them back in their pouch. Then, with a jerk of the reins, he wheeled the horse and kicked it into a gallop.

Forrest had to know that the Yankees had already crossed Chickamauga Creek and were coming this way. It wasn't supposed to be like this, Cory thought. The Confederate attack should have begun before the Union army had any chance to advance. But that wasn't what had happened. The delay in getting Johnson's division into position might prove fatal.

Forrest must have been able to tell from Cory's breakneck pace that something was wrong. The general rode out to meet him as soon as he saw Cory galloping along the trail.

"What is it?" he called when they were still several yards apart and reining their horses to a halt.

"Yankees! On this side of Chickamauga Creek! Coming this way, General!"

Forrest yanked his saber from its sheath. "By God! Let's hope it ain't too late already." He turned in the saddle and waved to the men behind him. "Come on, boys! There are Yankees up yonder!"

The cavalry surged forward with Forrest in the lead, Cory riding just behind him. They came in sight of Pea Vine Creek, a winding, shallow stream that was quite a bit smaller than Chickamauga Creek. The Union troops Cory had seen a few minutes earlier were on the other side of Pea Vine. They were infantrymen and were marching smartly along the road.

"Dismount and advance!" Forrest shouted. "Drive 'em back, boys!"

Cory dropped to the ground, pulled Dash's head around, and slapped the horse on the rump to send him trotting toward the rear with the other mounts. Orderlies would gather up the horses and keep them safely out of the battle while the dismounted cavalrymen advanced toward the enemy.

Forrest strode in front of his men toward the creek. He had his saber in his left hand and his pistol in the right. Though the range was difficult for a handgun, the general lifted the pistol and began to fire toward the Yankees, squeezing off his shots in a calm, deliberate fashion. Rifles began to rattle from the Federal ranks.

The battle had begun.

Cory lifted his carbine and fired then started reloading as he trotted along. He'd had to load on the move in previous battles. Less than half a minute later, he was nearly ready to fire again. He eared back the hammer, put a percussion cap on the nipple, and raised the weapon. He paused just long enough to draw a bead on the mass of blue before him, press the trigger, and bring the barrel down after the recoil of the shot kicked it up. Then he was moving again, stepping forward through the smoke that had gushed from the barrel of the carbine as he fired. His eyes and throat stung from the smoke. He ignored the irritation and started reloading again.

The fire coming from the Confederates was ragged but nearly constant. Only a few of the Yankees had reached Pea Vine Creek, and those who had now lay on the bank and in the edge of the stream, cut down by the deadly accuracy of the Southern riflemen. The rest of the Union soldiers began to fall back, fighting as they retreated. They were stubborn; Cory had to give them that much. Not as stubborn as Southerners, of course.

Cory had thought a great deal about the war during his spare moments, whenever he wasn't thinking about Lucille. He was no longer convinced that the Confederacy could win. Back during the early days of the war, right after the smashing defeat of the Federals at Manassas, all the talk had been that the war would be over quickly, and that the Yankees would lose. Shiloh had taught the South that the struggle would be long and bloody, but despite that, most people believed the Confederacy would emerge triumphant in the end. The loss at Sharpsburg had tempered that optimism, but the heady triumph at Chancellorsville had restored it. Then had come the twin defeats at Vicksburg and Gettysburg, and what had seemed so promising back in the spring was now a struggle for survival. Winning was one thing; not losing was another. The Confederacy could not conquer the North. Cory was sure of that now. But perhaps, if they could hang on and make the price for victory high enough, political pressure on the Lincoln administration could accomplish what force of arms could not. A negotiated settlement, a peace treaty, a degree of autonomy for the South . . . those were the goals now, and Cory was realistic enough to understand that.

But in a moment such as this, it was all forgotten. As the Union soldiers turned to run and the Confederate cavalry surged forward, Cory shouted a Rebel yell just like the rest of his companions. They were going to whip themselves some Yankees today!

Back through the woods, the Yankees retreated. Forrest and his men splashed across Pea Vine Creek, keeping up a constant fire as they went forward. A few minutes later, they emerged from the thick belt of trees and looked across the field toward Chickamauga Creek and Reed's Bridge. The span was a wooden affair built of planks and timbers, with low railings along the sides. The Yankees who had been running a short time earlier had stopped now and were congregating at the bridge. On the other side of the creek were even more of the blue-clad soldiers, a lot more. Cory stopped to stare, as did most of the men with him. The rout of the Federals appeared to be over before it even got started good.

Forrest, however, never broke stride. He sheathed his saber and reached beneath his coat for fresh cartridges to reload his pistol. At the same time, he never looked back to see if his men were following him.

The pause lasted only a second. Then, with a yell, Forrest's men went on the attack again.

A few of the Yankees flung themselves on the ground along the creek bank to present smaller targets, but most stood upright, out in the open. The Confederate cavalrymen, though fighting on foot like infantry, conducted themselves a little differently. Most of them went to one knee to aim their carbines and fire. As they started to reload, they came to their feet and took a few steps forward, until they were ready to fire again. Then it was back to a knee, lifting their carbines to their shoulders, squinting over the barrels, and pulling the triggers. Cory did that half a dozen times as the Confederates surged toward the creek.

Forrest stepped back so as not to be in the way of his own men, but he still paced among them as they advanced. He stopped from time to time to snap a pistol shot toward the Federals. He shouted to his men, exhorting them on against the Yankees, drawing his saber again and sweeping it through the air above his head.

The racket was terrible as Cory advanced with the other men. The rattle of musketry was bad enough, but soon the artillery on both sides came into play. Cannons boomed, so loud that the reports were like blows against the ears of the soldiers. Shells burst in deafening explosions that flung dirt and blood and body parts high in the air. The deadly metal debris from bursting canister shot whined through the air around Cory's head, along with the whip-crack of passing bullets. Under all the tumult, cries of pain and screams of dying men could be heard from both sides. So far this was just a skirmish, but that could kill a man just as dead as a full-scale battle.

Cory became aware that some of the Union troops were firing one shot after another without reloading. Those damned Spencer repeaters again! He wished he had one as he rammed bullet and wadding and powder charge down the barrel of his carbine. This wasn't a fair fight at all.

The irregular thudding of bullets into flesh echoed all along the Confederate line, sounding like badly timed ax blows against tree trunks. From the corner of his eye, Cory saw men falling around him, blood gouting from their wounds. One of them toppled forward, his lower jaw and the bottom half of his face blown off, but he crawled forward despite the horrible wound and tried to raise his rifle for one more shot. Not far away, a headless body writhed and gushed blood, the head taken off cleanly by a cannonball. Some of the bodies seemed barely touched, with only a small stain on their chests to show where a bullet had drilled a deadly path.

Cory's eyes saw all those horrific sights, but his brain refused to recognize them. Instead he focused his attention on the line of blue a couple of hundred yards away. Forward progress was slow but inexorable. He fired, reloaded, fired again.

Forrest, on horseback now, galloped past and shouted something. Cory didn't understand the words. He stood up and reached for his ammunition pouch as he shuffled forward.

A moment later, having reached the end of the line, the general wheeled his mount and rode back. As he neared Cory's position, the young man saw the horse's front legs fold up underneath it. Forrest was thrown from the saddle as the horse fell heavily. The sight of the general's being unhorsed broke through the haze of battle madness that had descended over Cory's brain. He sprang forward and leaned over to grasp Forrest's arm.

"General! General, are you hit?"

Forrest came to his feet with Cory's help, his long coat flapping like a cape. "I need another horse!" he shouted. "Somebody get me a horse!"

Cory didn't see any fresh blood on Forrest's clothes, and the general didn't seem to be in any pain. Of course, when the fever of battle gripped Forrest like this, he might not know whether he had been wounded or not. A moment later, an aide came running up holding the reins of another horse. Forrest snatched the reins out of the man's hand and vaulted onto the horse's back. It was easy to see why Forrest was known in some quarters as "the Wizard of the Saddle."

Now that Forrest's spill had broken through Cory's daze, he was more aware of his surroundings. The Southern cavalry had advanced about halfway across the open ground next to the creek. There was a tree up ahead, next to the road on the left, and with it a small stand of brush. That would furnish at least a little cover for the Confederate skirmishers so they wouldn't be such inviting targets for the Yankees. Cory started trotting toward the tree. Several men followed his example, then more and more of them until the entire force was shifting left.

This movement not only allowed the dismounted cavalrymen to use the tree and the brush for protection, but considering the bend in the road, it also gave them a better angle from which to fire at the Yankees who were trying to use Reed's Bridge and the scattering of trees along the creek bank for cover. When Cory neared the tree, he broke into a run and then bellied down behind its trunk. When people were shooting at him, he was damned if he was going to pace slowly toward them out in the open any longer than he had to. That might be the way they fought wars in Europe and places like that, but not in the Confederate States of America, by God!

Forrest swooped by, grinning. Cory supposed the general approved of the maneuver. Propped on his elbows, he cradled the stock of the carbine against his cheek, drew a bead, and fired. Above him, bullets smacked into the tree trunk, and tiny pieces of bark showered down around him. He waved a hand in front of his face to clear away some of the powder smoke then reached for his ammunition pouch again. General Johnson was sure taking his time about moving up with his division, but that was all right, Cory thought.

Hell, he could fight all day like this!

THREE HOURS later, Cory was reconsidering that hasty thought.

The barrel of his carbine was so hot it glowed red. He had to be careful not to grasp it when he reloaded, or he would burn his hand. Cory's mouth was dry as cotton and tasted like brimstone smelled. His eyes watered so much from the smoke that half the time he couldn't see what he was aiming at. His shoulder was numb from the kick of the weapon's recoil against it. And his bladder was just about to burst.

Here he was in the middle of a battle, he thought, and he was worried because he needed to relieve himself. Things sure got boiled down to their simplest level when a fella was fighting for his life.

Some good had come out of the afternoon, though. The Confederates had gained at least fifty yards in the past three hours.

But the Yankees were still holding firmly to Reed's Bridge.

Cory had left the dubious shelter of the tree when the Union artillery began using it for a target. The poor tree was nothing but a smouldering stump now. Cory knelt in a little ditch at the side of the road. It wasn't much cover, but it was better than nothing.

Forrest galloped by, as he had been doing all afternoon. Cory was pretty sure the general had had more than one horse shot out from under him today. Forrest wasn't just dashing around offering empty encouragement, though. He moved sections of troops here, there, yonder—ever nearer the bridge. And now, when he came racing down the road a moment later, he brought more than daring strategy and bold tactics. He brought help with him, for he was riding with General Pegram at the head of Pegram's division. Reinforcements had finally arrived.

Cory and the other dismounted cavalrymen surged up off the ground, yells ringing from their throats. Pegram's men left their saddles and charged forward, toward the bridge, and the infusion of fresh fighting men revitalized the men of Forrest's brigade who had been battling out here all afternoon. A glance back toward the trees showed Cory a flurry of battle flags and a cloud of dust rising around them. That would be General Johnson and his troops, closing in on Chickamauga Creek at last.

The Yankees had taken the stubborn battering for hours, but now they saw that the odds had swung against them. Men began breaking and running. Officers on horseback tried to keep the retreat orderly, but they failed. Cory saw one man pointing at the bridge and shouting frantically, and he guessed the Yankee officer was telling his men to destroy the bridge so the Confederates couldn't use it. There was no time for that. A couple of soldiers tried to pull up planks from the bridge, but bullets knocked them off their feet. When the rest of the Yankees saw that, they forgot all about trying to wreck the bridge. All they wanted to do was flee before the wave of butternut rolling toward them.

Cory fired one more shot and then lowered his carbine. Forrest's and Pegram's men were flooding across the bridge now, peppering the retreating Yankees with rifle fire to keep them running. Cory took a deep breath, choking a little on the smoke, and rubbed his watery eyes. He looked around for Forrest.

The general had withdrawn a short distance to let his men do their bloody work. Two men sat on horseback with him. Cory recognized General Johnson, but the other man was a stranger to him. He was also a general, with a full beard and a wounded left arm that rested in a sling tied around his neck.

As Cory walked toward Forrest, the general summoned him. "Lieutenant Brannon!" Cory picked up his pace and trotted over to the trio of officers.

"Lieutenant Brannon, find the rest of my staff and tell them that we're movin' south to Alexander's Bridge, at the request of General Hood here. Seems General Walker needs a bit of a hand down there."

Cory nodded his understanding. The third officer was Gen. John Bell Hood, a Kentuckian who led a division of hard-fighting Texans. Cory had heard of him but never seen him until now. More important, he knew that Hood's division was part of General Longstreet's command.

He ventured a question to Forrest. "Sir, does this mean that the reinforcements under General Longstreet have arrived?"

Hood answered instead. "That's right, Lieutenant. Our trains began arriving at Ringgold this morning. Troops were still unloading from those rattletraps when I left to come here." Hood looked over at Forrest. "This young man seems to have a good grasp of what's going on."

"He's like me," Forrest said. "Not much for soldierin' by the book, but a hell of a fighter when he wants to be."

"Thank you, sir," Cory said, flattered by the comparison. "I'll pass along your orders, sir."

"And when you're done with that, find me," Forrest said. "I reckon we've got some more scrappin' to do this afternoon."

"Yes sir!"

Cory had forgotten his weariness, his aches and pains. He would fight alongside Nathan Bedford Forrest anywhere and at any time!

As GENERAL Bragg's battle plan called for, Gen. Bushrod Johnson began moving his men across Reed's Bridge and into the country west of Chickamauga Creek. The only problem was that Bragg's schedule had called for this to happen in the early morning, instead of the middle to late afternoon. General Hood ordered Johnson to push on until the Yankees had been driven back a mile or more from the creek. When that had been done, Johnson's men would turn and face left to begin driving the Yankees before them and swinging the gate shut. That would have to wait until the next morning, though, because night was coming on too quickly to accomplish much more today.

Meanwhile, Cory and the rest of Forrest's men mounted up and hurried south toward Alexander's Bridge, where a Confederate division under Gen. William H. T. Walker was attempting to take the bridge and cross over the creek. So far the Federals had put up a determined defense. Walker needed that bridge to get his men and artillery across the creek in a reasonable amount of time. They would have to be ready to do their part when Johnson turned south.

The situation was reversed for Forrest's men at Alexander's Bridge. At Reed's Bridge they had been the first to arrive and had carried the brunt of the fighting for hours before help arrived. Here Walker's troops had been engaged first, and Forrest was coming to their aid.

Not that the cavalry was fresh and rested. Not by any means. Some of the men were wounded, and all of them were tired after the battle at Reed's Bridge. They would have been running low on ammunition by now, too, if they had not captured quite a bit when the Yankees retreated. Cory had replenished his own ammunition pouch from one dropped by a fleeing bluecoat.

As they approached, Cory heard the heavy booming of artillery, but mixed in with it was a sound that was becoming all too familiar—the rapid-fire cracking of Spencer rifles. "General," he said in frustration, "do all the Yankees have those repeaters now?"

Forrest shook his head. "Only one brigade of cavalry, as far as I know. Those boys must've dashed down here after they pulled back from Reed's Bridge. The Yankees are shiftin' around like we are."

Cory didn't like the sound of that. The Union cavalry wasn't anywhere close to being as good as the Confederate horse soldiers, wasn't as fast or as well mounted or as dashing. That was the way it had always been since this war began, and that was the way it was supposed to be.

"Don't worry, Cory," Forrest went on, as if reading his mind. "They won't never be the fightin' fools that we are."

A few minutes later, as Forrest and his men threw themselves into the battle around Alexander's Bridge, Cory saw living proof of that. Forrest had yet another horse collapse under him, mortally wounded. This time he landed on his feet, stumbling but not falling. He grabbed the reins of a loose horse whose rider had been blown out of the saddle and swung up on its back, hardly missing a beat as he waved his saber and shouted commands to his men.

This fight didn't last as long. As the sun hung low in the sky, almost touching the long ridges to the west, the Yankees retreated from Alexander's Bridge and General Walker's men began to pour across it. Cory, who had fought dismounted again, went looking for Dash. As he walked along, he became aware that the back of his left hand was burning. He looked at it and saw an ugly red welt that oozed blood in a few places. Something—a bullet, a piece of canister, God knows what—had scraped his hand without his even knowing it at the time. He had come that close to death. Hell, he told himself, he had probably come that close a score or more times today.

And for what? Two bridges, a little bit of ground, and a grand plan that was perilously close to failure.

Cory let his wounded hand drop to his side and hoped that tomorrow went better. He looked toward the ridges and hoped that tomorrow he would live to see another sunset.

Chapter Eighteen

CORY SLEPT SURPRISINGLY WELL that night. Gone was the nervousness of the night before, when he had been waiting for the battle to begin. Now he had been blooded—even though it was only the crease on the back of his hand—and had spent nearly an entire day smelling gun smoke and having the din of battle assault his ears. He had done good work. He was tired. He slept, heedless of what the next day might bring.

He woke up on Saturday morning where he had stretched out the night before, underneath a tree near a large building that someone said was a sawmill. When he sat up and rubbed his eyes and looked to the east, he could see nothing except heavy fog, but he knew that Reed's Bridge, where he and the rest of Forrest's men had fought the day before, was over there less than a mile away. After driving the Yankees back from Alexander's Bridge, Forrest had moved north with his troops, so that he would be in position to reconnoiter in front of Johnson's advance. The cavalry was still scattered, but Forrest had a good-sized force with him. Cory hadn't seen anything of Lieutenant Gardenhire since the previous morning. He hoped the Tennessean was all right, that he was just somewhere else on this sprawling field of battle.

The sun had risen already, though the fog dimmed its light considerably. Cory had slept late. He got up and went over to one of the small campfires that had several cavalrymen gathered around it. He took a cup of coffee, a square of hardtack, and a piece of fatback. He had eaten very little the day before because he just hadn't been hungry, but today his appetite was back. His stomach wasn't just rumbling and growling; it was practically howling.

Cory hunkered on his heels to eat the food and drink the coffee. One of the other men said, "We'll be movin' out soon.

Thought you was goin' to sleep the day away, Brannon. Man who sleeps that sound must have an untroubled conscience."

Cory sipped the hot, bitter brew in the tin cup then nodded. "Reckon I do."

"You don't have anything you want to get off your chest? Sins you need to ask the Lord to forgive? This ain't a good time to be carryin' a burden. Fella goin' into battle needs his heart an' soul as clean as he can get 'em."

Cory felt a prickle of irritation. He knew what the man was saying: It wasn't good to die with unforgiven sins. But he wasn't in any mood to be preached at this morning. He rubbed a hand over his gaunt, beard-stubbled jaw and said, "The Lord and I are squared away. Leastways, I think so. I hope so."

"Well, that's good," the other man said. "But if you want me to say a prayer with you, you just let me know."

Not likely, Cory thought.

But as he finished his breakfast, he couldn't help but muse back over his life. He supposed he had done a lot of bad things. He knew he had caused his mother quite a bit of pain, especially when he rode off and left the farm behind him. During his wanderings, he had drunk too much whiskey, and whenever he had enough coins in his pocket, he had spent some time with women of ill repute and easy virtue. All that hadn't seemed so bad at the time, of course. In fact, he had enjoyed his life until he ran out of money and prospects and nearly died on the docks of New Madrid. Since then, he hadn't been blameless, either. He had let himself fall in love with Lucille Farrell and gotten her to fall in love with him, and maybe that wasn't a good thing. Maybe she would have been a lot better off without him, Cory wondered. Of course, he hadn't meant to hurt her. He would never do anything intentionally to cause her pain or harm. But life had taught him that good intentions meant about as much as a bucketful of warm mule droppings. It was what a man did that counted, not what he meant to do. And since he had brought pain to Lucille, he was a failure, no matter what else he did in life.

Maybe it wouldn't hurt to say a prayer or two before the day's fighting got started, he told himself. But the darkness deep inside him told him that it couldn't help, either.

"Come on, Brannon. Time to mount up."

Cory gave a little jerk of his head as the voice broke into his thoughts. He drained the last of the coffee, set the cup aside, and stood up.

The war didn't wait for a man to waste time sitting around brooding.

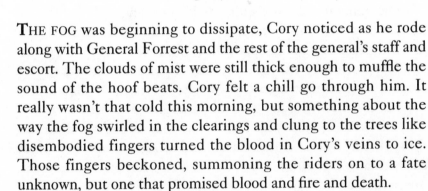

THE FOG was beginning to dissipate, Cory noticed as he rode along with General Forrest and the rest of the general's staff and escort. The clouds of mist were still thick enough to muffle the sound of the hoof beats. Cory felt a chill go through him. It really wasn't that cold this morning, but something about the way the fog swirled in the clearings and clung to the trees like disembodied fingers turned the blood in Cory's veins to ice. Those fingers beckoned, summoning the riders on to a fate unknown, but one that promised blood and fire and death.

Somewhere up ahead, the Yankees were probably feeling their way toward the Confederate lines. Or maybe they were just sitting back and waiting, waiting for the hated Southerners to come to them.

The fog began to lift even more. The wind freshened, shredding the mist and blowing it away. Though the fog was still thick in places, shafts of sunlight slanted down through it, and when Cory looked up he began to see bits of blue sky overhead.

The riders entered the woods, following the narrow road that led east from Reed's Bridge. Off to the left, some of the cavalry dismounted, took their carbines and rifles, and began working their way through the thick growth. This was a classic reconnaissance in force, though Cory knew from the way Forrest was talking that the general didn't expect to run into much opposition.

After being driven back yesterday, the Yankees had fled almost to the foot of the ridge that was now visible in the distance.

Without warning, guns began to pop. The firing came from the south, to the left of Forrest, Cory, and the other riders. Forrest held up a hand and reined in. "Our boys must've run into some Yankee scouts," he surmised.

As the moments passed and the firing in the woods grew heavier, a scowl appeared on Forrest's face. Cory knew why. From the sound of the shooting, the encounter to the south was developing into a battle. This was no sketchy clash of skirmishers and scouts.

The general suddenly spurred his horse ahead. "Stay here!" he called over his shoulder, but several officers, including Cory, ignored the order and galloped after him. They were not going to allow Forrest to run head-on into a mass of Federal troops alone. No one knew if that was what was really up ahead, but none of the men with the general wanted to take that chance.

Cory kept up easily on Dash. The road twisted and turned through the woods, and as it curved around a bend, Forrest came to a halt again, his horse's hooves sliding a little on the dusty road as he did so. The other officers came up and clustered around him, staring down the road at the unexpected sight before them.

Several hundred yards ahead, the road was full of blue-clad troops marching steadily forward. Not only that, but the trees thinned out up there so that Forrest and his companions could look to the south, and ranks of Union infantry stretched as far as they could see.

"By God, they've stolen a march on us!" Forrest exclaimed. "We were supposed to be beyond their left flank. Instead, they're beyond our right!"

"What are we going to do, General?" one of the officers asked.

Without hesitation, Forrest replied, "Dismount Davidson's brigade and move it up to reinforce our skirmishers. They sound

like they could use the help. Then you, Captain Anderson—"
He looked at another member of his staff. "Ride back to General
Polk and tell him to send Armstrong's division up here. We're
going to hold this ground and stop the Federal advance. That
way General Bragg will have time to move our boys around
accordin'ly."

That was assuming that Bragg would actually react to this
unexpected threat, rather than railing against it and doing nothing, Cory thought.

"In the meantime," Forrest went on as he drew his saber,
"we'll give those boys in blue up there somethin' to think
about."

With that, he swept his saber forward and kicked his horse
into a run. The men with him had no choice but to follow.

Cory's heart pounded like Dash's hooves striking the road.
This small party of cavalry was no match for rank upon rank of
infantry. Forrest wasn't turning back from the mad charge,
though, and if Forrest didn't turn back, none of the men who
rode with him would, either.

Smoke began to rise from the rifles of the men in the front
rank of the Union force. Cory heard the pop and crackle of gunfire. As bullets spurted up dust in the road, Forrest reined his
mount to the side. "Give 'em a taste of lead!"

The cavalrymen brought their horses to a halt and dropped
to the ground. Their rifles and carbines came up, and a volley
rang out. The range was still great, but Cory saw a couple of
men in the Union ranks drop to the ground, evidently wounded.
He began to reload.

The Yankees kept coming at a slow, steady pace. They kept
firing, too. Bullets clipped through the trees that pressed in
close on both sides of the road. To Cory's right, a man grunted
and took a step backward. He dropped his rifle as he brought his
left hand up to his bloody right shoulder.

Forrest rode up and down the left side of the road, heedless
as usual of the bullets flying around him. When the storm of

lead became too thick, he waved his saber. "Pull back! We need a little breathin' room."

What they needed was reinforcements, Cory told himself as he found Dash and swung up into the saddle, grateful to see that the horse was unharmed. In orderly fashion, the cavalrymen mounted up and rode at a fast pace back down the road to the east.

They hadn't gone far before they met General Dibrell's brigade hurrying to the front. Forrest reined in and greeted Dibrell. "Where is the rest of the division?"

"We're all that General Polk felt he could spare, sir," Dibrell answered.

Cory saw the fury on Forrest's face and expected an explosion of temper from the general. Instead, Forrest retained control of his raging emotions and asked calmly, "Does General Polk understand that the Federal forces have overlapped this end of the line?"

Dibrell nodded. "I believe so, General. We're still all he sent."

Forrest's head jerked in a curt nod. "Very well. Dismount your men and add them to Davidson's line. We have to stop those Yankees."

Within minutes, the orders were carried out and the line of dismounted Confederate cavalry that stretched through the woods south of Reed's Bridge Road was thicker and stronger with the addition of Dibrell's brigade. But it might not be strong enough to turn back the Yankees, Cory thought as he found himself a good position behind a bush at the top of a small rise. He stretched out on the ground and poked the barrel of his carbine ahead of him. He took off his hat and unslung his ammunition pouch, placing it where he could reach it with less trouble than if it had still been on his hip.

The Yankees came straight on, nothing subtle about it, crashing through the brush and stalking across the clearings, never deviating from their path except to go around trees and thickets too tangled to be passable. Waves of rifle fire swept out from them as they marched forward. The Southerners returned the fire, not in volleys now but every man shooting for himself, at his own pace.

Cory soon fell into a rhythm, losing track of time as he fought. He sighted over the barrel of the carbine, squeezed off his shot, hunkered down on the rise to make himself a smaller target, reloaded, thrust the barrel forward, sighted, and fired again. He felt that he was pretty safe where he was. The rise provided good cover, and he was never exposed for more than a few seconds as he picked out a target and aimed the carbine. Bullets whined through the brush above his head, but they all missed by several feet.

In the distance, artillery began to boom. A few seconds later, shells whistled down from the sky and slammed to earth along the Confederate lines. The explosions blew down some trees and stripped the leaves off of others. Cory frowned in what he had thought was his safe haven. The rise of ground might protect him from rifle fire, but it wouldn't do him a bit of good if a Yankee shell landed nearby—or right on top of him.

That thought made him remember what had happened to John Cullum and caused a sick feeling to clutch at his stomach. He hated artillery. He didn't mind so much fighting man to man. He could harden his mind to those dangers and even disregard them much of the time. But the idea of death falling on him from above . . . that had always made Cory queasy.

More cannon fire made the ground shake, but these reports came from close by. Capt. John W. Morton Jr., Forrest's young captain of artillery, must have arrived and brought his guns into play. That might help keep the Yankee artillerymen busy, Cory told himself, so they couldn't send as much havoc flying through the air at the Confederates.

From time to time, Cory saw Forrest talking to couriers who then galloped toward the rear. The general was asking for more reinforcements, Cory decided. They were badly in need of help. Outnumbered, their only advantage lay in the fact that they were on the defensive, while the Yankees had to come to them. That meant the Union troops were more in the open, making them better targets.

Cory kept up his steady fire. He couldn't see much because of all the smoke that hung over the battlefield, and he couldn't hear anything except the constant roar of rifles and artillery fire, blending into such a clamor that surely all the imps of hell could not have produced more of an appalling racket. The noise was one of the worst things about combat, Cory had discovered. It made his ears ring and filled his head until he couldn't even hope to hear anything else. The other men were the same way, he supposed. Commands had to be given by gesture, because no one could hear the shouting unless the officers were right beside them. Even then it was hard to understand. Confusion and chaos reigned.

Cory had dug little trenches in the dirt with his toes as he pushed himself back and forth at the top of the rise. He panted and coughed as he slid along the ground and winced as rocks dug into his knees and belly. Mixed with the stink of powder smoke that coiled around him was another smell, one very similar to new-mown hay. It came from all the branches and leaves that had been stripped from the trees and bushes by flying lead. The woods in the valley of Chickamauga Creek were being scythed by cannon and rifle fire. As that sweet tang drifted to Cory's nose, he felt an almost unbearable pang of longing to be back home on the farm. The place had never looked half as beautiful to him while he was growing up, as it would right this minute.

Two officers strode up behind Cory. He saw them when he glanced over his shoulder but paid no attention to them other than to recognize them as Generals Forrest and Pegram. He fired again at the Yankees and was reloading when Forrest kicked his foot.

Cory jerked in surprise and rolled over. Forrest gestured for him to follow and then turned to stride toward the rear with Pegram. Cory scrambled to his feet and hurried after them. Off to the right, an artillery shell burst.

Forrest and Pegram went behind a stand of trees that were very close together, forming a fairly effective shield from the Union rifle fire. "Hold this position no matter what might happen, General," Forrest said to Pegram, lifting his voice to be heard over the din. Pegram nodded his understanding of the order.

Forrest then turned to Cory and gripped his arm. "We're goin' for help. There are too many of those Yankees. Our boys can't keep holdin' out against them. If anything happens to me, Lieutenant Brannon, you find whatever officer you can and tell him to get some infantry up here in a hurry."

"Yes sir," Cory managed to say. His mouth was dry, and he had trouble forming the words. His mind was spinning. Forrest had been sending couriers to the rear asking for reinforcements for the past several hours, and none of the messages had done any good. Why did the general think he would be able to accomplish more than those other men?

Of course, Forrest was going himself this time, Cory reminded himself. He was just along for the ride, a poor substitute in case Forrest's fabled luck finally ran out and a Yankee bullet or artillery shell found him. That wouldn't happen, Cory told himself. Forrest would be just fine, and the Confederate commanders in the rear would listen to him at last and rush more men to the front.

Cory dragged the back of his hand across his mouth. Things had better work out that way. He didn't want the responsibility of trying to save the Confederate right to fall on his shoulders.

The two men hurried through the trees to the spot where the horses were being held. Cory found Dash while the general swung up onto the mount he was using today. With Forrest in the lead, they started off through the woods, moving as quickly as they could around the trees. Once they reached the road, both men urged their mounts into a gallop.

"We'll find General Walker's division," Forrest flung over his shoulder. "By God, he's a fighting man! He'll give us what we need."

Cory hoped so, otherwise the Confederates were going to be driven back all the way to Chickamauga Creek. The ground that had been won the day before would be lost.

The sound of firing faded somewhat behind them. Cory's hearing, which had begun to improve as soon as he was off the front line, grew even better, and he looked to the south as he heard more firing from down there. He saw a haze of smoke hovering over the trees.

"The battle's going on to the south, too, isn't it, sir?" he asked Forrest.

The general's keen eyes had already noted the powder smoke. "I reckon so. From the looks of it, we're tryin' to push across the creek in several places. Somebody must've figured out that Bragg's gate just isn't goin' to swing the way it was supposed to."

A short time later, Forrest and Cory came within sight of a large Confederate force. As they galloped up to the officers leading it, Forrest called, "What unit is this?"

"Wilson's brigade, sir, under the command of Colonel Claudius Wilson," an officer replied as he saluted. "We're part of General Walker's division."

Forrest returned the salute. "Do I have the honor of addressin' Colonel Wilson himself?"

"You do, sir."

"In that case, Colonel, I ask that you bring your men and follow me. My boys have got their hands full with the Yankees up there on the front."

Cory thought Colonel Wilson looked hesitant for a second, but then he nodded. Though it had been couched as a request, Forrest had just given him an order, and he knew it. "Yes sir. If you'll lead the way, we'll be right behind you."

Cory heaved a sigh of relief. He hadn't wanted the responsibility of bringing the infantry to the front, and now he didn't have to. All he had to do was ride with Forrest. He was a better follower than a leader, he thought.

The infantrymen picked up the pace of their march. They had to in order to keep up with Forrest. The noise of battle grew louder as the soldiers approached the front lines. Cory hadn't missed that racket at all. He swallowed hard, knowing that soon he would be in the middle of the clash once again.

"Move your men to the left, Colonel," Forrest ordered, waving a hand to demonstrate to Wilson where he wanted the troops to go. The infantry spread out through the woods, and within minutes, the firing grew heavier as these reinforcements joined the battle.

Cory stayed close to Forrest as the general made his way toward the front lines. They could feel the ground shaking from the artillery, and bullets were clipping through the trees around them before the general halted. From the top of a wooded rise, he studied the situation and watched the progress of the battle. About fifty yards in front of him was one of Morton's batteries. The guns rocked back on their carriages and belched smoke and fire each time a shot was touched off. Cory watched their crews going about their work and knew the gunners had to be hot and sweaty. Even in the middle of winter, when everyone else was in danger of freezing, artillerymen sweated as they worked around the hot barrels and breeches of their cannons.

"It's not goin' to be enough," Forrest said after he had observed the battle for a while. "We're still in danger of the Yankees pushin' us back to the creek." Turning to Cory, he announced, "I'm goin' back for more men. They won't listen if I just send a messenger, but they'll listen to me! You stay right here, Lieutenant Brannon, so I can find you. This is where I want the next batch of reinforcements to go."

Cory acknowledged the order. Forrest wasn't taking him along this time, and that had to be because Forrest was now confident that nothing would happen to him during the ride to the rear. Cory certainly hoped that turned out to be the case.

Forrest wheeled his horse and galloped away, leaving Cory there on the edge of the battle. The general hadn't said that he couldn't take part in the fighting, only for him to stay where he was. Cory swung down from the saddle and tied Dash's reins to a nearby bush. He moved to a tree, leaned his left shoulder against the trunk, and brought the carbine to his right shoulder. He saw a group of blue-clad soldiers making their way through a clump of trees a hundred yards away and drew a bead on them. If he didn't stop them, they might be able to flank that artillery battery and capture it. None of the gun crew seemed to have noticed the threat.

Cory squeezed off a shot and saw one of the Yankees drop. Even as that sight registered on his brain, he was already ducking behind the tree to reload. Bullets thudded into the trunk. His fingers moved with practiced ease, the reloading process going fast and sure. He turned, brought the rifle up, and fired. Another man fell, and the Yankees started going to ground, their advance blunted at least for the moment.

Cory reached for his ammunition pouch. No Yankees were getting past here, he told himself.

Not unless they went over his dead body.

⊂══◆══⊃

A HALF-HOUR later, Forrest returned with another brigade of infantry, this one belonging to Gen. M. D. Ector, as Cory found out later. He was still standing beside the tree when Forrest galloped up. With sweeping gestures of his saber, the general directed the new troops to their positions between Wilson's brigade and the dismounted cavalry of Pegram and Dibrell. The Confederate line was getting quite long now, and Cory began to wonder about the possibility of a flanking maneuver on the Confederate right.

Forrest pointed his saber toward four bodies in Union uniforms that were sprawled on the ground just outside the clump of trees in the distance. "Your work, Lieutenant Brannon?"

"Yes sir," Cory said.

"You've had a busy time of it."

Cory noticed that Forrest wasn't riding the same horse he had left on. That meant he'd probably had yet another mount shot out from under him. "As have you, sir," he said.

Forrest was dismounting when the ground rocked from a blast at the nearby artillery battery. When the smoke and dust cleared, Cory saw that a Federal shell had hit one of the Confederate guns. The blast had blown off one of the carriage's wheels and toppled the cannon on its side. One member of the gun's crew was down, but the others had already sprung forward to try to right it. Forrest strode forward with Cory just behind him as the artillerymen, red of face and grunting with the strain, heaved the big gun upright again. It was tilted because of the missing wheel, but at least it could be fired now. The gunners began reloading it, one man running to the muzzle to run a water-soaked cotton swab down the barrel while the others readied a powder charge and shell.

Forrest strode up and rested a hand on the carriage's remaining wheel. One of the crew members noticed him and started to salute, but Forrest stopped him. "Never mind that. Just keep on givin' 'em hell, boys."

Cory and Forrest stood there and watched the battle, and within minutes Cory was deafened again by the frequent blasts of the cannon. If he survived this war, he might not have any hearing left at all, he thought. That would be a small price to pay for living through such carnage, though.

After a while, another officer rode up with an escort, and Forrest turned to greet him. "General Walker, sir."

So this was General Walker, the commander of the entire division, Cory told himself. In a brisk, decisive voice, Walker commented, "You've done superlative work here this morning, General Forrest, but I was thinking you might like to take some of your men and try to turn the enemy's left. I'll remain here and follow the example you've set in holding this line. The rest of the division will be here momentarily."

A faint smile tugged at Forrest's mouth. "I've been thinkin' along those lines myself, General," he said. "General Pegram's boys are out there so far on the right now it might not take much to get them around the corner or even into the Yankees' rear."

Walker nodded. "Good luck to you, General."

Forrest headed for his horse. He didn't have to glance around and tell Cory to go with him. Cory was already beside him, leading Dash.

Within minutes, they were galloping toward the Confederate right. Forrest found General Ector's infantry first and ordered them to shift even farther in that direction. As that move began to take place, Forrest rode on and conveyed similar orders to Generals Pegram and Dibrell. With the Confederate right extended, they began driving forward toward a rise where several cannons and a brigade of infantry marked the extreme left of the Federal line.

These Yankees hadn't faced much action during the day, but they had plenty of trouble right in front of them now. The cannons began to roar and volleys rang out from the infantry as Ector's infantry and Forrest's dismounted cavalry started through the trees, firing as they came on toward the rise.

Forrest might have intended for Cory to stay with him, but Cory didn't know. Without waiting for orders, he slipped out of the saddle and started forward with the other men, firing then reloading his carbine as he trotted through the brush and weaved around trees. Shadows slid across his face as he crossed in and out of the areas where sunlight penetrated the thick foliage. A Rebel yell welled from his throat and joined the thousands of others that rose from the charging Confederates. Everything was instinct now, patterns of light and darkness, dreadful noise, the bite in the nose of powder smoke, the thundering of artillery and his own heartbeat. Cory fought on, even when it became obvious the charge wasn't going to be able to reach the top of the hill. The Yankees were pouring too much fire down into them.

Cory saw a Federal battery no more than thirty yards in front of him. He slapped the breech closed on his carbine, cocked the hammer, thumbed a cap onto the nipple, and raised the gun. He fired at the same instant that one of the cannons roared. Cory was peering over the barrel of his carbine directly into the muzzle of the cannon. He saw the flame and the billowing smoke—

Then he was falling, his foot catching on a tree root, and he sensed as much as felt or heard the tremendous disturbance in the air only inches above his head. That cannonball would have smashed the life from him if he hadn't fallen. He lay on his face for several seconds, the carbine under him and digging painfully into his belly, and he trembled from the reaction to this latest brush with death. Somewhere along the front of the Confederate line, officers were shouting for the men to fall back. The flank attack had failed. Forrest had not been able to turn the corner.

Still on his belly, Cory began crawling backward. He didn't try to reload this time. He just wanted to get out of there. There was no shame to the feeling. It wasn't cowardice but common sense that made him and the other cavalrymen retreat. Cory knew they had already accomplished a great deal today. The Yankees had been poised to sweep around the Confederate right in a flanking move of their own that would have allowed them to destroy Bragg's army if it had succeeded. Forrest and Cory and all the other men with them had prevented that and saved the Army of Tennessee, at least for one more day. They could be proud of that.

But pride would come later. Right now, Cory just wanted to get out of the hail of lead that was still crashing all around him.

⌐━━◆━━⌐

IT HAD been a long day for everyone in the valley of Chicka-mauga Creek, not just for Forrest and the Yankees who opposed him. That morning, the armies had been spread out facing each other, their lines at least four miles long. Once the fighting had gotten under way on the Confederate right and the Union left, it spread down the valley as the lines of blue and gray surged back and forth. Patrick Cleburne, a fiery Irishman . . . John Bell Hood, a Kentuckian who led Texans . . . Leonidas Polk, an Episcopalian bishop as well as a general . . . these and dozens of other Confederate commanders sent their men forward into battle, across La Fayette Road, across the stream the Cherokees had dubbed "River of Blood."

It lived up to its name today.

Only the fall of night brought an end to the battle. And even as dusk was settling over the rugged landscape, there was one last burst of noise as Cleburne's men launched an attack on the Union left that did not end until full darkness made it impossible to continue fighting.

The daylong struggle had settled nothing. Advances had been made and lost on both sides. The Army of the Cumberland and the Army of Tennessee still sat there, separated by mere yards, as the world seemed to hold its breath. Morning would bring more strife. Everyone knew that.

But until then, the soldiers could sit and rest. And they listened to the cries of the wounded and dying who had left their blood on the ground and in the waters of Chickamauga Creek.

Chapter Nineteen

CORY WAS STILL TREMBLING that night. He didn't know if it was from the fury of the battle he had endured that day, or the fact that a cold wind now blew over the valley. There was nothing figurative about that chill. It was real, and it reached all the way into a man's bones and rattled them.

The cavalry was camped once more along the road that led to Reed's Bridge. That road was strategically vital, because it ran eventually to Ringgold, where the thousands of troops General Longstreet had brought from Virginia were still arriving, trainload after trainload. Those soldiers would be important on Sunday, when the fighting resumed. They would be fresh and ready to go, rather than exhausted by two days of arduous combat. With any luck, they might give the edge to the Confederates. Cory had no idea how many men the Yankees had, but with all the reinforcements that had been pouring in on the Confederate side, the numbers had to be drawing closer to even. Before it was over, they might even outnumber the Yankees, he mused, though a week earlier he would not have believed that was possible.

He stretched out under a tree—he didn't think it was the same tree under which he had slept the night before, but it might have been—and tried to doze off. His teeth were chattering, though, and that helped keep him awake. So did the moans and cries of the wounded. The surgeons in the field hospitals were working as fast as they could, but there was only so much they could do. Shattered, amputated arms and legs piled up outside the hospital tents, grisly monuments to the day's violence. And still the wretched sounds went on.

Cory hugged himself, trying to will the cold to go away so he could sleep. His belly cramped. He'd had a cup of coffee and a piece of jerky for supper. His appetite had deserted him again. He wished he were with Lucille. He wished he were home. He

317

wished he had a drink, or a pipe to smoke, or anything that might take away the chill and the riot of bloody images that flickered through his brain in an endless waking nightmare.

Somehow, in the midst of all that, he dozed off. He woke up surprised that he had slept at all.

He pushed himself to his feet, relieved himself behind a bush, then went looking for General Forrest. He found the general engaged in a council of war with Pegram, Dibrell, Wilson, Ector, and several other high-ranking officers, none of whom Cory recognized. The commanders of the entire Confederate right were gathered here this morning, he told himself.

As he listened to the conversation among the men, Cory heard the frustration in their voices and realized that no orders had arrived from General Bragg as to what they were supposed to do this morning. One of the generals said in disgust, "He's left us out here on the right end to swing in the wind."

Forrest chuckled. "Always figured a gallows might be my destiny. Well, absent any orders to the contrary, I'm pushin' on. My scouts tell me there's a church up yonder, not far from where this road runs into the La Fayette road. I'm thinkin' it'd make a good headquarters once we run the Yankees off."

Cory frowned a little when he heard that. Not because of Forrest's intention to advance; that was all they could do. But he had signed on with the Army of Tennessee to be a scout himself, and so far in this campaign he had done precious little scouting. Instead, Forrest had taken to keeping Cory close by in case he needed him for some special task, and when he wasn't doing that, he was fighting with the rest of the dismounted cavalry as an infantryman. The failed charge late in the afternoon of the day before reminded him all too much of the futile attempts to take the Hornet's Nest at Shiloh. Cory didn't want to go through that again if he could avoid it.

So he went up to Forrest as soon as he had the chance. "General, how about if I go take a look around, see what the Yankees are up to this morning."

Forrest grinned at him. "Gettin' a little restless, Lieutenant Brannon?"

"I guess so, sir. I've always been fiddle-footed."

"Go ahead," Forrest told him with a nod.

Cory found Dash and got a saddle on him, then rode east through the woods, taking it slow and easy. The cold wind of the night before had died down to a chilly breeze, but it brought with it whiffs of wood smoke. Cory knew that smell came from the campfires of the Union army.

He didn't stop until he heard the ringing sound of axes biting into tree trunks. If the Yankees were felling trees, it could only mean one thing: They were erecting breastworks and other fortifications in expectation of a Confederate attack. They were digging in instead of getting ready to run. Rooting them out would be a hard, bloody business.

Cory dismounted and advanced on foot. He parted some brush and peered across the valley toward the foot of the long ridge behind it. Missionary Ridge, he had heard someone call it. Some of the Yankees probably considered themselves missionaries, he thought bitterly, because they had invaded the South to bring their own version of the gospel, the bloody gospel according to John Brown, to the "heathen" Confederates, delivering their message with fire and lead. What a waste, Cory thought. What a godawful, bloody waste.

He put those thoughts out of his head and concentrated on studying the Federal forces aligned along the La Fayette road. His field glasses showed him the church of which Forrest had spoken. Across the road from it was a small, neat house, probably where the preacher lived. Chances were, the church and the house wouldn't be that pristine when this day was over. And even though it was Sunday, there wouldn't be any psalm-singing going on in the chapel.

Cory backed away, mounted up, and rode back toward Forrest's position. Before he got there, he encountered the general, moving forward at the head of the cavalry. Cory told him what he had seen, and Forrest nodded, unsurprised by the news that the Yankees were getting ready to defend their positions.

"General George Thomas is in command over there," Forrest said. "He's a man who won't run."

"Yes sir," Cory agreed, although he didn't know the Yankee general or anything about him. Forrest seemed impressed by Thomas, and that was good enough for Cory.

Forrest turned in his saddle and said to one of his staff, "We'll be engaged soon, no doubt. Pass the word."

The cavalry moved forward again. Within minutes, the Federals were sighted up ahead, and the order went back for the men to dismount and advance with rifles and carbines at the ready. Cory did so, along with several thousand others. Off to the left, the infantry that had reinforced Forrest's cavalry the day before was still with him, stretching out through the woods in a line that surely would have been quite impressive if it had been more visible. The thick growth made friend as well as foe difficult to see and fully appreciate, though. This was going to be more like thousands of small battles rather than one large one, Cory thought as he tightened his hands on his carbine.

He walked in as steady a pace as possible through the woods, men close on either side of him. Rifles began to bark up ahead. Cory started to lift the carbine and then thought better of it and lowered the weapon. He couldn't see the enemy well enough. He needed to get closer.

Artillery roared, and a tree to Cory's right came crashing down as a cannonball splintered its trunk. More shells burst around the advancing cavalrymen, and the rifle fire grew heavier. The Confederates began to return that fire now, and the cannons that had been brought up by Captains Morton and Amariah L. Huggins spoke in a deep-throated bellow to the rear, flinging their deadly missiles over the heads of the advancing riflemen. Cory finally got a good look at a Union soldier about seventy-five yards away from him. In one smooth movement, he brought the carbine to his shoulder, aimed, and fired. The Yankee spun around and fell.

Cory didn't know if the man had cried out when he was hit or not. He couldn't hear anything over the cacophony of artillery and rifle fire. Once these trees had been full of birds instead of bullets, he thought, and their songs had filled the air.

The thought was fleeting. After that there was no time for anything except reloading and firing and trying to stay alive as he pushed forward through the trees and brush. Branches clawed at his face and hands, and creepers tangled around his feet and legs. The very foliage itself was trying to hold him back, but he would not be denied. Cory's heart hammered inside his chest like a mad thing trying to get out, but he kept moving forward.

Time had no meaning in a situation like that. Cory never knew for sure how long it took Forrest's men and the infantry fighting alongside them to push their way through the woods to the La Fayette road. But he knew when they broke out into the cleared space along the road. For the second time today he saw the church, and his guess was proven correct. The whitewashed sanctuary showed damage from bullets and artillery shells. But it was still standing, and it was surrounded by gray-clad troops who surged on across the road and past the house to a small spring. Many of the men fell to their knees to drink from the little pond. Nothing made a man more thirsty than breathing powder smoke for a couple of hours.

Forrest came trotting along the road on horseback. He gave Cory a curt nod, but Cory wasn't sure the general really took much notice of him. He could tell that the wheels of Forrest's brain were spinning as he tried to figure out where he could hit the Yankees next.

General Pegram solved that problem. He rode up in a hurry, and Cory heard him explain to Forrest that a large force of Federal troops had been spotted moving down the Rossville road from the direction of Chattanooga.

"That'll be the Yankee reserve," Forrest said. He looked off toward the south, where a great deal of firing could now be heard. "Our boys are pushin' across. We can't let that reserve get thrown in as reinforcements." He nodded as he came to a decision. "General, face your men to the north and throw them across the road as a barrier to the Yankees. I'll find Dibrell and Ector and Wilson and have them add their men to yours as soon as possible."

Pegram snapped a salute, wheeled his horse, and galloped off to engage the enemy.

Forrest looked around, and his eyes fell on Cory. "Lieutenant Brannon!"

Cory answered the summons quickly and came running to the general's side.

"Have you seen General Dibrell?"

"No sir. Not since earlier this morning."

"You heard what I just told General Pegram?"

"Yes sir."

"Find Dibrell," Forrest said. "Have him get his boys in position as soon as he can. I'm not goin' to let those Yankees get by us! I expect our people down along the creek have enough to do right now without throwin' any more Yankees into the fight."

"I expect you're right, sir," Cory said.

GENERAL BRAGG'S orders, as they had every day of this battle so far, called for a series of attacks, starting with the Confederate right and proceeding with one unit after another down the line to the left. The first action was to begin at dawn.

But dawn had come and gone, and miscommunication and garbled orders had hampered the Confederate effort, just as had happened on the past two days. Despite that, the battle had finally gotten under way, with a division under Gen. Frank Cheatham making a strong push against the Union lines.

Cheatham was reinforced by units commanded by Generals Cleburne, Stewart, and Polk. The woods were filled with fighting as the Yankees tried to hold on. Their line bent but failed to break. More Confederate troops were hurled against them, and still they held. It was beginning to look as if the Federals were going to be able to stop the Confederate advance.

But the men who had come to this corner of Georgia from Virginia with Gen. James Longstreet were still moving into position, including a division led by Gen. John Bell Hood. Some of these men had fought the day before, but many of them were fresh and unbloodied, ready to throw themselves into battle when the word came from their commander. Instead of a wide front, Longstreet arranged his men into a narrow but deep column. When the time came, that column would smash into the Federal line like a giant arrow, driving through it like a wedge.

All the Confederates needed was the right moment to strike—and for the reinforcements that were on their way to the Yankees to be stopped somehow.

CORY DIDN'T look for his horse. Dash was back on the other side of the woods with the rest of the cavalry mounts, more than a mile away. Instead, he hurried along the road on foot until he spotted General Dibrell. Cory had known the man since the cavalry raid into West Tennessee the past winter, so he didn't hesitate to call out to the general.

Dibrell was on horseback. He turned and saw Cory hurrying toward him. "Lieutenant Brannon, what is it?"

"Compliments from General Forrest, sir. He says to tell you that the Yankee reserve is moving down the road toward us, and he intends to stop them. He's already sent General Pegram up there, and he wants you to follow as quickly as possible."

Without hesitation, Dibrell nodded. He knew that Forrest had a great deal of faith in Cory and that his information was trustworthy. Tightening his grip on the reins, he said, "I'm on my way. What about the infantry?"

"They're to move up and join the fight, too."

"I'll see that they get the word."

Dibrell galloped off to get his troops moving in the right direction. Cory was left behind. He stood at the edge of the road and leaned on the butt of his carbine for a moment, gripping the barrel. He was exhausted, but he tried not to let himself feel his fatigue. He would have liked to find another tree somewhere and rest under it, but he couldn't do that. Not while the battle was still going on.

He took a deep breath, hefted his carbine, and started trudging north along the road. After a few yards his steps grew longer and faster, and it was only a moment later that he broke into a trot. He heard rifle fire up ahead, and he hurried toward the sound of the guns.

❦

GEN. WILLIAM ROSECRANS had been monitoring the progress of the battle all morning from his headquarters behind the right end of the Federal line. Around midday, one of his subordinates informed him that a gap had appeared in the middle of the line, presumably where a brigade had been shifted north to reinforce General Thomas, who had his hands full on the Union left. Rosecrans had been very slow to advance on Chattanooga in the first place, but now, faced with potential disaster, he responded without hesitation. He ordered the division under Gen. Thomas J. Wood to move north and close up that gap.

Only there was no gap. The Federal division that was supposed to be there still was, but the thick undergrowth and trees concealed them. However, when Wood followed Rosecrans's order and shifted his troops, that movement *created* an opening in the Union line, the very problem that Rosecrans had been trying to remedy.

And at that moment, in a stroke of luck that for once favored the Confederacy, Longstreet sent his massive column forward to the attack—at the exact spot vacated by Wood's division.

Three divisions of yelling, sharpshooting devils in gray and butternut came crashing out of the woods, finding little or no opposition. Twenty-three thousand men, all of them looking for an enemy, moved across the La Fayette road and into the cleared fields of a farm beyond. They took fire from the flanks, men stumbling and going down in the stubble of the fields as their cries died on their lips, but there were no Yankees ahead of them to stop the charge. Almost before they knew what was happening, the divisions of John Bell Hood, Bushrod Johnson, and Joseph B. Kershaw had split the Federal army and found themselves in the enemy's rear.

It was chaos, but glorious chaos. After fighting in dark woods for days, these men were in the sunlight again, and most important of all, they were winning. They swept on, overrunning and capturing Yankee artillery batteries, routing whole brigades of riflemen, turning gradually to the right so that they could drive up the west side of the valley, and pushing all the opposition before them. Shouts of victory rang from Confederate throats.

But there was still fighting to do. Hood was shot off his horse and suffered a bad leg wound. Already weakened by the limited use of his wounded arm, the fierce Kentuckian was lost for the rest of this battle, grabbed up by his men and carried to the rear for medical attention.

All up and down the line, Federal resistance crumpled. This was no orderly retreat. In a scene eerily reminiscent of what had happened in Virginia, along the stream called Bull Run, the Yankees broke and ran, many of them dropping their rifles so they could flee even more quickly. For two days, they had fought with a stubbornness that promised victory, only to see that chance snatched away by happenstance.

Not all the Yankees were running, however. Thomas was able to rally his men and make a stand on a small bluff that protruded from Missionary Ridge. This height was known as Horseshoe Ridge, and it ended in a slightly higher elevation called Snodgrass Hill. Thomas intended to hold here as long as he could . . . and still, perhaps, turn the tide of battle.

CORY FOUND Forrest's dismounted cavalry already engaged with the Yankee reserve forces when he arrived along with the rest of Dibrell's men. The infantry under Ector and Wilson was coming up quickly behind.

Forrest had placed all his artillery in a line across the road, facing north. Volley after volley roared out from those cannons, sending such a storm of shell and canister and shot up the road that trying to advance into it would be pure suicide. Therefore the Yankees had to try to go around, and when they did that, they found the Confederate cavalrymen ready to fight them on foot.

As Cory approached the front, he saw Forrest riding back and forth in plain sight, as ever daring the gods of war to strike him down. Cory wasn't sure, but he thought Forrest was mounted on yet another horse. How many could he have shot out from under him without suffering serious injury? Cory knew that Forrest wasn't invulnerable—he had seen the general wounded twice and heard stories of other incidents in which Forrest was hurt—but some sort of special providence did seem to shield him from any mortal wounds.

Gardenhire was wrong about Forrest's luck rubbing off, though, Cory thought. The number of horses he'd had killed while riding them was proof enough of that.

Cory moved up closer to the front lines and saw where a couple of men had fallen. He stepped into that gap and raised his carbine, which was loaded and ready to fire. The Yankees were no more than fifty yards away. Cory settled his sights on one of them and pulled the trigger. The man kept coming, so he knew he had missed. He started to reload.

At a moment such as this, a man's every thought could be his last. Cory knew that. His fingers handled the reloading without conscious effort while his mind turned to Lucille. He seemed to see her as she had been the first time he had ever laid eyes on her, as she stepped from the *Missouri Zephyr* onto the docks at New Madrid. She was the loveliest woman he had ever seen, with a fresh beauty that he would not have dreamed possible. He had known at that instant he was in love with her, though he never thought then that he could ever do anything about it. Later, fate had brought them together, but Cory had never forgotten his first sight of her.

The carbine kicked hard against his shoulder as it threw its .58-caliber ball at the enemy. He hadn't been aware of lifting the weapon, aiming, and squeezing the trigger. But now, as the pleasant memories vanished, he saw one of the Yankees fall. This shot had found its target.

Cory wondered what that man across the way had been thinking an instant earlier, just before he died.

He started reloading again. As he did so, something slashed across his upper left arm. Though the impact was glancing, it was enough to spin him around and knock him off his feet. He landed on his left side, jarring the wounded arm against the ground. More pain shot through him, and then the arm began to go numb as he tried to push himself up. He looked down and saw the blood on his sleeve. There was quite a bit of it, and the stain was spreading down toward his elbow.

Cory couldn't tell how badly he was hit, and there was no time to examine the wound. He had dropped the carbine when he fell. Now he searched for it, saw it lying on the ground a couple of feet away, and reached for it with his good hand. He closed his fingers over the stock and pulled it toward him.

Sitting cross-legged on the ground with the carbine across his lap, Cory finished reloading it. He tried to lift it one-handed, but the weapon was too heavy. He forced the muscles in his left arm to work. He had only thought the arm was numb. Now he had to grit his teeth against the pain as he used both hands to raise the carbine.

He fired, and the recoil almost knocked him over backward. His head was spinning, and he felt light, as if he might float up off the ground. He knew that was crazy, knew the only reason he felt that way was because he had lost quite a bit of blood. Using the carbine as a crutch, he struggled to his feet and balanced there for a second, blinking against the smoke that blew into his eyes. Slowly, he turned his head, looking first one way and then the other. The line of his fellow soldiers stretched to the road and the artillery on the right, and as far as Cory could see to the left. Smoke from the rifles and the cannons billowed over the battlefield, drifting forward until it mingled with the smoke from the Union guns. It was funny, Cory thought, that no matter which side it came from, the powder smoke looked the same, and once the clouds of it had swirled together, no one would ever be able to tell any difference again.

Blood was pretty much the same way, he realized, and then he thought again of Lucille and didn't even feel himself falling into the black void that claimed him.

FOR TWO hours in the middle of the day on Sunday, September 20, 1863, forces under the command of Gen. Nathan Bedford Forrest held back the reserve troops trying to come to the aid of Gen. George H. Thomas. Finally, the Yankees swung sharply to their right, toward Missionary Ridge, and were able to get around Forrest. But in the time the reserves had been delayed, Thomas had lost any chance of rallying enough men to launch a counterattack on the Confederates. All he could hope to do now was hold his position until nightfall and then retreat toward Chattanooga, as most of the rest of the Army of the Cumberland had already done. Indeed, orders came from General Rosecrans, who had already withdrawn to Chattanooga, to abandon Snodgrass Hill and Horseshoe Ridge. Thomas ignored them and stayed where he was.

CORY DIDN'T have to worry about his arm being numb when he woke up as dusk was settling over the valley. The arm hurt like blazes. But he was aware that a bandage was wrapped tightly around it, so he knew he had been taken to one of the field hospitals. He tried to take inventory of the rest of his body to see if he was injured anywhere else. Other than some aches and bruises, he seemed to be all right. He lifted his head from the ground where he was lying and looked around.

He was under a tree. In this thickly wooded landscape, it was difficult to be anywhere else. A tent was set up not far away, and judging by the screams he heard coming from it, that was the field hospital. The surgeons were sawing off mangled arms and legs, often when the patient hadn't had even a slug of whiskey to help fight the pain.

Whiskey sounded good to Cory right now, but water sounded even better. He sat up, braced his back against the tree trunk, and worked his way to his feet. A wave of dizziness hit him. He stood there and leaned against the tree until it had passed.

"Brannon!"

The voice was familiar, but Cory couldn't place it right away. He turned and saw a young officer hurrying toward him. The man's face was streaked with grime from the powder smoke that still hung in the air, but he wasn't wounded. In the gathering dusk, the man had to come closer before Cory recognized him.

"Gardenhire?" Cory's voice came out as a croak. His mouth was so dry it would barely work.

The Tennessean laughed. "We both came through the battle. I told you that you had some of General Forrest's luck, and I must've gotten some from you." He clasped Cory's arm to steady him as Cory swayed a little. "Are you hurt bad?"

Cory shook his head. "I don't think so." He moved his left arm to see if it worked. The muscles screamed a protest, but they obeyed his commands. "The bone's not broken. Reckon a bullet just grazed me."

"You'll be all right, then."

"Unless I get the blood poisoning." Gardenhire frowned at him, and Cory gave a hollow laugh. He went on, "What about the battle?" He had been listening for the sound of guns, but all he heard were scattered shots.

"A few of the Yankees held out all afternoon on a hill north of here. Snodgrass Hill, I think it's called. But they pulled back when it started to get dark." Gardenhire paused then said warily, "Listen . . ."

Cory did. At first he couldn't identify what he was hearing in the distance, but then he realized it was the sound of a Rebel yell coming from countless men.

It was the sound of victory.

The noise spread, and Cory forgot about how bad his arm hurt. He and Gardenhire joined in the yelping and howling as the Southerners celebrated their triumph. The Union army had chased them out of Chattanooga and thought to fall on them here along Chickamauga Creek and destroy them. But now it was the Yankees who were running away with their tails tucked between their legs. Vicksburg had fallen, and Gettysburg had been a disaster, but by God, they had whipped Abe Lincoln's hirelings here at Chickamauga!

The Rebel yells echoed down the valley for a long time, until well after night had fallen.

Chapter Twenty

D ESPITE HIS UNCERTAINTY OVER how Henry's marriage to Polly Ebersole would work out, Mac enjoyed his visit home in September. He could only stay away for a couple of days, though, before he needed to return to Camp von Borcke and report to Fitz Lee. He hugged his mother and sister, saying to Cordelia, "I've told you where the camp is. If you need me, send word there right away. If you have to, get on a horse and come get me yourself." He lowered his voice even more so that Abigail, who was standing on the porch, wouldn't be able to hear. "But be sure to carry a pistol with you if you ride off the farm. It might be a good idea to keep one close at hand all the time."

"You don't think the Yankees will come here, do you, Mac?" Cordelia asked.

"They haven't hesitated at going anywhere else they want to down here. Just remember that, Cordelia."

She nodded, looking solemn and even a little frightened. That was good, Mac told himself. These days, the smart thing was to be frightened, because there was a hell of a lot of evil loose in the Confederacy.

He swung up onto the stallion, waved to Abigail and Cordelia, and heeled the horse into a lope that carried him away down the lane. Mac didn't look back. He was afraid that the sight of the farm, looking much as it had before all this insanity began, might be too much for him to bear.

When he got back to Camp von Borcke later that day, he rode straight to Lee's tent. The general was sitting on a stool in front of the tent with several aides gathered around him. Everyone seemed to be in a good mood. Lee greeted Mac with a grin and an upraised hand.

"Ah, the return of the prodigal," Lee said. "Welcome back, Captain Brannon."

"Thank you, sir," Mac said as he dismounted and handed the stallion's reins to an orderly. "It's good to be back." That was a lie, but not too much of one. When he was with the cavalry, he missed the love and stability of farm and family. When he was on the farm, he missed the freedom and excitement of the cavalry.

"Pull up a stool," Lee went on, gesturing for Mac to join him. "There have been some changes since you left."

"Really, sir?" Mac sat down and removed his kepi.

"Indeed." Lee's grin broadened. "You're now an aide to Major General Fitzhugh Lee, commanding the Second Division, Virginia Cavalry."

Mac was impressed but not surprised. It had been rumored that General Stuart was going to reorganize his cavalry in the wake of the failed campaign into Pennsylvania. As one of Stuart's favorites, not to mention a highly capable officer, Fitz Lee had been in line for a promotion and an important command. "Congratulations, sir," Mac said. "Who's going to command the First Division?"

"Wade Hampton, as soon as he's recovered from his Gettysburg wound. He's a major general now, too. Until then, General Stuart will command General Hampton's division."

Mac nodded. Hampton was not only an excellent field commander, he was as morally upright a man as Mac had ever met.

Lee looked more solemn as he went on, "General Stuart has retained the rank of major general, so Hampton and I equal him in rank, but we are subordinate by our dates of rank and still under his command."

Mac imagined that arrangement might prove to be a little awkward over time. Stuart had been Fitz Lee's mentor for so long that it was unlikely Lee would ever become restless under Stuart's command, but the same could not be said of the North Carolinian, Wade Hampton. Hampton would do his duty, though, whatever it was. Mac had no doubt of that.

Lee put his hands on his knees and pushed himself to his feet. "I was just telling the boys to get ready for a review. We're going to be putting them on every day for a while, Beauty says, until we get used to the reorganization."

That sounded like a good idea to Mac. Besides, he knew how much Stuart loved to assemble his troops and have them pass in review. It was always a grand spectacle, and there was nothing Jeb Stuart loved more than spectacle.

For the next few days, that was the routine. The cavalrymen drilled and cared for their horses and got some rest after the rigors of the summer they had just gone through.

Then, early in the morning of September 13, Stuart called Lee to his tent for a conference. As a member of Lee's staff, Mac accompanied his friend and mentor. It was a glorious dawn, with a breeze whipping the colorful flags and pennants that flew over Stuart's headquarters.

Stuart sat his visitors down on camp chairs and stools and introduced a nervous-looking man who stood beside him as one of the surgeons attached to the cavalry. Mac had recognized the man's face but didn't know his name.

"The doctor has been home on leave," Stuart explained. "Our sympathy goes out to him in the unfortunate passing of his wife."

Murmurs of agreement came from the assembled officers.

"He has brought us important news, however," Stuart continued. "It seems that the enemy has become quite active again on the other side of the Rappahannock. You witnessed a great deal of troop movement from this side of the river, did you not, Doctor?"

The surgeon nodded. Accustomed to spending his time in field hospitals, the man was clearly uncomfortable at being part of a military strategy meeting. He affirmed Stuart's presentation of the facts.

Stuart went on, "Having been alerted to this situation, I sent scouts up to the Rappahannock this morning, and they just reported to me moments ago that the Yankees have crossed the river with two divisions of cavalry supported by infantry and artillery."

Mac tensed. Things had been quiet since the return from Gettysburg as both armies tried to recover from that terrible clash. Now it looked as if the war was about to heat up again.

"I suspect," Stuart continued, "General Meade is aware somehow that General Longstreet's corps have departed for Georgia to reinforce the Army of Tennessee. He thinks us to be undermanned. I've already ordered our wagons to the rear. Gentlemen, get your troops ready to move as soon as possible. We're falling back to the Rapidan River."

It was all Mac could do not to stare in disbelief. Stuart was retreating? Beauty himself, the Cavalier of the Saddle?

Something else troubled Mac even more. If the cavalry pulled back to the Rapidan, that would leave Culpeper County unprotected. If the Yankees swept through here, destroying everything in their path, the Brannon farm and everyone on it would be in danger.

Now that Stuart had issued his orders, he dismissed the meeting, and the officers returned to their commands to begin preparations for the movement. As Mac strode along with Fitz Lee, the general said, "I know what's wrong, Mac. You're worried about your family."

"Yes sir," Mac said with a nod.

"No one can blame you for that. We have our duty to carry out, though, and I can't spare you, even for long enough to ride over to the farm and warn them." Lee clapped a hand on Mac's shoulder. "I'm sure they'll be all right. The Yankees aren't monsters, you know. They don't make war on civilians."

"No sir." *At least not intentionally*, Mac added to himself.

But when the cannons began to roar and the bullets started to fly, intentions didn't mean anything. Anyone caught in the way of the war stood a good chance of dying.

He prayed that Cordelia remembered everything he had told her.

WITH A bucket in each hand, Cordelia moved from the well toward the house. The sound of hoof beats came to her ears, and she stopped and looked over her shoulder toward the lane that led to the house. A couple of hundred yards away, dust rose in the air. That much dust had to come from quite a few riders.

The handles of the buckets slipped out of her hands, and water splashed on the ground as the buckets fell. "Henry!" Cordelia called as she broke into a run toward the house. "Ma!"

Those were Confederates coming up the lane, she told herself, trying to calm her fears. But she didn't believe it, not really. The riders wouldn't be coming so fast if they were friendly.

The front door slammed open and Henry appeared, clutching a rifle in his right hand. He had surprised Cordelia and Abigail a little by bringing Polly back here with him to live after the wedding, but the decision hadn't come as too much of a shock. Considering how Duncan Ebersole felt about the marriage, it would have been too much to expect for him to offer a home to his daughter and her unwanted and despised husband.

"What is it?" Henry asked as his sister reached the steps. "What's wrong?"

"Riders coming," Cordelia explained. She came up onto the porch and turned to point along the lane. With her other hand, she reached for the pistol that was always in the pocket of her dress these days, as Mac had suggested before he left.

"Probably just some Confederate cavalry," Henry said.

Cordelia shook her head. "I don't think so."

"There's no reason to think it's Yankees."

"No reason to think it's not," Cordelia said. "We don't know what's happening these days. We don't even know where Mac is."

A couple of weeks had passed since Mac had returned to his unit. In that time they hadn't heard from him, nor had they been into Culpeper to hear anything about what was going on with the war. Coping with the fall harvest had kept everyone on the farm busy, even Polly, who was trying to pitch in and help as much as Henry would let her. He wouldn't allow her to do much, though, saying that her delicate condition made it unwise for her to work.

Henry put both hands on the rifle, and his fingers tightened as he stared at the approaching dust. "You're right," he said, his voice low. "Get in the house."

Cordelia pulled the pistol from her pocket. "I will do no such thing."

"Cordelia . . ."

The door opened again, and Abigail stepped onto the porch. She carried the old shotgun. Polly appeared in the doorway behind her, looking frightened. "Henry, what is it?" she asked.

"Damn it all! You women, get in the house!" Henry burst out. "I'll handle this."

"No," Abigail snapped. "Polly, you come out here and take Henry's rifle."

Henry stared at her. "Ma, have you gone crazy?"

"Polly, do as I say. Henry, give her the rifle and go inside. Stay out of sight." Abigail's tone was brisk and businesslike, but Cordelia could see the fear lurking in her mother's eyes. "You're a young man of military age," she went on. "If that's a Yankee patrol, they might try to arrest you, but they won't bother three women who are alone on a farm."

Cordelia saw Henry swallow and thought he was going to argue, but what Abigail said made sense. "What if they search the house?" he asked.

"Hide in the root cellar," Polly suggested as she came onto the porch. "Please, Henry, hurry. Do what your mother says."

With a muttered curse, Henry thrust the rifle into Polly's hands and then jerked the door open. He ran into the house. A moment later, Cordelia heard the rear door open and close and knew Henry had made it to the back of the house where the entrance to the root cellar was located. She couldn't hear anything else because the clatter of hoof beats had grown too loud.

The riders swept into the yard, at least twenty of them, Cordelia estimated. Even through the roiling clouds of dust, she could see their blue uniforms shining in the sun as they brought their mounts to a halt. After all these years of hearing about the Yankees, now she was seeing some of them face to face.

She was terrified.

She tried not to show it, however. A glance at her mother told her that Abigail was calm, even a little defiant as she stepped to the edge of the porch. Cordelia stayed where she was, a little behind Abigail, and Polly drew up even with her on Abigail's other side. Polly was even more pale than usual, and her features were drawn tight. Cordelia suspected she looked about the same way.

"What do you want?" Abigail said in a loud, unafraid voice, addressing the question to the man who sat his horse slightly in the lead of the other riders. He was young, with tanned, regular features and brown hair under his black hat. Cordelia thought the insignia on his uniform meant he was a captain. He rode a mouse-colored horse with a darker stripe down its back.

The captain touched a finger to the brim of his headgear. "Good afternoon, ma'am. Please don't worry. We don't mean you any harm."

"You Yankees harm us just by being here," Abigail said. "State your business and then get off my land."

A grin tugged at the corners of the young officer's mouth. He was amused by Abigail's attitude but was trying not to show it.

"Yes, ma'am," he said. "We're on a scoutin' and foragin' expedition. If you have any fresh eggs, we'd be much obliged if you were willin' to share a few of 'em."

There was something strange about the officer's voice, Cordelia thought. It had a definite drawl to it, but not enough to make him sound like a Southerner. There was a sort of twang, too, which was barely discernible. Of one thing, however, she was sure: This man didn't sound like any Yankee she had ever heard before.

"That's all you want?" Abigail said. "Eggs?"

The captain nodded. "Yes, ma'am."

"You're not going to steal what little stock we have left and burn our house to the ground?"

The officer looked genuinely shocked. "Now, why in tarnation would we do that?"

"Because you're Yankees!" Abigail practically spat the words at him.

Cordelia wanted to tell her mother to stop. This man appeared to harbor no ill will toward them, and it was foolish to bait him like that. Some of the other Yankee cavalrymen were beginning to look angry and impatient.

The captain, though, just grinned. "I'm on the side of the Union, ma'am, but I hail from Texas," he said. "The Rio Grande country, to be precise. So I don't reckon I'm too much of a Yankee."

Abigail frowned. "You just want eggs?"

"Yes, ma'am."

"We still have a couple of laying hens . . . I suppose it wouldn't hurt. The nests are out there in the chicken house. I'd appreciate it if your men would leave a few eggs for us."

The captain looked at one of the other riders. "You hear that, Sergeant?"

"Yes sir, Cap'n." The sergeant jerked his head toward the chicken house. "Curry, Tompkins, you go gather them eggs."

"Do we bring the chickens with us, Cap'n Pryor?" one of the Yankee soldiers asked. "It'd sure be nice to have a couple of layin' hens."

"You'd have to bring the rooster, too," the captain pointed out, still grinning. "No, leave the hens. Just get some eggs."

In a low voice, the sergeant asked, "Reckon we ought to search the place, Cap'n? Make sure there's no Johnny Rebs hidin' here?"

Before answering, the captain turned back to the three women on the porch and studied them for a moment. Then he shook his head. "I don't think that'll be necessary, Sergeant. I doubt if a brigade of Jeb Stuart's cavalry is hidin' in the parlor."

Cordelia took a deep breath and decided to indulge her curiosity and venture a question. "Captain?"

He looked at her. "Ma'am?"

"Can you tell us what's happening? With the war, I mean."

The grin disappeared, and the young man's tanned face became more solemn. He leaned forward in the saddle and thumbed his hat to the back of his head. "We crossed the Rappahannock about a week ago, and General Stuart has pulled back down to the Rapidan. There wasn't any fightin', if that's what you're worried about. We grabbed up a few artillery pieces, but that's all."

"Cap'n," the sergeant said, "I ain't sure it's a good idea to be talkin' about military matters with these civilians."

The Texan ignored the warning. "You have kinfolks in the army?" he asked.

"One of my sons is with General Stuart," Abigail said, pride in her voice.

"Well, we may be meetin' up one of these days, then."

"Another was a member of the Stonewall Brigade. He was wounded at Gettysburg and is in a hospital at Richmond."

"I'm sorry to hear about his injury," the captain said, and he sounded as if he meant it. "Any other sons?"

"One out west somewhere . . . and another who we lost last year at Fredericksburg."

"I *am* sorry, ma'am. I truly am." The captain reached up and took his hat off. "I'll be mighty glad when this war's over and we can all go back to bein' countrymen."

"That will never happen," Abigail said. "Confederates will never be countrymen with the likes of you."

"I hope you're wrong about that, ma'am. I surely do."

Abigail didn't say anything else, and neither did the captain. After a few minutes, the two men who had been sent to the chicken house came back holding their hats. Cordelia saw a few eggs in each man's hat. They handed the hats to a couple of the men still on horseback and swung up into their own saddles.

Still looking serious, Captain Pryor continued, "I think you ladies will be all right here, but you'd better stick pretty close to home. We'll have patrols out on the roads, and some of the boys are a mite jumpy after all the fightin' we've seen. I'll pass the word, though, that you're to be left alone."

"Why would you do that?" Abigail said. "We're the enemy, aren't we?"

"No, ma'am," the captain said. "We may be on opposite sides in this fracas, but no American can ever really be an enemy to me."

With that, he touched the brim of his hat again, nodded, and wheeled his horse. The rest of the cavalrymen followed him as he rode out of the farmyard at a fast trot.

Abigail, Cordelia, and Polly watched the soldiers leave. When they were gone, Polly observed, "Why, he didn't seem so bad at all. For a Yankee, he was almost . . . nice."

"Don't let him fool you with that sweet talk," Abigail said. "They all hate us and think they're so much better than us. If they didn't, they never would have invaded our home, now, would they?"

"No, I suppose not." Polly didn't sound convinced, though.

Cordelia didn't know what to think. She had been so scared, but then the young officer had been so nice, just like Polly said. He was almost gallant. Surely it was impossible that *all* Yankee soldiers were evil. Their politicians and their generals were out to destroy the South, but most of the soldiers were just plain, ordinary men, not that much different from the men of Culpeper County. In fact, Nathan Hatcher had gone north to fight for the Union, and although Cordelia still felt an ache in her heart when she thought about that, long ago she had come to realize that she could never despise Nathan as a Yankee. And the young Yankee captain was from Texas, one of the places Cory had always talked about wanting to see. According to his letters, Cory had managed to get there, at least into the eastern part of the state.

Captain Pryor was from the Rio Grande country, he'd said. Where was that? Down around Mexico somewhere? Cordelia wasn't sure.

The only thing she was certain of was that when the captain smiled like that, it would be awfully hard to hate him, no matter where he was from.

Abigail turned toward the door. "They're gone now," she announced. "Let's go find Henry and let him know it's safe to come out."

THE GOOD news reached the cavalry camp on the Rapidan River near Liberty Mills on September 22. Two days earlier, the Army of Tennessee had clashed with the Federals down in northwestern Georgia, not far from Chattanooga. Along a stream called Chickamauga Creek, the two sides had fought back and forth through the woods for three days, and finally the Confederates had prevailed and sent the Yankees running for their lives back to Chattanooga. Cheering erupted as word of the victory spread through General Stuart's camp.

The celebration didn't last long, however, because scouts raced in with more news. Union cavalry was moving toward them from the direction of Madison Court House.

Like everyone else in camp, Mac hurried to saddle his horse as the order came to prepare to move out. When he was mounted on the stallion, he rode quickly to the headquarters of Fitz Lee's division and found the general full of excitement, as he always was when there was action in the offing. Lee was already on horseback, ready to ride as soon as the order came.

"About time we had something to do again," Lee greeted Mac. "Running from the enemy doesn't sit well with me."

That was as close as Lee was going to come to criticizing Stuart, Mac knew. He simply nodded. "Yes sir."

A few minutes later, Stuart was on his way north with a good-sized force, leaving only one brigade behind to guard the camp. They rode hard over the rolling Virginia hills and didn't stop until they neared a crossroads where a blacksmith shop stood. Stuart, in the lead with Fitz Lee, signaled for a halt and looked down the slope toward the crossroads. Approaching the smithy from the other direction was a division of blue-clad cavalrymen.

"There they are, gentlemen," Stuart murmured. "What are we going to do about it?"

"Attack them, sir," Fitz Lee said with cavalier enthusiasm, as much a firebrand as ever.

Stuart drew his saber. "I concur," he announced gleefully. "Gentlemen, prepare to charge!"

The bugles blew and the guidons waved, and suddenly the two mounted forces leaped ahead, surging toward each other with a thunder of hooves and a cloud of dust. Mac was close by Fitz Lee, his saber in his hand. The stallion galloped ahead in a fluid pace, responding instantly to the slightest pressure of the reins or from Mac's knees.

Over the past two years Mac had grown to know the sounds of a cavalry clash all too well: the shouted orders, the ringing of steel against steel, the cracking of pistols, the crash of horse against horse, the screams of wounded animals, the cries and curses of wounded men. Those noises filled his ears now as the two groups of riders came together. As always in such a melee, confusion reigned. Dust billowed and swirled and made it difficult to see. Figures loomed up, and if they wore blue, they were the enemy. Mac slashed left and right with the saber as the lines tore through each other, and suddenly the foes that had been in front a few seconds earlier were now behind him. He wheeled the stallion in time to see General Stuart's horse going down, blood welling from a wound in its side. Mac's heels jabbed into the stallion's flanks and sent the big horse leaping forward. He sheathed his saber and reached out to grab Stuart's arm, hauling him to safety before the dying horse could fall on him.

Mac pulled the stallion to a halt. Stuart did not hesitate; he climbed onto the animal's back behind Mac. "Find me a horse, Captain!" he shouted.

Mac headed for the edges of the battle, figuring it would be easier to locate a riderless mount there.

As he and Stuart rode out of the dust cloud surrounding the combat, Mac spotted several men galloping hard toward them along the road from the south. These weren't Yankees, Mac realized. They were some of the scouts Stuart had sent out earlier to keep an eye on their back trail.

"General, scouts coming in!" Mac called over his shoulder. "Looks like there might be more trouble!" Maybe those men were riding so hard because they wanted to get in on the fight, but somehow Mac didn't think so.

"Head up the hill and meet them!" Stuart ordered.

Stuart slid off the stallion as soon as Mac brought the horse to a stop at the crest of the hill. The scouts raced up and didn't bother saluting. One of them shouted, "More Yankees on the way, General! They're behind us!"

Stuart looked unperturbed, but Mac knew the general had to be surprised by this news. Stuart wouldn't have knowingly ridden into a trap. He turned to Mac. "Captain, tell the artillerymen I want their batteries placed upon this hill with half of the guns pointing north and half pointing south. Then find General Lee and tell him to break off the engagement and rally here."

Those were tall orders, but Mac knew he would have to do his best to carry them out. He snapped a salute in acknowledgment and went off in search of Fitz Lee.

The horse artillery had not gone into action yet and was still nearby, so it was no problem to convey Stuart's orders to the men in charge of the guns. They began positioning their batteries as Mac galloped down the hill.

In another stroke of luck, the fight was breaking up already. Mac knew when he saw the Yankees pulling back that they hadn't set a trap for the Confederate cavalry. They wouldn't be breaking off the attack if that were the case. It was just bad luck that had put Stuart in a position between two groups of Federal cavalry. That was troubling in itself, though, because Mac recalled a time when bad luck had never dogged the general, when it seemed like fortune smiled on Stuart no matter what he did.

Mac spotted Fitz Lee and raced over to him. "Yankees coming up from the south, sir!" he reported. "General Stuart says to rally on top of the hill!"

Lee grasped the situation immediately and nodded. He shouted orders to his staff, and within moments, the horsemen were riding hard toward the spot where Stuart waited. Seeing what was going on, the men of Hampton's division followed suit without waiting for specific orders. Less than a quarter of an hour had passed before Stuart once again had his forces massed atop the hill.

The other group of Yankee cavalry was in sight now. Stuart stood at the crest of the hill, arms crossed, looking first one way and then the other. A smile played around his mouth. "Well, gentlemen," he said, "it looks like we're going to have to charge both directions at once."

"We're ready, General," Lee said.

"Very well. Fitz, you take the south. I'll handle the north with General Hampton's men. We'll give them a volley or two with the artillery, and then we can commence with the charge."

The cannons began to roar, slowing but not stopping the Yankees as they closed in from north and south. After a few minutes, Stuart gave a curt nod, and his divisions charged down opposite sides of the slope toward the enemy. Again, Mac found himself in the middle of a desperate fight as he joined the rest of Lee's men in trying to clear the road to the south.

The stallion whirled and leaped and carried Mac out of danger countless times during the brief engagement. His sword was daubed with crimson from the slashes he had made through Yankee flesh. He had a cut on his right arm and one on his left leg, but neither injury was serious.

After several minutes that seemed much longer, the resistance on the road to the south crumbled, and Lee's men broke through. They had split the Federal force blocking the road, and now they were faced with the task of keeping the path open as Hampton's division and the artillery tried to escape from the box in which they had found themselves. The pounding of hoof beats was deafening as the troopers raced to safety.

Mac found Lee in the confusion and stayed at his side, sheathing the saber and drawing his pistol instead. Lee's division kept the Yankees occupied while the rest of the Confederate force streamed by. Then it was time for them to make their own mad dash back toward Liberty Mills, fighting a rear-guard action as they went. The Yankees pressed them closely from behind, but as they drew near the camp at Liberty Mills, a Confederate infantry division that was bivouacked there heard the shooting and came running out to join the fight. As the Yankee cavalry encountered a deadly volley from the riflemen, they realized they were getting into more than they could handle. As Lee and Mac reined to a halt at the side of the road and turned their horses to watch, the Yankees began retreating.

"They're going hell-for-leather the other way now!" Lee exclaimed. His face was flushed, and he sounded like the cavalry had just won a great victory.

Mac couldn't quite see it that way. True, they had successfully extricated themselves from a tricky, dangerous situation, but they hadn't won any ground. In fact, when the Federal cavalry stopped, they would probably find themselves in possession of territory they hadn't controlled that morning. As far as Mac could tell, the engagement rated as a stalemate at best. More likely most people would consider it a defeat.

He didn't say anything about that to Lee, however. It was best to let the general enjoy this moment and take from it what pleasure he could . . . because Mac suspected that from here on out, the Yankees were going to be giving them grief every chance they could.

Chapter Twenty-one

GEN. NATHAN BEDFORD FORREST was not a man to stand still for long, or to waste time savoring a triumph when there were more victories to be won. Knowing the general as he did, Cory was not the least bit surprised when he found himself in the saddle before dawn the next morning after the battle of Chickamauga, riding north toward the small village of Rossville with Forrest and four hundred troopers to make sure the Yankees were still retreating.

In the gray predawn light, Cory and several other scouts ranged ahead of the main body of cavalry. While all his senses were alert for any sign that the routed Federals might turn back and attempt to mount an assault that would take the Confederates by surprise, Cory allowed his brain to wander a bit. He thought about Colonel Thompson. He was more than curious about Lucille's uncle—he was worried. He hadn't seen the colonel since the night before the battle had begun. As far as Cory knew, General Bragg and his staff had remained out of harm's way during all the fighting, but it was hard to be sure of such things. There were always stray bullets flying around a battlefield, not to mention artillery shells that went wild or carried farther than they were supposed to and exploded in the rear. He had been too exhausted the previous night to go searching for Thompson, but he vowed that as soon as he got the chance, he would find the colonel and make sure he was all right.

The rapid clatter of hoof beats jolted him out of that reverie. Riders were moving up ahead, and he knew there was no Confederate cavalry this far north except him and the other scouts. That meant Yankees. Cory turned Dash and galloped back through the fading night to report to Forrest.

Other scouts were coming in with the same news. Forrest reacted to it just as Cory expected him to—by ordering a charge.

The four hundred riders swept ahead toward Rossville, eager to do battle once more.

Several minutes later, they came in sight of the Federal cavalry. The sun was peeking over the eastern horizon now, casting light over the scene, but enough shadows remained so that the muzzle flashes of the Yankees' guns could be seen clearly as they fired a volley. Cory was riding at the head of the column beside Forrest, and he felt something hot spray across his face. When he lifted a hand to wipe his cheek, his fingertips came away red with blood.

Fearing that Forrest had been hit, Cory jerked his head toward the general. He saw that Forrest's horse was the victim instead. Blood poured from a wound in the animal's neck, and its steps were beginning to falter.

Forrest leaned forward in the saddle. The wound was within reach. He jammed his finger into the bullet hole in the horse's neck, stopping the flow of blood. With his other hand he held the reins and guided the horse as its stride lengthened once more and strength returned to it.

Cory wiped away the rest of the horse's blood as best he could while galloping along the road next to Forrest.

The Yankees had fired that one volley and then turned to run. Behind them lay the gap in Missionary Ridge where Rossville was located. They rode for it as hard as they could, fleeing like the very devil himself was after them.

And maybe he was, Cory thought as he looked at Forrest stopping up that wound with his finger and urging the last bit of speed out of his dying horse.

As the cavalry climbed a slight rise, Cory spotted something in the branches of a tree that stood on the crest. "Look, General!" he called to Forrest. "An observation platform!"

The Yankees had laid planks across some branches to form a crude platform high in the tree. Now two of them were trying to climb down and flee, but they were too late. Forrest's riders raced up to the tree before the Union duo could reach the ground.

Cory reined in and aimed his carbine at the two men, and dozens of his comrades did the same. If the Yankees foolishly tried to put up a fight, they would be shot to pieces before anything could happen.

So the two men did the sensible thing, dropping their rifles to the ground and raising their hands in surrender. The captives lowered themselves from the tree.

Forrest took his finger out of the bullet hole in his horse's neck and swung down from the saddle. No sooner had his feet touched the ground than the gallant mount fell. Its legs kicked once in a dying spasm, then it was gone. Forrest, a lover of good horseflesh, spared the horse a glance of regret and turned to the tree and its observation platform. To Cory's amazement, Forrest reached up, grasped one of the lower limbs, and began to climb.

"Toss my field glasses up here," he called to Cory when he was partway up the tree.

Cory reached over and took the glasses from their pouch attached to Forrest's saddle and carefully threw them up to the general. Forrest caught them, slung them around his neck, and kept climbing. When he reached the platform, he perched there and lifted the glasses to his eyes to scan the scene laid out before him. Cory figured that from up there, Forrest could see Chattanooga itself and all the ridges that lay around it, encircling the town along with the Tennessee River.

"It's a rout, by God," Forrest said after several minutes. "I've never seen the Yankees in such a state of confusion." He called down to his adjutant. "Major Anderson! Take down this message. Date it 'On the Road, September 21, 1863,' and address it to General Polk. 'General: We are within a mile of Rossville. Have been at the point of Missionary Ridge. Can see Chattanooga and everything around. The enemy's trains are leaving, going around the point of Lookout Mountain. I think they are evacuating as hard as they can go. They are cutting timber down to obstruct our passing. I think we ought to press forward as rapidly as possible.' Sign it, 'Respectfully, etc.'"

Forrest paused then said, "Add a note requesting that the message be forwarded to General Bragg."

A lot of good that would do, Cory thought. Bragg's army had won a great victory the day before, but as far as Cory could see, Bragg himself had had little or nothing to do with the outcome of the battle.

Forrest climbed down from the tree as the major finished transcribing the message. As a courier galloped off with the dispatch, another member of the general's staff asked, "What do we do now, sir?"

"Just what I suggested to General Polk and General Bragg," Forrest said. "We press forward. Somebody find me a horse!"

THAT MORNING, with the enemy retreating before him, was the beginning of a time of great frustration for General Forrest, Cory thought later. Some of Forrest's men skirmished with the Yankees still withdrawing through Rossville, but Forrest held back most of his force, thinking word would arrive at any time saying that the Army of Tennessee was on the move again and would come roaring up the valley to fall on and crush the retreating enemy.

Instead, except for establishing a headquarters in a log hut atop Missionary Ridge, Bragg did nothing. The army sat and waited, just as it had done so many times before while Bragg nursed old grudges and tried to decide what to do next. All that day and during the days to come, Cory heard mutters of discontent not only from the common soldiers who hated to quit once their fighting blood was aroused, but from the officers, too, especially Forrest. The general wore a dark look on his face all the time and seemed to be seething inside.

The delay, however, gave Cory a chance to search out Colonel Thompson. That was about the only good thing he could say about it. Getting permission from Forrest to do so,

Cory rode to the top of Missionary Ridge and along the crest to Bragg's headquarters, thinking he was most likely to find the colonel there.

Seeing several officers standing in front of the hut Bragg was using, Cory reined in and saluted. "Excuse me, sirs, I'm looking for Colonel Charles Thompson. Have any of you seen him?"

"Thompson?" one of the men said. "Tall fellow, graying hair? Talks a little like a professor?"

Cory nodded. "That's him."

"You'll find him down at the field hospital. He was hit on the third day at Chickamauga. Shell fragment."

Cory stiffened in the saddle, feeling his insides turn to ice. "The colonel was wounded?"

"That's what I just said, isn't it?" The officer sounded impatient now.

"How bad?"

"I don't know, Private. What's the colonel to you, anyway?"

"My wife's uncle, sir. And a good friend."

The officer's expression softened a little. "Well, you go on and see about him. He wasn't killed, I know that much."

"Thank you, sir. Where's the hospital?"

"Back down the ridge about half a mile."

Cory nodded. He remembered passing the hospital tent on his way up here. He hadn't dreamed at the time that Colonel Thompson was there.

He saluted and turned Dash to ride hurriedly back along the ridge. When he came to the large tent that served as the field hospital, he dismounted and grabbed the arm of the first medical orderly he saw.

"I'm looking for Colonel Charles Thompson."

The orderly shook his head. "I don't know any names. You'll just have to go in and look for him if you want to find him."

Cory approached the tent's entrance and hesitated. He heard the groans and cries of agony from inside, and along with the wretched sounds, an odor of rotting flesh came through the opening between the canvas flaps. But he had to know how badly the colonel was hurt, so he turned his head, took a deep breath, then plunged into what might as well have been hell.

A few cots were scattered around inside the tent, but most of the wounded men lay on the ground, either on the dirt itself or on threadbare blankets spread beneath them. Most had lost arms or legs or both. Bloody bandages were wrapped around the stumps of those amputated limbs. Some of the patients had head injuries, and they were so swathed in bandages that their faces were completely covered. Everywhere men groaned and cursed and prayed and begged for water.

Cory had been in field hospitals before, so he couldn't say that he had never seen anything like this, but no one ever grew accustomed to such horrible sights. He felt sick, and he knew he would be haunted for weeks by what he was seeing here today.

The wounded men were arranged so that people could walk between them in aisles that were barely wide enough for one man. As Cory moved past, some of the more alert men called out to him, and a few even clutched at his legs. He pulled away from them as gently as he could. He searched every face he could see, hoping to recognize Colonel Thompson.

One of the surgeons stopped him. "What are you doing in here, soldier?"

"Looking for a relative, sir," Cory answered. He figured that was only a small stretching of the truth. He and the colonel were related by marriage, after all.

"His name?"

"Colonel Charles Thompson."

The surgeon frowned in thought then turned and pointed with a bloodstained hand. "Try over there in the back corner. I think there are some officers over there."

Cory thanked the man and hurried to the corner the surgeon had indicated.

Sure enough, the second man he checked was Colonel Thompson. Cory felt relief flood through him as he saw the colonel's unmarked face. Thompson lay on his left side with his head on a folded blanket. His eyes were closed, and he seemed to be asleep. Cory knelt beside him and placed a hand on his shoulder, and when Thompson didn't stir, he had a bad moment during which he thought that maybe the colonel wasn't sleeping at all. Maybe he actually was dead.

Then Thompson opened his eyes and lifted his head a little to look around. His eyes lacked focus at first, but then his eyes fastened on his visitor. "Cory?"

Cory squeezed Thompson's shoulder. "It's all right, Colonel. I'm here. Everything will be all right now."

That was a bold statement to make, he thought. And a foolish one as well. Thinking back on his life, nothing had ever been all right simply because he was there. In fact, situations usually grew worse whenever he involved himself in them.

"Cory," Thompson said again. "Thank God you're all right. You *are* all right, aren't you, lad?"

Cory nodded. "Yes sir, I'm fine. Came through the battle with just a few scratches."

"Would that . . . I could say the same." Thompson rolled a little more onto his back and raised his right arm so that Cory could see his midsection. "They've torn the guts out of me."

Wide bandages crisscrossed Thompson's middle. They were stained with blood and a bad smell rose from them. Cory stared in horror. Most major wounds were fatal, but belly wounds were some of the worst. Men nearly always died from them, and they took a long time doing it.

"Oh, Lord, Colonel," he whispered. "I'm so sorry. I'm so sorry."

"Not your . . . fault. No one's fault . . . except the Yankees. And the bad luck . . . that sent a Federal shell near me."

Cory leaned forward, trying to force the grief out of his mind. "Listen, Colonel, you're going to be fine. I've never known anybody tougher than you. You just need to rest up for a while—"

Thompson's hand found Cory's arm and closed over it with surprising strength. Cory was reminded of that awful day at Fort Donelson when Ezekiel Farrell had died. Farrell had clutched at him like that, too, before slipping away.

"We were . . . wrong to come here," Thompson said. "We should have tried to . . . go west. To Texas. The war is . . . lost."

Cory had never heard words like that from Thompson's mouth before. He said, "We won yesterday, Colonel. We whipped the Yankees and sent them running back to Chattanooga as fast as they could go." Maybe that good news would make the colonel feel a little better, he thought.

Thompson gave a weak shake of his head. "This battle . . . means nothing. The Yankees can lose . . . again and again . . . and still win in the end. There are too many of them . . . too many . . ."

With that, he sighed and rolled over so that he was facing away from Cory again. His eyelids slid down. His breathing was raspy but fairly regular. The colonel had just run out of strength, Cory realized. He was sleeping again.

Cory pushed himself to his feet and looked down at Thompson. The past few days had aged the man at least ten years, he thought. Thompson was ready to give up on both the Confederacy and his own life. He was ready to die.

He wasn't going to let that happen, Cory decided. He would do everything in his power to see to it that Thompson was reunited with Mildred and Lucille.

He found the surgeon he had spoken to earlier, grasping the man's arm as he tried to move past. "Doctor, what about Colonel Thompson?"

The surgeon looked confused. "What about him?"

"Is he going to be all right?"

"I don't remember the specifics of the colonel's case, but I sincerely doubt it. I doubt if any of these men will ever be all right again, even if they live. Which in most cases is also highly in doubt."

Cory wanted to take a swing at the man's florid face with its muttonchop whiskers. The surgeon didn't care. These poor wounded men were nothing but meat to him. With an effort, Cory restrained his anger. Instead, he announced, "I want him to have the best possible care."

"Of course. We do everything we can—"

"You don't understand," Cory said. "I'm holding you personally accountable for the colonel's survival."

The surgeon's eyes widened in surprise and anger. "What the blazes! Have you lost your mind, boy? You can't talk to me like that!"

Cory pressed his face closer to the doctor's and said, "I ride with General Forrest."

He could see that this simple statement meant something to the surgeon. The men of Forrest's cavalry had a reputation as being somewhat wild, daredevils who cared little for military protocol or niceties. Forrest was known for his skill with a bowie knife and his fiery temper, and his men were noted for their own violent excesses.

"I'll do what I can, of course," the surgeon said. "Everything I can. You have my word on that."

"Good," Cory said. "I'll be back to see the colonel. Every day, if possible."

"Certainly. Don't worry about him. He's in good hands."

Cory gave the surgeon a curt nod and left the hospital tent. He stopped outside to raise his arms and press the balls of his hands against his eyes. That bit of bravado inside meant nothing. He knew that. The colonel would live or die—probably die—according to his fate and no amount of threats would change that. All Cory had accomplished was to make himself feel better for a few seconds, but he could already tell what a hollow victory that was.

Nor could he forget what Thompson had said about the South being doomed to lose the war. In his darkest moments, Cory had thought the same thing, but it was something else again to hear it from such a staunch supporter of the Confederacy as Col. Charles Thompson. Was Chickamauga a hollow victory, too? Was the war already over with the twin defeats at Vicksburg and Gettysburg, and the South just too damned stubborn to admit it?

Cory didn't want to know the answers to those questions. He didn't even want to think about them. It was bad enough that he allowed doubts to plague him.

But in the back of his mind, a tiny voice had begun to chant *All for nothing, all for nothing.* He tried to close his brain to the words, but they wouldn't go away.

What he needed was a good fight against the Yankees, he told himself. In the midst of battle, a man didn't have to think.

All he had to do was fight to stay alive.

A WEEK DRAGGED by, broken up only by a few inconsequential clashes between patrols from each side. The week allowed even a makeshift soldier like Cory to sense that the great advantage won at Chickamauga was slipping away. Finally, as far as Forrest was concerned, the worst blow fell. General Bragg relieved him of command of most of his division, leaving him only a single regiment. The rest of Forrest's men were to be transferred to the command of Gen. Joe Wheeler to augment Wheeler's own division for a raid north of Chattanooga that would cut the supply lines into the town.

When Cory heard that, it was clear to him what Bragg planned to do. He had seen the same thing from the other side in Vicksburg. Bragg was going to lay siege to Chattanooga and starve the Yankees out.

The tactic had worked for the Union forces under Grant at Vicksburg, and Cory wasn't enough of a military strategist to say whether it could work here or not. But it seemed to him that Bragg had frittered away an opportunity to win an outright victory over the Army of the Cumberland. He knew that Forrest felt the same way, and in addition, Forrest was livid over having his men taken away from him and given to Joe Wheeler, a commander for whom Forrest had little respect despite the fact that they had once been friends.

Forrest wrote an angry letter to Bragg protesting the decision to reassign his troops. In return, he received assurances from Bragg that as soon as Wheeler was back from the raid, Forrest's troops would be returned to him. Somewhat mollified by Bragg's response, and at loose ends for the moment, Forrest left the camp and headed for LaGrange, Georgia, to visit his wife, whom he had not seen for eighteen months.

Cory remained at Missionary Ridge, visiting Thompson in the field hospital every day as he had promised. The colonel's condition didn't improve, but he didn't seem to be getting any worse, either. Sometimes he woke up for a short time while Cory was there; at others, he slept through the visit and Cory just sat beside him in silence.

A few days after Forrest's departure, Cory was grooming Dash when the general appeared on horseback and trotted past. Forrest's face was dark with fury. Cory hadn't even known he was back from LaGrange. Startled by Forrest's appearance, he called out to him.

Forrest reined in. "Find Dr. Cowan," he snapped at Cory. "I want him with me when I see General Bragg."

"Yes sir," Cory answered then hesitated. "If you don't mind my asking, sir . . ."

"I received a dispatch from General Bragg while I was in LaGrange," Forrest paused and said curtly. "He must have sent it not long after I left here. I'm bein' stripped of the rest of my command. Joe Wheeler's gettin' all the cavalry, and he's not givin' any of it back."

Cory was shocked. How could Bragg do such a thing? General Forrest was the most successful Confederate commander anywhere in the West, the only one to win any real victories.

"I'll find Dr. Cowan, sir," he stated and turned and ran across the camp.

J. B. Cowan was Forrest's chief surgeon and some relation to the general as well, though Cory didn't know the details of that. Cory saw him frequently at the field hospital and found him there now. Cowan looked just as surprised as Cory had been to hear that Forrest was back from his leave of absence. With Cory trailing him, he hurried across the camp to join the general.

Forrest had dismounted and was pacing, impatience evident in every move he made. He clasped Cowan's hand. "I'm goin' to see Bragg. It's time he heard some truth."

"Bedford . . . ," Cowan began, but one look at Forrest's face must have convinced him that arguing wouldn't do any good.

Forrest swung up onto his horse. "Cory, throw a saddle on your mount for Dr. Cowan," he ordered.

Cory sprang to follow the order. A moment later, he had Dash saddled and ready to ride. Cowan mounted and spurred the animal to follow Forrest.

So did Cory, following as fast as he could on foot. He wasn't sure what was going to happen, but he knew he didn't want to miss it.

When he arrived at Bragg's headquarters, he saw Forrest pushing past a sentry into the log hut. Cowan was close behind him. Cory hurried up to the doorway and joined the startled sentry in staring at the scene inside.

Bragg was seated behind a campaign desk. He stood up and tentatively offered his hand to Forrest. The Tennessean, however, ignored it and planted himself in front of the desk, fairly quivering with anger. Suddenly he jabbed the index finger of his left hand toward Bragg.

"You robbed me of my command in Kentucky," Forrest began. "Men whom I armed and equipped from the enemies of our country! You drove me into West Tennessee in the winter of '62 with a second brigade I had organized, with improper arms and without sufficient ammunition."

Cory remembered that trip all too well, including Ham Ryder's death.

"In spite of all this I returned well equipped by captures," Forrest went on as Bragg stared at him. "And now this second brigade, organized and equipped without thanks to you or the government, you've taken from me as well." He leaned forward, and despite the desk between them, Bragg retreated a step, his eyes wide under the bushy eyebrows.

"I have stood your meanness as long as I intend to! You've played the part of a damned scoundrel, and if you were any part of a man I'd slap your jaws and force you to resent it. You may as well not issue any orders to me, because I won't obey 'em! I hold you personally responsible for any further indignities you try to inflict on me. And if you ever again try to interfere with me or cross my path, it will be at the peril of your life."

Bragg sank into his chair as Forrest's tirade came to an abrupt end. He had not said a word during the dressing down, nor did he now as Forrest turned and stalked out of the building. Cory moved quickly to get out of the general's way, as did the gawking sentry. Cowan followed after Forrest.

"Now you're in for it," Cowan said quietly as they reached the horses.

"No," Forrest said. He grasped the reins and stepped up into the saddle. "He'll never say a word about it. He'll be the last man to mention it, and mark my word, he'll take no action in the matter. I'll ask to be relieved and transferred to another command, and he won't oppose it."

"I hope you're right," Cowan said.

Cory followed them, not hurrying this time. He knew Cowan would leave Dash at the cavalry bivouac. Cory's mind was spinning. If General Forrest was right about Bragg's reaction to the outburst, Forrest would soon be leaving the Army of Tennessee. Cory had expected to stay with Forrest for the foreseeable future, but that was before Colonel Thompson had been wounded. With the colonel in such bad shape, how could

Cory leave him now? Abandoning Thompson would be almost as bad as abandoning Lucille.

He had managed to do that plenty of times in his quest for adventure, he reminded himself. His family had always come off second-best to his restless nature, his thirst for action and glory.

But that was in the past. He had seen enough war now to know that there was nothing glorious about it. Nor could he rationalize a decision by saying he was doing what he could to help the Confederacy. The Confederacy might well be beyond his help now, especially considering the fact that he was just a common soldier, not a general or a strategist.

Of course, he couldn't help the colonel, either, he reminded himself. He wasn't a doctor. Even if he had been, there wasn't much he could do. Thompson's injuries were too serious for anyone to help him, other than keeping him as comfortable as possible and hoping for a miracle.

But at least he could do that, Cory told himself. A cool cloth, a comforting touch, a prayer . . . those things he could offer to his friend and the beloved uncle of his wife, and that was what he was going to do. Forrest could order him to leave, but somehow Cory didn't think it would come to that.

He walked on, firm in his determination . . . and hoped that nothing would come up to make it waver.

Chapter Twenty-two

PRESIDENT JEFFERSON DAVIS INTERCEDED personally in the dispute between Braxton Bragg and Nathan Bedford Forrest but failed to resolve it. At one point, Forrest offered his resignation, but Davis refused it. Instead, he approved Forrest's request for a transfer, and in the middle of November 1863, with a small force of three hundred men, Forrest departed the camp at Missionary Ridge and rode off toward Rome, Georgia.

Cory Brannon was not with him.

As Cory had suspected, Forrest did not order him to go along, though the general wasn't pleased with Cory's decision to stay behind.

"You're such a damned civilian at heart, it wouldn't do any good to make you come with me," Forrest said as he shook hands with Cory just before leaving. "You never did want to join the army."

"No sir."

"But you're still one of the fightin'est boys I've ever run into. Good luck, Cory." Forrest added, "You're goin' to need it if you stay here where Bragg's in command."

With that, he mounted up, waved a hand in farewell, and rode off to whatever awaited him elsewhere in this war.

Cory thought about what Forrest had said about luck and General Bragg. As far as Cory could see, the greatest danger the Confederate army atop Missionary Ridge faced was dying of boredom. General Wheeler's cavalry raid to disrupt the supply lines into Chattanooga from the north had been a rousing success. What few reports the Confederates got from spies inside the city said that the Federals were slowly starving to death. Soon they would have no choice but to give up.

Cory was glad the siege was going well, but at the same time, he felt sorry for those trapped in Chattanooga. If the soldiers were starving, that meant the townspeople were in even worse shape. He knew that from bitter experience.

As always in war, the situation changed from day to day. The great bends of the Tennessee River created several points of land, including Moccasin Point just west of Chattanooga. Two miles away on the western side of the point, where the river curved around it, was Brown's Ferry. West of there, on yet another bend of the river, was Kelley's Ferry. Kelley's Ferry could be reached by steamboat from the town of Bridgeport, Alabama, and a passable rail line still ran from Nashville to Bridgeport. A couple of weeks earlier, the Yankees had captured Brown's Ferry from the small Confederate force holding it. Now, with supplies coming by rail from Nashville to Bridgeport and by steamboat from Bridgeport to Kelley's Ferry, a backdoor route into Chattanooga was opened as the supplies were taken overland from Kelley's Ferry to Brown's Ferry and across Moccasin Point to Chattanooga. Word from the city said that this new supply route was known as the Cracker Line, after the crates of hardtack that were transported over it. The amount of supplies the Yankees would be able to bring in by this route was limited, but the city wasn't completely cut off anymore. Chattanooga's defenders might not have an abundance of food just yet, but they had something almost as important: hope.

When Cory heard about the Cracker Line, he was reminded of the supply route he and Thompson and Pie Jones had set up from Vicksburg across Louisiana to Texas. The cutting of that line by the Yankees had meant the inevitable surrender of the city. If they had been able to establish something like the Cracker Line, there was no telling how long Vicksburg might have been able to hold out. The siege of Chattanooga didn't seem like such a good idea anymore, at least not to Cory. General Bragg seemed determined to continue on with it, though.

Fresh supplies weren't the only things new to Chattanooga. Rumors went around the Confederate camp that General Rosecrans had been replaced as the commander of the Union army.

The Yankee War Department had placed U. S. Grant—old Unconditional Surrender himself—in command of all the Union armies in the West. Grant had relieved Rosecrans and replaced him with Gen. George Thomas, who was already being called the Rock of Chickamauga because of his stubborn stand atop Snodgrass Hill on the third day of the battle. Cory didn't know much about Thomas, but he knew the man had put up a better fight than anyone else in blue on the field of battle that day. Thomas's promotion didn't bode well for the Confederate cause.

Another worrisome rumor was that Grant was acting to bolster Chattanooga's defenses by bringing in reinforcements over the same route that the supply trains were now using. A large force under Gen. William Tecumseh Sherman was said to be on the way to the besieged town. And the Confederate forces were shrinking instead of growing, as they should have been. General Longstreet's division had already been dispatched to the northeast to try to wrestle the city of Knoxville out of the hands of the Federals under Gen. Ambrose E. Burnside, who had failed so dismally at Fredericksburg the previous winter. And now Forrest was gone, too.

The only bit of good news as far as Cory was concerned was the improvement Colonel Thompson was making. As the cold, damp days of late fall set in, the colonel began to rally, taking not only Cory by surprise but the surgeon who attended him as well.

"It was always a good sign that the colonel didn't develop blood poisoning and die in the first couple of days he was here," the doctor explained to Cory. "I don't have any explanation for it. Belly wounds are almost always fatal, if not sooner, then later." The man shook his head. "But Colonel Thompson is a stubborn man. He has the will to live."

Cory wasn't so sure of that. It had seemed to him that Thompson was giving up back when Cory had first found him in the field hospital. How had the colonel summoned up the strength to hang on this long and give himself a chance to start healing at last?

Cory didn't want to dwell on it, but maybe his presence had had something to do with the colonel's improvement. Maybe his almost daily visits had provided Thompson with an anchor of sorts, something to cling to during the dark moments when it would have been easier to just let go and slip away. Cory felt uncomfortable as those thoughts crossed his mind. He would have done almost anything to save the colonel's life, but he didn't want to give himself credit, even in his own mind, for something he'd had nothing to do with.

"What are you frowning about?" the doctor asked him.

Cory shook his head. "Just thinking."

The doctor grunted. "Perhaps that's your problem. You think too damned much." He jerked his head toward the back of the tent where Colonel Thompson rested. "Just be glad the colonel's alive and go say hello to him."

Cory managed a sheepish smile. "You're right. I'll do that."

An orderly was winding clean bandages around Thompson's midsection when Cory came up. Cory caught a glimpse of the ugly scar that the ragged wound had left on the colonel's body. The flesh around the wound wasn't inflamed anymore, as it had been at first. Thompson was even able to sit up this morning.

When the orderly had finished and left, Thompson extended a hand to Cory. "Help me stand up. I want to get out of this place for a few minutes."

"I'm not sure that's a good idea, Colonel," Cory said.

"Why not? Take a deep breath. That's the smell of death. This place is full of it. You can't honestly say that it's good for anyone, can you, lad?"

Cory couldn't argue with that. He looked around, saw that none of the surgeons was paying any attention to them, and took Thompson's hand. "All right, Colonel," he said. "But just for a minute."

With Thompson's hand clasped in his and his other hand under the colonel's elbow, Cory helped him to his feet. The colonel was pale and shaky, and Cory worried that he might pass out. But after a moment Thompson was able to take a deep breath, and some of his strength seemed to return. "I'm all right now," he said. "Let's go out the back."

Cory led the colonel to the rear entrance of the field hospital and pushed aside the canvas so they could step outside. Moving slowly and carefully, they made their way over to a tree. Thompson leaned against it and sighed. He was bareheaded, and a cool breeze riffled his gray hair. He wore a tattered uniform jacket over his bandages, and Cory pulled it a little tighter around his shoulders to protect him more from the wind. From up here on Missionary Ridge, they could see a long way. The Tennessee wound on its leisurely way below them. Chattanooga was in plain sight on its banks. To the west, the long, impressive bulk of Lookout Mountain loomed. Mist clung to the valleys, ghostlike streamers of white that drifted and swirled in a slow waltz of phantoms. The sky overhead was slate gray with the promise of winter in it. Thompson dragged in a deep draft of the raw November air.

"My God, I never dreamed anything could ever smell so good. I've smelled death for so long I was afraid it was all that was left in the world."

"They say Fighting Joe Hooker's troops are over there on the other side of Lookout Mountain," Cory commented, but he fell silent when Thompson lifted a hand.

"Don't talk about the war," he whispered. "From up here I can't see it. I don't want to see it. I just want to look out over these mountains and the river for a few moments."

Cory nodded and stood there in silence as the colonel leaned against the tree and looked around. After a while, Thompson said, "I was born in Tennessee, you know."

"No sir, I wasn't sure where you were born."

"In a cabin on this side of the Cumberland Gap. My father knew David Crockett quite well. They hunted together sometimes. I remember Colonel Crockett letting me shoot his rifle once, when I was a boy." Thompson's voice had a soft, dreamlike quality to it as his memories ranged back to his childhood. "I've always loved Tennessee. I hated to leave Nashville and go to Vicksburg." He looked over at Cory. "We're in Tennessee now, aren't we?"

"Yes sir. The way I understand it, the border's a little ways south of us."

Thompson nodded. "I'm glad. I'm glad to be home." He sighed again and looked away, into the distance. "Mildred," he said softly and then fell silent.

Cory stood there for several minutes, waiting. When Charles Thompson didn't move or say anything else, Cory said, "Colonel, we'd better get you back inside before the doctors get riled up."

Thompson didn't reply. Cory said again, "Colonel," and put a hand on Thompson's shoulder. He took a step so that he could get a better look at Thompson's face, and he saw that the colonel's eyes were closed.

"Charles?" Cory breathed. And then he felt tears stinging his eyes worse than any cloud of powder smoke ever had. He whispered, "Colonel . . ." even though he knew it was no use. Thompson wouldn't be answering.

Cory put his arms around him and held him and cried for several minutes before lowering him gently to the ground.

THE SURGEON said that Thompson must have started bleeding inside from his wound. That answer made as much sense to Cory as any could have. All he knew was that the colonel was gone, and he felt as alone as he ever had in his life.

A burial detail took Thompson's body down off Missionary Ridge and laid him to rest in the valley of Chickamauga Creek, among the hundreds of other graves that had been dug there. Cory went with them and made sure the spot was still in Tennessee. Thompson had been glad to be back in his home state, and Cory saw to it that he got to stay there. It was late in the day before he trudged back to the top of the ridge and sat down on a rock to try to figure out what he was going to do next.

His official assignment had been to Forrest's brigade, but that didn't exist anymore. He supposed he should report to one of the units under General Wheeler, but he wasn't sure which one. Besides, he was only one of thousands of Confederate soldiers on this ridge. Who would miss him if he just walked away, or rode off on Dash? He could tell the sentries he was going on a scouting mission, and likely they would believe him.

Could he do that? Was he really capable of being a deserter, a horse thief? He hadn't wanted to join the army in the first place. He didn't mind a fight, but he couldn't stand being tied down.

Somewhere out there, farther west, his wife was waiting for him. By now Lucille and Mildred and the Carters had reached Texas. Had they settled down there, started making a home for after the war? Or had they run into trouble along the way, maybe even danger? It was possible that Lucille was dead. The very thought of such a thing made him sick. He tried to put that possibility out of his mind. Lucille was fine, he told himself. He would just have to repeat that over and over.

He could go west . . . or he could head southeast, the direction General Forrest had gone. He knew Forrest planned to put together another cavalry brigade, and then he would take the fight to the enemy. Forrest could do nothing else. He was born to battle. Some men were like that, Cory reflected, but he wasn't one of them.

On the other hand, Forrest had been his friend, and while there was little or nothing Cory could do here at Chattanooga to make a difference, if he was riding with Forrest again he would have a chance to accomplish something. Not to win the war for the Confederacy; he was convinced that was a goal that was out of reach now. But maybe if Forrest and others like him could inflict enough damage on the Yankees, it would make it easier to negotiate a settlement of some sort. Grant's motto might be

Unconditional Surrender, but from what Cory had heard of President Lincoln, that wasn't his attitude. Lincoln might welcome some way to bring the Rebel states back into the Union with a minimum of hard feelings that could prolong the bloodshed . . .

Cory rolled up in his blankets and went to sleep that night still not knowing what he was going to do. He would think about it in the morning, he told himself, and come to a decision then.

CORY WOKE to the sharp crackling of rifle fire and the booming of an artillery bombardment. He struggled up out of his blankets, throwing them aside and reaching for his carbine. He looked around wildly, thinking that the Yankees had gotten on top of Missionary Ridge somehow and were attacking the camp. He saw plenty of men running around in confusion and near panic, but they all wore butternut. No Yankees were in sight.

It was a cold, misty morning, with fog once again hanging thickly in the valleys between the ridges. Banks of clouds shrouded Lookout Mountain and muffled the clamor of battle, but as Cory stood on Missionary Ridge and peered into the cottony mass that blocked his sight, he could tell that the sounds were coming from that direction.

The only explanation was that the Federal troops under Joseph Hooker, which had moved into the valley on the far side of Lookout Mountain, were now assaulting the long, rugged height.

Cory stood there with his heart thudding. All his pondering the day before meant nothing now. If the stalemate had continued, he might have been able to talk himself into slipping away and leaving the army. But to run off in the face of the enemy . . . he could never bring himself to do that. It would be utter cowardice. Now that the fight had begun, he had no choice but to stay and do his part.

He was not far from General Bragg's headquarters. Officers went in and out of the log hut, and after a while Bragg himself came out, mounted a horse, and rode off with his staff, probably bound for somewhere they could get a better look at what was going on. Cory didn't think they were going to find such a place. As the morning went on, the fog grew thicker and thicker. Lookout Mountain was no longer visible at all.

Cory went to a spot at the edge of the ridge and posted himself there. If anyone paid any attention to him, they would probably assume some officer had ordered him to take up that post. He stood there and waited, from time to time wiping beads of condensation off the barrel, breech, and stock of his carbine. There was no telling what might come out of that fog and start up the hill toward him.

He wished the colonel was with him now. Thompson would have been able to interpret the sounds of battle and get an idea of what was going on. To Cory, the cacophony sounded like chaos over there. More men moved up on the rugged overlook with him. He didn't know if they had been ordered there, or if like him they had just found a place to wait and see what was going to happen.

One of them edged over beside Cory. "I hear ol' Hooker's tryin' to get his artillery up the mountain over yonder."

"I wonder if he's having any luck."

"Hell, no! Those slopes are too steep." The Confederate soldier sounded confident. "Our boys'll push him right back down the hill. He couldn't beat us at Chancellorsville, and he can't beat us now."

Cory nodded, even though he wasn't nearly as convinced as his companion. True, Hooker had been defeated at Chancellorsville by Robert E. Lee and Stonewall Jackson, but this was a new day, a new battle. The gods of war might smile on Hooker today. Lord knew they smiled seldom enough on Braxton Bragg.

The morning rolled past, cloaked in fog, and gradually the men on Missionary Ridge became aware of what was going on at

Lookout Mountain as reports came in. Hooker's forces, thousands of infantry and dozens of artillery pieces, were indeed trying to ascend the slope. The Confederate defenders were putting up a gallant fight so far, though, and the progress of the Federals up the ridge had been slow.

The firing died away for a while, and Cory wondered if the battle was over. Then it started again as the fog thinned, and he realized that the two sides had stopped shooting at each other because they couldn't see anything. Now, as visibility improved, the killing began again.

More than once as the day dragged past, those intervals of silence came when the fog grew too thick for a man to see his hand in front of his face. But the moments of quiet always ended, and the roar of guns started up again.

That afternoon, more fighting broke out at the northern end of Missionary Ridge itself. There was a knob up there called Tunnel Hill, Cory recalled—a different Tunnel Hill than the one where Forrest had made a stand on the railroad near Ringgold. The Yankees must be trying to capture this one. Again, he couldn't see the battle, only hear it. His nerves were stretched taut by the tension of listening to the clash of phantoms. There was nothing ghostly about the battles themselves, though. Men were dying out there in the fog, and the fate not only of armies but also of nations might hang in the balance.

The rumbling of Cory's stomach reminded him that he had not eaten all day. He dug a small bit of hardtack out of his pocket and gnawed on it, drawing no satisfaction from it. He washed the stuff down with a swig of water from his canteen as he listened to the artillery batteries blasting away. His hunger didn't seem any more real to him than did anything else on this dreamlike day. He had the bizarre sensation that he was floating somewhere outside himself, detached from his body, an observer of this scene but somehow not really part of it.

Then he saw wounded men being carried past on stretchers bound for the field hospital . . . bloody, screaming wreckages of human beings . . . and once again he knew the reality of what was happening. This was no dream, no trance.

Given the time of year and the thick fog, it was no surprise to anyone that night fell early that day. As dusk settled in, though, the fog finally began to break. A brisk wind sprang up, hastening the process. The moon rose a short time later into an almost clear sky. The air lost its dank, heavy feel and became crisp and frigid.

As Cory stood there on Missionary Ridge, still waiting as he had been all day, the cold made his breath plume in front of his mouth. He looked out across the valley between the ridges. Confederate campfires still burned atop Lookout Mountain.

"Lord," one of the other men said in a hushed voice. "Look at that."

For a moment, Cory wasn't sure what the man was talking about. Then he became aware that the silvery moonlight washing over the scene was growing dim. He looked up into the sky and saw a black arc cutting into the glowing disc of the moon. His breath caught in his throat.

He'd had enough education to recognize an eclipse. Cory wasn't exactly clear on the celestial mechanics that caused such a thing, but he knew it was a natural phenomenon. Ancient peoples had regarded such eclipses as portents of disaster, though, and maybe they were on to something there, Cory thought, reflecting on the events of the day.

The moonlight grew more and more dim as the blackness cut into it, until finally nothing was visible of the moon itself except a thin crescent of light. Everywhere along Missionary Ridge, men stood and stared at the sight in silent awe, and the hush that hung over the ridge was deep and profound. If this wasn't a bad omen, then Cory had never seen one.

Then came the inevitable and steady retreat of the darkness. The moonlight grew brighter once again, casting harsh shadows. Cory's hand shook a little as he dragged the back of it across his mouth.

With everything that had happened today, it was almost too frightening to think about what the morning might bring.

⊙▬▬◆▬▬⊙

No one got much sleep on Missionary Ridge that night. General Bragg, faced with an enemy that wasn't content to just sit and be starved into death or submission, was forced into action. Convinced that the greatest threat lay on his right flank, where Sherman had moved into position during the afternoon and captured a sizable band of Confederate pickets below the slope of Tunnel Hill, Bragg shifted his forces in that direction. Two divisions under the command of Gens. Patrick Cleburne and Carter Stevenson were withdrawn from Lookout Mountain and moved to Tunnel Hill.

In fact, all the Confederate forces on Lookout Mountain were withdrawn under cover of night. The lunar eclipse, evil portent or not, may have helped conceal the movements of the army by deepening the darkness. In the predawn hours of November 25, 1863, when Fighting Joe Hooker's troops renewed their assault on the top of Lookout Mountain, they found it deserted.

By this time, Cory was at Tunnel Hill. No one had given him any orders to go there. When Cleburne's men had marched by during the night, Cory had simply gone with them. He didn't know if Bragg was right about the main thrust of the Federal attack being directed at Tunnel Hill, but Sherman wasn't sitting down there for nothing. When morning came, so would the Yankees. Cory was convinced of that.

Like all the other ridges and hills in this part of the country, Tunnel Hill was rugged and covered with boulders. Cory found a spot in a nest of rocks where he could aim his carbine down the slope. Several other soldiers joined him there. He wondered if they were acting on their own initiative, as he was, but he didn't bother asking. It didn't matter what reasons any of them had for being here. Fate had brought them to this spot, and here their destiny would play out, whatever it might be.

As the sky lightened to the east, Cory leaned his carbine against a rock and rubbed his hands together. He was chilled to the bone, and he needed to get some feeling back in his fingers. They would warm up soon enough when he started firing the gun, he supposed, but he didn't want to wait that long. He wanted his first shots to be as accurate as possible.

The sun rose, and as its rays washed down through the clear sky over Missionary Ridge and Lookout Mountain, Cory heard something he hadn't expected to hear. Somewhere in the distance a band began playing. The sound seemed to be coming from the west. He straightened up in the rocks and craned his neck, peering in the direction of Lookout Mountain. Suddenly, at the very point of the mountain, a flag was unfurled. It was the Stars and Stripes, and Cory recognized the music now as "The Star-Spangled Banner." Cheers floated through the air at the sight of the flag, cheers from the throats of thousands and thousands of Yankees. The flag flapped in the cold wind, its colors brilliant. Cory felt his chest tighten. Once that had been his flag, that song his anthem. The United States had been his country. But that had been taken away from him by the arrogance of the Northerners who thought to dictate to the rest of the country and impose their will on their Southern neighbors. The invasion of the Confederacy was the greatest theft of all, because the Yankees had stolen the very soul of what should have been one country. Cory swallowed hard and felt tears well from his eyes and roll down his cheeks. That it had come to this was unbelievable. Nor did he blame the Yankees alone, he realized. The Southern leaders had been just as stubborn, just as blindly determined to have things their way. There was plenty of guilt to go around.

Cory blinked away the tears and tightened his grip on the carbine. These men atop the hill with him were his countrymen, now and forever, and he would stand with them against the enemy, even an enemy that never should have been. He crouched there in the rocks and listened to the distant music and waited for the Yankees to come.

BUT A couple of hours dragged past after that unforgettable moment when the Federals unfurled their flag, and still the attack had not begun. The strain of the long, tense night before began to catch up with Cory. Though he wouldn't have believed that he could sleep under these circumstances, he found himself nodding off. Unable to fight the drowsiness, he leaned his carbine against the rock beside him, crossed his arms over his chest, and lowered his head. Within moments, he was sound asleep.

Mere minutes later, he was jolted out of that slumber by the sound of guns. Sherman had launched his attack.

From where he was, Cory could see the tracks of the spur line that led right up to the hill and then through it in the tunnel that gave the height its name. Confederate defenders were clustered above the tunnel and spread out in wings on either side of it. As he looked down the hill, Cory was a little to the left of the tunnel entrance and about a hundred yards above it. Ranks of Union infantry pressed forward, and behind them smoke rose into the morning air as the cannons began their bombardment. The Confederate artillery answered shot for shot.

Cory brought the carbine to his shoulder and sighted along the barrel. When he had drawn a bead on one of the Yankees rushing forward, he squeezed the trigger. The carbine cracked and kicked against his shoulder. Cory saw the soldier stumble down below then fall, carried forward by his momentum. His rifle, with bayonet attached, slithered away from him.

Cory reloaded, found another target, and fired again. Off to his right, an artillery shell burst, flinging rocks and dirt high in the air. He ignored the pebbles that pattered down around him and loaded again. Grapeshot and canister whined past. Bullets sent splinters of stone and rock dust flying from the boulders in which Cory and his companions crouched. The high-pitched scream of ricochets added to the chaos.

With cold detachment, Cory continued loading and firing. He knew from previous battles that he had to force himself to remain calm. If he gave in to the true feelings lurking inside him, he would start gibbering in fear and would be no good to anyone, least of all himself. So he took his time and focused as much of his attention as he could on the details of what he was doing. He concentrated on ramming home the powder charge, the wadding, and the .58-caliber ball; then the hammer was cocked and the percussion cap thumbed onto the nipple, and the carbine was ready to fire again . . .

The sun climbed higher in the sky and reached its zenith, hovering directly overhead as Sherman's troops continued to assault Tunnel Hill. Midday departed and the blazing orb started its long slow slide down the western half of the sky, and Sherman's men were no closer to the top of the hill than when they had started that morning. The Confederate defenders under Cleburne and Stevenson were holding firm.

Cory had been right about warming up. Between the sun and the heat rising from the barrel of his carbine, he was hot enough so that beads of sweat sprang out on his forehead. When they threatened to start trickling into his eyes, he paused long enough to sleeve them away then went back to fighting. As he wiped off the sweat, he had glanced around and seen that three of the men holed up with him in this nest of rocks had been hit. Two were dead, and the third had a chest wound that made every strangled breath wheeze and bubble in his throat. Cory knew the man wouldn't live much longer.

His only injury so far was a scratch on his cheek from a flying splinter of rock. A few drops of blood had welled from it, but that was all. The stinging pain was easy to ignore.

A part of his brain wondered what else was happening along Missionary Ridge. He didn't believe that this attack on Tunnel

Hill was the only tactic the Yankees were trying today. Hooker was somewhere on Lookout Mountain—at least he had been early that morning—and Cory guessed that Fighting Joe's troops were striking at some other point on Missionary Ridge. And there was Gen. George Thomas to consider, too. He had a lot of men under his command. What was he going to do with them?

Giving in to his curiosity, Cory turned and looked back along the rugged spine of Missionary Ridge as it ran to the south. Sure enough, a thick haze of powder smoke hung over the entire length of the ridge. That much smoke meant a full-fledged battle was going on down there, as it was here at the northern end of the ridge. There was so much noise around him he couldn't hear anything else, but he knew the guns were blasting on the center and the left of the Confederate line, too. Could the defenders on top of the ridge hold their positions? Or were they spread too thin?

Cory couldn't answer those questions. He might wonder about them, but for all practical purposes, his world had boiled down to Tunnel Hill and the ground around it. He couldn't do anything about something that was happening somewhere else.

Down below, the Yankees pulled back, and the fighting tapered off for a while. Cory was glad of the chance to let his carbine's barrel cool. He sat slumped against one of the boulders and drew deep breaths. He was weary all the way through, in mind and body both. His eyes slid closed, but he knew he wouldn't doze off this time. Too much energy was pumping through his body for that to happen. His heart pounded in a wild rhythm.

He allowed himself to hope that the Union withdrawal meant the Confederates had won. Maybe the Yankees would pull all the way back to Chattanooga or even abandon the city and head north to Nashville. If that was the case it would mean the Confederacy had accomplished a great victory today.

But after a short time, the sounds of gunfire and artillery blasts welled up again, and Cory knew his hope had been a futile one. The breather was over. The attack was still on. He lifted himself into a crouch and thrust the barrel of the carbine over the rock to draw a bead on one of the Yankees.

More time passed. Three men knelt behind the rocks with Cory. One of them went down, drilled cleanly through the head. The storm of lead grew worse, and another man cried out as a ricochet ripped into his belly. He doubled over, fell to the ground, and mewled in agony. Cory and the remaining man exchanged a glance and kept firing. Their time was coming, and they both knew it.

Suddenly the other soldier took a stumbling step backward. He looked down at his chest. Blood welled from a wound there, a slow, thick stream of crimson. He could only say, "Oh, hell," and then he collapsed.

Cory spared the dying man a glance while reloading. Now he was the only one left in this little pocket of resistance. He thought about leaving, but for some reason he couldn't. The deaths of the men who had stood with him bound him here.

A clatter of hoof beats made him look around. An officer on horseback paused just above and behind the rocks. "Fall back!" the man shouted, waving his hat over his head. "Fall back to form a rear guard!"

Then he was gone, dashing on to give the order to the other defenders on Tunnel Hill. Cory found himself freed. He could leave this place without dishonoring the men who had fallen beside him. In a way he still felt that he owed them a death . . . but it was a debt he would not have to pay today.

Scrambling out of the rocks, clutching his carbine, he hurried away from the point of the hill and fell in with other troops who were gathering a short distance back from the crest. He asked one of them, "What happened? Why are we pulling back?"

The man's face was completely black from powder smoke. His eyes were wide and haunted. "The Yankees broke our center awhile ago, is what I heard. Twenty thousand of the bastards come straight at the ridge, and they never stopped no matter

what we threw at 'em! After a while, our boys broke an' run."
The man shook his head. "Can't say as I blame 'em. One fella
who was there told me they kept yellin' *Chickamauga! Chickamauga!* as they come up the hill. Those Billy Yanks are crazy!"

No, not crazy, Cory thought, just determined to avenge their
defeat a couple of months earlier. If he had seen those grim figures coming at him, he might have turned and run, too.

Later, he heard that a Federal artillery shell had landed in a
direct hit on Bragg's headquarters, blowing the hut to kindling.
Bragg was not there at the time and so escaped destruction. The
retreat from the center and left of Missionary Ridge was nothing
short of chaos as the Yankees washed up the slopes of the ridge
like a blue tide. Only on the Confederate right, at Tunnel Hill,
had a successful defense been mounted. And with the rest of
the ridge falling to the Yankees, the men of Cleburne's and
Stevenson's divisions would have been overrun and destroyed if
they stayed put. Instead, they moved quickly down the eastern
side of the ridge and formed into a protective screen to cover
the retreat of the rest of the Army of Tennessee. The Yankees
might still overwhelm them, but at least they would continue to
put up a fight as long as breath remained in their bodies.

Late in the afternoon, Cory and the men with him reached
the tiny railroad depot known as Chickamauga Station. It was
chaos there, too, but Bragg's officers were struggling to restore
some order. Trains were waiting to carry some of the troops
away, and the others would continue the retreat on foot. They
were headed into Georgia, Cory heard someone say. Another
man added that they might not stop until they reached Atlanta.

Cory stood beside one of the flatcars that lined the tracks
and looked back to the west, where Missionary Ridge was still
visible in the distance, masking Lookout Mountain beyond it.
General Rosecrans had come to Chattanooga to chase out the
Confederates and send them scurrying into Georgia. Everything
hadn't worked out the way Rosecrans had planned, and yet in
the end the results were the same. The victory at Chickamauga

had been wiped away by the bitter defeat. A lot of good men had lost their lives, including Charles Thompson, and still the Yankees had won. Not only that, but Cory now found himself farther than ever from Lucille, with no way to get to her.

"Want a hand?"

Cory looked up. The flatcar was already crowded with men, but one of them was offering his hand to Cory, offering to help him up. The man was gaunt and grimy and bloody, but he managed to grin. "Come on. There's room for one more. I'll give you a hand."

Cory reached up and clasped the man's wrist. He climbed up onto the flatcar and perched on the edge of it, holding his carbine so that its barrel was between his knees.

"Hell of a day, weren't it?"

Cory nodded. "Yeah. A hell of a day."

With a shrill whistle and a blast of steam from its locomotive, the train lurched into motion. Cory gripped the edge of the car's floor with his free hand to steady himself. The cinders of the roadbed began to move past below his dangling feet.

"Don't you worry," the man beside him said. "We'll whip the Yankees next time. We'll be tusslin' with 'em again 'fore you know it."

Cory looked toward the ridges fading from sight behind them as the train picked up speed.

"Yes. I expect we will," he admitted.

Chapter Twenty-three

NATHAN HATCHER SHIVERED AS he sat slumped against the stone wall of his cell. The cold of December went all the way into his bones. When he had first come here to the Rock Island prison camp, he had listened to the constant *drip-drip-drip* of water until he thought he would go mad from the sound. But since winter had set in, all the water was frozen, and it was quiet in this tiny cell. All Nathan could hear was the rasp of his own breath and the chattering of his teeth.

He pulled the thin blanket a little tighter around him. The cell was four feet wide and five feet deep. He could never stretch out full length. A barred window no more than six inches square was set into one wall just below the ceiling, allowing a little light and air into the cell. He was fed only once a day, through a slot in the heavy wooden door. Once a week the door was unlocked and he was taken out under heavy guard for ten minutes in the open air. While that was going on, his slop bucket was carried out and dumped. He didn't see a single human being from one such occasion until the next.

He was unsure how long he had been here. Eternity, perhaps?

Like the captain of the Yankee patrol that had captured him, he had expected he would hang for his part in the escape. For some reason, though, his life had been spared and he had been brought here to Rock Island rather than returned to Camp Douglas. Back when his brain had still worked at something approaching a normal level, he had wondered if Louisa Abernathy's Quaker friends had had anything to do with it. Perhaps they had pleaded that he be spared. He didn't think about it anymore. Now, he had very few coherent thoughts at all. He had gone mad from the solitude.

Or at least he thought he had.

He didn't look up when footsteps sounded in the corridor outside the long line of cells where the worst prisoners were kept. He didn't even notice them until they stopped outside his door and a key rattled in the lock. Then, slowly, Nathan's head lifted from his chest. He looked at the door, not really curious. He didn't care what happened.

The door swung open. Two guards stood there in the corridor, their rifles leveled at Nathan as if they expected him to come roaring out of the cell and attack them. As if he weren't mostly starved to death, half-insane, and no danger at all to anyone.

An officer was with them. "Nathan Hatcher?" he asked.

Nathan blinked against the bright light. It really wasn't all that bright; in fact, the corridor was dim and shadowy. But to Nathan's eyes, the glow from the lantern at the other end of the corridor was harsh.

"Nathan Hatcher?" the officer said again when the prisoner failed to reply. "I know that's your name. There's no point in denying it."

Nathan managed to grunt. He hadn't spoken any words in over a month now.

"How would you like to get out of here?" the officer said. "For good."

Nathan didn't know what the man was talking about. This was his place. He had never been anywhere else, never would be anywhere else. Oh, sometimes he seemed to remember another life, other places, other people, but those were just dreams. Phantoms conjured up by a shattered brain. This cell was all there was.

"I can arrange your release," the officer went on, talking just like he thought Nathan understood what he was saying. "All you have to do is sign an oath of loyalty to the Union and agree to serve in our army. Don't worry, we won't make you go fight other Rebels. We're putting together an outfit to go west, to Arizona, to pacify the hostiles there. You won't really be a Yankee." The man chuckled. "Well, maybe a galvanized one."

Like the water that had oozed and dripped in this prison before the freeze, the man's words slowly trickled into Nathan's brain. He struggled to grasp their meaning. He wanted to give up and return to the stupor from which this man's visit had roused him. But something about what the man had said prodded at Nathan. He frowned, and under the thick beard, his jaw and his throat muscles fought to form words. Finally he was able to croak, "Out?"

"That's right. I can get you out of here." The officer began to sound impatient as he went on, "I'm not sure why you were recommended as someone I might be able to use. I need good fighting men, men who can stand up to rugged country, bad weather, and a bloodthirsty enemy. What about it, Private Hatcher?"

Nathan raised his head a little more and blinked his eyes. His vision cleared slightly, and his thoughts were clearer now. Perhaps the walls of this four-by-five cell *weren't* the boundaries of the universe. Maybe there was something else out there.

Maybe he had a reason to live.

He lifted his arm, held out his hand. "H-help . . ."

"If you can't get up on your own two feet, I can't use you."

Nathan put his other hand against the wall. He pressed hard against the stone. He could barely feel his feet because of the cold, but he managed to draw them underneath him. Stringy muscles contracted, and his bones creaked like he was a hundred yards old, but ever so slowly, he pushed himself upright then took a stumbling step toward the corridor.

He was going out.

"Consider this a present," the officer said. "It's Christmas, you know."

CHRISTMAS 1863 was not a very festive occasion in the Brannon household. Will was still in a Richmond hospital, slow to recover from his Gettysburg wound. But at least the family knew from the letters written by a woman named Dorothy Chamberlain that he was well cared for and was gradually regaining his strength. He hoped to be able to come home sometime after the first of the year and complete his recuperation there—before returning to the army.

Mac had spent the autumn fighting up and down the Virginia countryside with Jeb Stuart's cavalry. There had been battles with the Yankees at Auburn, Buckland, and Brandy Station during October and early November. In late November, General Meade had tried once more to thrust his forces south across the Rappahannock, but Gen. Robert E. Lee had his troops dug in at a small stream called Mine Run. Thinking better of it, Meade had turned back before there was any serious fighting. Mac had been able to pay a short visit to the farm a few days before Christmas, but now he was back at Stuart's headquarters near Orange Court House.

Word had reached Virginia of the victory at Chickamauga and the subsequent defeat just outside Chattanooga. Abigail insisted it didn't matter. She held fast to the belief that the Confederacy would prove triumphant in the end. Henry, Cordelia, and Polly weren't so sure.

Henry stood in the parlor on the evening of Christmas Day and told himself that despite everything, life could be a lot worse. There was a blaze in the fireplace warming the room, and the family had made a decent supper on corn bread and a bit of ham Abigail had saved back.

Abigail sat in her rocker, her Bible open in her lap. Henry didn't think she was actually reading the Scriptures, though. She looked to him like she was dozing.

Cordelia and Polly were on the divan, doing some mending and talking softly. From where he stood near the fireplace, Henry looked at his wife and sister and was glad to see that they were getting along so well. He knew that Cordelia had always had doubts about Polly. But in the months Polly had lived here, the young women had grown closer. The baby probably had something to do with that, Henry thought. Polly's stomach was gently rounded now with the new life growing inside it, and Cordelia responded to that. She wouldn't have been female if she didn't, he told himself. He smiled as Polly gave a soft laugh. She laughed a lot these days, despite the hardships the family had to endure. Henry figured that had something to do with the fact that she hadn't seen her father in months. As far as he was concerned, the longer Duncan Ebersole stayed away, the better. The old man could sit there on his plantation and rot.

A knock sounded on the front door. Henry looked that direction, frowning in surprise. It was a raw, cold night, and Christmas to boot. They weren't expecting visitors.

"My Lord, who could that be?" Abigail said as she roused from her half-sleep. On the divan, Cordelia and Polly looked surprised as well, and a little worried, too. Abigail went on, "Henry . . ."

He reached up and took down the shotgun from the pegs over the mantel. "I'll see who it is," he said.

He stepped to the door. The shotgun was tucked under his arm as he reached for the knob. Pausing, he called, "Who's there?"

A woman's voice came back. "Is this the Brannon farm? Oh, please, help us!"

Henry's frown deepened. He looked at his mother again, and Abigail motioned for him to open the door. He shifted his grip on the scattergun, holding it ready just in case as he twisted the knob with his other hand and swung the door open.

An icy mist blew in and brushed Henry's face. He saw two ragged figures huddled there on the porch. The man was bent over, and the woman had an arm around him to support him. The man shook as a wracking cough went through his body.

"Thank God," the woman said. Her face was thin and haggard. A few strands of red hair escaped from the shawl she had wrapped around her head. "I thought we would never get here. Help me get him inside. Please. He's so ill."

"Who in blazes—" Henry began.

Then the sick man lifted his head, and Henry stared into the gaunt, bearded face of his brother Titus.